Darkest Before Dawn
A Guardian's Diary

Amelia Hutchins

Darkest Before Dawn Copyright © October 14, 2014 by Amelia Hutchins

All rights reserved. No part of this publication may be reproduced, distributed, or transmitted in any form or by any means, including photocopying, recording, or other electronic or mechanical methods, without prior written permission of the publisher, except in the case of brief quotations embodied in critical reviews and certain other noncommercial uses permitted by copyright law. For permission requests, write to the publisher, addressed "Attention: Permissions Coordinator," at the address below.

ISBN-13: 978-0-9911909-9-7

ISBN-10: 0991190998

Amelia Hutchins

P.O. Box 11212

Spokane Valley, WA 99211

Amelia-Hutchins.com

Ordering Information: https:www.createspace.com

Quantity sales. Special discounts are available on quantity purchases by corporations, associations, and others. For details, contact the publisher at the address above.

Orders by U.S. trade bookstores and wholesalers, Please contact Amelia utchins ameliahutchins@amelia-hutchins.com

Printed in the United States of America.

10 9 8 7 6 5 4 3 2 1

Also by Amelia Hutchins

THE FAE CHRONICLES

Fighting Destiny (Book One)

Taunting Destiny (Book Two)

Escaping Destiny (Book Three)

Warning

This book is not suitable for anyone under the age of eighteen. This book is intended for those who enjoy dark humor, and a wild ride. There is adult language and scene's that may leave you tying up your partner and making him or her, very happy. This book is a series, but has a happy for now ending. There are no zombies in this book, but should my imagination place a few in the next book, do not worry, I will kill them off shortly. Not intended for anyone who doesn't enjoy being taken for plot turning, panty soaking, and edge of your seat wild ride.

Acknowledgments

I'd like to thank the fans for their continual support and unwavering trust. To everyone who helped this book be all it could be, and more. To the family who moved on to greener pastures, God Speed. And last but not least, to the bloggers who give us endless hours of their time and are just truly amazing. You are the reason little authors can make their big dreams come true.

Darkest
Before Dawn
A Guardian's Diary

Prologue

Some things will stay with me forever. Some things I wish I could forget. Those days—when it all began early last spring—are a big block of memories that I would like to hit delete on and start over.

The news had run on a nightmarish, surreal loop. Terrifying stories of the fast moving virus and the devastation it had left behind. The World Health Organization as well as The Center for Disease Control had been at a loss because this virus spread so quickly that within a week, at least half our nation's population was wiped out. Other countries hadn't fared any better than ours did. With time passing, and no cure in sight, the government made an announcement; those who hadn't been infected should seek shelter and avoid other humans, or anyone they might suspect of being infected.

I was one of the lucky ones, but only because my father had been prepping for the end of days since my mother had been killed almost ten years ago. He had been working on an underground bunker, one large enough to sustain our entire town. Like the Old Testament stories of Noah, most of the town's people thought he was crazy. Guess who's laughing now? Not my dad, that's for sure. I would often catch him mumbling something about the whole thing being a criminal shame.

He trained me and my brother mercilessly in survival techniques for years before the virus hit, almost like he knew something we didn't. Not too long ago, he went out in search of help, and we haven't heard from him since. I suspect his kindness was his undoing. I was left with my brother, my best friend, and a handful of those who listened to my dad. We have added to our count survivors from all across the country; however, I would only take in those who I felt I could trust.

I don't trust easily, not since I witnessed acts of violence that were so grotesque and inhuman that I spewed my lunch soon after. Basic services such as public utilities and emergency services broke down within weeks of the virus outbreak. Random gangs roam the countryside and no one is safe anymore. We save who we can, but every day it grows more desperate, and I often question why we are prolonging the inevitable.

Someone once told me that silence was golden. They lied. It's deafening. There are no planes in the skies, no kids in the parks playing, no car horns blaring anymore. Although my father warned me what the aftermath to an event like this would be like, the reality is far different than the theory.

Darkest Before Dawn

A few weeks after the virus left millions dead, news of other creatures roaming the land hit the radio. At first we thought it was a joke, but then I wondered why anyone would joke about something like this after the virus. We chose to ignore it, because our minds just couldn't comprehend it.

Not until I met him.

He is my salvation, and my damnation. He watches me, and he's not like anyone I have ever met before. Maybe I'd been waiting for him? Maybe fate works that way, because until him, I never cared what anyone thought of me, but I would find myself watching for him. I would actually go out of the shelter, just hoping to catch a glimpse of him.

If I had known then what I did now, I mean really *believed* that life as I knew it would forever be changed, I'd have taken a chance with him sooner. Maybe I wouldn't have been afraid of living, or loving. I found out the hard way that life really is too short to hold back and constantly second-guess yourself.

In my darkest hour, he was my dawn. His kind is dangerous, but in the world we now live in, he was and is my best chance of survival. Other creatures exist, and while I've made a choice to accept it, I haven't always found that acceptance came comfortably or easily. Each new revelation I discovered would shake my foundation a little more than the last. To keep those I care for alive, and thriving, I'll have to do so much more than I could have before. Still, my darkest hour is yet to come, and

I'll keep fighting until we've won.

    I'm getting ahead of myself. For you to understand it all, we need to start at the beginning. The day the virus hit our town. The day the world as I knew it ceased to be, and a new world began.

Chapter ONE

The day the virus came to town.

"You can't be serious," Addy laughed.

"Dead serious," I said as I checked my watch for the fifth time. Grayson would be out of school in the next hour, which meant my shopping buddy needed to move her ass.

"So how many more hours of clinical do you have?"

"Five, and then I start an internship at the hospital. I worked my schedule around Grayson, but I'm hoping Dad will snap out of his prepper state and man up."

"You know that won't happen," she said as she grabbed popcorn and turned to head to the dairy aisle. "So, what's he say about that virus?"

The virus was bad, and the news was just depressing. Rh Viridae or 'Pacers Flu' had hit Europe hard; hospitals there were overflowing with the sick and the morgues couldn't keep up with the dead. "He says it's the end of days, but he said that about the war in Afghanistan, too. I just hope they find a cure for it before it can get this far."

"Chocolate, or no chocolate?" she asked as she wiggled her eyebrows.

"You have to ask?" I mocked.

"You're right," she said as she added a few bars to basket. "So, is he all prepping or…"

"Or," I said as I reached for a gallon of milk, and put a few cartons of yogurt into the cart. I was still dressed in my plain blue scrubs from the hospital, which did nothing for my figure. I caught Miss Smith watching me, her eyes narrowed on the items in my cart.

She was one of the teachers at the high school, and had always struck me as pretentiously prim and proper. She'd also been the one to report my father to Child Protective Services because she believed Grayson would have been better raised by a 'normal' family, instead of our little broken one. I gave her a sharp look before I purposely added more flavors into the cart.

I had been failing school back then, so I knew where she had been coming from. Did I care? Nope. He was my family, and while my dad seemed crazy to everyone else, I knew he had his reasons for what he did. He wanted to protect us, and I think it was his way of coping with my mother's death. He'd started his prepping the week after her funeral.

Darkest Before Dawn

I'd only been eleven when she had been brutally gunned down and killed in a robbery gone wrong. It had been a low point in our lives, but we'd dealt with it. Grayson was only two when she'd been killed, so to him, she was just gone. He'd been a surprise to my parents who thought they couldn't have any more children. Hence the huge age gap. He was twelve now, and in fifth grade. I pretty much raised him, and so far, I think I've done a good job of it.

Grayson was a normal twelve year old boy. He got in trouble once in a while, but managed to keep his grades up. Unlike me, he had more than one friend, and was outgoing. I was more of an introvert. I loved Addy, but I had never been much of a social butterfly. I was driven, and had plans.

"We should invite some guys over tonight. Dillon has been asking about you. You know he likes you. I don't see why you keep refusing to go out with him."

"He isn't interested in me, he's only interested in something new," I said dropping Captain Crunch cereal into the cart. "I think he has three more to go until he beats Brad's score."

The problem with small towns was everyone knew what everyone was doing. I have to agree with my dad sometimes when he says that boys act like some sort of weird species that are best avoided until they grow out of the phase where the little head does more thinking than the big one. In a small town, their competiveness can take on a bizarre twist. Brad and Dillon were best friends, and we'd gone to high school with them. Dillon had chased me up until Candace had moved to town. He immediately stopped chasing me and started chasing after her, right up until she gave it up to him. The very next day he was after me again. "I'm not interested in being used."

"It's just having fun, for crying out loud," she mumbled as we headed to the register with her back a little stiffer than it had been. "You should try it sometime."

"No way on the Dillon thing, and there's a ton of things I know I'd find to be more fun. Half of our graduating class is hopeless! They barely managed to graduate because most of them already had children. Look at Tabitha, she slept with Dillon and nine months later she's jobless, a mother, and on welfare. Worst of all, I know she was on birth control because I was there at the clinic when she got the shot. I just don't get why people would play with their lives like that. There is so much more out there, and we can do anything we want to. A child or a disease is so not on my to-do list right now."

"Are you done preaching yet?" Addy said as she turned to look for anyone to ring us up. "Where the heck is everybody?" she asked and I looked around the store.

The clerks were gathered around a TV monitor at the far end of the store. I tilted my head to see what had them careless enough to the leave the registers unattended. There was a beautiful news lady on the

Darkest Before Dawn

monitor, with what looked to be a hospital behind her that was taped off with bright yellow quarantine tape, and workers busy setting up barricades.

I left my cart and moved closer until I could make out what was being said.

"At one o'clock, the Deaconess Hospital announced it had eight new cases of Rh Viridae and out of the eight cases, only one patient remains alive. The CDC is asking that only those with life threatening emergencies come to the emergency room, and those who can manage it, to go to Sacred Heart and avoid Deaconess at this time. Patients inside Deaconess are being secured in their rooms while the emergency room is being locked down to prevent the flu from spreading. Again, they are asking that you avoid Deaconess and seek other hospitals …" she continued on, but I was done listening.

"Ray? Can you ring us up? Please?" I asked one of the cashiers.

"Oh, sorry, Emma, I got caught up watching the news. Can you believe this? New York and Florida are reporting that a ton of folks have already died overnight. They're saying the flu that was in Europe is here in the States now." He gestured back at the monitors as he walked with us to his register.

"Crazy," I answered while a shiver ran up my spine.

"They say it's moving really fast, just like it did in Europe," he continued.

"Crazy," I said again, because I couldn't think of anything else to say.

I waited for Addy to get through with checking out before I paid for my groceries and we loaded our few items into her car. "Can you drive me by the school? I want to get Grayson and get him home. I have a bad feeling about this."

Addy looked at me cautiously as she tossed her purse in the car and pulled her long blonde curls into a ponytail. "Should we be worried?"

"They were watching a reporter from Spokane," I explained.

"Shit," she said as she slid into the driver seat of her Volkswagen bug which she had named Satan. The car was named aptly, since it had a tendency to break down when she needed it the most. "Yeah, let's go grab him. You think we should go buy more food?"

"No, I think we should get him and then get home. Dad is probably at the shelter already. Might be a good idea to grab some things and meet him there."

"Emma, give it to me straight. No bullshitting!"

"I'm starting to think my father was right to prep, and I think we should get Grayson and your parents to the shelter, right now."

"My mom's in Spokane with my dad; he's getting another treatment at Deaconess."

Darkest Before Dawn

My heart chose that moment to plummet to my stomach. I had a feeling that this flu was something bad, really bad. "Try to call them when we get to the school, you can use my phone."

I took out my phone from the side pocket of my purse and checked the list of missed calls and voicemail messages. I hit the play button on the first one, and listened to my father as he barked out orders like any good drill sergeant. "Emmalyn, this is your father," duh, Dad, "I picked up Grayson, where the hell are you!? Get to the house and grab your bags; have Addy do the same. I packed one for her and put it in your closet last week. Tell her I reached her mom, and she's fine. She's with her dad, and he has to stay overnight because of the quarantine order. She said for us to take Addy with us, and she'd keep in touch..." the message ended so I clicked on the next, "Grab a gun from the house, use the back way to get to the shelter, and be careful."

"Change of plans, head to my house, Addy. Your parents are stuck at Deaconess, but they want you to come with us. Your mom says they're fine, but stuck until they lift the order."

"What order?" she asked as she flipped the bug around and headed back in the direction we'd just come from.

"Quarantine; they have him at the hospital so he's probably started his chemo."

Fuckitty fuck! Chemo took your defenses against

viruses down because it killed your immune system. Her father was stuck at Deaconess, where the news lady had been reporting from. I did my best to keep the worry I felt from showing. Addy was delicate already from her dad's cancer coming back, but this would make her strong façade crumble.

"What the hell does that mean?"

"Means they are playing it safe, and trying to keep him away from the flu."

At my house, we both jumped out of the car and headed inside. It was quiet, with the exception of the television which had the news on. My dad must have forgotten it when he bugged out with Grayson to the shelter. I walked over to it quickly and turned it off. "You want to grab some movies and I'll grab the bags?"

"Sure," she said, and I smiled reassuringly. We'd been through drills before. Not like this though, and I had a bone-deep worry that this time was different than the other bug-outs we'd done. Addy had been a true friend staying with me even when my father ran drills daily. At the most random of times, he'd make us practice escaping to the shelter.

Even though most of the kids we'd grown up with had made me the brunt of their jokes, she'd stood beside me and defended me when the need arose, and I loved her for it. The jerk-weeds didn't tease me just because they thought my dad was crazy. No, my hair had that weird orangey thing going on as a kid. Fortunately,

Darkest Before Dawn

I'd grown out of that and it was now more of a long strawberry-blonde mess that was always in my way. Them thinking my dad was nuts wasn't anything I could grow out of, though. I walked down the long hallway and into my room, where I threw open the closet door and grabbed both of the heavy bug-out bags. I opened mine and tossed a few more clothes in, then gave my room a quick once-over.

I wasted no time in heading to the safe where the handguns were kept, and punched in the code. I stuck one of the guns in the back waistband of my pants, and added back-up ammo clips to each of my pockets, then closed the safe and picked up the bags. I stopped in the hallway, and set the bags back down before I grabbed some of the photo albums my mother had made; they held some of the only photos with her and Grayson in them.

I met Addy by the door to the pantry and smiled as she held up bags of snacks for Grayson which I'd implemented in the last bug-out we'd had. There was nothing worse than a cranky preteen who had to go without his snacks and was convinced he was going to have to eat MREs. Together we headed back to the car.

"Did you want to stop by your house?" I asked.

"No, this is a drill, only a drill," she snapped, and I lifted my eyes to hers.

"You sure? We could stop for you to grab a few things. Just in case; you never know, right?" I hated that she was going to say no. I knew it before she answered.

"No, it's only a drill. It won't hit us like it did Europe. This is the United freaking States!"

I didn't point out that Europe had amazing medical facilities, or that they had some of the most skilled doctors on the planet. She was grasping for straws and I understood why. Her parents were in a hospital that was currently under quarantine for a deadly virus. They were in the eye of the storm, and her brother was in the Army. He was currently deployed to Iraq, and on his second tour.

"I love you, bitch," I said and watched as her lips curved into a soft smile.

"Love you too, whore," she said, and started the car.

"You know, I'm not sure you can call me that."

"I know you well enough that I can call you whatever I want. I know you are a whore deep inside where it counts. Just because you don't advertise your deviant ways, doesn't mean I don't know the real you," she snarked with a mischievous glint in her soft brown eyes.

I smiled back, even though I was consumed with worry for my family and hers.

We hit the highway just in time. I looked over at the town of Newport as shit hit the fan. Cars were lined up, and it looked like some of the people from town were heading out. Why would they leave Newport? It was

Darkest Before Dawn

less likely to be swamped with infected people, and yet it seemed like they were all heading to Spokane from the looks of it.

I looked over to Addy who also noticed the line of traffic, and I wondered what she was thinking. Fortunately, she normally voiced her opinion pretty loudly, so I didn't have to wonder what was on her mind for very long.

"They're idiots. All of them."

Blunt and to the point; yet another reason why she was my best friend. I closed my eyes and sent a silent prayer that this would pass. We made it to the shelter in record time, and I smiled as I mentally high-fived Addy for being so vigilant through the bug-out drills we'd endured through the years.

The shelter was an abandoned missile silo my father had purchased from the government. When he got it, the silo had been nothing more than piece of crap metal fortress. It now had solar panels, and my dad had paid to have the well that fed it cleaned and rebuilt. It had over a hundred rooms, and seventeen levels. Most of the levels had rooms with sleeping quarters, but some of the floors he'd used to store food, ammo, weapons and pretty much anything else you'd need to sustain life for quite a few years in the event of an all-out emergency.

"Thank God!" My dad wrapped his arms around me the moment I stepped from the car and smacked a wet kiss to my forehead. "I was so worried," he continued and then did the same to Addy. He grabbed the heavy bags as we grabbed the groceries. Inside, Grayson was reading and looked a little pissed off, but he'd always hated being pulled from school for anything related to the shelter.

Cool kids didn't bug-out.

I smiled as he raised his eyes and waved. "Dad pulled me out of school. Again."

"If he hadn't, I would have this time, buddy," I said as I walked to the makeshift kitchen all the way down the hall, through three other rooms. Dad hadn't made this place for comfort, and that had been his reply every time I'd complained about the kitchen being so far from the media room, as I referred to it. Addy followed me, and helped me get the food put away.

I sat on the counter while she prepared popcorn smothered with extra butter, and grabbed the wine from the refrigerator. We were so close to the twenty-one milestone that Dad would indulge us once in a while as long as it wasn't done without him present. She poured three cups, and once the popcorn was done, we headed for the media room.

Dad had locked us in, and I knew nothing from outside could get in unless we let it in. The door to the shelter had three layers, and the outer, being the strongest, was made to withstand pretty much everything. Inside the main room was a large table that had a few old computers built into it which were pretty basic and

Darkest Before Dawn

controlled much of the shelter's functions. There was also a flat panel TV that was digital, but according to Dad if the grid went down, so too would the internet and our visual link to the outside.

I chose to sit beside Grayson on the couch, and watched the news from there. It was grim, and there was a new reporter now, who was telling us how her co-anchor had become sick, and was now deep inside the quarantined area. The news was getting worse, and when Grayson lifted his head, I could see the worry in his gaze. Grayson and I took more after our mom with our red-blond hair and blue eyes than Dad's dark brown hair and gray eyes. Some of our nastier neighbors referred to us as the 'Milk-man's kid's' which didn't help things growing up, either.

"It's going to be okay, kid."

"You can say that, Emma, if it helps you sleep better at night," Grayson said as he stood and grabbed his Game Boy. "I'm going to my room. Wake me up for dinner, Ems?"

"Sure thing," I said and watched as he left the room. I shot an irritated look at my dad. "You shouldn't be playing this with him in here."

My dad didn't budge, didn't turn around or even acknowledge that I'd spoken. He flipped to the next channel, and shook his head as a reporter and his cameraman were wading through long white plastic-looking bags stacked inside of what looked like a tent. I squinted to try and make out what I was seeing past the news ticker at the bottom of the screen that was running statistics of dead in cities like Seattle, Olympia, and Spokane. The reporter reached down with a box cutter, and sliced the bag open.

"Oh my word," Addy whispered in a horrified tone as a face came into view. There were thick, black-looking lines that had spidery black tendrils fanning through his face where I knew his veins should be. The man had dried blood caked to his nose, eyes, ears, and lips. I didn't think they could show something like that on TV. Was this reporter trying to pull a 'Geraldo' or was he honestly trying to report what was going on?

I wanted to throw up, because I knew what the rest of those bags had inside of them now. They were bodies, hundreds of dead bodies being stored in the ventilated tents because the hospital morgue was too full to take anymore. "Turn it off," I said, downing my cup of wine without realizing it. I reached for the bottle. "I should be at the clinic."

"No way! Emma, I agreed to let you get a job there because that knowledge is needed, but no way in hell are you leaving this shelter."

"You didn't *let* me do anything! I'm needed there; those people need help!" Panic and despair welled up in me with the need to do *something* to help.

"They won't make it, and if you go out those doors, Emma, neither will you!" he snapped angrily as his wide eyes turned to me, full of worry.

    I sat stunned, but it only lasted briefly as Addy's sobs sounded from beside me. I wrapped my arms around her tightly and promised her everything would be okay, even though I knew it would never be okay again.

Chapter Two

Present Day

Six months had gone by, and while most of the town's two thousand plus inhabitants had died, some had survived. Some others had managed to escape town and now lived on its outskirts or deeper in the wooded mountains surrounding us. Some of them we took supplies to since they'd refused to come to the shelter. Newport is a small town that butts up to two other small towns and sits on the border of Idaho. Our town is so small; you could literally walk from Washington to Idaho in less than twenty minutes if you were so inclined to.

My dad had begun the process of burning the dead and had led us around town, showing us what needed to be done as far as cleaning up and foraging for supplies. With the breakdown in services and information, all bodies were burned to prevent the possible spread of the virus or diseases like typhoid. Winter wasn't too far off and we had to gather as many supplies as we could, especially with the growing numbers in the shelter. Since there were mostly girls in our little group, we'd

Darkest Before Dawn

all trained with him. He also was the one who came up with the idea for us to wear disguises since we'd been privy to a few cases of rape, and other abusive scenes which we'd saved a few women from. We all wore black hoodies with sugar skull masks that hid our hair and features. The sugar skull masks were a find that we scored on one of our earlier trips to Spokane. We'd found a case of them in an abandoned costume shop and altered the intricate masks to a more masculine version with Sharpies to hide our gender. While we appreciated the protection of the hoodies and masks, it wasn't very pleasant when the temperature hit 106 in the summertime.

We'd cleaned out the stores and other shops to prevent the goods from being taken out of town. Luckily, a supply train for the stores in town had stopped in Priest River, and no one else had noticed it hidden deep in the thickly wooded area. The only thing we lacked was meat, but that was easily hunted for. Soon after the discovery of the train cars, we'd received increasingly desperate radio distress messages from a group trapped in Montana and my father had left to find and help them make their way here, to the shelter.

I'd been his second in command and knew how to do everything he did on a daily basis. He'd been gone for almost a month, and with each passing day, I was losing hope. He'd said two weeks at the most, but I knew trekking through the mountains to avoid marauders and lawless men was dangerous. Time kept passing, and he could be hurt, or worse. Dead. I'd refused to acknowledge that thought, but everyone else whispered it when they thought Grayson or I couldn't hear them.

I knew the possibility of him being alive was slim, but I also knew miracles happened... But did they happen to me? Probably not. Did it mean I should give up on the man who everyone called crazy, who saved us all in the end? Nope.

He was the reason I was out tonight on patrol, looking to help anyone who needed it while protecting the shelter from anyone finding it. He was the smartest man I knew, and had taught us how to survive, which was what I was doing now. Surviving the 'end of days' with a pack of pissed off women. We were fortunate that the few other men in the shelter hadn't decided to go with him, preferring to risk the possible bitch-a-thon that occasionally broke out inside the shelter, to the possibility of death outside of its sanctuary.

I adjusted the mask and hoodie as I made my way through the town. I flexed my gloved hands and waited for a lone car to pass me. It wasn't like we got much traffic in our remote location; it was just that some of the people that came through here had been pretty bad and it was wise to be wary of any newcomers. When this had begun months ago, we'd thought our biggest problem would be finding food. Wrong; it was the creeps who decided they found lawlessness appealing and made victims of those who had survived the virus.

I'd been watching this car circle around for the last hour; it had three occupants. A woman and two mean-looking men. The woman looked scared and pretty much

Darkest Before Dawn

broken. She had bruises on her face, and scrapes on her lips as if she'd been abused. One of the men kept up a steady stream of verbal abuse at the woman, confirming my suspicion that these two assholes were responsible for her current condition.

Hmm, bow or gun? Bow; it was silent. I needed the element of surprise. Besides, ammo was hard to come by and I could make more arrows. I pulled out the crossbow, which had been attached to my backpack for easy access on a pull cord. I flicked my finger over the button to silently auto-cock the string, and nocked the arrow onto the guide as I peered through the white skeletal mask. I needed to get the guys out of the car and away from the woman. I smiled as one exited the car to enter a darkened store, which was empty; I knew because I had cleaned it out last month.

I slipped into the darkness through the back door, and waited in position, watching through the crossbow scope, for him to shine his light in my direction before I released my arrow. There was stunned shock on his face as he took in my black Misfits hoodie, which matched the skull mask I wore.

"What the fuck?" he asked, and stepped forward. I released the arrow and watched as he hit the ground without another sound other than the thud as he hit the tiled floor.

I knew what I looked like; a freak. The hoodie was thick, and looked bulky from the lightweight Kevlar vest I wore beneath it. I wore black cargo pants which matched the black combat boots that protected my feet. I had a pack attached to my back, since sometimes it was impossible to make it back to the shelter and hiding out was required.

I searched the dead body, and found one handgun which I shoved into one of the many pockets of my pants. I secured the crossbow back on the cord, and pulled the heavy corpse back into the shelved storage room to hide it. I retrieved the arrow from his larynx. "Should have been a nicer guy," I whispered to the corpse. "Lesson? Don't be a dickhead, you'll live longer."

I liked keeping the odds in my favor, and one was always a good number. I heard footsteps, so I pressed my back to a shelf as I snatched my crossbow from the pull cord, and grabbed a fresh arrow rather than use the one I had pulled from his buddy so the blood wouldn't muck up my aim. I inhaled slowly, and controlled my heart rate as the man called out for his friend. He continued walking into the dark as if he didn't have a care in the world.

I guess it was easy to think like that when you preyed on the less fortunate or weaker beings. Once again I auto-cocked the string and slid my arrow in, as I used the scope to aim between the shelves. He was smaller than the first guy, but his eyes were hard and his hands were fisting with irritation.

"You better get your ass out here; don't think I won't leave you and keep the girl to myself! Was tired of sharing her with you anyway!" he shouted as I pulled the trigger. I enjoyed the sickening crunch of muscle and tissue as it ripped apart his heart.

I stood up and walked to where he was bleeding out. "And I'm sure she was sick of being shared with the both of you, too," I snapped and ripped the arrow out of his chest. I'm not into forgiveness or rehabilitation. I have enough on my plate without worrying about those who hurt others.

I walked out to the car, and the moment the woman saw me, she screamed. I rolled my eyes. Overly dramatic much? I walked to the car, shimmying off my pack, and opened the door. I shoved my pack onto the passenger side and slid into the driver's seat, thanking the powers that be; those idiots had left the keys in the ignition. I could drive this heap and ditch it when I came back for my bike. The woman had been handcuffed to the door of the backseat and was now in full hysterics, probably thinking she'd ended up in the hands of yet another monster, but I didn't have time to waste right now. If I had to pick between my motorcycle and her…Let's just say I'd pick the bike. It helped me to protect and feed those in the shelter, and was a necessity. It was a Ducati, which my father had personalized for just about any type of apocalyptic scenario. It had off road tires, and could actually go off road as most four wheelers could. I'd hand painted on the camo-green skulls, and airbrushed the rest of the bigger details onto the gas tank. Needless to say, this bike had both necessity and emotional attachment.

I parked a few feet from the shelter and pulled my

mask off to look at her. The moment I did, she stilled.

"You're a woman!"

"Last time I checked," I smiled and watched as tears slid from her eyes. "Who were those men?"

"They killed my baby, and shot my husband," she said before she started her hysterics again.

"Look, I'm sorry for what they did. You're safe now and they won't be hurting anyone else ever again. You gotta stop crying so I can explain a few things before I allow you into the shelter." I gave her a moment, because personally, I couldn't imagine what she'd been through. "Got it together?" I asked and when she nodded her dark head, I continued. "My family is in there, and some others we found in similar positions as yours. You can stay here, but if you do, you'll be asked to help. We all work together there and we all help out. No free rides."

She nodded emphatically. I felt a twinge of regret knowing she'd lost a child.

"We have children here, ones who we found alone, or found with bad people. They need reassurance and love, so you know, love on them, or whatever. They are alone in the world, and depend on us."

"Were they found with men like…" she couldn't finish her sentence and I didn't need her to.

"Some; some we found in homes around here curled up with their parents' remains. It's sad either

Darkest Before Dawn

way. Everyone has lost someone from the flu but unlike us, they don't understand what's happened. They don't need to know yet. No good can come from it."

"You have food and water?" she asked.

"First things first, name?"

"Cathleen," she whispered.

"I'm Emma. It's nice to meet you. Wish it had been under better circumstances. Now you need to know one thing, Cathleen, if you fuck with my family or hurt anyone we have promised to protect, I or one of the others in the shelter will kill you. We've all sworn to protect those who are in there. You can be one of them. The alternative isn't something you want to find out about."

I handed her off to Addy, who met us armed with a trusty pair of bolt cutters, and took off in the car. I made it back to my bike, which was still there, thankfully. I exited the car with mask and hoodie securely back in place, the weight of my pack on my back, and suddenly felt the additional weight of a stare. I looked around but could see nothing. I wasn't alone, though I was sure of it. I climbed on the bike and did a once over of the area around me. Nothing.

Decision made, I would probably go someplace to hide tonight, rather than take the risk of bringing trouble back to the shelter. I headed up the old river road and released the throttle. If anyone was following me, they wouldn't be for long. When I reached the river, I climbed off the bike and pulled my crossbow from its resting place on the pack before I moved to the water.

I could still feel the stare on the back of my neck, but that was impossible. I turned and eyed the bushes as a branch snapped. My eyes strained to see into the dark terrain. I could hear something, but it sounded more like a wild animal than a piece of shit human. I reached down and pulled out a flashlight, shining it into the thick brush.

It was hard to see in the dim light through the mask. However, I was not removing it. We'd saved countless women from rape, and worse. Don't ask what the worse was. It was pretty rank, and just disgusting.

The bushes moved, and I involuntarily stepped backwards. Great, Emma, just friggin' great! Crossbow in one hand, the flashlight held firmly in the other. If it's a bad guy, maybe you can club him to death with a crossbow, or better yet, light his way to you! I clicked off the light and brought up the bow, resetting it and glared at the bushes, daring them to move wrong.

Bushes; I was warning bushes, really? Get on the bike, Emma! Choices, shit, choices were overrated. I could see a few here, though.

One: Stand here like a blooming idiot and shoot the bushes.

Two: Get on the bike and pretend I didn't threaten to murder bushes. Well, in my head I did.

Darkest Before Dawn

Three: Go into the bushes and search out what had moved and kill it.

I moved toward the bike and lowered the crossbow. Well played bushes, well played. I straddled the bike and started it. Once I secured the crossbow to the bike's saddlebags, I took off again. I headed back to town. It was safer there because there were a lot more places to hide. I needed to check the fish traps and then make sure they still had bait, but I wasn't giving away their location to any animals, or friggin' bushes! It would just have to wait for tomorrow.

In town it was deathly quiet. It was weird sensing the silence. It was one thing to wish for it, but another to hear it. Crickets were the loudest, but on a calm evening, you could hear frogs, birds, and other critters rustling around in the night. Tonight there were only the sounds of crickets and my motorcycle. I climbed off the bike in front of one of the houses I knew needed to be cleared. I had been here earlier today and had to abort what I was doing when I heard that car going through town.

Inside were four bodies. Mr. and Mrs. Jameson, and their once beautiful twins, all of them had died in that house. No one was sure how the Rh Viridae virus had picked its targets, or why it had allowed some of us to live. There was no rhyme or reason to how it selected to kill us. It just did.

I walked into the house and stepped right back out. Yuck. The dead stank! You'd think after all this time I'd be used to it. No such luck! I brought out the coroner's cream and lifted the mask only far enough to place it on my upper lip and then dropped the mask back into place. I scanned the area as that tingling sensation of being watched came back.

If someone was out there, they were keeping their distance. Which suited me just fine, but it still made me itch to figure it out. I went back inside the house and carried out the twins, one at a time, in a sheet, and just barely managed to keep the tears in my eyes. I'd known this family, and had babysat the twins for extra money on the weekends. I placed them on the wood pile I'd stacked earlier today, and then went back inside for their parents. Mrs. Jameson was easy, but Mr. Jameson had some extra weight which sucked. I got him out, placed him with his family, and looked around the street.

Where was this person hiding? The houses on this block all had dead corpses still inside, which would make it unbearable to sit inside, or hide. Not to mention the diseases that came from the dead, from not being able to bury them correctly. I brought out the fuel and splashed it over the unfortunate family and then got on my knees and said a quick prayer to the heavens that they be accepted with only my humble blessing to send them on.

When I got back up to my feet, I brought out the book of matches, struck one on the cover and tossed it in. The flames leapt to life, and tears fell for the family. They'd been damn good people, and no one had deserved what had happened—no one.

Darkest Before Dawn

Flames as big as this in the night would be seen a long way off, so it was time to go. I would probably come back with a team of girls tomorrow and finish the next few houses. I turned to head back to my bike, but someone was standing close to it. On instinct, I pulled one of my handguns from its holster and aimed straight for his heart. I couldn't speak, because I'd give myself away. I tilted my head, and cocked the weapon.

He held up his hands and smiled. "Now, now, little boy. I come in peace."

As if. *Boy!* I lifted my brow even though he couldn't see it. He had long blondish-brown hair which was pulled back into a ponytail which gave him a 'Huntsman' look. His eyes and skin tone were hard to make out in the moonlight and the shadows flickering off the bonfire behind me; it was creating an enchanted feeling inside of me.

He scanned me briefly before he spoke and it felt as if his eyes were looking right through my disguise and straight into my soul. I shivered briefly before narrowing my eyes beneath the mask. It was impossible for him to see me, or determine anything else with the baggy clothes I wore.

"Do you speak?" he asked, and I shook my head. "No?"

I didn't bother to move the second time, minus lining up and adjusting the gun sights better. The more he spoke, the more noticeable his faint accent became.

I couldn't quite place it, but it sure wasn't from around here.

"A mute, then?"

Man, he was thick!

"Okay, I'll play. This town, how many people are left?"

He stepped closer, and I stepped back and the heat of the fire grew hot against the clothes I wore. He moved around until he was able to lean against the house.

"Use your fingers, I'll count."

I held up my middle one.

He grinned, but it was lopsided. "One?"

He pushed off the house and I fired, aiming for the right, next to his head. Close enough that it nicked his hair. His eyes grew wide, and then narrowed. "You missed," he growled, and I shook my head. "You didn't miss?"

Another shake as I smiled beneath the mask.

"Alright, I'll play it your way and tell you what I have observed so far," he grinned knowingly. "You don't kill unless you have to, and yet you kill if the need arises to help someone, mostly women and children, but I think you would help men if they need it. Personally, if they aren't strong enough to save themselves, you should let them die. I've been watching for you awhile today, and I haven't seen you take off that mask yet."

It was time to go. He'd been watching me *all* day? How had I missed that?

"Tell me, are you helping to gather slaves for someone?"

I almost cussed, but caught myself before I did so. Oh, he was crafty! Wait, I was craftier. I tilted my head as I aimed my weapon at his head, again. He watched my hands, and for a moment, his eyes captured mine through the mask and held them. Time stood still, and something inside of me kicked into overdrive…my heart?

"Shit, you can't be over sixteen with those baby blues."

I blinked, and considered shooting him. It would solve the issue of him being too close to my bike. Would also work to wipe that charming grin off his entirely too kissable lips.

"Tell me, why be alone? We have room for you. We have rules, of course. Not many, but we could make a man out of you yet."

Thanks for the offer, buddy, passing! Besides, I was pretty sure he couldn't make a man out of me. I was just grateful that he hadn't seen anyone else from the shelter today or followed me there earlier.

I turned and gave the family one last look before

moving to my bike, but it had been a mistake. His hand gripped my shoulder, and I brought the gun up, and tried turning in his direction, but his viselike grip prevented it.

"I wouldn't do that," he chimed, as he leaned closer and...*sniffed me.* I felt violated, but the moment his nose touched my throat, I felt something kick inside of my belly, and heat pooled down there. *Oh, Emma, be a boy! No getting wet, not now, now ever, pull it together!*

Oh my word, he'd sniffed me! Like a friggin' dog! What the hell was wrong with people? I turned around and faced him, forcing him to release my arm. He narrowed his eyes, and tilted his head, mirroring my earlier assessment of him.

"You don't smell like a teenage boy," he mused.

Shit. Shit. Shit!

I tried again to raise my gun, but something in his posture made me hesitate. He wasn't aggressive, but he was dangerously curious. I stepped back and widened my pose, seeing if he'd do the same. Instead, his eyes slid down to my legs and back up at me.

"Go kid, before I change my mind," he said and I wasted no time getting back onto my bike and leaving him there. I didn't go home, because if I did, he'd follow and I knew it. Knew it like I knew today had sucked monkey balls. I made it about a mile from the shelter and once again got off the bike to look around. I didn't feel the eyes on me, and after a few moments, I pulled

Darkest Before Dawn

out the hand held radio and radioed in to Addy.

Nope, I didn't speak, because it was vital that I keep my gender to myself. Instead, I used the code my father had taught us, to let her know I'd be sleeping in the big red barn on the Johnston's property.

"Stay safe, and don't do anything stupid, over."

Beep, beep, beep. *Love you, too.*

I pushed the bike inside and set up the cans which would alert me if anyone tripped the fishing wire. With the bike secured, I crawled up to the loft and sprawled out on the hay. I'd killed today, and even though it had been for a good reason, it left behind a darkness that bothered me. How many people would I have to kill before this was over? When would this be over? It had been months, and it was only getting worse.

Lying there in the blackness of night, it almost seemed normal. Until you listened to the silence and it sank in that nothing would ever be normal again. There would be no going back; the government was gone and those small factions claiming to be there to help you couldn't be trusted, nor could the distress calls like the one my father went to go answer. I'd heard plenty of reports of people going to them, only to never radio back just like my dad didn't. To me, it was a dead ringer for a red flag of trouble.

I closed my eyes without removing the mask, and slept.

Chapter Three

I woke up with the sun just rising. The smell of hay was rank, but what else had I expected? I sat up and looked around as I got my bearings. I'd dreamt of the man from yesterday, and it had left a tingling sensation in the pit of my stomach. I shrugged it off and reminded myself of what happened when men found women alone. Nothing good.

I stretched my arms, climbed out of the loft, and opened the huge doors before pushing my bike outside and closing them. I did a perimeter check with my eyes and when I was satisfied I wasn't being watched, I climbed on the bike and headed home.

I walked in and was pounced on by Addy.

"Bitch! I was so worried that I barely managed to sleep at all," she whined, and kissed my cheek.

"How's Cathleen settling in?" I asked, changing the

subject. I didn't want to discuss why I had hay in my hoodie, pants, and boots, and well, let's just say it was pretty much everywhere.

"She's adapting. I asked her for her story for the record books." The record book was where we kept the tales of everyone who we helped or saved along the way. It only had a few pages filled out, but eventually, we would write more. "She's from Boise, and was the mother of a two year old who those men killed. They also killed her husband of five years, and she's not ready to talk about it, but she seems to be healthy. She was definitely abused, but healthy."

"Good," I said as I pulled off the mask and shrugged the heavy pack off. I needed a shower and to change my clothes before I went back on patrol. "How many are up and about?"

"Kaylah, Jillian, and Greta are awake. I can wake the others if you need them."

"Do so," I said stretching my back where it hurt from the night spent in the barn. "I want more of the dead burned, but we also need to grab some more supplies. We might need to make a trip into Spokane again."

Spokane was the closest large city, but going there was always dangerous. "Has there been any news from Kameron or anyone from his group? He should have contacted us by now."

"Nope, Jimmy and Grayson are working the radio this morning, and nothing has come across yet," Addy said as she tied her long blonde hair into a tight ponytail. She'd been popular in school because she was outgoing, leggy, and beautiful, where as I was quiet and tended to hide in her shadow. Hey, if they can't see me, they can't make fun of me. Not like I cared what they thought; it's just the taunting and insults can wear on you after a while.

I left her with a few orders and headed to my room. Inside, I peered at my tired reflection. My hair was getting long, and the once strawberry-blonde hair had turned darker without the sunrays to keep it light. My eyes were the color of the sky on a clear, brisk day. I was medium height, and medium build. Short when compared to Addy's five foot eight frame. My breasts hadn't come in till late, and while I'd been a late bloomer, they were at least decent but still easy to hide when needed.

I peeled off the vest, and worked the pants off until I was able to breathe again. It sucked to hide from the sun. It wasn't like I wanted to tan; I just wanted to feel it shining on my face, to feel it heat my flesh. I missed being able to walk down the street. I missed simple things, but in the end, those things were huge. I'd always heard people say that most simple things were often the most missed…I hated that it was true.

I grabbed my shorts and slipped them on before grabbing everything I needed for the shower. We'd begun to make our own soaps and other necessities. It was easier than we had thought, but Maggie, one of the few I'd saved, was an amazing survival fanatic, and knew which herbs and natural greenery worked for what. The soap she made was priceless now.

Supplies were limited, and we tried to make what we could. It took a good deal of time to collect what we really needed to survive. I mean, how hard was it to grab a handful of flowers from the meadow, compared to walking through a dark store with no idea what was lying in wait to mess with you?

Shampoo was harder for her to make, and considering my hair went to the middle of my back, and seriously needed conditioner, I did make those hard runs to obtain it. Most of the girls had chopped their hair off, but I had my own reasons for keeping mine long. Eventually, I would have to cut it, but not today.

I showered and changed into clean black cargo pants, and a Misfits tank top. I braided my hair and pinned it into a tight bun. I scanned my reflection in the mirror and grunted. I looked tired, and the black circles beneath my eyes were only getting darker with each passing day.

Dressed and ready for the day, I headed to the media room. Grayson was watching a monitor with Jimmy by his side. No one else was hanging out in there yet so it would hopefully give us a chance to catch up.

"Ems, check this out," Grayson smiled as he pointed to a map of the United States that had been spread out on the table. Red pins indicated locations we knew there was people still alive in, as well as blue for supplies we'd left for survivors. "More red."

I looked to the marker and narrowed my eyes. "California?"

"Yes, now can we go away from here?" he begged.

"You want to just pack up and leave? Because it's *so* safe out there, Grayson," I mumbled. For a preteen, he was a good kid. Often times I would risk it and hook him up with some comic books and other items. His entire room was filled with stuff I'd brought back for him.

"I would settle for a trip to town," he whined.

"No; I told you, not until you are fully trained."

"You and me trained with Dad for years, and now he's gone! You don't have time to train me anyway; you spend all of your time training the girls!"

"That's because they're older than you are, Grayson! You're also my responsibility to care for, and I can't be out there watching after you when I'm hunting. I train the girls because together, we work well. I need you to be here so I know you're safe. It's the only way this works."

"I hate it here!" he shouted, and I cringed.

"More comic books? What do you want, Grayson?" He seemed to be doing this more and more as of late.

"I want you to look at me like I'm old enough to

Darkest Before Dawn

take care of myself! I was taught by Dad, too. I know what to do, Emma. I'm not stupid. I can learn to fight so that I can help you!"

"You are! But smart people don't want to go outside; they don't ask to go outside because it's not safe!"

"You do!"

"I do it because I have to. Dad taught us how, but he also said you needed more training and to be able to control your temper more before you'd be ready to go out. I'll see what I can find for you today, and I'm planning on going to Spokane soon, so I'll make sure to hit up the comic book shop."

"Promise?" he begrudgingly asked.

"I promise, and, Grayson. Try not to be in such a hurry to go out there. What you see on those monitors is only half of what happens. I love you, brat."

With Grayson settled down, I headed to the main room. I'd redone a lot of the inside to make it more efficient. I walked to the wall of mask, as we referred to it and pulled down a modified sugar skull mask.

"How many are coming out?" I asked to no one in particular. I didn't have to, because they knew if they didn't pitch in, we wouldn't survive the winter.

"Kaylah, Greta, and Jillian wanted to go. Who else?" Addy asked as she bounced into the room in a whirl of color. She had on yellow leggings, a blue shirt, and red skirt with hot pink *Nike* shoes. I smiled and wondered at her choice of clothes, but I wasn't judging. Oh who am I kidding? Holy friggin' rainbow!

"I'm not going," Bonnie said as she flattened herself out on the couch.

"Well then what do you plan on doing?" I asked as I folded my arms over my chest.

"I don't feel up to anything," she complained.

She complained a lot. "Bonnie, you can either work here, or you can come with us. No one gets to sit around. No one."

She glared at me, and I had to remind myself that while mentally punching the spoiled brat in the face was allowed, hitting her in front of everyone? Not such a smart plan.

"Who the hell died and left you in charge?" she snapped and I flinched.

"My father," I whispered with venom dripping from my lips. "You want to try your chances on the outside? Go for it."

Jillian and Bonnie were Towners as we called the people from our town that had joined our group here in the shelter. They had come here for help and we'd allowed it. We had a few others, but mostly we'd accepted the elderly or the young who had been abandoned or orphaned by the flu.

Darkest Before Dawn

Bonnie glared at me, but it didn't faze me one little bit. Little did anymore, and it was getting worse. The only thing I'd felt in the last week was the unexpected response from the mystery man. That, however, was unsettling. I'd never felt my body respond to any male like it had to him, and I'd made a mental note to take a break from reading romance novels for a while.

They were my guilty pleasure, which made me curious, but not enough to jump on the first male I saw. Not that my mystery man wasn't jumping material, because he was. He was jumpable, but he also thought I was a gangly boy. I shook my head and turned my attention to the problem at hand. "You know the rules. You either help out, or get out, Bonnie. This place works because we all work on it; if I let you lounge around, others will try it, and I can't allow that."

Yes, I was taking the high road and being nice. Did it mean I wasn't mentally punching her in my head? Nope. I was beating the tar out of her. She'd been a spoiled brat all through high school, and had been Jillian's shadow. I watched as she twirled her dark blonde hair in her fingers and considered what I'd just said. Seriously, she had to consider it?

"I'm not doing laundry, or dishes," she said as she stood up.

"Then tell me, Bonnie, what *are* you going to do?"

"No clue, but I refuse to do either of those chores."

"Maggie!" I shouted and waited for the fortyish

woman to pop her head in.

"Yes, Emma?" Maggie asked as her green eyes glowed with happiness; it told me she'd been playing with the children again.

"Bonnie's clothes are not to be washed. If she wants them washed, she is to do them herself. Also, she's volunteered to help you in the kitchen tonight, and would love to help you do the dishes. If she protests, she's to be given more chores."

Bonnie puffed out a groan but I ignored it and turned my attention to the group who was leaving the shelter with me. "Okay ladies, reminder time! Once we go through those doors there is to be no vocal cord usage. We use the hand signals for communications. We stick together unless I signal otherwise, and if you need a moment, you signal us and we will wait for you. Any request on the logs?" I asked Addy who was in charge of taking requests from those who couldn't go outside of the shelter.

"Cathleen asked for a pregnancy test. Brent asked for more wires, and black tape. The duct tape is low, and Nana asked for more ointment for her rash."

"Crap, that sounds like a hospital trip," I said and scrunched up my nose. I hated going to the hospital. It had yet to be cleared out of the corpses, and was a cesspool of disease. I could find all those items there, and we had antibiotics on the ever growing backlist. Why? Because I'd put off going there in hopes of clearing it.

Darkest Before Dawn

I'd also have to go in alone. There really wasn't any reason to take a group deep into it and I knew the layout like the back on my hand since I'd done my clinical there.

"I will do the hospital, and you guys can start the burnings," I said as I watched them all gear up to match my outfit. I slipped on my Kevlar vest, gloves, and then the lighter hoodie I'd grabbed when I was in Spokane last. It made it easier for me to haul tail through tainted areas. I grabbed my pack and emptied it of my last haul, which wasn't much. I checked to make sure the quiver was full and that the crossbow was clean and working, as well as adding a handgun and a few knives to the holsters I'd created just for them.

By the time we were done, we looked like group of punk kids who had a serious Goth fetish. Each girl used the coroner's cream, and no one complained about what they would be doing. It was life now, and if we didn't clean the houses out, we would all eventually end up sick. We couldn't bury them, because we couldn't embalm them to prevent the disease from contaminating the ground.

I pressed the code into the buttons of the panel and opened up the doors, and waited until everyone had passed through before I turned to Addy. I gave her the sign for I love you, and blinked three times.

"Love you too, mute; in fact, I really like you mute!" she smiled as I raised my gloved middle finger.

Outside, Greta had the camouflaged tarp off of the Humvee, and was folding it up already. When we went out in large groups, we normally used the Humvees we'd stolen after the military had left Newport. No reason to leave them there for someone else to steal. I waited until they were loaded up, and climbed on my bike. I gave them the hand signal for them to move out, and followed behind them.

I waited until we hit the edge of town before moving in front of them and signaling which side of town they should hit first. It only made sense to clear the dead out of one side and work our way across it.

I sat with my feet on the pavement as I watched them head in the opposite direction of the way I needed to go. I did a scan of the surrounding area and looked for a place to hide my bike. I would walk most of the way to the hospital, since I couldn't chance being caught there. The place was full of those who had sought treatment for the flu, but it was a small hospital and the waiting and treatment rooms, beds and morgue were full of the dead.

I ended up parking it in the bushes of one of the houses beside the highway, and glared at the sundial/thermometer in Mr. Linksys's front yard that said it was a blistering ninety-five degrees today. I passed through the yard, with kid's toys scattered through them and hated knowing that these houses still had those poor, innocent souls inside of them. Ones we would have to burn eventually. You would think that more people would have gotten out of town, but it was as if they'd gone into shock and just tried to ride it out at home.

Newport hadn't boasted of many residents. Sad part was, it was one of the largest cities in Pend Oreille County. It hadn't even been considered a city until the late seventies.

I reached down and picked up a discarded Newport Minor paper, and then let it drop to the ground. I scanned the dark corners of the buildings down South Washington Ave, and listened. Even though it was a small city, it had once been alive.

Now, it was a ghost town. I brought up my crossbow and slipped an arrow from my pouch into my hand. The silence of the town was unnerving and set me on alert every time I came to it. It was silent today, and deafening. Bodies had been littered all over the streets for the first few months after the flu had had ravaged the town.

Dad had said in the panic, the overwhelming numbers of people who'd come out from the smaller towns for help, Newport had been the rally point for those in need. It ended up being a mass grave site when the CDC had announced that there was no vaccination for what was killing millions of people.

I wasn't even sure we still had a CDC anymore. If we did, they'd gone to ground. I peeked around the corner and eyed the hospital, which looked exactly the same as it had before. The cars were in the same places, as well as the few items I'd placed to be able to tell if it had been disturbed. When I was sure it was safe, I started forward.

At the doors, I paused and listened again. Silence. I hated silence. Once, I used to want it. I had a younger brother who was both annoying and loud, and I could remember thinking how blissful it would be if I could only have silence. Well folks, it isn't golden…it sucks.

I stepped through the broken glass doors, and tried to avoid the crunching of glass my boots made as I stepped on the unavoidable remains of the windows. It was darker inside, but luckily it was early enough that the sun was working with me. I passed the emergency room, and made my way toward the pharmacy.

I stepped over the dead body that was leaned against the doorframe and pulled out the key I had from my clinical here. I'd been so close to getting my degree, and Mr. Kenan had agreed to hire me. He had even given me keys to the locked areas the day before the world had gone to hell. He was here, in his chair, with his body decomposing. He'd worked until he hadn't been able to from the looks of it. I slid the key in, and turned it until the door to the drug room slid open.

I added a few bottles of this and that which would be needed. I grabbed Phenergan for nausea, along with pain killers just in case we ever had need for them. I grabbed the pregnancy test as I sent a silent prayer to heaven that God wouldn't be so cruel as to do that to Cathleen. I also grabbed a few bottles of prenatal vitamins just in case God wasn't listening to me.

Darkest Before Dawn

I was almost out when I heard a strange noise, which sounded almost like an animal. It wouldn't be unlike animals to come and feed off the dead; I'd seen it a lot actually. It was a danger I was also trying to prevent. Birds like crows and vultures couldn't get in here, but bobcats, coyotes and foxes sure could. I peered out of the room and started toward the main doors, but as I moved closer a growl sounded from entirely too close to where I stood.

There in the middle of the hospital was a huge red timbre wolf, his fangs huge and pristine as they dropped saliva. He hadn't seen me yet, but I was willing to bet he'd smell me before he saw me. I stepped back, and winced as my foot crunched on something littered in the hall. Friggin' hell! I turned and ran, but the moment I did, the beast let out a haunting howl, and gave chase.

I was just passing the elevator and moving further into the darkening hospital and the patient rooms when an arm yanked me sideways, into one of the many rooms. The door slammed shut, and I stepped away from my savior. I could hear the beast outside, its nose blowing hot hair under the thin door.

"That was stupid, kid." It was the mystery man again.

I eyed the window and noted that it was broken. My pack was secured to my back and not too full yet; if I was fast enough, I could get out of it before he even noticed I'd left. Instead, when he turned and looked me over, I was stunned. Last night he had been hot, but

Amelia Hutchins

today? Today he was friggin' gorgeous.

I met and held his turquoise eyes. Eyes that made the air expel from my lungs as they searched my face intently. He was covered in shadows, but his eyes were in just the right amount of light that they looked positively stunning. They reminded me of gentle swaying of waves as they crashed against sandy beaches. They were the most beautiful swirls of tropical greens and blues that created the perfect shade of turquoise. Those eyes of his sent butterflies into my lady parts, and I wasn't sure why it felt like there was a party in my pants; I only knew there was one.

"You really don't talk, do you?" he asked as scraping and snarling sounded from the other side of the door. I tore my eyes from his to where the sound was getting worse. "Shame, I'm betting you could tell me a little about this town."

Yup, I could. I just wasn't going to. I watched as he stepped more into the light, and wondered if I should be making an exit soon, but when the sun fully exposed his body, my mind went to hussy town, and I followed it.

My brain turned over and I changed my mind from my earlier assessment. His eyes were the shade of a Caribbean ocean in full summer with the most beautiful mix of blue and greens, and his hair wasn't as dark as I had first thought it to be. Instead, it was a dark blond color that reminded me of the wheat fields in Washington State, and it fell to just above his wide shoulders. He towered above me by a foot at least and looked to be in his late twenties or early thirties. He looked like he belonged to another age in time, as if he'd stepped out of a Viking movie and right into my path. This guy could give Thor a run for his money, and Thor was a serious hottie in my book.

He wore a white T-shirt and loose-fitting jeans with black biker boots. He had guns strapped across his chest, and another tucked into his belt which was held together in the front with a silver skull.

"Do you sign?" he asked as he turned back to face me, which put his features back in the shade, and gave my hussy-fried mind a break. I shook my head, but his lips tipped up in the corner, as if I'd just given something away.

Crap!

Chapter Four

"Funny, most mutes can sign."

I pointed to my throat, and shook my head. His eyes however, slid down my body slowly making my libido kick into drive, and that stupid heartbeat was back, and throbbing between my legs. He smiled, and bit softly into his full bottom lip.

"As a matter of fact, you don't smell like a boy, either," he continued casually, reiterating the statement he'd made the day before.

I didn't smell like a boy? *Note to self, roll in dirt next time.*

"Remove the mask," he said, and I shook my head slowly as I stepped back. He followed. "Scared I won't like what I see, boy?"

Oh friggin' hell bells! He was gay, and I was playing a boy! It friggin' figured that I'd find the only hot gay guy left on planet earth and it seemed only fitting that said gay guy thought I was a boy! Someone in hell was laughing pretty damn hard at my misfortune, I was sure of it.

I shook my head and took a step closer to the window. The door was being chewed open, and I made a mental note to put an ASAP order on removing the dead, because we had enough crap to worry about. Wild animals putting us below them on the food chain was just not one of them.

"I'm guessing you do speak, but for some reason, you won't," he tipped his head, and his blond hair met the sunrays. I tried to keep my eyes locked to his, I really did. However, they went to the golden strands, and it took effort not to remove my gloves and test their silkiness. "I don't bite too hard." He grinned as he moved closer to me.

I tore my eyes from his hair and palmed the knife in my holster at my hip.

"I wouldn't try that," he warned, but I was being backed into a corner, and I wanted out. "If you pull that, I will kill you."

Between the door being attacked by a hungry wolf, and him warning me about my impending doom, I was freaking out. He stepped closer, and I at the pulled the knife, only to find myself slammed against the wall. I cried out, and he stopped. His eyes widened as his hands made contact with my chest.

"Fucking hell, if I didn't know better, boy, I'd say you have a perfect set of breasts," he grinned. He palmed them as his hands slid beneath the vest I wore. I growled, and took advantage of his brief distraction, pulling the knife. I held it against his throat, and then pressed harder when he just continued to grin at me.

"Back up," I said and continued to hold it against his flesh. "I said back up!"

He did as I asked, but only a step or two.

"You're female, so why hide it? Why not use it to your advantage?" he asked without blinking.

"And what? Become someone's whore? Or be raped by some loser until nothing of me is left but some mindless, sobbing mess? No, I don't think so," I replied. It was sounding like the Cujo that was growling, slobbering, and clawing at the door had a few friends join him and they were trying to eat it now.

"Remove the mask," he purred.

"Hey buddy, notice the knife?" I warned. Man, he was so not gay! I was trying to remember how to breathe while working my way to the window inconspicuously.

"Yeah, I see the knife. Not worried about that. I'm more curious to see why you wear the mask? I'm thinking it's because you're scarred, or hideous?" His head shifted from side to side with curiosity trying to get a look behind the mask.

Darkest Before Dawn

I snorted. Seriously snorted and shook my head in disgust. Did he think he could goad me into removing it with that?

"Hands up, or I'll shoot!" Greta's voice said from outside the window.

The man slowly placed his hands on his head, but it looked like a sexy relaxed pose instead of a worried one. "That's my cue," I said, and smiled beneath the mask.

"More of you masked ladies? I think I might like this town," he grinned as he stepped back and I replaced the knife in the holster.

"I wouldn't stay here," I warned, feeling cocky again.

"You planning on kicking me out?" he asked, and for a brief moment, I caught a warning in his tone.

I turned and looked at Greta, who had been stripped of her gun and was now between two beefy men. I went to reach for my knife, but I was pressed up against the wall, and my mask was lifted, baring only my lips. One moment I was about to scream, and the next, I was being kissed. By kissed, I mean it was curling my toes, and the moment his tongue pushed past my lips, I moaned. Hello Hussyland! I am your new leader. Follow me!

His mouth was clean and tasted of mint. His kiss was soft and yet hard as he demanded I open my jaw wider to accept his kiss. I was lost in it, as if the world had been sucked down a black hole, and only he and I remained. When he finally pulled away, his eyes were wide as if he was as shocked as me by the electrical sizzle that had shot through my entire body.

"You kissed me," I said in puzzlement. He hadn't even removed the mask fully, and yet he'd kissed me! "You kissed me!" I said with more anger. How dare he think it was okay to just go around kissing women!

"I did," he replied mockingly. He smiled, and I narrowed my eyes behind the mask. "And I'm already making plans to do it again."

"You wouldn't," I said indignity rampant in my tone.

"Oh, I would. In fact, watch this," he replied huskily before he pushed the mask up and kissed me again. This one was in no way soft. This one was fierce and his teeth scraped across mine as he held my face immobile. He growled from deep in his chest, or hell, maybe it had been me. His tongue captured mine and they danced, as if there was a musical beat only they could hear. His hands lowered and cupped my face even with the mask in the way. When he pulled away, I didn't need to see his lips to know he was smiling. Nope, they were still against my skin, and I felt them move into a smile. "You kissed me back," he whispered and pulled away from me. "Bjorn, Sven, let the girls go," he said to the men outside.

"The guns?" one of the two beefcakes asked.

Darkest Before Dawn

"They're only women and they need them for protection. They won't use them against us, will you…?"

I considered saying yes, but ammo was hard to find, and guns was nearly impossible. "I can only promise that if you promise not to kiss me again."

"Why would I stop kissing you, when you respond like that?" he asked incredulously as he folded his tattooed arms over his wide chest.

"Because I told you to, and I wasn't kissing you back. I was just planning on how best to gut you."

"You can lie to yourself, sweet one, but I know when someone is kissing me back and when they're planning to kill me."

"Get that often do ya?" I smiled as I said it.

"The kissing part? All the time," he replied casually and I felt something furl in the pit of my stomach at the thought of him kissing someone else as he had just done to me. The door chose that moment to splinter open, and wood shot through the air. I was taken to the floor hard, and the wind was knocked out of me painfully. "Kill!" he shouted, and bullets exploded from guns from outside, as the sound of shells hitting the ground echoed in my ears.

"Stay still," he warned, as I looked to the right where a pile of wolves now lay. "It's almost over," he assured as his thumb rubbed the soft tissue of my cheek. "I should have known this skin was too pretty to belong to a boy."

"Is that so?" I said without lifting my eyes. The wolves were huge, and didn't look right. I wiggled my hips against the pressure of his body and the hard floor. And froze. "Please tell me you have a banana in your pants?" Because it was large, favored left, and holy friggin' cat snouts! He was hard and on top of me! I pushed against him struggling to get out from underneath him.

"A banana? No sweet girl, that's a cock," he mused.

"Get off me!" I shouted and hit panic mode. With the last of the shots fired, he allowed it. He was huge, and I felt seriously uncomfortable with Mr. Happy poking my ass!

"Hey, it's okay. I was serious; we don't mean you any harm," he cautioned with his hands held up in mock surrender. "For now, anyway."

"Is that a threat?" I asked, and then wondered why I was wasting time. There were dead wolves in a pile, my girls were outside with men who looked like they'd been models for muscle magazines…Okay, that part wasn't that bad, but still, I needed to get out of there. "Don't answer that," I supplied and moved to the window. When I got through it, I looked back at him to find him watching me openly.

"See you around, Sweet Lips," he taunted and grinned at me.

Darkest Before Dawn

Sweet Lips? Next time, I'd bite him! It would stop that name from ever leaving his mouth again.

"Doubt it," I replied and looked at Greta who was currently eye-banging one of the men. "Let's go."

We headed away from the men, but as we entered the parking lot of the hospital, it was to find about twenty more men, and a couple of scantily dressed women watching us curiously. I didn't blame them, or the men who watched us with caution. We walked past them without any problems, and the moment our feet hit the blacktop, we bolted as if the hounds of hell were chasing us.

We made it to my motorcycle without any problems and took off in the direction of the girls. "You came for me, why?" I yelled over the motorcycle and then resented my tone.

"You took too long, and you're never late," she shouted back. "I worry about you, ya know? You hold us together and I know you have to do certain things which are going to leave their mark on you."

"Thank you," I whispered and wondered if she had heard it over the quiet purr of the bike.

She held on as we rounded the corner and found the others slowly piling the bodies of the town's less fortunate into a pile. I waited for Greta to climb off before I joined her. My lips still burned from his kiss, and the tingling in the pit of my stomach hadn't stopped yet. The cold reminder of why we were here did little to cool the ardor in my system.

We walked in silence, absently slipping back into our roles as we moved to help the others with the bodies. I wasn't paying attention, because if I had been, I would have heard the music from the car that was sending dirt up in the air. I raised my hand, pointing it straight in the air. It was the signal for the women to hide. Nope, I had been contemplating that kiss, and its electrical pulse which had managed to slip into my panties and stay there.

When they had slipped into the shadows, I followed them. I was between a building and a house when the Jeep slowed and then stopped by the pile of bodies. Had I been paying attention, we'd all be close together instead of scattered. The occupant of the Jeep got out and pulled on a thin length of leather. I had to swallow the bile that tried to come up as a small, thin girl who could be no more than thirteen climbed out and went to her knees in front of him.

The guy looked methed-out, and his words were slurred as he smiled cruelly at the girl. They seemed to be alone, which worked out well, considering I was out of range for hand signals.

"This looks like a good enough place to pass the night, whore," he sneered and held out his boot which she then lowered her face to—and licked. Oh my God, he was so going to die for that. He kicked her and told her to clean it better, and I couldn't stop myself from lunging and walking out to meet him.

Darkest Before Dawn

"What the fuck is this?" he asked. "You want some of my cock too, boy? I really couldn't give a fuck less as long as it's tight. Right, whore?" He didn't even look shocked that I was wearing a mask, or that I was dressed in all black. Most people who saw us had the instinct to run, or try to kill us. Him? Not so much; his reaction was to abuse me. Yup, he was either on drugs, drunk, or both. I was going with both.

I narrowed my eyes and pointed at myself. This guy had to be on something, because he couldn't keep his attention on me or the poor girl for more than a few seconds. Drugs are bad, m'kay?

Yep, it was official. Only the scum had been spared from the flu, and lived. He kicked her in the face and she cried out as she fell back. "I'll do better, master, I promise. Please don't do what you did to Diana to me, I'm a better whore!"

"Nasty little bitch, you'd do anything for me, wouldn't you?"

I gagged. She nodded, and from the crazed look in her eyes, I believed she would do anything he asked her. She probably had done unspeakable things just to stay alive.

"Go suck that boy off, while I fuck his ass," he smiled coldly revealing blackened teeth.

I pointed at myself again and tilted my head; he was serious!

Yup, time to die. I pulled my crossbow from the cord and nocked an arrow before he could blink.

"What the hell do you think you're doing, you weak little piece of shit!" he screamed as spittle ran down his face. I knew the moment the others stepped out from their hiding places, because he turned white. "You won't get away with this! My friends are coming! They will kill you *all*, but not before they make you feel pain." I pulled the trigger, releasing the arrow, and watched as he fell to the cold ground with the other dead people.

I wasn't ready for the girl when she attacked me, and Greta had to pull her off of me. "You killed him! You killed him you fucking punk!" she screamed and clawed at Greta as she tried to get at me. Ok, up close and personal with crazy, I now saw that she was closer to seventeen or eighteen.

"I did you a favor. He can't hurt you anymore!"

"I'll kill you! I'll kill all of you! I'll sell you to Ted and I'll become his main whore! I'll never want for anything again!"

I shook my head, and then looked at Greta.

"Can you change? *Will* you change?" I asked with desperation in my voice.

"I'll kill you!" she screamed and the moment she lunged, I pulled the knife and slipped it between us. Tears left my eyes to stream down my cheeks as she cried against my chest. "Kill...you." My stomach clenched and rebelled against me.

She gurgled, and when I could no longer feel her breathing, I picked her up and carried her to the pile. Mercy killing, but it left a mark on my soul, one I'm sure I'd remember forever.

"You couldn't bring her home with us, and you couldn't chance letting her go to bring men back here to us," Greta said softly and the others agreed. This was why she was worried, and I understood it. This poor girl wasn't my first mercy kill, and unfortunately, she wouldn't be my last.

"It's done," I said, and stopped them from saying more. I couldn't handle the look in their eyes, or their pity. I cocked my head to the side and listened as the sound of vehicles moving swiftly traveled through the air. "Get to the top of the building, go!" I shouted as I moved to the saddle bag on my bike. I grabbed it and ran for the Humvee, lifted the hood and pulled out a handful of cords so it wouldn't start. If they took the gas, so be it, but they were not getting the damn thing.

Next I ran to my bike, pulled out the keys, and booked it up the front set of stairs to hide behind the door, but the cars had been moving faster than I'd predicted. Shit!

"Look....what the fuck!" A male's deep voice tore through the air. "Spread out, and find who did this! I want their heads!"

"And if it's a woman?" someone else asked.

Amelia Hutchins

"Then bring her to me, alive, she's *mine*."

I made myself flush against the wall as I pulled out a grenade from the saddlebag. I pulled the pin and stepped into the doorframe, then tossed it like I was bowling for pins. I slipped silently back into the shadows and listened as I counted.

"What the…." Boom! I dropped the bag, since I'd only counted four men outside, and I knew at least one was dead. I pulled the crossbow from my bag, set it and aimed at the man furthest from me. It struck him in the chest, and he looked down, surprised that it was there.

"Run!" one of the other men shouted, but as I lifted my crossbow, reset it and took aim, I caught a glimpse of a shadow stepping out from behind one of the abandoned cars on the street. I released my breath and watched as my mystery man swung a wicked looking axe and cleaved the unsuspecting guy's head in half. He didn't hesitate as he went after the other guy. I watched him as he swung his axe again, and removed the guy's head. Ewww, he was so cleaning that one up.

I stepped from the building to survey the damage. The car they'd driven here in was toast. Pieces of the leader were scattered on the ground. I looked up to the top of the building to find the three candy skull masks still staring down at me. I turned my head as mister sexy walked back up to me, his axe still dripping blood.

"Get your girls, and get out of here. This group has more people, and I'm willing to bet they are on their way here," he said as he stepped over the body pieces and walked up until he was nose to nose with me. He lifted the mask with no warning, exposing my lips again. His thumb trailed over where a single droplet of blood remained from being hit. "Be careful, there are bad men out on your streets, my fierce Valkyrie."

"Why did you help me?" I asked, because this wasn't the first time. I'd have been puppy chow earlier, and he had plenty of time to attack me between his men and Greta getting there.

"Is it wrong to help people?" he asked, surprised by my question.

"If you expect something for it, it is."

"Have I demanded anything from you?" he countered as he stepped closer. I pretended not to be intimidated, but I was. I whistled for the girls, and watched him as he continued until he was inches from me.

"You will, and when you do, remember, I have nothing to give you."

"And what if I only want your name?" he asked softly.

"Emma, you want us to head back?" Greta asked as they walked out from the building and joined us.

I shook my head. "Well, I guess you have it now."

"Emma." He tested my name on his tongue and for

some reason; it rolled through my vagina and bounced off my rib cage before hitting my nipples and turning them hard. I may have been a virgin still, but my body belonged to a slut! Moisture pooled between my thighs, and the only thing he'd done, was say my name. "I guess I'll have to think of something else you can owe me," he smiled and walked off, leaving all the girls drooling in his wake.

"He has got some friggin' nerve!" I snapped.

"Look at that ass!" Greta said.

"Um, if I have to choose between going back to the shelter, and him, I'm choosing him." Jillian whipped her hair back, which was her signature move for flirting—it had been since first grade.

"Momma wants some!" Kaylah chimed in.

I tore my eyes from them, back at him just in time for him to look back and wink at me. "Get in the hummer," I growled.

"I'd give him a hummer," Jillian laughed.

I shook my head; yup, it was official. I had a land, it was called Hussy, and I was its queen.

Chapter Five

I spent the next day handing out care packages to the families that lived deep in the woods. I'd brought the ATV, since most lived in places cars and my bike wouldn't reach. I was at my last stop for the day, and the sun had already begun to set for the night. I rounded the bend and turned off the ATV, but even from the distance I had parked away from my destination, I could tell that something seemed off.

If I'd been smarter, I would have run. Really, my brain was playing that annoying eighties song asking: should I stay or should I go now. Yup, I was a dork that way. I had theme music for every kind of situation. If the Jaws music started playing, I was seriously out of here.

I rounded the corner of the cabin, and stopped cold. Blood! Danger! I was torn, because I knew this family. I'd gone to school with Karen, and she'd just had a baby. I could hear whimpered cries from inside, but the amount of blood that was dried and caked on the porch told me someone had died…gruesomely.

I strained my reserve and my spine, which was bent and twisted and wanted to run away, and pulled out one of my knives. I crept slowly up to the door, and listened. The whimpering noises were faint and other than that, the house was silent. I turned and peeked my head inside, only to gag as the smell of death hung putrid in the stale air.

There were a few things you got used to in this new world. The smell of death however, wasn't one of them. Seeing children left parentless with no one to defend them was another and if I was right, Sarah was alive. Or there was a cougar in here hunting me. The second option seemed dismal as the house's set-up was pretty open which left no place for a cougar to hide.

I braced myself for what I knew I would find, and walked inside. There in the corner was Joseph, dead. He was torn to shreds, as if a wild animal had done it. I walked over to the blinds and pulled them, and blinked back tears at the destruction I found. They'd fought hard, but in the end, whatever had attacked had won.

From the gnawing marks, and the way their bodies were mutilated, I was willing to guess it had been an animal, and not humans. Karen was in the doorway to the only bedroom in the cabin. Her body lay torn and ripped into pieces as Joseph's was. I fought the tears, and won. I scanned the room, looking for the smallest of Danvers. But I couldn't see little Sarah anywhere.

Darkest Before Dawn

I stepped over the grisly remains and looked around the room. The whimpering had stopped, but it was more than possible that the baby was among the remains. She was a tiny little thing. I sent a silent prayer and turned to leave when I heard the faint whimper again.

I swung back around and looked through the room. I walked over the window and tossed it open for more light. There were several items for the baby, which meant Joseph had gone on a run before they were attacked. I searched around, but still couldn't find any sign of her. I walked to the bed and pulled off the bedding, but she wasn't there. I stepped around the bed and as my foot slid on something white and oozing, I felt the loose floorboard.

They wouldn't have put a baby in a floor, right? If I'd been Karen, I'd have put her anywhere I thought she'd survive...I stepped back, and leaned down to remove the board. There in the small space was Sarah, her big blue baby eyes looking up even as she squinted from the light.

I closed my eyes in relief as pressure left my chest as I expelled the breath that I hadn't realized I'd been holding. "Hi, Sweetling Sarah, you've had a tough day, haven't you?" I cooed softly. I'd often heard her mother calling her Sweetling, so I figured I'd try to comfort her with it. Babies liked familiar things...right? I wasn't baby friendly, what the hell was I supposed to do now?

I put my hand down to check her breathing, but as I did, she wrapped her tiny little hand around my finger. I carefully pulled her out, and held her against me. Wow, she reeked. "Poor thing, how long have you been in there?" I waited, right up until I realized I was expecting this little being to talk back. I looked around the room until I found a sheet, and walked to the bed. "Don't move," I told the tiny, mewling infant, as if she was going to get off the bed and run away.

I collected a few things and placed them in my pack, like formula, and diapers. I didn't see any bottles, well, correction. I saw one that hadn't been gnawed at. Obviously the bigger animals that had killed the family had come and gone, and then little ones arrived after and had decided to tear everything else apart. Poor little Sarah fell asleep. She must have been fussing all day and conked out from exhaustion. I brought out the knife again and quickly shredded the sheet as I made a makeshift baby sling. I arranged her so I could easily get to the AR-15 if I had to.

Mmm, I'd seen women wearing them in the front, but if I was attacked, she'd be in front of the vest... the back it is! I reached down and secured the tiny being in the cloth and then brought her up as I tied the sling around my chest. She wasn't crying, but that was probably because she was relieved I wasn't some long toothed animal.

I grabbed the pack and walked to the front door as I mentally assessed the room again. Teeth marks; check. The bloody paw marks looked canine, and that pissed me off since they'd just tried to eat me yesterday. I looked to the corner and smiled. I could tell that some of

Darkest Before Dawn

the prints were old, and some were new. Which meant, the wolves had come back to snack on the corpses after the kill.

I knew Joseph had been trapping animals for fresh meat, and I also knew he'd worked at the fish and tackle shop, which doubled as a hunting shop as well. I found the unused traps in the closet and made fast work of setting them around the bigger pieces of the bodies. Wolves by nature were smart animals, cautious if they could smell humans. Obviously these ones were hungry enough to ignore their instincts.

I walked out of the cabin, and stopped cold. My heart dropped to my feet, and my breath froze in my throat. I stepped back towards the house, but it was filled with traps. In front of me were about ten or more men, all looking at me strangely. I had my mask still in place, so I guess that only made sense. I mean, I had a skull face, and had a ripped up sheet wrapped around me; even I'd pause to do a double take.

"And what ye be doing in there?" the leader asked. He wore no shirt but he had it hanging from his pants, and his torso was covered in tribal tattoos. His hair was black, and his eyes, even from this distance, popped with a deep emerald shade. The men behind him all held guns, which of course were pointed at me.

I took a step closer, and another one. *Please, Sarah, not a peep!*

I remained silent, as I worked my way closer in the

direction of the path. If I could just make it to the path, I could run to the ATV. I was fast, but I wasn't fast enough to dodge bullets, and I couldn't turn and run because I had a sleeping infant on my back attached to me, and my pack weighed heavily on my arm stuffed with all of the supplies I had taken for her.

"I wouldna do that," the hulking leader said in what sounded like a Scottish brogue, as he sniffed the air. At about the same exact time his eyes landed on me, a painful scream ripped from inside the house. I turned in horror as a male came limping out, white and pale as he collapsed to the ground with a bear trap clamped wickedly around his foot and ankle.

"Liam!" The taller of the men shouted.

He was bleeding profusely. He'd passed out from the shock and pain. I had a choice to make, since I knew how to save him.

"What the fuck did ye do?" the leader asked angrily as he stepped closer.

"Don't move," I said and watched as shock registered on his face. "I can help him, or he can bleed out—" the baby wailed and the entire forest froze. I waited to see their response, before I spoke over the screaming infant. "He'll bleed out unless you allow me to help him. I was in nursing school, and also working at the hospital in Newport as a surgical technician. If I help him, you let me go, deal?"

"What happened inside that house, lass?" He asked

Darkest Before Dawn

instead of answering me.

"Animals ate Sarah's family—she was hidden—and I need to get her to my people so I can examine her."

"Deal, save him," he growled.

I turned and slowly walked back up the steps, and then kneeled down to where the black haired male was just opening his eyes. "I won't hurt you if you don't hurt me."

He nodded; his face remained strained with pain. How he was managing to not scream was beyond me. The metal teeth of the trap were buried in his flesh at his ankle. I ripped off my sweatshirt sleeve to be able to stop the bleeding. It wasn't until I tried to remove the trap that I felt a flash of panic.

"I need help," I said turning to eye the leader. I hated that I needed it, but without help, I couldn't manage it. It was an old trap, rusty and one that had to be held open to release the animal, in this case, this man's foot.

The leader stepped forward, and for a brief moment, I wanted to dart into the forest to keep Sarah safe, and yes, myself too.

"Easy, lass," he said as he moved to kneel beside me. The wind was rustling through the leaves as the sun began to slowly dip into the sunset. It was also blowing the stench of death to us from the open window, and blowing it out the front door, too. "What the—"

"The couple in there, or at least I think it was only one couple. Can't be sure, Lach, they are in bloody pieces. Looks like rogue wolves tore them apart," the pale man said in a similar brogue to the leaders, his teeth chattering from the pain.

"That's nae good," Lach said as he manhandled the trap and held it open. I looked at his hands, and up at his face. He wasn't straining in the least, and this trap was exerting at least a hundred pounds of pressure.

"A little further," I said as I continued to watch his face. He was lighter skinned than my mystery man was, and his eyes were a deep shade of emerald. His muscles, which should have been straining, were the same sleek, muscular build. He had a tribal tattoo that went down his left flank, and dipped lower into his pants.

"You gonna eye-fuck me lass, or help my brother?" he asked and watched me as I did just as he'd said.

"I wasn't eye-fucking you," I retorted haughtily.

"Ye were and I dinnae mind ye ken," he argued.

"I was sizing you up, and weighing my options." I pulled the mangled ankle out of the trap, noting a few things.

One: The man with the mangled ankle was regaining color, and hadn't made a sound of discomfort since regaining consciousness.

Two: His brother either had experience with traps,

Darkest Before Dawn

or deep inner strength...or both.

Three: Someone had either replaced my eyeballs with permanent beer goggles, and it was making all of the men around here look like Greek Gods.

Four: Or, my ovaries were on overdrive, making me hallucinate.

"I think he passed oot again, lass," he said with an annoyed look on his face.

"It's probably for the better," I mumbled as I took in the damage. I placed the material around the injured flesh, which had somehow managed to already stop bleeding. My fingers trailed up the bone to see if there was a break in it, but if there was, it wasn't palpable. "Are you seeing this?" I asked as the wound started to scab at the edges. Impossible! It took hours for wounds to dry enough to scab.

"Lass," he said and I lifted my eyes to his from where I'd been fascinated by the rapid healing. I met his eyes, and then rough hands grabbed my arms, and I was pulled up.

"She's only a baby! If you do anything to her, I *will* kill you!" I growled.

"Hold her still Declan, Ian, careful nae to harm the bairn," he said softly. "Let's have a look beneath the mask."

"No!" I shouted, but the men behind me laughed. It

wasn't until a familiar voice rose over the laughter that I felt my anxiety escalate.

"And what do we have here?"

"Jaeden," Lachlan said, as he looked from the mystery man and back at me. "Thought we'd find ye close tae here, smelled the stench of death all the way from my mountains in Montana."

"Lachlan, good to see you again, sort of hard not to smell death these days; seems to be about everywhere. And Montana, was it...really? Seems a little far from your homeland," Jaeden snorted disbelievingly. For some reason, I wanted to test his name on my tongue as he had mine. "Now let poor Emma go. She doesn't like to take off her mask," he said as he winked one of his turquoise eyes at me.

"Nae further than yours, Jaeden," Lachlan growled. "She was in this house of death," he said as his eyes landed on me and then my exposed arm where I'd ripped off the sleeve instead of undoing the makeshift baby sling to get the materials in my bag. "We followed the stench, which led us here. This was done by a rogue pack which seems tae be sticking around this area."

"We met a few of them yesterday in the hospital in Newport, didn't we, sweet Emma?" he waited for me to nod, instead I just watched him. "Anyway, we dispatched them. More seem to be converging on this area. You have any info on why they would come here?"

These two knew each other, yet their posture said it

Darkest Before Dawn

wasn't by choice.

"It's why we came, but if ye think I'm going tae discuss pack business in front of a mortal, ye are dead wrong, leech."

Okay, there was a few things wrong with this conversation. One being *mortal*; we're all mortals, right? Pack business? Was he in some kind of cult? Rogue pack, like a big bad pack of rabid wolves, or could it explain the drop dead beef cakes that seemed to be crowding in on my tiny little city? Leech? Did Jaeden suck…? And if he did, what exactly *did* he suck? I was so lost.

"Hey, if you two are going to compare dick sizes, can I go? I'm unequipped to participate," I said with a smile hidden beneath the protection of the mask. Both men looked down to the location in question, and I felt a blush rise from my stomach all the way to my cheeks.

"So, Jaeden, what does the lass look like behind the mask? Hideously scarred?" Lachlan asked.

Jaeden grinned as his eyes did that quick search of my eyes that felt as if he could see through the mask I wore and was looking into my very being. "No idea, but I couldn't care less what she looks like." He said as he sidled up next to me. "What is that smell?"

"Probably the dead bodies?" I offered.

"What the hell is on your back?"

"A baby," I said. "Can I go? She needs to be taken care of. She's been alone for at least one day from the smell of those bodies. I still have to find some things for her."

"I'll come with you," he said, and I had to push the urge to scream 'hell no' down from my throat where it sat, waiting to come out. "Lachlan, I trust you and your pack will be staying in the area?" Jaeden questioned casually.

"Someone has tae guard the race, and since ye feast upon it, I guess that leaves me," Lachlan said just as easily, while his men grunted in agreement.

Feast upon it? Like a zombie? I narrowed my eyes on Jaeden, and of course they slid down his body. Today he wore camo pants and dark leather boots. He had on a long sleeved black shirt, thankfully. It made it easier to breath around him. He didn't look like any zombie that I'd ever seen in the movies and then my mind drifted away wondering how much it would hurt if he took a nibble at me. I gave myself a sharp mental shake at that. *Gross, Emma, just gross.*

"You don't need to follow me," I said to Jaeden who had inched closer towards me. He ignored me, but Lachlan smiled as I said it, as if he found it funny.

"The lass says nae, leech," he smiled as he said it.

"The *lass* doesn't have a choice in the matter, dog."

I looked from one male to the other. "Again with

the name calling? Maybe you guys should go to couples therapy?" They raised their eyebrows, and I narrowed my eyes at their twin looks of surprise. "Just saying," I smiled, but it was still hidden beneath the mask. "I'm leaving; this baby needs care."

No one stopped me, but Jaeden followed me until I reached the ATV. "It only seats one," I said as I turned to look at him.

"Liar, two can easily fit on it. Besides, you need help protecting the baby."

"Fine," I replied as I adjusted the baby to my front and straddled the ATV and waited for him to climb on it. The moment he placed his arms around my waist, I shivered. "Problem?" he whispered against my ear. "I personally like it when women drive…"

"Is that a sexual innuendo?" I asked, smiling even though I shouldn't have been.

"Tell me, Emma, do you like to drive?" he continued on.

"I like the purr of the engine, the way it feels between my thighs…" I smiled as he growled. "And the way I can run shit over," I whispered, and listened as his lungs expelled a disappointed sigh. I took off, not waiting for a signal that he was ready, but then I really didn't care if he fell off. It would solve the issue of the butterflies currently attacking my insides.

We drove for several minutes in silence before he

Amelia Hutchins

started talking, which I pretended to ignore. It wasn't until he turned on the bike and his grip tightened that I slowed and made a point to listen.

"Don't slow down! Fucking hell, they must smell that thing's diaper," he growled and one hand released me as he pulled a gun from the back of his pants. "There's a hunter's perch about a mile up from here, can you make it there?"

Make it there? I turned and caught sight of what had him on edge. There were wolves running right at us. I floored it. "Protect the baby!" I shouted as we hit a bump, but fortunately the ATV corrected and we continued towards the perch. "Hold on," I warned as we hit a hill, which I normally would have gone around because it was steep. The wolves would be more winded though, and it would give us time to climb the perch. I knew where it was, but the woods could be tricky at dusk.

"There," he pointed to it as he narrowly missed a low hanging branch. I stalled the bike, clicked off the gas, and shut it down before jumping off the ATV and running to the back to grab the food. I tossed the duffle bag of army rations to Jaeden and climbed up the wooden ladder at a swift pace. Sarah was crying, and I couldn't blame her; the poor thing had been through hell. The sounds the wolves were making would have scared anybody.

I finished climbing and reached for the bag as Jaeden handed it off to me. I tossed it into the corner and started to undo the sling. Then I was turned around, and Jaeden

Darkest Before Dawn

was there helping me to undo the knot so I could secure Sarah safely in the small pile of hay hunters would sit in while waiting for prey. I kissed her little forehead before wrapping one of the thin shirts I kept in my pack around her.

I pulled up the AR-15 and moved to the lookout window. The perch was bigger than most, but hunters around here took their hunting seriously. Hundreds normally converged to these mountains for hunting since it was teeming with wild life. These perches were built to last, as well as for comfort.

I snapped the red dot on, and clicked the scope open before looking through it. "Eight wolves," I said, and waited for Jaeden to say what he saw. When he didn't, I turned to look at him. "See anymore?"

"Holy hell," he whispered as he moved closer and his finger traced my cheek softly.

I blushed to my roots. My mask had come off somewhere between laying Sarah down, and grabbing the gun. "Stop it, and pay attention!" I growled. I felt naked and exposed under the heat of his eyes.

"Twelve wolves, eight you can see, four are lagging behind. Three brown and the rest are gray, and you're beautiful."

I blinked and looked out into the woods. It was getting dark fast, and I couldn't see much, so how had he? I peered through the scope at the trees and sure enough, there were stragglers in the bushes. The wolves

81

closest to us had their ears tight against their heads as they peered up at us.

I aimed the gun at the front-runner, and fired a shot into the dirt, inches from his front paw. He growled instead of yipping, and bared huge fangs. "That isn't normal," I mused out loud. "Wolves cower when we shoot at them…these ones looks like they wanna chew off my face, rather than run."

"Shoot it," he said as he brought up his gun and took aim at the leader of the pack. Right when he was about to shoot, a large pack of wolves burst through the brush and lunged at the pack circling the perch. "Fucking mutt," he mumbled.

I couldn't look away from the wolves as they savagely attacked each other. It was eerie, and yet even though I knew I should, I couldn't look away. The biggest of the new wolves, a black one, attacked the biggest of the brown ones, and I knew without a doubt that the brown one was going down.

It was a grisly sight, but the moment the black wolf made the kill, the others took off as if hellhounds were hot on their asses. "Wow," I whispered, which caused the black wolf to turn and look up at us. The sun had almost set, but even through the dimly lit forest, the emerald eyes were unforgettable.

They sent a shiver through my skin and a frown to my lips. "Since when do wolves have green eyes?" I asked myself.

Darkest Before Dawn

I was about to turn and see if Jaeden had the answer, when he pulled me close to his body and his mouth captured mine. His kiss wasn't just a kiss. He was declaring ownership of Hussyland with his mouth. His tongue pushed past my teeth and captured mine. I moaned against his lips as his hands came up to hold my face, while his tongue made love to mine. I pressed on his chest, fully intending to stop the madness.

Madness…there was madness in my panties, in my stomach and I was pretty sure it was madness that my hands had dropped lower, until I was pretty sure I was groping him. The wolves howled, and I jumped, biting his lip as reality came rushing back.

"You taste like heaven, woman," he whispered huskily.

"You kissed me," I replied, dazed.

"Jeg har tenkt å gjøre det igjen, og mer, søt jente," he replied with a wolfish grin. *

Oh yeah, wolves! And had he just called me dirty names in a foreign language? And if he had, why was I all giddy over it, when I shouldn't be? Oh yeah, 'cause it was sexy as hell!

~~*

"Jeg har tenkt å gjøre det igjen, og mer, søt jente."

Translation: "I plan to do it again, and more, sweet girl."

Chapter Six

The wolves had disappeared into the woods, so I made myself busy tending to Sarah. Jaeden had insisted we stay put until morning, since the wolves still howled all around us. They were close enough to keep us stuck here until it was light enough to see them.

Sarah had a rash, but that was a given since she'd been wearing the thing for more than a day as far as I could guess. What little remained under her onesie was laughable. I was reassuring her, and telling her everything I was doing as if she was an adult.

"You do know she doesn't understand anything you're saying, right?" Jaeden said. He was sitting up against the wooden wall of the perch. He sat with one leg extended and the other bent at the knee. He looked relaxed and uncaring, despite being stuck in the hunter's perch for the entire night.

"You think I don't know that? Why don't you do

Darkest Before Dawn

something useful?" I asked and picked up the flashlight to check Sarah for wounds. Her mother had given her life to ensure this child survived, so I'd do my best to ensure that her sacrifice hadn't been in vain. "Can you hold the flashlight?"

He accepted it without question, and I started a full examination of the infant. I finished it, satisfied and relieved that she only appeared tired and dehydrated. "She's a little dehydrated, but that's about all, minus the rash." I scooted the hay around into a little bed and set her down in it. I quickly made up a bottle of formula using the bottled water from my pack. Not exactly sanitary, but then again, what was these days? I sat down in the hay, pulled her back in my arms, and touched the nipple to her lips. Poor little starved thing latched on and suckled with long, greedy pulls, her little eyes drifting between concentration and contentment. "She's obviously got an angel watching over her," I mused and smiled as the child once again clasped her tiny hand around my finger. "Your mother was so brave," I whispered to the child.

"How do you figure that? She died," Jaeden said.

"Yes, but not before she hid the most important thing in her world, and made sure it was safe," I replied, looking up into his eyes—that was a total mistake. Once I looked into them, I felt as if I was drowning. I absently chewed my lip, which kinda hurt, but I was too busy doing sexual things to those beautiful sea green eyes. I started to say something, but forgot what I'd been about to say, and his lips curled into a knowing smile.

"You keep looking at me like that, and I won't be responsible for what happens," he said as he lowered his mouth. I threw myself backwards, making the content baby start from her drowsy state.

"Stay there!" I warned loudly, which scared Sarah and tore a cry from her throat. Shit! I tried to pat her back and console the baby, but Jaeden reached out and gently, but firmly, took her from me, startling the little thing into silence. My guess was she too got lost in those seductive eyes. Poor girl. "What are you doing?"

"What does it look like I'm doing?" he asked as he pulled off this own shirt. "I think she's cold," he mused, and tucked the shirt tightly around her. God help me. I had to force my jaw to remain up as he cradled the baby in his arms. "That's better, little one," he cooed, patting her back until she made a wet burp.

"So what was the name calling between you and Lachlan?" I asked curious as to how they knew each other.

"That's a long story," he said as he leaned back with Sarah in his arms. From here I could make out a black raven perched on a skull on his right pectoral muscle. He had words written on his ribs, but it looked as foreign as the words he'd said earlier.

I looked around and then back at him. "Like we don't have enough time right now?" I know; pretty smart-assed thing to say, but really, we had time to kill. I sat back down in the hay and made myself comfortable.

Darkest Before Dawn

"He took something that was mine," he stated, but didn't elaborate.

"So he stole a toy? What, were you both five?"

He smiled. "He helped himself to someone I once cherished. It's not something I like to talk about."

"He stole your girlfriend?" I knew my eyes were wide, but I was pretty sure this history they had started way before Rh Viridae had even been heard of, before the world had fallen apart.

"He and I were friends once upon a time," he continued. "Until she chose him, and then everything went to shit."

"How do you know she chose him?" I asked.

"She taunted me with it for a long time. Sometimes bigger things happen and you're forced to work together. That doesn't mean I have to like the mutt."

"How long ago was this?" I asked softly.

"I said I don't like to talk about it," he snapped angrily, his funky accent becoming more pronounced. Sarah started to protest, but he whispered softly to her and she closed her eyes again.

I reached for the duffle bag and dug through it for two bottles of water. I offered one to him, but he shook his head. When I offered him the jerky Addy had made, he smiled.

"You should eat it. I had a rather large meal before coming out to find you," he said quietly as he absently rubbed the sleeping baby's back.

"You do know that stalking is against the law, right?" I ridiculed.

He lifted a single eyebrow and looked around at the mountain terrain. "Who's going to press charges? Or enforce them, sweet girl?"

"You think I need someone to help me kick your ass?" I smarted off, and then considered the fact that I was alone with him, other than an infant, who wasn't going to be much help.

"You wanna try it? I'm up for it," he said, setting Sarah down gently in a small bed of hay. "Rolling on the ground with you to see who wins, well let's just say I'm up for the challenge."

"Are you crazy?" I asked and scooted back.

"Absolutely," he grinned as he stood up, his muscles bulging from the subtle movement. "Come on little she-devil, pounce."

He was serious! I waited for him to step close enough before I swung my leg out and kicked his out from beneath him, which wasn't an easy feat, but somehow I managed it. Only thing was, I didn't plan on him launching himself at me, or being taken to the hard wood beneath him. The wind from my lungs whooshed out, but he'd lessened the pain of the fall, and before I

Darkest Before Dawn

could figure out what had gone wrong, he was kissing my neck.

"I win," he whispered huskily before his lips kissed my neck seductively. I wrapped my legs around his, and tightened them right before I flipped him over. "Mmm, I like fighting with you," he rumbled with a wicked smile curving his lips. "I'm guessing I'll like fucking you even better."

I looked down at him with a disgusted look on my face. "In your dreams, buddy," I countered.

"That's a given," he said as he flipped me easily, as if I weighed no more than Sarah. He gripped my hands, and held them both easily above my head before lowering his mouth to my ear. "I've already dreamt of fucking you, and that was before I knew what beauty you hid behind the mask."

I swallowed and closed my eyes. He'd just said I was beautiful, and while it was a little disturbing that he'd dreamt of me, I was turned on by it. "Sure you don't have a mask fetish?" I asked and then cried out as his teeth nibbled against my soft lobe. His tongue traced where his teeth had bitten. The sensation was erotic, and sent heat flushing through me.

"I have an Emma fetish," he grinned against my ear.

"Obviously," I said as I tried to scoot my ear from him, which wasn't easy considering he was holding me down with his body, while his mouth violated my ear and his hands held mine captured above my head. "You do know there's a baby here, right?"

"She isn't interested in us," he assured me. "Look at me, Emma," he commanded, hoarse. I trembled from his tone as his hot breath fanned where he had just nibbled. I knew I shouldn't, but I looked up and was instantly aware of a few things.

One, he was hot!

Two, his eyes turned darker when he was turned on.

Three, there was something between us, and it was growing.

Four, it was hard, hot, and pressing against me in a place I was pretty sure had floodgates that had been opened.

"This is how it will work. I'm going to kiss you. You're going to kiss me back, and make those delicious little noises while doing so," he rumbled decisively.

"Is that so?" I asked. I couldn't recognize the voice that came out. It wasn't mine, that much I knew. This voice was thick, lusty, and full of seduction. I could have turned my head, but I found myself captured and held prisoner by his eyes. His lips grazed mine. His teeth nibbled my lower lip before sucking the fatty tissue between his teeth. He groaned right before he released it, and invaded my mouth. His kiss was searching, and the moment I moved my tongue against his, he growled and the kiss became hard and fevered.

Darkest Before Dawn

My body ignited as he pressed his growing erection against me. I moaned and parted my thighs as if my life depended on it. His hands released mine as he pulled at the vest I wore. It was a reality check that snapped me out of this compliant, drug-like state. I pushed against him as his lips left mine. "No," I whispered as I fought to get up; he allowed it. I moved to sit beside Sarah, who was sleeping blissfully.

"I didn't mean to scare you," he said as he sat opposite of me. "You should sleep. I'll keep first watch."

I blinked at him as I absently trailed my fingers over my swollen lips. He'd kissed them hard enough to leave his mark on them, and he kept doing it. I knew he had to be suffering right now from his erection; having felt it against me, I was certain of his discomfort. Hell, I was suffering for stopping it. But no way in hell was I losing my virginity in a hunter's perch, with a stranger to boot.

I lowered myself to the wooden floor of the perch and curled my legs up as I cradled the sleeping baby. I wasn't sure how I would manage to sleep with over six feet of I'm-so-sexually-charged-male sitting inches away from me. I could feel his eyes watching me, and the reminder of what had just happened was there where his hands had touched me. My kiss-swollen lips, where his mouth had left scorch marks from the heat of it.

Eventually my mind drifted to Sarah. What kind of life would she have? I'd found her, and wasn't sure if this world was fit to have a child in. I had one can of formula, a bottle, and a dozen diapers. What would I be able to give her after that? I touched her cherubic cheek and watched as her small lips puckered, for more food probably. She was so tiny and defenseless.

"She has a brave protector in you," Jaeden said as he smiled.

"I saved her, but for what? This isn't a world kids should grow up in. It's hard enough to find food for the group, but for an infant?"

"You shouldn't worry about what will happen tomorrow, only what you can do for her today."

"Winter's coming and finding supplies will be hard enough; now I have to look for formula and diapers. I've never wanted to be a parent, but with my brother it was different. I had help, even if my father was busy prepping for the end of days; he still made time for him. This little one doesn't have parents, and will never know her parents loved her enough to give up their lives. It just seems this world is too cold for such a small little thing."

"So you think, but even in the tragedy of her parent's death, she found you. She found someone to care for and protect her. You have a shelter, and a place to keep her safe. You've managed to help others, and I'm guessing if anyone can keep this child safe and loved, it's you. Now stop worrying and get some sleep, you can only do what you can, until you can't."

"You're an asshole, you know that, right?" I whispered with a small grin.

Darkest Before Dawn

"So I've been told," he wiggled his eyebrows but it was short lived as growling sounded from below us.

I sat up and looked down, and almost screamed. I somehow managed to prevent it from tearing from my lungs, but wasn't sure how. Below us prowled at least seven wolves, with glowing red eyes. What the friggin' honey buckets! "What the hell are those things?" I whispered unevenly.

"Rogue pack," he said in the same quiet voice I'd just used. My heart hammered wildly as I continued to look into blood-red eyes.

"Wolves with rabies?" I wondered out loud.

"Worse," Jaeden said as he stood and looked down at them. "Sit down, Emma, and protect the child." He walked to the other side of the little shelter and pulled out a cell phone. He punched in a number and a beeping noise sounded from the other end of the phone.

"Your phone works?" I asked with wide eyes. How the hell did it work? All the towers had been down for weeks, and even the internet had crashed.

"It works well enough," he said as he watched the surrounding woods as the wolves continued to growl.

"But how? The towers are down, right?"

"I'm magic," he said without looking at me. What was he waiting for? I didn't have long to wait for the answer as twenty minutes later, shots rang out in the distance, and moved closer. He turned to look at me and smiled. "You should reconsider having children," his eyes lowered to where I held Sarah protectively against my chest. "My people are coming. I thought we could wait until morning, but that doesn't seem the best course now. I'll have them follow us back to your shelter, but you and the babe should ride in the SUV with me."

"I'm not telling you where I live," I said defensively. He stepped closer with a twisted smile on his lips. "The other day wasn't the first time I had seen you. I've followed you home a few times," he replied. "I've known where you sleep," his voice dropped low. "You are curious by nature, sweet Emma, but if you want to know anything about me, all you have to do is ask. I'll even show you to my bedroom and let you play with my toys."

"That's kind of disturbing," I admitted.

"I like to know everything about the women I plan to fuck, and Emma, I plan to fuck you."

Chapter SEVEN

A week had passed since I'd been stuck in the hunter's perch with Jaeden. Sarah had found a new champion in Cat, as she preferred to be called now. She gave up Cathleen, as the name reminded her of the family she'd lost. The moment she'd seen me carrying in the small infant, she'd offered to help with her. Since then, she'd revealed that her breast milk had yet to dry up and even though I thought it a little weird for her to be feeding Sarah, it solved the issue of formula.

She'd taken to loving the child, and had agreed to be the one to watch over her. It was as if fate had handed her a second chance with being a mother. I watched her as she held the little girl up and whispered sweet encouragements to her. I guess they would eventually both heal one another's wounds as time moved on. Toxic; this world was toxic right now, but even with the toxicity, hope was blooming even with the diversities.

"I'm heading out," I told Addy as I grabbed a mask,

and slipped into my vest.

"Alone?" she asked, and I nodded. "You've been going out a lot on your own lately," she said with a knowing look. "Does this have to do with a certain, hot male?" she smiled.

"No," I said emphatically and when she laughed, I winced. Okay, even I didn't believe myself.

"You know, Emma, you deserve it. You spend all your time trying to be this super worker bee, but you deserve some sexy time too."

"Sexy time? Who says shit like that? And I'm not even into him. He's a stalker who even admitted he was! Yes he's absolutely gorgeous, but let's face reality for a moment, Addy. Men like him don't date girls like me. They bag and tag em', and you know it. I'm not into the whole catch and release thing."

"You like him, he likes you. I don't know if you've noticed this, but the selection of men these days is between scarce and scary. You have the ugly, the uglier, the creepy, and the creepiest. You found one who according to the ladies, is panty-dripping-jump-on-my-cock-hot. Jump on it sister, or I will. Shit, Jillian and Bonnie left an hour ago to find him and try and see if he'll play stuff the muffin with them, so start running. If those sluts get to him first, I'm going to be pissed. Only reason I'm not all on it is because of you. You deserve a good go 'round in the grass," she said as she wagged her finger at me.

"Did you say Jillian and Bonnie left?"

"That's all you got out of that?"

"Addy! Did they at least take their masks?" I asked, but I had already turned to find their masks still hanging from the wall. "Shit!" I zipped up my hoodie, dropped my mask over my face, grabbed my bag, and swung it onto my back as I headed for the doors. "How long ago did they leave? And why wasn't I told before now?"

"They've been gone for only an hour, which isn't exactly a long time on foot," she shrugged.

I punched in the code to the door and growled as I slammed it shut. I took off on the Ducati, once again thanking the powers that be for my dad choosing this bike for me. The bike was fast, but had only a little vibration and wasn't noisy. It was sort of the perfect bike for everything I did these days. I made it to the edge of town in time to hear screaming. My heart sank into my stomach, and together they sank to my knees.

The scream came again, only this time it was muffled and sounded more like a laugh. I parked the bike and pulled up the AR-15, holding it at the ready as I approached. The giggles, shrieks, and male voices sounded like they were coming from a row of homes that dotted the edge of town. I turned the corner of the block and found Jillian and Bonnie flirting with Jaeden's men, and considered pulling the trigger.

I started forward, but the moment my foot moved, Jaeden came out from behind one of the dark SUVs, holding a bottle of water which he handed off to Bonnie, who twirled her hair around her finger. Oh no she did not just use her I'm-a-bimbo move on him.

"So why she's so hard?" he asked.

"Her father was insane, and her mother died when she was young. You remember that right, Jill? I mean the entire town called him crazy. Emma just takes after him. She's cuckoo; I mean, who spends their summers prepping instead of at the beach, right?"

"She's driving us all bonkers at the shelter, and if she'd just get laid already—"

"She'd what, Jillian? Even if she got laid she'd still be insufferable. She expects us all to work our asses off. We clean, and hunt, and worst of all, she makes us burn the dead like her crazy ass father did."

"Why does she hide behind the mask? You ladies didn't wear it today," Jaeden continued as he leaned his tall frame against the SUV beside Bonnie who twirled her hair a little faster with his close proximity.

"She's a freak. She and her dad thought that by hiding that we're women, we'll survive longer. I think she just wants the rest of us to be hidden so she can actually get a man," Jillian snickered and Bonnie laughed with her.

I slid the gun around to my back, and stepped forward, pissed that their entire talk was about me. I knew the moment Jaeden sensed me coming, because he smiled and nodded his head subtly. Neither of the ungrateful bitches noticed me coming.

"I mean if you really want someone more… enjoyable, we are available," Bonnie said.

"We do everything together," Jillian said.

"Oh, I'd agree on that considering both of you witches got Chlamydia together. Jarrod Patton, right? Jocks; you two just couldn't get enough of them!" I chimed in with a sickeningly sweet tone. "Also, if you'd been paying attention in class, we wear the masks to gain the element of surprise, but it's also to prevent you from being raped. I'm not crazy, and neither was my father considering if he hadn't prepped, you ungrateful bitches would be dead. You have ten seconds to start back towards the shelter, or stay the fuck out of it. Your choice," I snapped. "And you," I growled at Jaeden. "If you want to know something about me, ask me. Otherwise, fuck off."

I turned and started moving, but his viselike grip fingers caught my arm and tightened around them. "Emma, stop."

"Go to hell!" I snarled. I wasn't sure why I was so pissed, only that he shouldn't have been asking them about me, or anything else.

"Only if you're coming with me," he growled. He was pulling me to one of the empty houses, and I knew I should fight harder, but I didn't feel endangered, yet. He pulled me behind him up the cement stairs, and once we were inside, he closed the door and pressed me against it. "Jealousy suits you."

"You think I'm jealous?" I wasn't. Okay, if I was to be honest, maybe I was…but I wasn't ready to be honest, not about that anyway.

"Tell you what, how about we flip a coin? Heads I'm yours. Tails, you're mine," he quipped.

"As if," I said and watched as he leaned his chest against mine.

"I knew you were there; your motorcycle isn't exactly silent," his hands lifted the mask and removed it. He tossed it across the room to a dusty couch. Next he unzipped the hoodie and bulletproof vest, and for some reason, I didn't stop him. "That's better," he whispered. His turquoise eyes scanned mine, and he smiled. "I wish you could have seen the look in your eyes as they spoke of you. They thought harshly of you, Emma, why?"

"We weren't exactly friends in school," I admitted.

"No," he said thoughtfully. "You would be above them. Your kind doesn't hang with the trashy girls."

I smiled as I looked up at him. "Above them? They're the ones boys went after, and me? I was the one they avoided."

"Because they were nothing but little boys, my little Valkyrie; idiots go after the easy fucks. Men go after the ones who are worth the chase. Like you. Even before I saw this enchanting face, I knew you were a diamond among a pile of rocks. You have something they will never have."

"And what would that be?" I asked feeling unsure of myself.

"Balls," he said. It was the last thing I'd expected from him to say. "Now that I have you alone and at my mercy...I plan to make you tremble...are you ready?" he smirked.

"I don't think so," I said, but he pulled my body against his.

"Oh I do, because I know you want it. I can smell the sweetness of your readiness. You were jealous, and I know what it is you want. I know what your body craves."

"Does this shit work on actual girls, or do you just practice it in the mirror and then try it on unwilling participants?" I smarted off because I was nervous. My legs had already become weighed down with lead, while moisture built in my panties.

"You tell me," he said as he cupped my chin. "I'm going to tell you what I want to do to you, and you tell me if it works when I am done with you."

"I don't—" his hand slid to my breasts, and cupped the heaviness of them.

"Fucking perfect size," he said as his other hand slid down to my stomach where he trailed his fingers over the top I wore. He pushed my body between his and the hard wall. "I promise to stop, but only when you ask me to. Otherwise, you tell me when you get wet and I'll see if it's wet enough."

I didn't answer him. Instead, I fought just to remember I needed to breathe.

"I'm going to touch you—a lot. I'm going to tell you exactly what I want to do to you," he said as one hand lifted my face to his until our eyes locked. "I'm going to start."

He untucked the shirt I wore, and the feel of his fingers against my flesh made me quiver for more. "Would you shiver when my fingers tangle in your hair? Like this?" His voice was low and captivating as his hands pulled at my hair, and as if on cue, I shivered. "Would you shut your eyes if I pulled you against me? Like this," his hands reeled me in even closer, and his breath fanned my ear. My eyes closed, as if by his will alone. "Would you moan for me, when I bite your bottom lip like this?" His teeth grazed my lip and he bit gently. Sure enough, I moaned even as I tried not to. "Would you try to stop me if I reached down and pulled your panties down to your knees? Would you resist me when my hands parted your trembling legs? Would you moan as my fingers found your waiting wetness? Would you sigh for me as I wrapped your legs around me? Would you bite my lip back, when I finally pushed my hard cock inside of you? Would you, sweet Emma? Would you come for me if I asked you to?"

Darkest Before Dawn

This was bad, so bad! I was sopping wet, and his nostrils flared as if he was fully aware that he'd succeeded in his mission. I was embarrassed because his eyes hungrily roved over the twin traitorous peaks of my hardened nipples. My breathing was ridiculously labored, and his wasn't. He leaned in and pressed a kiss to my forehead.

"That, sweet Emma, is how you tell the boys from men. Men know how to get a woman soaking wet without doing a single thing. Boys have to touch and caress with their hands…real men can make you come with words alone." His eyes smiled knowingly. "Tell me, how many men have you allowed between those silken thighs?"

I blinked. None? I so wasn't admitting that to him! In fact, I wasn't opening my mouth because if I did, I was sure I'd moan, or worse.

"None?" he guessed.

I swallowed, and refused to speak.

"Gone mute again? I can change that," he said as he pinned me between his arms and captured my mouth in a heated kiss. He pulled away as another moan stole from my lips. "Lust is heavy when tongues crave a taste of heaven. Tell me, Emma, does your tongue feel heavy? Does it lust for another taste of mine?" His eyes searched mine and he licked his lips seductively. "I take that as a yes, so I won't make you wait," he whispered before he claimed my lips and held my face pinned in his hands, helpless at his touch. His kiss was heady and intoxicating. His touch left me boneless, and I was surprised at just how much I wanted him to continue just like this.

His hands slid lower until one pulled against my shirt as it worked it over my breasts until the only thing between us was the skimpy lace of my bra. He lifted it, and his tawny head lowered until his lips kissed one nipple, and then the other. I moaned and arched my back like a little slut, ready to beg him for more. I needed him to make the dull ache that was centered between my legs stop. The burning heat in my lower stomach had a palpable heartbeat which seemed connected to my clit.

His teeth grazed my nipple and I cried out. He continued to tease me, his tongue slipping over the delicate flesh, and then from the other one came pain. His fingers rolled and pinched my nipple, painfully. I cried out, but then he switched, and his mouth was kissing the tender flesh better, and the sensation was off the hook. He pinched again, but this time his mouth landed on mine as he lifted my legs and wrapped them around his waist.

He was walking us somewhere. I held on, kissing him back until I felt as if I was suffocating, and I couldn't have cared less if I died like this, with him. It wasn't until my back hit a wall and I watched as he lowered himself to his knees as his hands began to work the buttons of my fatigues that I knew I was a goner.

Pounding started at the front door, and I ignored

Darkest Before Dawn

it, up until someone shouted 'wolves' from the other side. Jaeden and I both paused, and that's when it hit me. With my dignity gone, and my mind nothing more than mush, reality came rushing back. My breasts were both exposed, and my nipples were swollen from his mouth and hands. His chest was naked, and I blinked, wondering when he'd removed his shirt.

My gun had been removed, and I hadn't even felt it! It lay with my vest beside the door, and I had to wonder if his mouth was a dangerous weapon. It must have been a weapon of mass destruction against my brain, obviously.

"Get dressed," he said as he unwound my legs and stood to retrieve his shirt. I slid to the floor, and stayed there for a minute.

He turned and looked down at me, his gaze hot enough to singe my flesh with his eyes. "This isn't finished, Emma, not by a long shot."

Oh. What. The. Hell. Emma! You slut, what the hell had you just allowed to happen? Hussyland was open for business, and my vagina was its entrance. And who had the key? Jaeden! I snapped out of it and pulled down my shirt before rushing over to my vest as I slid my mask back into place.

Wolves! There were crazy-ass, red-eyed wolves outside, and I was so busy considering my vagina's eagerness to welcome Jaeden's Mr. Happy that I'd lost it for a moment. I pulled back on the confidence and sass

I hid behind and leveled him with a cold look through the eyes of the mask. "This is over; it doesn't happen again," I stated firmly.

"We'll just see that about, now won't we?" he said with an air of confidence that shook my own.

Chapter EIGHT

His men waited just outside the door, armed with various guns and swords...because swords were in these days, I guess. I looked in the direction that they all faced and walked through the men. Were they seriously *sniffing* the air? I moved to where Jaeden stood, and sniffed to see if I could smell whatever it was they had.

Nothing.

I moved to my where my bike had been and almost growled out loud when I couldn't see the markers I had left around it when I hid the bike. Those bitches! It was a full mile back to the shelter. Jaeden turned his head and looked at me carefully. "Keep the mask on, Emma," he said as we all started forward as a group.

"Always do," I whispered and then scrunched up my face as I heard how stupid it sounded. We walked through the woods for what felt like forever, even though I knew it had only taken us moments to reach the bloody scene.

I spotted my bike on its side, with blood splattered all around it. Jillian was sightless, her head turned at an awkward angle in death. Bonnie was nearby in the grass, her legs spread wide, as if her assailant had tried to do more than just rip her apart. Her shirt was ripped open and her pants were gone, as well as her underwear. I swallowed down the saliva which threatened to become more. My stomach rolled with what I was seeing.

They'd been ripped apart, literally. This hadn't been a kill for food, but a brutal show of strength. Tears filled my eyes as I walked closer to where Jillian was staring into the sky, as if her killer had stood above her, taunting her. I followed her eyes, and then looked to the damp ground at huge paw prints that seemed to be everywhere around her body, but also, foot prints—bare *human* footprints.

I walked over to Bonnie, who had the same prints around her body. Bloody handprints covered her thighs as if they'd been held apart. Wolves didn't work with humans…right? They'd been ripped apart, and yet Bonnie had been raped. The proof was there for everyone to see. The next question was, had she been dead before they'd raped her corpse or was she raped and then killed? Did the wolves show up after the humans had raped Bonnie and killed them both? And why was only Bonnie raped? My mind whirled with scenarios, none of them making any sense.

"What kind of sick bastard would do this?" I

Darkest Before Dawn

whispered, horrified as I turned to find Jaeden and his men staring at me. I knew that look, it was the one that said at any moment they expected me to shatter and break into a million pieces. I wouldn't; instead I was disgusted. I was disgusted at what I was doing while this was happening. How long had I been in that house, being seduced by Jaeden?

I didn't know shit about him, and for all I knew, I could be standing beside the killer. I doubted it, since they looked as disgusted as I felt about what had occurred here. I kneeled beside Bonnie and reached for her leg to close it, to give her some resemblance of dignity in death, but when I grabbed her leg, it detached from the body. Muscle gave way, and the sound would haunt me forever. Bone had been severed by something besides the wolves. It was a clean break, and as I looked to her arms, I realized they too had been set back in place.

"Emma," Jaeden said gently as he held out his hand for mine. I glared up at him as I ignored his hand and reached for my handheld radio.

"Addy, call everyone in. Now. I want a full head count of every soul that belongs to the shelter. No one goes out, and no new person comes in. Lock it down," I ordered.

"Everything okay out there, Ems?" Addy's distant voice came back over the radio.

"Bonnie and Jillian are dead, and I need you to issue

that order, now."

"Will do, and Ems, be fucking careful. Bring them back if you can, please," Addy said.

"They're in pieces, Addy, actual pieces. I can't bring them back like this, it would only cause panic. I need everyone inside and do a headcount. I'll be back as soon as I can."

"Bitch, are you safe?" she growled and I could hear her panic even over the radio and static.

"I'm with Jaeden and his men," I admitted.

"Be safe, and if he doesn't keep you safe, I'll cut his balls off and feed them to him!"

I caught sight of Jaeden wincing but ignored it. "Call it, and lock it down."

"Sending it now," she said.

I knew the moment she did it, because Jillian's radio went off.

"Get the fuck back here! Two down, call out!" Addy shouted to the radio. I listened as one after another sounded off. Jaeden's eyes narrowed as he listened as men and women sounded off. Yeah, I had a large group. He'd had no idea of just how big that group was. After some fifty people sounded off, I responded.

"Get back to base, and be safe. We are no longer safe in the woods. Once inside, you are to stay there.

Darkest Before Dawn

Addy and Jimmy will do a head count. If at that time, we find others missing, I will find them."

The radio seemed to explode with chatter, everyone asking questions at once. "Enough; you'll be told when we are all back and safe. For now, all you need to know is we lost two and I won't lose anymore. God be with you, and watch your six, over."

I turned to Jaeden and nodded. "Let's find the sick pieces of shit," I said and watched his face clear of all emotions.

"Come again?" he asked with a serious look on his face.

"I'm finding who did this, with or without your help," I bit out crisply as I did a check of the ammunition I had on me. He seemed to consider it briefly before making up his mind.

"These were wolves, Emma, very dangerous ones at that."

"Yeah because we all know wolves are in to fucking humans, and raping them? Since when did wolves become able to unbutton pants? Someone put them back together. Wolves don't do that, not even rabid ones." I watched as his eyes narrowed at my quiet sarcasm.

"Good point," he said, but I got the feeling he was either hiding something or covering it up. I also had a feeling he wasn't used to being questioned.

"What is it you aren't telling me?"

"Nothing," he said as he stepped closer, and I stepped back. "Don't do that, Emma."

"Do what?" I snapped.

"Don't pedal backwards with me. I don't regret what we did, and neither should you."

"Shouldn't I? I was with you when I should have been with them! I could have helped them!" I was ashamed of what I'd done. I'd been so close to having sex! I'd let my guard down, and they had paid for it. I was so sick of this shit! Too many people were being killed, and while I hadn't been a huge fan of either of the girls, I wouldn't wish this kind of death on anyone.

Life kept throwing curve balls at my head, and the only thing it was doing was improving my skill in dodging them. I was tired of dodging, I needed a friggin' bat. It was time to knock a few home runs out of the park, and after all, I had home field advantage. This was my town. I knew it like the back of my hand, and had lived here for my entire twenty-one years of life.

"You should go home," Jaeden said with a tinge of anger lacing his tone. "Try to think of it as this; if you'd been with them, you'd be lying beside them in pieces right now. What we did? It saved your life."

"You don't know that," I said as I met his soul-piercing eyes. "I'm a fighter, Jaeden. I know everything there is to know about this town, and for all you know, I could have stopped this from happening."

He smiled but it was cold. "You need to face reality, little lady. You're small, and while I've seen you fight, you wouldn't win this one. This was a pack of rogue wolves. They are deadly, unlike any other animal you've ever met."

"Well since I haven't met many wolves before, that tells me absolutely nothing. Wolves are wolves, and I have never heard of any kind of wolves doing anything like this before."

"Emma, go home. I'll let you know if I find the animals that did this," he snapped.

"Those are my girls on the ground, Jaeden! I'm either coming with you to help kill the monsters that did this, or I'll go out by myself. You can't stop me!" I seethed. Who the hell did he think he was?

"Bjorn?" he said as he focused his attention on his handgun and checked the magazine.

"Yeah?" An extremely tall man with jet black hair and cold, blue eyes stepped up.

"Secure Emma, and protect her with your life. Lock her in my bedroom if you have to, but don't let her out of your sight."

I snorted. Right! Not gonna happen—I was captured in a bear hug before I'd even noticed him move. He tightened his hold on me even as I kicked his legs and screamed. "You're an asshole! You have no right! You can't do this to me!"

Jaeden smiled as he slipped his handgun into the back waistband of his pants. His eyes lifted to mine, and he strolled over to where I was thrashing in the giant's arms. "Cease struggling, sweet Emma, before you hurt yourself," he replied. His hand came up to touch my cheek before his thumb traced the fullness of my bottom lip. "I'll see you when I get home from hunting, honey."

Chapter Nine

I was shown to a massive bedroom and none too gently reminded to stay put. Jaeden and his group had taken over the old manor house which had been built for one of the owners of one of the biggest logging companies that helped our town establish its footprint in Pend Oreille County. This meant the house was ancient. Ancient, but beautifully crafted. Much of the place had been falling down, which made many of the kids in Newport believe it had been haunted; they only went in it on a dare. Just before the flu wiped out the town, the mayor had led a renovation project on the estate that would be managed eventually by Pend Oreille County Historical Society as an extension of their museum complex.

The room I was in was gigantic, and must have been part of the finished wing, since it had a huge, black four poster bed that had a billowing canopy of white silk and gauzy panes that draped to the floor at each corner. The room was masculine, yet looked as if it had a woman's touch to it. The bed had a gray silken duvet with black trim and matching silk sheets, with an insane amount of pillows of the same material scattered against the headboard. The walls were painted in a darker shade of gray, with black crown molding around the ceiling.

There was a huge settee at the end of the bed, which was silver in color, and had a white fur throw placed over it. I ran my fingers over it and smiled. "PETA would have a field day here…" My eyes landed on the massive tub that took up a corner of the room, already filled with water. I walked over to it and stuck the tips of my fingers into the blissfully seductive depths. It was warm…

I smiled. A bath. I couldn't remember the last time I'd taken a bath. We only had showers at the shelter. It was ideal for the amount of people we had there, but I missed bathing. Did I dare? I did, but first things first. I walked to the door and tapped on it.

Bjorn was just on the other side of it, so I knew he'd hear me splashing if I indulged, and I didn't wish to have him walk in on me. "What?" he asked gruffly.

"The bath in the room, may I use it?"

"If you wish to use it, I can abide giving you privacy," he said with a stern look. "Do not make a mess for Jaeden to return to."

"Okay, are there towels? Do you know how long he will be gone?" I asked as an afterthought. No way in hell was I going to chance having him return to find me all naked in his tub.

Darkest Before Dawn

"Step aside," he ordered, and I quickly obliged. He was either a soldier by nature, or had served his country, based on his stance. He was aware of where I stood and what I did, even as he moved around the room to a locked armoire and pulled out some items for me. "Is there anything else you need?'

"No," I replied looking at everything he'd brought out. There was a tray, and on it, an iPod, washcloths, a towel, and several bars of sweet scented soap as well as an assortment of bath salts. Based on where Bjorn pulled these items from, either Jaeden had found these items here, or he'd planned on entertaining women here.

"Do you require sustenance?" he continued.

"You mean food?" I asked, wondering who the hell referred to food as sustenance in this day and age. Hell, maybe Jaeden had found Bjorn here with the house and resurrected him or found him in a dusty old home in his old country. Bjorn had the same odd accent Jaeden did.

"I'll bring you food when you finish bathing, mistress."

Mistress?

I waited for him to shut the door, and then smiled. A friggin' bath! I did a happy dance around the room with a grin from ear to ear covering my face. I was dancing around when I caught sight of the huge stones beneath the black clawfoot tub, and paused. No way. I walked over and yes, I got on my stomach to look at the huge boulders. It was friggin' genius! I reached out to run my finger over one of the round stones and cried out. "Ouch!" It was hot!

Okay, so obviously it was genius, and I was an idiot. There was no faucet, but there was a cold bucket of water that was close enough to the stones beside the tub that the water wouldn't be ice cold. I looked around the room as if I expected Jaeden to jump out at any second.

He'd gone hunting, which meant I had time to enjoy the tub. I felt bad for not mourning the girls, but they'd screwed up, and even though it hurt to know they'd died as they had, I couldn't change it. I was still pissed that Jaeden had detained me as if he owned me, but more than an hour had passed since our confrontation and with the distance and time, the anger had dissipated.

I finally scrounged up the courage to undress, but not before I'd sprinkled bath salts into the water. I placed the tray at the end of the tub and slipped into the water with a groan of absolute pleasure. My pussy still ached from his touch, which was where my hands wanted to go. I shoved away the urge to finish what he started, but barely.

I wasn't a prude, and I knew what sex was. I just hadn't wanted to be used and discarded like some play toy. I'd made myself explore every curve of my body, and knew the difference now between how his hands felt, and my own. His made my body go into a state of emergency, while mine just did what was necessary for relief.

Darkest Before Dawn

I closed my eyes, but the idea of music and a bath was seductive. I hadn't charged my iPod in ages and wondered how many generators they were using to keep the electricity going in this place. I reached for the headphones, and slipped them on over my head. After I'd looked through the playlists and had found one labeled 'slow submission', I smiled. On it was a ton of hard rock, but there were also other songs which both relaxed and seduced my senses.

It was stupid, I knew it. I was in his room, listening to his playlist…or one he'd made for another woman. I felt like an interloper, and yet I didn't care. The smell of rose in the water was provocative, and eventually, I placed the iPod which was in a waterproof case—handy—on my chest, while my hands skimmed over my flesh.

I moaned low in my throat, and then reminded myself of whom and where I was. I closed my eyes as I felt my nipples harden while the image of Jaeden flashed in my mind. The way his touch sent my body into overdrive, with a simple look or touch. One of my hands slipped beneath the surface to explore the ache between my legs, while the other played with my nipples.

The idea of getting off in his bedroom was both intoxicating and arousing. He'd never know what I'd done, because I was the only one here. I listened to the beat of the music as Puddle of Mudd's *Control* played through the buds in my ears. My fingers found the beat, and I gasped as my fingers stroked the small bud in the junction of my legs.

He'd turned me on, and left me unsatisfied. It wasn't his fault of course, because I'd have stopped it...or I'd like to think I would have. The idea of a man like him between my thighs drove me wild, but it could be because I'd yet to experience what he could do. That might explain why it was so easy for him to turn me on. I was a twenty-one year old virgin. Probably the only one in my town before the flu hit, and probably the oldest living one in the world now.

I allowed a finger to slip between the folds, and rocked my hips against it. My lips trembled as my nipples turned into hard pebbles. I could come so easily. A single finger slipped inside of me, and I gasped and opened my eyes to make sure the door was still locked, but it wasn't the door I should have been worried about.

Nope, it was the six foot five male who was watching me with intensity so dark and hot in his eyes that instead of closing my legs, they fell open with a knee resting on both sides of the tub. I didn't stop. I should have, but his eyes feasted on my bare pussy, and what I was doing to it.

"Fucking hell, Emma," he growled. It was the only warning I got before he strolled to the tub and pulled me out of the water. "I expected you to be pissed. Instead, I come home to a fucking nymph in my bathwater."

"I wasn't...it wasn't...where are you taking me?" I sputtered with a guilty blush spreading over me from head to toe. I landed on the bed with a whoosh of air that escaped my lungs. His mouth devoured mine as his

Darkest Before Dawn

hands took over what mine had just been doing.

"I love the way you tremble for me," he growled. "The way your skin grows flushed, and your pussy weeps with the need to be fucked," he murmured as he kissed his way down my flesh.

"Jaeden, what are you doing—" his mouth found the sweet nub of my core and my hips bucked against his mouth and the deliciousness of what he felt like there. "Oh, wow…" I moaned and made incoherent noises as the sound of his mouth sloppily sucking and licking my flesh echoed in my ears.

"You taste like heaven," he replied as his mouth continued to ravish my sex. It wasn't until he slipped a single finger inside of me that I knew I had to stop this. It was too much, the feeling intense and overwhelming. I wrapped my legs around his shoulders, baring myself to him until I felt exposed, and instead of being embarrassed, I called his name and encouraged him to do even more.

"More," I ordered and listened as he laughed without removing his mouth from my very wet, very close to coming pussy. "Yes! Oh God, that's so good!"

Another finger was added, and soon I was riding it until I thought I would break into a million tiny pieces. I called his name, but then he was gone. I looked around the room, and felt the weight of his stare. Something was still touching me, and yet it wasn't him.

I sat up in the tub and looked around. Jaeden sat in

a chair on the other side of the room, watching me. I looked down at my body, and found my hand still buried in my naked flesh. My nipples were hard, but the iPod continued to play, something slower than it had been. "I was asleep," I said to myself. I'd dreamt of him, and he'd been in the room with me as I had!

"Tell me, Emma, why were you calling my name in your sleep?" he asked from where he sat in a dimly lit corner. He stood and walked towards me, until I could see he was half undressed. His belt was undone, and his shirt was gone. I could see his massive length, hard and ready beneath the jeans.

"Nightmare," I whispered as I chewed my bottom lip and looked up as he came to stand beside the tub. His eyes greedily consumed my flesh as he looked into the still-warm water of the tub.

"You normally masturbate while having nightmares?" he asked with a cocky grin lifting his lips.

"Is there a bad time to masturbate?" Did I really just say that!?

"I'd think that it would be a bad time to finger-fuck that sweet flesh in front of a man you almost fucked today. Considering I wasn't finished with you," he said as he knelt down and splashed water into my face. I brought my hand up to wipe away the water, but as I did, his hand replaced mine. "Don't move," he ordered. His finger found my folds, and slid between it. I moaned and tried to close my legs. "I said do not move. Do not come, either. Not unless I tell you to, my little minx."

"Jaeden, I can't...Oooh," I moaned as his finger found the spot and pressed against it. Addy said most guys couldn't find the spot, and that's why people made million off writing guides, and yet he'd found it in seconds.

"Can't what, Emma? Come? You can and will for me, many times," he said as his smile grew hard and heated. "Fuck, you have a tight little sheath, don't you?" he whispered as he added another finger. He pulled them out, only to curve them as he plunged them back inside. "When's the last time this tight, sweet haven was plundered?"

He increased the speed, but even as I teetered on the brink of no return, I pushed him away. "Stop, I don't want this." It lacked conviction.

"That's too bad," he said as he shoved his fingers in deeper, only to pull them out abruptly and stand up to his full height. "Do you normally play hard to get, or is this just for me?" he sounded angry.

"There was a towel here," I whispered embarrassedly. I'd been imaging him, and here he was. Yet I still couldn't go through with it.

"It's over there," he hiked his thumb over his shoulder to where it lay on the chair he'd just moments ago vacated. "Get dressed, cock tease. I set out clothes for you. It's too dangerous to go home tonight, so you'll stay here."

"I'm not a cock tease," I snapped. "If I thought you'd be back in time for the show, I wouldn't have done it."

"You were turned on by what we did today, and so was I. I want to fuck you, Emma. It's as simple as that. Why deny yourself what you want?"

Oh well, because, one, I'm a virgin. Two, I don't even know much about you besides my body heads straight to Hussyland when you are close to me…Yup, couldn't say those!

"I'm not playing hard to get, Jaeden. I don't need a man to make me come."

"Do it, I'll watch," he challenged as I sat up and crossed my legs over my naked vagigi. "I might even join in, and let *you* watch *me*."

"Can you hand me the towel?" I asked and watched as his eyes lowered to where my boobs were barely submerged in the water. I could feel the iPod in the water, the buds floated but barely.

"Nope," he said as he walked to the bed and plopped down on it. "Get it yourself, little girl."

As if I wouldn't? I stood from the water, watching as his eyes lowered to my shaved vagigi. I stepped from the bath, uncaring of the water that splashed over the edge in my anger. I walked over to the towel and picked it up to slip it around my body.

On the back of the chair was a sheer white nightie.

Darkest Before Dawn

"I'm not wearing that!" I looked around for my clothes, and gear. "Where are my things?" I had back-up clothing in my bag.

"You sleep with me tonight. Unless you prefer another of my men?" he questioned.

"So I have to sleep in your bed, with you? No thanks. The floor looks good enough for me."

"That wasn't an option," he warned. "You don't like taking orders, do you?"

"Does anyone?" I scoffed.

"Put the nightgown on, and get in this bed. It's an order," he said as his smile faltered and his eyes grew heated.

"No," I snapped as I fisted my hands on my hips in nothing but a towel.

"Now," he said, and the single word held enough command that I felt a push to do as he said. I shook my head.

"I'm not fucking you," I snapped angrily. "My pussy? It's off limits to you."

"Is it? Because I'm pretty sure that is the second time it almost came from me barely touching it. You need to be fucked, and hard. I'd like nothing more than to chain those pretty legs to my bed and torture that sweet cove with my mouth, my fingers, my cock, and my tongue…for hours."

I shivered and shook my head. "You do know what no means, right?"

"You do know you have sweet juices dripping down your leg from your readiness to be fucked, right?" he mimicked me.

"Then I guess I better clean it up, because you won't be."

"Is that a challenge?" he asked as he sat up, his pants slipping even lower on his tapered hips. "Because, Emma, I fucking love challenges, and right now? You're the only challenge I see."

"I'm still not fucking you—" He was off the bed before I could finish. I ran to the tub and around it. He strolled toward me with long, angry strides.

"I like it when women play hard to get. Never been one to take the easy pickings. So please, Emma, play hard to get with me."

He trailed my movement with his eyes as I kept the tub between us. I held the towel to my chest as I watched him. "I don't want to fuck! Period! No challenge, no hard to get. No fucking!"

"I don't make love if that is what you're asking for. Love is for idiots, little girl. You can't play with fire and not expect to get burned. You were still moving those sweet delicate little fingers into your succulent

Darkest Before Dawn

flesh when I walked in. Those noises? Enough to drive a sane man insane. You called my name, *several* times. Tell me, was I fucking that sweet flesh good? Was I pounding my hard cock in deep enough for you to come while imagining it? I watched those sweet tips turn darker as they grew hard from what your own fingers were doing."

"You shouldn't have been watching me! It's called privacy!"

"I'm sorry, but when there's a woman in my own bath, in my own room, fucking her tight little pussy, clumsily at that, I'm not going to turn away from it. Not when it's *my* name leaving her sweetly parted lips as she uses her fingers, trying to get off. You were trying to come, were you not?"

"Still not fucking you—" He caught me and took me to the floor. His mouth found my lips and claimed them hungrily.

"How many times have you come while picturing me?" he asked when he lifted his head.

"None," I said truthfully. "I would have come once, but it wasn't you I was imagining. Bjorn was...how should I put this..."

"Dead, if you finish that sentence." There was no laughter in his tone, and his eyes turned dark without the heat which had just scolded my flesh. "I won't share you with my men, unless of course, you want to fuck all three hundred and fifty two of them. I'm not sure this tight, sweet pussy could handle it though. I could be wrong though. Am I wrong? Shall I call them all in?"

"You're a fucking asshole!" I growled through tears that filled my eyes and threatened to fall.

"I know I am," he whispered as he sat up and released his hold on me. "Hunting gets the adrenaline pumping, and finding you as I did, well it sent me on the hunt for you."

His eyes lowered to where the towel had come undone, and my entire anatomy was open for his inspection. "I love the knowledge that this sweet flesh is hairless," he said as he stood up and walked to his dresser and opened one of the drawers. He tossed me a long shirt, and then left the room before I could call him back.

"That was brilliant, Emma!" I belittled myself as the tears fell. I was such an idiot. I'd been fucking myself, and instead of getting off, I'd fallen asleep! I slipped the shirt on over my naked curves and eyed the bed. This was crazy. I couldn't sleep with him, not in any sense.

He walked back in with a bottle of cognac. He strolled over to the dresser and pulled down two crystal snifters before he moved to the bed. He placed them on a tray I hadn't noticed earlier in my angry tirade. He poured two glasses to the rim, and then re-corked the bottle before placing it on the dresser. Next, I watched as he moved around the room with his sleek abs and muscular back.

Darkest Before Dawn

He pulled out a pair of shorts, and then removed his pants. A smarter woman would have looked away, not me though. I was an idiot tonight, obviously. I watched as he turned and pointed his one-eyed gun right at me. Or, maybe it was a missile because it was huge, and I was pretty sure the Sex-Ed teacher had gotten it all wrong. I swallowed a groan as he carried his shorts to the bed and sat on the edge of it without putting them on.

I was gaping. I mean, my eyes actually bobbed as he'd walked to the bed, and I was pretty sure my mouth was open wide enough he could have slipped that missile inside of it without a problem. I'd seen men naked before, because Addy and I had hidden in the boy's locker room once. Okay, it was more than once, but who wants to admit that?

I absently took a step closer to it, before remembering I wasn't wearing panties, and was currently dressed in his clothing. I lifted my eyes, and found him watching me.

"If I didn't know any better, I'd say you've never seen a cock before."

"I've seen many cocks. I mean, I've seen a few at a time," I whispered breathlessly. I wondered at my own words, why the hell had I said that? I had helped with some of the high school physicals when I was beginning my nursing courses. I'd seen them limp, fat, hard, and, well, limp. I'd never seen one this size, or of this magnitude. I'd never seen one I wanted to lick before, either. I absently licked my lips as I listened to him growl.

"So what you're saying is, you've taken cocks before, but you won't take mine?"

"Yes…uh, no. No."

"Is it too big?" he asked with a wide grin.

"It's huge!"

O. M. G. I was talking about his cock! With him present! And it was pointing at me! The thing was staring at me, and I swear to God it was bobbing, and waving a firm hello!

"It's big, but I promise you could take it. I've seen smaller women take bigger cocks. Just means some positioning would be needed until you grew accustomed to it. Real men get their women excited first. They suck those sweet lips until the flesh is soaked with her come, and then her body will accept anything she tried to take inside of it. But you already know that, what with your curiosity to play with that sweet pussy. You have men at the shelter. Tell me, Emma, do they serve your needs?"

My head snapped up from my eye-fucking his massive cock at his words. "I don't sleep around."

"There's nothing wrong with finding release."

"I'm not like that, at all."

"So you have toys?" he countered.

Darkest Before Dawn

"Toys?"

"Sex toys, dildos, balls, that kinda stuff. Please tell me you're not allowing that sweet, succulent pussy to be neglected. Besides, you shaved for someone."

I had; for myself. I'd been shaving for a while, but that had been because everyone else was doing it. After Addy had called it a forest, I'd shaved it and then had just kept doing it to avoid the itchiness that came with it growing out. "Most women shave these days."

"Do they?" he smiled knowingly. "Tell me, does it grow in the same color of your hair?"

"That's none of your business," I growled. This was crazy! His cock was aimed at me, and I wasn't wearing any panties! I was in his room, when I should be demanding my things and leaving. Instead, I was ogling his Mr. Happy Whacker, and drooling over it!

He raised a brow as he took in my state of dress, and his state of undress. He was made for this, what with his sex God body, and tattoos that were located in places my tongue wanted to trace…that was it! I was tossing out every erotica book I'd obtained from houses. This was insane! I wasn't a slut, and yet I felt the need to get on my knees and wipe that glistening pre-cum away from his magnificent cock with my tongue! I was a friggin' virgin, who had a huge imagination and a slut between my legs that said pound me!

"Get dressed!" I cried and then winced. He smiled.

"Does it bother you? Or are you fighting the urge to be naughty with me? I'll even let you sit on it if you ask me nicely."

"Naughty? Would you cover Mr. Happy Whacker up?"

He burst out laughing, and yes, I watched his cock go up and down before I forced myself to turn away. I was fighting to get my pulse and my breathing under control when he came up behind me. "Don't touch me. Just don't do it, please," I whispered.

"You've already named my cock," he whispered as he pulled me back against him. "No one has ever named him before," he said with laughter in his voice.

"Did you find the monster responsible for killing my friends?" I used 'friends' loosely as I changed the direction of this conversation.

"No, but we have an idea of where they are. We will be going out again in the morning."

I turned to face him. "I need my things. I think it best I leave, before I do something I will regret in the morning."

"Like fuck me?" he pulled away and glared at me.

"Exactly."

"Get in the bed, Emma. I didn't take you as a prude, but I guess I was wrong. You can have a night cap with

Darkest Before Dawn

me, and then sleep. Tomorrow is soon enough for you to go home. Drink," he said as he handed me the glass.

"I'm not drinking it," I said as I held it.

"It's not drugged," he assured me as he tipped his up and took a swig from it. He set it on the dresser as he carefully and very slowly put his shorts on over his firm ass. "I'm not trying to get you drunk either, or take advantage of you," he said as he turned around and faced me. "You saw some pretty hairy shit today. The alcohol is just so you can sleep without seeing it."

I eyed the glass and then brought it up to my lips and sniffed it. I wasn't a big drinker, but he had a point. I didn't want to dream about what had happened to Jillian and Bonnie. I just wanted to sleep and forget it before I had to face reality again. I took a big drink and coughed as it burned my throat. "Holy cat balls," I sputtered.

"Drink it slowly; won't burn so much."

"You tell me this after I drink it," I said with a sour look on my face.

"I'm going to kiss you, before we sleep."

"Is that so? What if I don't want you to kiss me?" I asked, lowering the glass as the feel of alcohol swept through me.

"Then you should probably stop kissing me back. It's hard to not kiss you when you react the way you do. It makes me think you want my kiss."

Maybe I *was* a cock tease? Because I had just licked my lips like a two-bit hussy who was ready to examine that thing in his shorts with my tongue, and he'd said kiss...not head! "I'm not a hussy, and I don't go around just kissing people."

"Good to know; that tells me a lot about you. That when you respond and melt beneath my touch—and you do melt—that it's me and not just every male in the general vicinity."

"Well, I'd have to kiss a few more people to compare these feelings to," I said, smirking as I took another sip.

"Is that so? You think I'd allow it?" he asked as he drank the rest of his glass, and set the empty on the dresser. He lifted the covers on one side of the gigantic marshmallow bed and slid under them.

"I'm not yours."

"Yet; you're not mine yet. You will be."

The single word said with so much confidence sent my heart hammering against my rib cage. "That's a little cocky, don't you think?"

"It's called confidence," he said and eyed my glass as he brought his hands up behind his head. "You need to know the difference, because with the way you kiss me, sooner or later, it's going to end with us fucking."

"I know the difference between being cocky, and being confident. And maybe I'm just desperate?" I

Darkest Before Dawn

smiled and wiggled my eyebrows.

"If you were desperate, you'd have jumped on my cock when I left it undressed and so brazenly displayed for you."

"You make a good case, but say I found it lacking? Maybe I'm used to something so much bigger."

I took another sip and smiled.

"Bigger? I felt how tight you were. You couldn't handle bigger, little girl. You live in a small town where boys are just that, boys. I promise you that I am all man, and I also promise you this, Emma; I will have you. The only question is when it will happen, and how hard I will fuck you."

What the hell was I supposed to say to that? I mean, I could come off with some shit, I was sure of it, but I think I had just experienced a word-gasm! I opened my mouth only to close it and repeat it. "That's straight up cocky."

"Yes, it actually was, but I'm also confident that you want me. I think my bluntness scares you and it should. I know what I want, and I go after it balls to the wall. I want you. It's as simple as that, little girl."

"Is that so?" I asked, and felt the heat from the alcohol as it warmed me from the inside, or maybe that was him. "You want me, and yet you keep calling me little girl. So you are either a huge pervert, or well, I forgot what I was saying." I paused. I looked at the now empty glass and back up at him. "This isn't a fair fight, and you promised to not take advantage of me."

"I didn't say anything about kissing you, or making you come tonight, *little girl*."

"I'm not coming," I said as I narrowed my eyes on him.

"Not yet."

"Not tonight."

"Who says?" he asked.

"Me!" I growled but it came out seductive. Oh holy crap. I was drunk! "You got me drunk."

"Yes, I did," he grinned, unrepentant.

I smiled. But no coming. I could be drunk, but I couldn't allow him to get that close to make me go mindless. "I'm going to bed."

"With me," he said huskily.

I plopped down on the bed and crawled across it. It wasn't until I reached the other side and turned to judge the distance between us that I remembered I had no panties on. I remembered because he was looking as I had, when I'd stared at Mr. Happy Whacker.

This, by the way, was a horrible name for a penis. I laughed, and his eyes left my naked backside to meet my eyes. His lips curved up into a beautiful smile.

Darkest Before Dawn

"Do that again," he said as I remained on all fours.

"I'm not showing you my ass again!" I laughed as I sat down.

"I like the sound of your laughter, sweet Emma."

I lost the smile and blinked at him. "Not much left to smile or laugh about anymore."

"Just because the world has gone to hell doesn't mean you can't live."

"True," I said, even though I didn't believe it. I'd felt guilty for living when so many had died. It seemed unfair that babies had died, and those of us who had lived longer, well, lived. "Do you ever wonder why God allowed some to live, but took innocent lives? Like the babies. They didn't deserve what happened to them. They hadn't even lived yet."

"You think God did this?" he asked as he continued to watch me from his lazy pose with his arms resting behind his head.

"Or Satan. I mean, what kind of God would allow this to happen? At first I thought it was a wakeup call. So many people had stopped living. In school, everyone spent most of their time checking updates on Facebook, or their phones. We'd stopped living, and between the internet and electronics, we'd become introverts."

"That's pretty deep," he said as his lips curved up into a smile.

"I'm serious," I said vehemently.

"Come to me," he said in a tone that commanded me. I shivered from the intense heat that burned in his eyes.

"No funny business. You promised."

"Do as I told you to," he said not moving from his pose. "I said I wouldn't fuck that tight, pretty pink flesh...yet. I told you I was going to kiss you."

I was moving before I had any idea I was. I paused and looked up at him, once again back on all fours. I felt like a puppet, drawn to him! As if he held the strings which seemed to be attached to my vagigi. I was trembling, and when I stopped inches away from him, he smiled.

"Now lie down beside me, Emma, and part your legs for me," he said with confidence burning in his eyes.

"You said you wouldn't bang me tonight."

"I said I was going to kiss you. I just didn't say where I would place that kiss."

Chapter Ten

I did as he'd told me to, unsure of why I did it. I only knew that his self-assurance brooked no argument. The look in his eyes commanded obedience, and I was curious to see where he would kiss me. I was on my back when he sat up. His eyes held mine captive with their turquoise heat. His fingers trailed up my thighs slowly, and rounded to the sensitive flesh of my inner thighs.

The multitude of sensations mixed with my uneasy emotions as his fingers danced over my flesh. I felt my nipples as they grew hard, ready to be kissed. My core grew moist, slick with desire. My hands fisted at my sides to prevent me from touching myself. He was only touching my skin, and barely doing that!

"You like it," he whispered huskily, "when I touch you, like this." His hands slid up my inner thighs, both hands on each leg at the same time, until they skimmed over my nakedness. He never removed his eyes from mine as he ran them slowly back down to my knees. My instinct was to close my legs. I'd never been this far with a man. I was so far out of my league.

"Are you wet?" he asked and I shook my head in denial. He smiled as if he knew I was lying, but since I was currently on display, he could probably see the proof. I tried to put my knees together, but his hand caught them and held them apart. "If you lie to me, I will punish you for it. In this room, I want the truth. Now tell me, sweet girl. Are you wet?"

I nodded, and watched as he lifted my leg with one hand and pulled his other hand back. It slapped against my ass, and I cried out. Was he serious!?

"Are you wet?"

I nodded again, and he smacked it, again. "Stop that!"

Slap.

"Now!"

Smack! Only this time, there was no pain, but pleasure. I moaned and felt even more wetness leaving my pussy. I moaned as his hand smacked down again. The sound echoed through the room. I considered nodding again, just to see if it would revert to pain instead of pleasure. I was turned on, yet pissed that I was. He had no right to spank my ass, even if it had made me wet.

Darkest Before Dawn

"Are you wet?" He asked again with more force in his tone. His eyes left mine to look at the now saturated folds. "Damn," he whispered breathlessly.

"Yes," I replied, and felt his hand as it returned my leg to the bed. My hand absently reached down, knowing it wouldn't take much to get the screaming orgasm out of my system. I didn't care if he watched. That's how wound up and turned on I was.

"Good girl," he whispered before he caught my hands and held them prisoner against my legs. He worked them down farther, until my hands were trapped against my ankles. His eyes came back up to meet mine as his head lowered between my legs.

I felt a mixture of absolute horror, and fear as his mouth touched against my flesh. "What are you doing?" I wiggled my ass as I tried to get away.

"Kissing you," he replied before his mouth opened and hot breath fanned my swollen lips. Why would he…Ahhhhh! His mouth touched my core as his tongue licked the folds in a long, slow trail that started at the soft nub, and ended at my opening. His tongue continued to do it for several moments while I made inhuman noises. His tongue pushed inside and I felt the storm building out of control as he continued to ravish me with only his tongue.

He sucked and kissed and continued to pull with his lips as he kissed my core, slurping and licking until I was moaning so loud, I was pretty sure I would have no voice come morning. I fought to get my hands free, because one single flick of the swollen clit between my legs would send me over. He pulled his mouth away, and the moment his hand released mine, I tried to get it to where I needed it. He didn't allow it. Instead, he rearranged himself between my legs, took my wrist back, and captured it, along with my other wrist, in his much bigger hand. His hand brought both of my wrists up, and held them firmly against my belly.

A single finger slipped over my swollen flesh, exploring the wetness he'd created. "I want to fuck you so bad right now," he growled as his finger slipped into my opening. "You're so fucking wet and ready."

"Mmm," I mumbled as I moved myself over that finger.

"You like that, don't you?" he asked hoarsely as yet another finger joined and then another until it became painful. He was stretching me, and I had to move to keep from screaming from it. I lifted my hips to meet his thrust, each one penetrating my soul. I cried out, and lifted my head to look at him and then at what he was doing. "Fucking hell, you're tight and so hot right now, so sweetly fucking my fingers with that tight sheath. You want to come, don't you, good girl?" he asked and I nodded emphatically.

"Please," I begged.

"Please what?" he countered as he watched the heated skin he was currently fucking.

Darkest Before Dawn

"Make me come," I whispered as I looked to where his eyes had locked onto my flesh. "Oh God," I cried as the orgasm started to unfurl inside of me. I pushed and pulled with my hips to bring his magical fingers deeper into my slick heat. "Oh hell," I screamed as his hand released mine and his mouth lowered to allow his tongue to flick hard and slow over my throbbing clit.

He moaned against my core as my body shook with a force unfamiliar to me. I was coming undone, or dying. Either one was okay, because this was heaven. His fingers slipped out, and his mouth took their spot as he moaned and moved his mouth over my juices as if he couldn't get enough of them. His hands lifted my ass, and pulled it up until I was there for him to feast on. The sucking and sounds of what he was doing sent me over that precipice again.

My eyes closed and yet he continued to suck from me, his teeth grazing my flesh as he did so. I felt boneless when he'd finished, and moving was so far out of the question that it wasn't even an option. He climbed up my body, and at that moment if he'd tried to fuck me with his hard cock, he'd succeed.

"You've never been kissed like that before, have you?"

"No," I whispered through dry lips.

"Good," he replied as he claimed my lips and pushed his tongue inside. I could taste myself on him and it was hot. I moaned again as he ravished my mouth, his cock rubbing against my stomach. I could feel its silken flesh from where it had escaped its captivity in his shorts. He pulled up, and smiled down at me. "I keep my promises, but I am going to dry fuck you, hard. Look what you did to me," he said as he drew my eyes to his cock.

Dry fuck? He rubbed his cock over my skin, and pushed it back inside of his clothes. He held my legs apart, as he rubbed his erection between the cleft of my core. I moaned at the sensation of what he was doing. His eyes locked with mine as his hand captured my chin, and held it in place. We were both making noises, as he used my body for relief.

"Don't take your eyes off mine," he growled when I tried to close them. "Good girl," he said when I met his. "Fuck, you're perfect. You've never been controlled before, have you, Emma? You've never had your pleasure held, or controlled by something like me."

"Jaeden," I whispered, unsure of what he was asking, but not caring. I was lost in the feeling of what he was doing to my body. He stopped, and pulled on his cock. I tore my eyes from his to see what he was doing, as fear trickled up my spine.

"Eyes," he snapped.

I ignored him, watching him as his hand worked his cock. He used it to slap my pussy—hard. I cried out in surprise, but kept my eyes on it as it slapped my exposed flesh again. I was wet, so the sound exploded when he continued to use it on me. I lifted my hips, wanting, needing more. His hand moved from my chin to my throat, where it tightened enough that I lifted my eyes to his.

"I'm going to come all over your swollen pussy," he said, as his lips curved into a wicked smile. "You don't get to see it."

"I want to see it," I whispered.

"I know you do, that's why I'm not allowing it."

I struggled against his hold, but his fingers tightened. It wasn't painful so much as it was erotic. At any time, he could strangle the life out of me. His thumb rubbed over my carotid artery, as if he was testing my pulse while he continued to beat his cock against my flesh.

It turned me on to know he was using his hand, when he could have been easily buried deep inside of me. Instead, he was keeping his word. I had a feeling that even if I begged him to fuck me, he wouldn't tonight. I was almost there again, just from the knowledge of his impending orgasm. His flesh slapped mine hard enough that I screamed and then moaned.

"That's it, sweet girl, you like my cock beating your flesh. Knowing I could fuck it at any moment. I could bury this," he slapped my flesh harder. "At any fucking moment in this perfect cove and you know it. It turns you on, doesn't it?"

I moaned and then when his cock slapped against my clitoris again, I exploded.

"I'll take that as a yes," he smirked knowingly and continued to beat his silken flesh over my pussy. "Open your eyes," he commanded. I did, and watched as the muscles in his neck tensed, and his shoulders grew stiff. He growled and as he did, hot spurts of liquid jutted out onto my swollen flesh.

He leaned over, and rested his forehead against mine. "Next time I come, it will be inside you."

I lay beside him, spent. I'd gone from virgin, to virgin whore in a single day. He had cleaned his come off with a towel, and then crawled in bed after changing into sweatpants. My legs remained open, because I didn't have enough energy to close them.

I'd come hard the last time, and when he wrapped his arm around my waist and pulled my body up close against his, I didn't argue it. He was already hard again. I closed my heavy lids, and fell asleep to the absolutely mindboggling emotions I was now feeling.

"You should know this, Emma, I plan to have you. I will have you. Tonight was only the first of many lessons you will receive, until I decide to bury my cock in your sweet flesh."

"Lessons?" I asked, but he just smiled against the curve of my neck in answer. "I don't understand what you mean."

"No, but you will when I teach you."

Darkest Before Dawn

~~*

I felt safe with him, even though I shouldn't have. Being next to so much raw masculinity should have scared the shit out of me. His arms had wrapped around me protectively during the night. I could feel his breath fanning against my neck as I lay there with him.

I closed my eyes again, only to wake up the next time with something pressing against my lower back. I swallowed nervously as I ran through the options of what it could be. The process of elimination was, of course, how I managed it.

Option one; a snake had crawled into his shorts and decided to hang out on my back.

Option two; he'd shoved a hard object in his pants, which he'd then placed against my ass and back.

Option three; a bee had flown in and stung his junk, which had caused it to swell massively.

Option four; he'd changed into a motorcycle and he'd produced a stunning kick stand.

Option five; and this was the most likely, he had some serious morning wood!

Now for the options of what to do about the woody in the ass?

Option one; pretend I don't notice said woody

poking my ass.

Option two; run screaming from the woody.

Option three; hire someone with a skilled woodpecker to reduce said woody to normal size.

Option four; make use of said woody and become a woody woodpecker and peck that woody! *Seriously, Emma?* Okay, so that option wasn't even on the table.

"Morning," he whispered against my ear.

"Woodpeckers!" I shouted without thinking it over.

"Come again?"

"No thanks!" I sputtered as I made a complete ass out of myself and moved away from the woody before I started pecking. "Pecking is bad!" I continued like a dumb ass. *Shut up, Emma, just shut it!*

I obviously had wood on the brain because I couldn't look away from where his sweats had a thick bulge showing through the flimsy material. I felt his eyes on my face and could see him smiling with the knowledge that I'd just freaked the hell out over his morning wood. "Sorry about that."

"M-uh-huh," I mumbled.

"Not used to sleeping with men?" he asked.

"I don't spend the night with them normally," I whispered and then raised my eyes to his. "I mean I sleep, I just don't...ya know, feel wood." Oh my god! Had I just said that?

He threw his head back and barked with laughter.

"Sure, laugh at my expense," I said irritably.

"You want to touch it?" he asked jokingly, which of course, I didn't catch until I'd considered actually touching it!

I left the bed, knowing my ass would be exposed. "I need to go home, check on my people. Do some other stuff." I was rambling. I did it when I was nervous, like when I woke up after a night of debauchery with a deadly, sexual male, like Jaeden. Okay, so yes, this was the first this had ever happened to me, but still!

"Get dressed, Emma, I'll have Sven bring you to my office when you're finished."

"I need to go home," I replied.

"You can, but first I want to discuss something with you."

Chapter ELEVEN

Once I was dressed, I checked the door and hall and didn't see Sven anywhere, so I slipped out on my own without looking for Jaeden or his office. I didn't wait to see if I was followed, or if Jaeden had given chase. I just knew if I stayed close to him, I'd be up shit creek with Mr. Happy Whacker. Who needed a paddle when you had a man who looked and acted like that?

I made it to the shelter and flashed the camera a cheesy grin. Addy met me at the door and threw herself at me. "I was so freaking worried! Why didn't you respond?" she demanded.

"I was…busy," I replied with guilt burning in my cheeks.

"You slut!" she said as she pulled back to look at me. "You gave him the V-card?" she grinned hugely.

"Not exactly," I replied warily.

Darkest Before Dawn

"I'm confused," she paused and looked at my rumpled clothing. "Did you have sex?"

"Sorta," I replied and started towards my room.

"Bitch! Explain how you sorta had sex with him?" she narrowed her eyes and followed closely at my heels.

"He kissed me."

"Um," she said as she grabbed my arm to stop me. "I think we need to discuss the birds and the bees."

I rolled my eyes. "He kissed me *down* there."

"Sweet baby Jesus!" she smiled as though the rapture had just come. "And?"

"He, well, he likes full control. I'm not sure he's an option for a first timer." I answered her honestly because let's face it, I knew zero about this shit, and he was a fucking pro.

"Is he a Dom?"

"Yes, no, I don't know!" I was in so far over my head I was drowning. I scrubbed my hands over my face in frustration as I tried to gather my thoughts. "Look, he was all ready to bang me when the girls were killed, Addy. I don't have time for guys considering there are rabid wolves out there. If I hadn't been almost handing him myself on a platter, they might still be alive." I knew I was rambling, and for some reason couldn't stop.

"Oh please, don't give me that bullshit. Those girls

went out to try and steal him from you. They took everything they owned when they left. They weren't coming back, Emma, period. I'll bet they were trying to worm their way into what they thought was an easy life with Jaeden or one of those hot guys they said he was with. They left us without even a thank you for saving their spoiled, lazy asses to begin with! They deserved what they got for being selfish pricks," she snapped angrily.

"No, no one deserved to die as they did, Addy. They were torn apart, and Bonnie was raped, and the worst part? I couldn't tell if it was before or after she was in pieces!"

"Oh, well shit. That's disturbing…" her expression softened a little as it looked like her thoughts warred between outrage, horror and disgust.

"Exactly."

"Still, was he huge? Did you go down on him?"

I blinked at the rapid rate of her words and disturbing change in conversation. "I didn't go down on him," I blew out exasperatedly and headed to the level where my room was.

"Why not? Need to practice it? We have men here, and I've read *50 Shades of Grey*, if he's all controlling, sign me the fuck up!" Her arms were waving in excitement as she hustled to keep up with me.

"You read that book?" I asked.

"Five times already. I can't stomach that romance shit. You think E. L. James survived the apocalypse? I hope she did, I need more books."

"You seriously need your ADHD meds," I snorted as I tried to keep my eyes from rolling.

"Yeah well, so what."

"Oh look! Squirrel!" I said with a smile on my lips.

"Did he at least get off? You know if you don't help him out, he gets balls which are blue and actually painful according to Daniel Anderson."

"You slept with Anderson?"

"Why do you always call people by their last names? It's disturbing, and no, how do you think I found out about his balls being blue?"

"What the hell did you do to give him blue balls?"

"I licked it, but I didn't finish it. Kid wouldn't get done and my jaw hurt. His loss." She shrugged. "I was in a hurry to get home before Dad found out I'd snuck out. Told him he'd have to be fast, now I know that's not such a good thing. Lesson learned."

"Oh, well…slut."

"Proud of it," she smiled. "One of us has to be adventurous."

"I need to shower and then I need a scouting party. I

think Jaeden knows where the wolves are, and I want to make sure that issue ends."

"So, you were going to fuck him? Or did you just part your legs and say hey baby, lick these cobwebs!" She waggled her eyebrows mischievously.

"I don't have cobwebs," I bit out.

"No, but you have to be the oldest living virgin left in America. So I have to make fun of you, even if you are my bestie."

"Yeah…well, scouting party, and don't get distracted by a squirrel."

I entered my room and closed the door on her curiously eager face. I slid down it and yes, I thought about his mouth and where I wanted it. Soon. I'd never experienced anything like it, or him, and I wanted what he could give. I just wasn't willing to let it cost another life.

I headed to the showers and did my business as fast as I could. Once back in my room I decided to dress as if it was any other day, only a day with the living still in it. I skipped the shapeless black fatigues for a form fitting pair of jeans. I shimmied into a slim grey tank top and layered it with a black skull one. I then slid on the few necklaces I had left, and then set to putting on the harnesses for my weapons and gearing up. A quick brush through my hair and a French braid had me feeling a little more my old self.

Darkest Before Dawn

I left the room without my mask or the black hoodie. It was late summer, and I was tired of hiding. Yes it had worked to protect us, but I wasn't hunting or hiding from men. I was hunting wild animals. I heard the others whispering as I walked through the shelter, and knew the moment Addy caught sight of me.

"Hot damn! It's the old I'm-a-badass-Emma!" She whistled.

"Sure, party ready?"

"Honey, if you plan on landing in his bed, I suggest you wear a skirt."

I shook my head at her. "We are going to the woods. Wearing *skirts* will just slow us down."

"Whatever," she whined.

"Scouting party?" I asked.

She pointed behind me. I turned to find a huge group dressed as I normally did. "No masks today, we aren't going into town. We're hunting wolves. If you see a wolf, you shoot to kill. They may look like big dogs, but they're not. They tore the girls up and it wasn't for food. We will be setting up bear traps as well, it might catch them. If not, we'll have more meat for winter. You will go in groups of four, and stay together. The rest of you, stay in touch with each other. Turn the walkie talkies to channel five and check in every fifteen minutes. Got it?" I just couldn't bring myself to tell them that Bonnie had been brutally raped. I was sure of it, but the whole scene was too improbable.

When they agreed and each group grabbed a set of traps, we headed out. I set out on foot, with the others, but when they went into the woods, I stayed to the fields. When I finally hit the section of woods on the other side, it was only to hear what sounded like grunting coming from one of the many houses there.

The sound wasn't coming from inside one of the houses though. One of Jaeden's men had a woman pressed against a tree. Her legs were wrapped around his back as he drove himself inside of her. She screamed with pleasure as he grunted. One of his hands held both of hers above her head as his mouth covered her neck.

I could have moved.

I could have stopped watching as they took advantage of the end of the world and got it on in the forest.

Instead I stood there and allowed my body to respond to what it was seeing. Heat furled in my stomach, and my mouth watered. My back arched as if it was me against that tree and Jaeden between my legs. I bit into the fullness of my lip to stifle the moan which almost broke free. I needed to leave, I reminded myself.

I should have looked away sooner, but by the time I gave myself a mental shake and turned to move, I was stopped by a hand snaking around and covering my mouth. I felt my stomach drop sickeningly until Jaeden's voice whispered softly against my ear.

Darkest Before Dawn

"Enjoying the show?"

I shook my head but his reply was a throaty laugh that sent heat pulsing through my body. Instead of moving his hand from my mouth, his other hand dropped from my chest to press against the V between my legs.

I moaned against his hand as I tried to avert my gaze, but his hand held me there, watching as the huge male drove his need into the willing woman. My nipples hardened as moisture pooled where his hand was cupping my sex. I felt my body go tight with want, as more cries erupted from the female.

"You like watching?" Jaeden continued as he pulled my body against his. "You're already wet, and your body is wound up with unspent need. Let me fix it, Emma, let me take you," he whispered huskily as he walked me backwards from the couple carefully. It was a good thing he held me up like I was nothing, because I didn't think my legs could've held me up, much less been useful.

When he stopped, he pulled me around until I was facing him. His mouth pressed against mine, and his tongue slipped between my lips and captured mine. Before I knew what he intended, I was on the leaf covered floor, and one of his much larger hands held mine captured above my head as his mouth wiped all reason from my mind.

I moaned against his mouth as I kissed him back. His free hand worked my jeans until he had them undone, and his hand slipped in to press against the dampness. His skilled fingers slipped into my panties, and one entered me. I arched my hips to allow him better access without realizing it. I cried out at the pressure he created, and his mouth swiftly smothered my cries. He pumped his finger inside of me to a steady beat that complimented my heart's rapid tempo. A fever spread through me, as even more tension built in my core.

I could have stopped him, but I didn't want the pressure to ease, to end. Instead, I kissed harder, and spread my legs for his touch, ignoring the awkwardness that the too-tight jeans were creating as he fought against them to slide another finger inside of me.

"You're so fucking wet," he whispered as he continued to bring me toward the storm he was creating. "So tight, so fucking greedy. Can you feel your sweet pussy sucking my fingers off? I want it to be my cock," he murmured as his mouth lowered to my neck and sucked softly against the artery there.

I moaned louder without his mouth preventing it from coming out. He inserted yet another finger until I became uncomfortably full. I cried out at the ecstasy of his touch. What *the* hell was I doing? Why wasn't I fighting him? I should have been, but instead I lifted my hips and rolled my head from side to side with the intense feeling his touch was igniting inside of me.

He was stretching me. Filling me. I gasped as the sensation swept over me, consuming the need to fight him and replacing it with the need to accept what he

Darkest Before Dawn

offered. I cried out as he moved his fingers in and out of me, creating more wetness. It was painful, and yet in that moment, when he started really moving them, a fire tore through me as something *more* started to build inside of me.

"You feel so good. So fucking wet and tight, little one," he whispered against my ear as he pulled his fingers out and slid them back inside slowly.

It was insane; we were on the forest floor and he was making me feel things I didn't understand. Things I'd never dreamt of, and I was allowing it all over again. I felt desire burning in my lower abdomen, building as his fingers worked magic that shouldn't be possible. He lifted his head, and looked down at me with a heat burning in his eyes that left me breathless, and boneless.

"Jaeden," I cried out as I yanked my hands out of his bigger ones and brought my hands up to his chest.

"Is this what you need?" he asked, as his finger sank inside of me again. "I think it is," he mouth came down to hover over mine as his hot breath fanned my mouth. He caught my bottom lip between his, and sucked on it and then bit the tender flesh, enticingly. Pain lingered with passion and pleasure, and mixed together to cause an earth shattering combination. I was coming undone. He was in control, and I wanted it. I wanted this, and it terrified me that I trembled for him. I was embarrassed by my own behavior and yet I wasn't stopping him. I would, in a minute...or a couple...

"I could destroy, and you'd let me. Wouldn't you, sweet girl?" he breathed.

"Yes," I whimpered.

I moaned as his fingers stretched me further, and he added another which made my entire body go tight like a guitar string. I moaned and arched my back for his touch, wantonly. It was as if I was starving and couldn't get enough of it. Then, as suddenly as it started, it stopped, leaving me a writhing, heaving, sweaty, frustrated mess.

He stood above me, his feet planted between my legs as he watched me struggle to put myself back together. I was wet, down *there,* again because of him. I was fighting for control over the feelings his touch had created. I couldn't get up, and I wanted him to come back down and finish what he'd started. God help me, I wanted him now. It wasn't what came out, because his words about destroying me were playing in my head.

I watched him bring his fingers that had been inside me to his mouth, and one after another, he licked them free of my juices. It was erotic and exhilarating as he sucked them clean while I watched him.

"You can't admit what you want," he said as he continued to watch me as he sucked at his long tapered fingers one by one.

"I can," I lied.

"Is that so? Then tell me why you are soaking wet from my touch, and yet unsatisfied. Tell me why you allowed me to fuck you with my mouth and fingers, and yet nothing else, and answer me this; why the fuck didn't you stop me sooner? You're either a fucking cock tease, or a selfish bitch."

"Who keeps starting it?" I demanded, ready to punch him in the nose. Okay that was fair enough, but why was he being such an asshole? I felt a mixture of raw emotions boiling up. "We don't belong together," I said on a whisper. "You'd fuck me, and then you'd walk away without looking back, it's what people like you do."

His eyes narrowed on me. I was pathetic. I felt it all the way to my toes. I had leaves in my hair from rolling on the ground with this man, and the things he made me feel were crazy.

I made it back to my feet and glared at him. "Don't ever touch me again, Jaeden," I snapped when he didn't argue with what I'd pointed out. "It'll solve everything."

It was stupid. That snippy comment may as well have been a red flag waving at a bull. He moved so fast that I didn't have time to turn and run away. I didn't have time to think before I was pressed against a tree and his mouth was on mine, ravishing it. He pulled away and looked down his nose at me.

"How can I stop when you respond to my kiss like this, every fucking time? Some days I smolder with the images of you in my bed, other days I *hate* you. I hate that you occupy my mind when I lie down to sleep, or that you are inside my mind at all. Then it hits me, Emma, I want to fucking *destroy* you. I want to take you to my bed and destroy you for every other man alive. I want to watch you come undone for me. I want to watch as you come, for me. I don't like fucking games, not ones that don't end with you filled full of me, sweet girl. I should bend you over and take what I want; you'd let me. Wouldn't you?"

"Please," I begged unsure of what I was asking for. I wanted him. That little voice inside my head told me to run, while my body screamed how stupid I was for leaving *this*. They didn't make men like him anymore, and I wanted him. Like some spoiled little child wanted a toy.

"Tell me what's stopping you from saying yes right this second, Emma," he demanded.

"I can't do this, Jaeden." Common sense said run, and that I'd never met anyone like him before. I wasn't prepared for what he could do to me. He scared the crap out of me, and I wasn't into taking chances. I had too many responsibilities to consider that were so much more important than having sex. He wasn't asking for a relationship, he wanted to fuck and it was as simple as that to him. Meaningless sex, that's all it would be. Addy wouldn't have to think twice about jumping him. Me, I was a different story. I just wasn't made that way and I wasn't sure I could ever be all right with just scratching an itch.

I wasn't sure if the pros were outweighing the cons.

Darkest Before Dawn

On one side, I knew virtually nothing about him and his men and where the heck they'd come from, not to mention, something was seriously off about all of them. Then there was the chemical reaction he and I had together. I remembered the speech my father had given me when Bradly Allen had stood me up. Bradly had invited me out to one of the school dances, and I'd stood there decked out in my dress waiting for him until well after the dance had ended. I had really liked him and was devastated.

My father had pulled me into the house, and explained to me that love couldn't be forced. He'd told me *"You can't force chemistry to be there if it isn't there. You can't make someone love you; it's just not how it works. It's the same for when you find it; you can deny it. You can even lie to yourself, and pretend it isn't there, but it is. Someday my, Emma, someone is going to make you feel as if you've been sleeping for your entire life, waiting just for them to find you."* I missed my dad, and his wisdom.

Jaeden just watched me as I got lost in my own head. I closed my eyes as he expelled what sounded like a rapid fire spattering of cussing. "Why are you out here?" he asked as he adjusted his pants and stepped away from me.

"I'm hunting the wolves."

"What if I could show you where they are? What would you be willing to give me?" he asked with his eyes on my mouth.

"What would you want?"

"I want to ride you for hours, to fuck you until you can't scream anymore because your voice is gone from screaming my name; until your throat is fucking raw. I want to shove my hard cock inside your soft wet pussy until it's ruined you for every other man's touch."

Is that all? Sign me up and pin a tail on my ass! No, Emma, bad Emma.

I wasn't aware that my mouth had dropped open until he raised his hand and closed it. "That's what I thought. That's my price, Emma. You, for one entire night, doing anything I command you to," he replied hoarsely.

"Name something else," I whispered not recognizing my own voice.

"Get on your knees, and suck my cock."

"Why are you being such an asshole, Jaeden?" I shouted in frustration. I was soaking wet from his touch, from his fingers being inside of me. My nipples were as hard as pebbles and throbbing, which was new since I'd never once felt them do that before I met him.

"Why are you telling me no when your body wants it?" he shrugged as he took a step toward me, and I took a giant step backwards.

"I'm not that kinda girl," I growled. Or at least I hadn't been until I'd met him. When I was with him I lost my grasp on reality, and did things I'd never have done otherwise. I wasn't the kinda girl who spread her legs in the dirt and really wasn't sure I wanted to.

"Oh but you're the kinda girl who watches as a couple fucks? Tell me, Emma, when you watched them, did you pretend it was us? Did you want me to press you against a giant oak tree and ride your soft flesh until you exploded on my shaft?"

"No," I whispered hollowly.

"Little liar. I can see you struggling to ignore what is happening between us, but sooner or later you will give in to me. Call it intuition, or whatever you want to call it. It's going to happen, and you'll scream for me. And it won't be a *no* coming out of those beautiful lips, it's going to be *more*, and *harder*," he continued relentlessly.

"Why are you doing this?" I asked with a thickness in my throat from the hurt I felt at his words.

"You know what your problem is, Emma? You still expect people to be nice. You expect them to behave as they did before the world went to hell. Problem is, they were always this way, now there's just no one to stop them. I'm used to getting what I want. Maybe that makes me shallow in your book, but I'm not taking you by force as others will do. I'm trying to be understanding, but it's against my nature. I was never a good guy, so don't expect me to be one now." I flinched at the anger burning in his voice.

"You're an asshole!" I shouted as I fought against my eyes tearing up.

"I'm an asshole? I'm the one who keeps saving your pretty little ass. Grow up, Emma. Go back to the safety of your shelter and shove that pretty little nose back into the romance novels you read. That's the kind of man you're looking for, right? You're looking for someone to wipe away the tears and become your knight in shining armor?"

"I never said I wanted anything from you! I asked about the god damn wolves so they don't kill anyone else. I didn't look for you because I wanted a friggin' hero! Fuck you! You're nothing but a bully," I cried as I turned to march off. Something was off about him, and I didn't like this Jaeden at all.

He was an arrogant prick!

"Walk away, Emma!" he shouted.

"I am!"

"Watch your back little girl, there's monsters moving in!" His parting words sent a chill down my back.

Chapter Twelve

I'd given Jaeden and his men a wide berth. Almost a month had passed with several more attacks by wolves. I no longer needed to head into town, because the Towner's in hiding who hadn't been killed had come to the shelter. Even those who had been hiding in the woods trickled into the shelter just to be on the safe side. It just wasn't an option to live outside anymore. Jaeden had been right, there were monsters here. After that encounter in the forest, I'd decided to include him on that list as well.

No one went out alone or unarmed anymore. It was a safeguard that helped eliminate a lot of problems for me, especially with the possibility of running into Jaeden and turning into a mindless slut. Today, Addy was out with me to forage some of the remote locations for wild fruits and vegetables while most of the able bodied from the shelter were out hunting game or looking for cattle that had been left in the pastures and chickens that had gone a little wild in abandoned farms. With more people showing up, the food was slowly trickling to the basics and the MREs. Winter in the Pacific Northwest—specifically in our little corner of the world, could begin as early as October and were notoriously harsh, so everyone was scrambling to collect what they could.

"My nails are never going to be the same again,' she grumbled as she dug up a wild patch of strawberries from the roots.

"Use soap," I said offhandedly.

"Ha-ha," she snarked. "What was that?" she asked, and I lifted my eyes from my own patch of berries.

"What was what?" I asked pushing my mind away from what had happened with Jaeden. I looked around at the edge of the woods but saw nothing. There was a fifty foot cliff behind us, so there wouldn't be any surprises coming from that direction. Below the cliff was a fast running river.

"You didn't hear that?" she asked as she wiped her dirt-covered hands on her jeans and stood up. I hated heights, but she loved them. She looked over, which made my stomach roll. "Wow, is that him?"

"Is that who?" I asked stepping closer. I felt my heart skip a beat as the sight of Jaeden and his men, along with some women playing in the shallow water of the riverbank came into view. "Asshole," I whispered.

"Which one is he?"

Darkest Before Dawn

"The one without the shirt on, with the bimbo splashing him," I sighed as I pointed him out to her.

"Are you serious? You turned *that* down!? Do you by chance have brain damage?" she asked with wide eyes.

"Obviously—"

I didn't get to finish as something smashed against the side of my head. I closed my eyes and touched my hand to where I could feel warm blood trickling from. I could just make out Addy screaming, but couldn't tell if she was a mile away, or further.

Rough hands groped me, and I knew I was being searched for weapons. It was obvious from the hoots of men as they found my three guns and four knives. Addy was behind me, as my hearing came rushing back I knew she was fighting off an assailant. We knew better than to take our eyes off our surroundings even for a second, and now we were going to pay for that lapse.

I turned my head to see her, and tears leaked from my eyes, or maybe it was blood. I struggled to my feet as hands groped and prodded me. I faced Addy and her attacker, and made a choice. He was ripping her clothes off, as if he couldn't get her naked fast enough so he could rape her. Thoughts of Bonnie skated across my mind. Were these the men who raped her? Dazedly, I wondered where the wolves were. I struggled and broke free from the hands that had tried to hold me down. I launched myself at Addy and her attacker, shoving them both, and watched as my best friend in the world fell to the bottom of the cliff. It was better than what they would do to her. She at least had a chance of escape since she was the best swimmer I knew.

"Fucking whore!" A man from behind me screamed, seconds before I was hit in the back of the head again. I fell to my knees as the world went black and white, and crawled in the direction of the cliff. I wasn't a strong swimmer, and heights scared the crap out of me, but again, it was better than what they were planning.

My fingers found the edge, and I peered down to see Addy swimming towards Jaeden's group and smiled knowing she'd be okay now, she was safe. I looked to where he stood, and knew the moment he saw what was happening. He shouted my name, and I smiled with regret. I should have screwed his brains out. I was now going to die a virgin....which sucked.

I was flipped over, and punched in the face. "Fucking bitch killed Jason!"

I grabbed his arms with what I thought was strength, but it wasn't. He didn't wince, didn't blink. I could barely make out his features. He was missing teeth, the rest that remained were rotten. He smelled putrid, as if he hadn't noticed all the water in Washington State which was readily available to bathe in. He ripped at my pants and I shook my head.

"Fucking whore, I'm gonna have fun with you and then you'll join Jason on the rocks below."

Darkest Before Dawn

I kicked out, and got to my feet unsteadily. I felt his hands latch on to me at the same moment I jumped backwards—off of the cliff.

They say you see all sorts of shit when you are about to die. Like your entire life flashing before your eyes. Not me, I saw the toothless asshole and the fear in his eyes. I pulled him close, laughing briefly before I rolled, turning him below me in the air—and we hit the rocks…hard.

I smashed my head against his, and went blind with pain as something cracked in my arms and stomach. Landing on top of toothless only lessened some of the impact. I could hear Jaeden shouting and Addy's screams, and knew I was dying. Or I thought I was. Bullets rained down from the cliff the moment I raised my head. I pushed myself from the bloody corpse and felt the cool water as I slid into it, and sank quickly.

I didn't want to die, but my chances of living were getting slimmer with every passing moment. Every inch of my body seemed to scream with pain. I pushed off the bottom knowing I had to get air, but I had nothing left. I felt arms as they wrapped around my waist and took me to the surface.

I leaned my head against the last person I'd expected to save me. I couldn't speak, and my lungs felt as if they were on fire. I pulled in huge gulps of air, as he laid me down on the riverbank and spoke. "Damn, lass, ye look like hell."

I looked into Lachlan's eyes and tried for a laugh, which only came out as a sob.

"Och nae, lass, none of that now," his voice was a gentle croon as he began to look over my many injuries.

"Emma!" Jaeden shouted as he rounded the bend, with Addy close behind him.

Addy fell to the ground beside me bawling. "Emma, get up!" she cried as she fisted her hair in her hands as she stared in despair at me. She was about to lose it, and I couldn't fix it. I didn't have enough in me to reassure her that it would be okay because it wasn't.

"No," I whispered even though it hurt like hell to say it. "Something's not right," I whispered.

I felt broken, as in everything was on fire. I was pretty sure I was knocking on heaven's door, and there wasn't going to be any do-over's. "You know what to do if it happens," I rasped to Addy as I started to cough up blood.

"No, get the fuck up bitch! You don't get to leave me! I can't do what you can, I can't, Emma. I need you! Grayson needs you! Get up! You don't get to die! We have to grow old together, you promised. I'm not as strong as you are." She was sobbing, and pulling on my useless arm. "You're all I have left, you can't leave me here alone, Emma, please get up!" she wailed.

"That hurts," I whimpered.

Darkest Before Dawn

"Lachlan, take her friend," Jaeden ordered and I lifted my eyes to him.

"No," I answered for Lachlan. "Home," I said sternly. "They need me," I said before trying to move my useless limbs.

"Emma, don't do this to me, you have to get up. Let them help you, you don't look good. Grayson can't see you like this. They're right. You look really bad," Addy sobbed the words out.

"Not…dying, just—a scratch. Walk…it…off," I struggled to continue. Addy's eyes were wide with horror as she looked at me. It wasn't a scratch; even I could hear the death rattle in my chest.

*~*Jaeden*~*

She'd been lucky to survive the fall; her body was a mass of broken bones and damaged flesh. I picked her up, listening to the faint beating of her heart as she lost the fight to stay conscious. I watched her eyes grow slack, as her life threatened to leave her. "Take her," I snapped at Lachlan who was allowing the thin wisp of a woman struggling in his arms to win against him.

"Ye cannae do what I ken yer aboot tae do without her consent….dinnae do it. She doesna deserve tae become what ye are, Jaeden," Lachlan's voice was an angry demand.

"You owe me this much," I spat out.

"Jaeden, that was long ago and I dinnae know. Ye ken I didnae plan on what happened." He sounded reasonable, maybe he didn't plan on it, but it changes nothing. I already had Shamus riding my ass to let it go. He isn't exactly free of betrayal either. It still burns and festers to think of it even after all this time.

He waited for me to respond for a few moments and when it became clear I had nothing further to say, he bit out a curse, and picked up the small struggling woman and carried her away. Her grief stricken wails faded with Lachlan's departure and the noise of the river.

I kneeled to the cold ground and ripped my wrist open with a sharp fang. I placed my wrist over her lips and pulled her mouth open, forcing her to drink my blood. "Drink, Emma," I begged her, I couldn't allow someone with so much fucking life to give up. Bringing her back as something like I am, well, it beat watching her die in my arms.

"Are you sure you wish to sire her? We are at war, and a neophyte is something we don't have time for," Bjorn grumbled as he kneeled beside us. "She's losing this battle, old friend. Maybe it's best to let her go."

"That's what they said about you, Bjorn, and I refused to leave you bleeding out on the battle field. I've never regretted bringing you over, yet," I responded grimly.

Darkest Before Dawn

I massaged her throat, working my tainted blood into her system. Her organs were damaged, her heartbeat was faint, and fading faster than my blood could repair it. I knew the moment it reached her organs, because she jerked in my arms. I remembered the fire, the burning of every cell as it was reborn. Her eyes grew wide with the pain. Her body convulsed, as she tried to push my wrist away. Her arms were shattered in the fall, and unable to do much of anything.

"You broke your new toy?" Sven's bright blue eyes narrowed at the sight of her broken body as he moved closer. "Shit," he whispered as he looked over the extensive damage.

Her skull was cracked and blood oozed from her scalp and dribbled from her nose. There were deep cuts and scratches all over her face; one showed the damage to her facial bones. Her heart had taken too much damage from the impact of the rock's unforgiving surface, and the sound of it trying to push the blood was sickening. Her insides were a fucking mess.

"She took a leap off a cliff to escape being raped," I replied as I felt her lips finally latch on. Good girl. I closed my eyes as the sensation of her feeding from my wrist made my cock stand up at attention. Feeding led to fucking, and she was a fucking mess. I moaned, uncaring of the men standing close to me. They knew what it was like, because they'd each made their own fair share of toys, as they called them.

My balls stretched taut as blood pulsed in my

erection. Easy boy, she's not available for you yet. She would be a hard turn, normally they weren't this close to death. She was barely breathing, and even as I fed her, everything in her body was either bleeding out or shutting down.

"Get the truck; she needs more blood than this and we're too exposed out here."

"You got it," Sven said as he turned and walked back through the thick brush to where the SUVs awaited us.

I continued to force the blood down her throat, even as she thrashed against my efforts. "Come on, sweet girl, you can do it."

The sound of the engine as it turned over and headed this direction was a relief. She needed more blood than I alone could give her, and she needed sleep. Tonight she would sleep with me, and when her body turned cold, I would place her in the ground for the change.

"Shamus should be here tonight; you think he's going to approve of your new toy?" Bjorn asked as he helped me secure her in the backseat.

"You think I give a fuck? He may be in charge of the Northwest, but he isn't my maker. I've lived by the rules, Bjorn. It's been over a thousand years since I've changed a female over to our world. He's made several, including Cayla. I have only brought one female over, and she's currently stuck on his dick."

"Astrid was your wife," Bjorn said calmly. "What

she did to you was unforgivable."

Unforgivable? I'd married her while I'd been human still. She'd been the pampered daughter of nobility, and my obsession. I'd earned the right to claim her in marriage, and I had to leave her with my seed just barely swelling in her body to serve my king. Not to go Viking like my father—and his before him—but to hold and defend a God-forsaken shit hole an ocean away. I had plenty of land and wealth from my family, but serving my king was paramount, so with promises to her of chastity and abstinence that would have made me a laughingstock to my forefathers, I left her to do my duty.

When I had been left for dead after the battle for control of York in Northumbria, and changed, I'd gone back for her. It was only after I had changed her that I discovered that while I had been serving king and country, she had been seeking the favors of every male with titles, land, or both that would pay her attention. My child wasn't lost to miscarriage as I'd been led to believe, but deliberately killed in her womb as no man would look at her with my seed growing there.

She'd taken many men to our bed, fucked them, and took great delight in telling me after. It wasn't enough for her to attempt to seduce any man I called friend; she would try and kill any female I showed affection to. She wanted my attention and she wanted my jealousy and would do anything to obtain it. The bitch was psychotic, spoiled, and unstoppable, and yet she'd found protection with Shamus. Wisely, he tried whenever possible to keep her away from me.

"Help me secure her, and open your vein," I told Bjorn before climbing in the back with them. "Anything from Lucas?"

"They captured the four men that were with the one she cliff dived with. They have been taken care of." He reported quietly as he helped me situate her over my lap. Sven began the drive back to the estate, the rest of our convoy following behind us.

"Good," I whispered as I cradled her head to his open wrist. The sight of his eyes as they grew round with lust from her lips touching his skin made anger radiate through me. I knew the moment his cock grew hard, because he shifted in the seat. His hand moved to grope her breasts, but the inhuman growl that tore from my throat stopped him.

"Habit," he said as he reached in his pants to fix his own growing erection. Mine was hard as a rock, pulsing with the need to pillage her sweet, pink flesh.

Knowing a woman was coming over, and drinking of blood was an aphrodisiac to our kind. The sound of sucking mixed with blood, rich in the air, had every male in the car hard and ready to fuck. Her heartbeat was sputtering, and her temperature was already dropping. I pulled her away from Bjorn's wrist as he moaned at the sensation of her mouth against his flesh.

Possessiveness wasn't a trait I had felt in a long time, and yet I felt it with her. She had an innocence to her that women lacked these days. The fire in her eyes when she was angered was seductive. The fierceness of her dedication to protect and help those she loved was unique in this day and age.

There was also the fact that I wanted to bury my cock deep inside of her perfect body and fuck it until she couldn't walk. I wanted to kiss her swollen flesh, knowing it was sore from what I had done to her. To kiss it and watch as she squirmed against me from the pain as it mingled with pleasure.

The first time she came for me, with my lips sucking her succulent juices, it took every ounce of strength to prevent my fangs from piercing her flesh. I could sense when she was nervous, embarrassed, turned on, and better than that, when her sweet pussy grew moist with the need to be fucked. I could smell her sweet little bud as it grew slick with the need to be plucked.

The first time I'd smelled her arousal had been unnerving. I'd wanted nothing more than to strip her bare and fuck her flesh until she knew she wanted no other. The only thing that prevented it was her. The fear I'd smelled at her body's reaction to me. She had been shocked by her response, as if she hadn't felt anything like it before.

Hopefully she lived, to allow me to explore her body and mind. Her heart slowed to a final stop and restarted within a few minutes. Bjorn noticed it and looked at her curiously. He shrugged his wide shoulders, as Sven did the same. Once we were back at the estate and in my room, I stripped her bare, and covered her up with a sheet as I worked to putting her body back together, setting her limbs so that her bones when she finally woke, would be healed correctly.

She was quite the temptress, even as she lay dying. Her legs were parted, and the smell of her pussy made my cock stand up erect for the fifth time since I found her broken and battered. I had Sven pull up a chair to be her next donor and within moments of setting his wrist to her lips, she latched on and sucked dreamily at it as I set her body to rights. He's not shy about looking at her beauty, even with the amount of damage that had ravaged her.

"She's not dying," he points out as her nipples grew erect against my touch.

"She has internal damage. Her heart stopped in the truck, but it started again…it should stop soon. Can you ready the crypt after you feed her?"

"As soon as I find some willing flesh and fuck this need out of my cock. She's a greedy little wench, with lips I'd like to—"

"I'd think really fucking carefully about how you finish that sentence, my friend," I warned with a fierceness that surprised even me.

"And if she has needs to match Astrid's? Will you control her and allow her to fuck us, or chance history repeating itself?" Sven asked, as he replaced his wrist with his thumb to keep her mouth working. "Fucking hell," he groaned as she latched on and moved her mouth on it.

Yeah, okay, it was hot. She was moving her head as if it was his cock instead of his thick thumb. "If she wishes to be fucked by more than just me, she will have to earn it and I will be present for it. I don't like sharing, and I need full control in the bedroom. Besides, there are other ways to fill each hole these days."

"There were other ways when your wife took those men to her bed, Jaeden. Astrid likes to be worshiped by men. She likes to control them with her body. She still tries to control you with it."

"Yes, well that wore off long ago and I have seen her for what she is. Astrid I want nothing to do with, but Emma is a different story. Emma is different. She was raised in this town. She's unskilled, and I become more certain each time I am around her, that she is untried by a man. I'm sure one cock will be enough for now. If later she decides she wants more, I'm sure I can find enough men to scratch that itch. For now though, she's my toy, my plaything, Sven. When the time of her hunger comes, I'll make sure to invite those who helped sire her."

"Good, because if she sucks cock like she sucks fingers, I want in," he mused as he worked her pretty little mouth with his thumb.

"I can take over now, her bones have been set," I snapped. The idea of having to share her pissed me off. I hated that they knew of Astrid's hunger for male attention. That they knew of the cunning deceit that hid behind her beautiful face. It had driven me mad with rage in the beginning. It was one of the reasons I demanded control in the bedroom. It had fed my need to withhold, and give pleasure. I'd become a fucking master of seduction, and a control freak in the process. The pictures in my mind—which included Emma—made my cock twitch.

Her sweet legs held open by ropes, showing me what was mine. Her hands bound behind her head, with her subtle movement opening her legs more...I'd have it. Soon. I placed my fingers in her mouth, two at first, and felt her sucking them off. No bloody wonder the others had been hard. I moaned at the sensation of her tongue as it curled around them, caressing them. Her head moved in the seductive dance, pulling them deeper, and then letting up.

My mind wandered to how many men had felt her sweet mouth curve around their cock? How many had pounded her pink flesh, and made her scream? None could do it as I could, and I would. It would be so easy to take her sweetness right now, but for the first time she's with me, I want her completely lucid and aware of everything we do.

"Soon my sweet girl, I will make you beg to come. I will tie you up and fuck you until the need to climax is so overpowering that you're wild from the need of it. When I'm finished with you, you will beg me to use you often, and I will."

Chapter THIRTEEN

I awoke to a strange noise and it took me a few moments to orient myself as to where I was. Classical music softly played in the room, soothing and yet it made my ears pound along with my head. I looked down at the bed, and flexed my limbs. I should hurt, and yet I didn't. I tested my eyes, and closed them against the blinding light that streamed through the giant windows. I sat up, only to discover I was naked, and my hands and chest were covered in…ewww, blood.

A dream; that was the only explanation. This had to be a very bad dream. I lay back against the pillows, and closed my eyes against the heaviness of them. Sleep stole my mind, and when I woke the next time, he was there.

I could feel his naked body wrapped around mine. He held me tight and whispered things I couldn't understand against my ear. He held me through the night, and when the sun's bright rays shined into the room, he tried forcing some thick, vile liquid down my throat. I fought against him, but in the end, he won.

He did it several times, and each time I felt myself growing stronger. Sleep pulled me under, and refused to allow me to wake up on my own from whatever it was that had happened to me.

"Shamus, this is Emma," Jaeden's voice drifted in, barely penetrating my muzzy mind and sounded like it was far away.

"Mmm, she smells divine. How long since she lost her human pulse?" the stranger asked in a deep voice that had an Irish lilt to it.

"She didn't," Jaeden's answered quietly. "Her heart only stopped the one time. She has few of the markers for the change. Have you ever heard of something like this?"

"You're sure she wasn't of another species?"

Another species?

"I'm sure of it; she was human."

I was dreaming still. It was the only way this conversation made sense.

"Strange, she looks human. Have you tasted her?"

"I've tasted her flesh," Jaeden confirmed, and I felt my body grow flush with the memory of his *tasting* me. "She accepted the transfusion of my blood, and the others. No ill effects, either. She is healing rapidly, and yet she hasn't regained consciousness."

"Did she sustain a head injury?"

"Yes," Jaeden conformed. "She suffered many severe injuries on top of that."

"Head wounds can make them come back different... like Cayla. You sure you want that?" Shamus asked. "She's a handful, what with her imaginary friend and all. It's like siring a child."

"Cayla was damaged before you changed her, we all knew it. You just refused to acknowledge it."

"Be that is it may, that piece of shit father of hers had beaten and raped her for years before I changed her. She was worth it with her abilities. Even damaged as she is, she's an asset."

"If Emma comes back unhinged, I'll end her misery," Jaeden said tightly.

"No, if she comes back unhinged, she'd still be a welcome addition to my bed; damaged minds in the bedroom are hot as fuck." Bed? Addition? Go back to sleep, Emma, this is a nightmare! "When she wakes, call for me. I'd like to taste her after you have. It may help in solving the mystery."

"Has there been any word from the elders?"

"None, but with technology crippled and only

the pagers up and running, it's a task to get messages through. She is wet; have you not satisfied the need from the change?"

"I would rather she be awake when I fuck her, so she knows who is claiming her. Unlike you, I prefer my partners to be awake and willing."

"Your loss; I find them irresistible when they are crazed with the change pulsing in them. They can't distinguish pain for the first few months and you can have so much fun. They can take anything you dish out, and more. Cayla was positively stunning in her change; she took me for hours and still begged for more. By the time she was done, she knew who had ruined her for other men. If you decide her mind is too far gone, call for me."

I listened as they left the room. Once I was sure they had gone, I slowly sat up. I felt my face and throat—I felt filmy, as if someone tried to clean me up, but didn't do the best job of it. I felt as if my body was on fire. My insides clenched with hunger as nausea rolled through it.

I looked down to find myself wearing a thin white nightgown that had been dotted with dark red splotches. I tested my weight, and then stood to move to the bathroom that was just off of the main room. I shuffled to it slowly and once inside, I flicked on the light and tried to look at my reflection. I was as white as a ghost, and my mouth looked like there was blood in the corners. Had they gave me said transfusion through my mouth?

Darkest Before Dawn

Images flashed through my mind of the cliff, and what had happened. I'd almost died, or *had*, according to Jaeden. He'd saved me? Did that mean they had medical staff on hand? Probably. I couldn't see any cuts or scrapes, which was weird. I walked on wobbly legs to the shower and turned it on, and blinked as my eye latched on to every droplet, my vision swimming before me.

I fell to the floor as my legs gave out from my weight. I crawled forward until I was beneath the cascade of droplets. I trembled as other images flashed in my mind. Addy; I'd thrown her over. Had she survived, or had I killed my best friend? Tears welled up and slid down as a sob racked my body.

I lay down, unable to hold myself up.

"Emma?" Jaeden's voice filtered in from the bedroom. He found me on the floor, and picked me up, uncaring that he was getting soaked from the shower. "You shouldn't be up yet," he whispered. "Your body hasn't fully healed from the change."

"I'm starving," I whispered as he wrapped me in a towel and carried me into the bedroom. I shook from the cold, but the feel of his arms wrapped around me took some of it away.

He sat us down on the bed, and didn't allow me to get up. He brought his wrist up, and sliced it open with his teeth. I cringed and barely held back the need to throw up. How the hell did he do that? I shoved my face into the crook of his neck and then looked up at him. What the fuck was wrong with these people?

"You need to feed, Emma," he urged.

"On blood? Are you fucking high? Gross!"

"Feed," he said and held his bleeding wrist closer to my mouth. I pushed it away and lunged for the bathroom, tossing up everything in my stomach into the toilet. It all looked like blood. Strong arms wrapped around me, as a soothing cloth was pressed against my face. "What are you hungry for?" he asked hesitantly.

"Fruit, a Big Mac, but I'm pretty sure that in no possible way am I hungry for blood!"

"Emma, it's normal—"

"In what friggin' world is it normal to crave blood, Jaeden?" I asked as I stood up and turned to face him—which ended with me face planting his chest, which was now bare. "That isn't normal; you aren't normal!" Jaeden's expression seemed torn between surprise and confusion.

"It doesn't call to you?" he said carefully.

"There are a lot of things that call to me, none of which are your blood."

He narrowed his eyes, and looked at me as if *I* was the alien. "I'm tired," I said as my lids grew heavy again and I could feel my legs giving way. He caught me,

Darkest Before Dawn

picked me up, and carried me to an oversized chair in the room. I watched as he cleared the bed off, and then stripped out of the rest of his clothes. I was too tired to protest sleeping naked with him, so when he gripped the edge of the nightgown, I allowed it.

He picked my naked ass up, and walked to the bed. He laid me down, and I watched as his hand moved to his large, throbbing cock. My eyes latched on, and for some reason, I wanted him to come with me watching him. It was official; I had massive brain damage.

"Do you have any idea how hard it was to sleep with you, naked, knowing you were oblivious to me?" he asked in a tortured tone.

"No, not if I was oblivious," I answered absently as I continued to watch his hand work over his silken shaft. "Did you do that while I was asleep?"

"No, but I promise you that now that you are aware, I plan to have you."

"Is that a threat? How did you save me?" Yes, I switched that subject fast!

"If you haven't figured it out, then I don't think you are ready to know yet," he whispered as he released his cock and crawled over the bed. When he was beside me, he grabbed my hand, and wrapped it around his huge cock. "You are ready to earn your place though, minx. I'm dying to taste you."

I moaned even as my eyes closed. My grip loosened

on his shaft as he moved down my body, and the sensation of his mouth on my pussy made my brain do funny things...like spread my legs for his mouth.

"I can smell your arousal, and it smells like heaven," he rumbled.

That was nice of him to say. I smiled, and made some weird ass noises which made my head spin. Something punctured the flesh of my upper thigh, and I screamed, but then the burn of the piercing was replaced with a mind numbing pleasure that made more sounds erupt from my throat that I am positive never came out of my mouth before. I heard him slurping, and an image of his wrist against my mouth came back. I was remembering something, but then my body jackknifed with a pleasure so deep and profound that I thought I was dying.

His fingers entered me harshly, and I dropped my knees to take them further inside of me. I listened to the sound his mouth as it sucked against my thigh, and the noise my body made as he pushed his digits inside of me. I was floating and mindless. I felt his hand stop the moment his mouth did, and I tried to lift my head to see what was wrong, but I was too far gone.

"What the fuck are you, Emma?" he whispered. I could feel his eyes burning into me as he climbed up my body.

"I'm—me," I whimpered.

He cupped his hands around my face and I opened my eyes a sliver. I was so tired, and the fire burning in

Darkest Before Dawn

the pit of my stomach for him was overwhelming.

"What the fuck are you?" he asked again, this time there was a hint of uncertainty in his tone.

He dropped his hold on my face and I heard the door as it was slammed open. I fisted the sheets as I struggled with my waning strength to pull them up. My breasts were still exposed as he returned, but he wasn't alone.

"Taste her," he growled and the sound that left the other male made my skin crawl.

This time, it hurt far worse. I screamed as the piercing pain shot into the inside of my upper thigh and through me. The strange gurgling noise was back, and I felt light headed. The pain eventually turned to pleasure, and I moaned as I moved my hips, needing more. Needing him there. Between my legs. Fucking me. "Please," I whimpered.

"You didn't take her, Jaeden, is it your intention to torture her?" another male voice said from the doorway.

"She isn't aware of what we are doing," Jaeden ground out, his voice a mixture of irritation and impatience, irritation and anger. "Enough, Shamus," he growled.

"Fuck her, or I will," the one named Shamus warned. "Her pussy is soaking wet with need, and she won't notice it. She won't sleep without it either. She needs the drain that comes with fucking."

"She's mine. I'll decide when she's ready to be fucked."

Somewhere in the bickering, I passed out.

When I awoke again, I was alone. The room looked the same as it did on my first visit. My mind flew through all the mental images and I wasn't sure what was real and what must have been a hallucination. I pushed off the sheets and looked at my pristine thighs. It really must have been some sort of drug induced hallucination. I rolled out of bed and looked around the room and when I was sure I was alone, I searched through his dresser for clothes.

I pulled on one of his large shirts, and used a belt to keep it in place. I walked to the window and quietly slid it open, before climbing out and lowering myself to a second story rooftop. I tried to hold on to get to the other roof that sloped nearby. Something wasn't right with Jaeden or any of the people here, and until I could figure it out, I needed to get away from them. I slid down the roof until I found an overhang, which was low enough to the ground that I could jump safely. I didn't land gracefully; instead I landed on my ass in a bone-jarring fall. I stood up and pulled most of the leaves from my hair before turning to the woods.

I set off in the direction of the shelter, with the hope that Addy was safe and unharmed, that I hadn't killed my best friend in an attempt to save her.

Chapter FOURTEEN

The walk back to the shelter was an intense experience that took every scrap of patience and self-control I had. The sun was blinding and the sound of nature was deafening. I could hear the bugs, the animals, and see every tiny detail of the things that I had never noticed or were hidden to me before. I tripped several times, and each time I struggled to get back up as I made my way through the dense forest. It was a bit of an out of body experience as I felt like I didn't have complete control over myself, my limbs, or my senses. Nothing. Maybe this was what it was like to be reborn. I covered my ears with my hands as I got closer and the shelter and the blaring noise of music assaulted me.

When I got through the brush, it was to find all of the residents of the shelter outside, with Lachlan seated at a picnic bench with Addy. In his lap no less! I struggled to make my legs move, and when Lachlan's eyes zeroed in on me, it was intense. He stood too fast, which deposited Addy flat on her ass. Good, she deserved it for leaving me with Jaeden.

"Emma, stop. Dinnae make me do something we will both regret," he warned.

I blinked at him in confusion. "This is my home!" I growled.

"Emma," Addy whispered and tried to get past Lachlan as he held her back. His men stood with weapons at the ready. To attack me?

"What the hell do you think you're all doing here? I've only been gone one night and you all move in? I seriously think you should reconsider shit." Oh yeah I was angry, years of hard work, training, everything I knew was being tipped over and trampled on.

Addy stopped struggling and looked at me in shock. "Emma, you've been gone for over two weeks." My heart stuttered as my head swam at this news.

"Bullshit," I argued.

"Emma," Jaeden called as he walked in on the precariously volatile situation. "Why'd you leave my bed?" His voice was filled with concern as I tried very hard not to reach out and throttle him.

I blushed from head to toe before scowling at him. I heard the gasps and comments which started to buzz right after the words slipped from his lips. I shook my head, and fought against the tears of anger. "Tell them it's only been one day that I've been gone!"

Darkest Before Dawn

"Emma," he said as his eyes moved to Lachlan with a nasty glare that should have flattened him.

"Tell them!"

"Emma, you were severely injured," he explained. "It took us a long time to fix you."

"And she's *fixed*, isnae she?" Lachlan spat out as if it was distasteful on his tongue.

"No, she's just as she was before," Jaeden looked meaningfully at Lachlan. "It's a fucking miracle."

"That's bullshit 'n ye ken it," Lachlan growled.

I watched as Lachlan cut his forearm open and held it up in my direction.

"That's crazy!" I snapped, pointing at Lachlan in disbelief. "Why the friggin' hell would you do that?" I watched as his eyes narrowed and then grew wide. Addy stepped a good foot away from him, and looked from Lachlan to Jaeden. "I'm not sure what the hell you guys' fetish with blood is, but it's seriously disturbing."

"That's impossible, I saw her fall. Nae one could live through that," Lachlan snapped.

I turned and looked at Jaeden as he watched me carefully. Was he expecting a reaction? Was I? I felt different; weird, strange, changed, and yet I was still me. Not that he could change me, but something inside was very different. I felt more alive, and more aware of my surroundings. I could also taste the anticipation and turmoil coming off Lachlan's men, as well as uneasiness from Jaeden, directed at me.

I turned and looked at him. Really looked at him. He was beautiful, but deadly. I knew he was deadly, just not why he was. He could fight, sure. I'd seen him in action. He'd saved my ass, and yet there was something else I should know, but didn't. There was something far more than the surface showed. I tilted my head, and watched as his eyes lowered down my body. There was something in the back of my mind that wouldn't come out. Something that I should remember, but didn't.

I could hear his heart beating, but I had to determine mine from his. I stepped closer, but then caught myself. "What type of blood did you give me exactly?" I asked as the weakness started to take hold of me again.

"I gave you a transfusion," he replied, but I could tell that there was a gigantic something he was leaving out. I could hear it in his tone, in his voice. "You should get dressed in something other than my shirt, Emma."

I looked down and yup, I was pretty damn sure it was still his shirt I wore while I argued with a bunch of men. I'd stolen his shirt and snuck away from his house like a thief. I wavered on my legs and he was there, catching and holding me upright. He barked out orders, which my people jumped into action with. He was a natural born leader, unlike me who fumbled with it.

"You can't order them around," I whispered as I

Darkest Before Dawn

lifted my face to his. His blue green eyes locked on to mine and he smiled.

"Just did," he confirmed.

"I feel funny," I admitted.

"Horny? Or just funny as in strange, Emma?"

"Why would I be horny?" I asked as heat flushed across my face at his question.

"Do you have any idea how hard it was to treat your naked body, without touching it? Even when you begged me to do it," he whispered against my ear.

"If I was dying to the point I needed a transfusion, why the hell would I be begging you to bang me?" I whispered back, way beyond confused at the weirdness of this conversation.

He smiled, his lips pressed firmly against my ear as he opened his mouth to tease it. I moaned and jerked back from him as if he'd set fire to my skin. I was flushed, and wet, which sucked since I wore nothing under his shirt. His touch sent every nerve in my body to the ready, and he knew it. I could see it in the confident look he awarded me with.

"I saved your life, Emma," he whispered.

"I know that," I replied. I did, but if he thought that was going to get him laid, he was wrong. Why was my body on fire? By fire, I mean I felt as if I was burning alive. Moisture had pooled between my thighs along with a hammering heartbeat that was pulsing in my vagina. I wiped the sweat from my forehead which made the shirt rise.

He was fast as he pulled it back down and looked over my head. "I'll expect you to come to me when you are fully healed, or if you have questions of how you are alive."

"Why would I question the fact that I'm alive? I'm thankful, Jaeden, really, I am. I'm not gonna do the humpty dance with you as a thank you. I've told you before, I'm not that girl. If I want to fuck you, I will."

"Do you want to? Fuck me that is," he smiled seductively.

"That depends on if you really bit me." I swallowed hard as I recalled an image from his bedroom and my time there.

His face went blank, and Lachlan, who I hadn't heard move at all, placed his bleeding arm in front of my face. "Eww! What is your problem? Seriously! Stop it." What the fuck did they think I was a vampire...? I snapped my eyes at Jaeden accusingly.

"You bit me! The blood, and oh my god! Please tell me you didn't feed....wait!" I looked from Lachlan who I had a flash image in my head of green eyes of the wolf in the woods. I turned to Jaeden who was watching me. "Am I on pain medicine?" I asked; because that shit could make you think some weird shit. It had to be meds; it was the only thing that made sense. Because right now, I was seriously tripping.

"I gave you something for the pain, yes," Jaeden supplied cautiously.

"Emma," Addy came up behind me with a robe. "I've been so worried about you," she breathed as she threw her arms around me. "I thought you were dead, and nobody said anything!" she sniffed, holding back tears.

Jaeden hadn't told her I was alive? Didn't he think I would make it? I looked over her head at him and narrowed my eyes. "Why didn't you tell her anything?"

"Because we didn't know if you'd make it or not," he replied simply.

"Right, but nothing? You couldn't tell them anything at all? Dick move," I bit out.

He smiled but other than that, his eyes just watched me. I could smell everything about Addy, her fear, and happiness. I sniffed her, and caught myself doing it. "You're fucking him?" I asked and leveled a murderous look at Lachlan.

"How did you know that?" Addy whispered as she pulled away and sniffed herself.

"I don't know," I said as I turned to Jaeden in confusion. I was about to collapse, and I kept getting bombarded and overwhelmed with things that I was suddenly noticing. I could smell everything, right down to Jimmie who refused to shower on a regular basis, which was disgusting. I could see the details of the brush on the hilltop which was as at least a mile away from us, and I was pretty sure I shouldn't be able to.

I knew Lachlan and his men were agitated by my presence, but why? Jaeden was on edge, but more than that, I knew he wanted me. I could *feel* it. I turned in his direction and walked to him; his eyes watched me. As if he knew what I planned to do before I did. I lifted myself up on my toes and kissed him.

The moan ripped from my throat, right before his hands lowered to my ass and pressed me against his hardness. He smelled intoxicating. His rich, masculine scent was mixed with spices and sex. His sex was hard and ready to do damage. He brought his hands up to my face, framing it as he deepened the kiss. He groaned as I pulled away from him.

"I can smell you," I whispered.

"I can smell your readiness too, my sweet girl."

"*Why* can I smell you?"

"I'm not sure, Emma, but if anything else strange happens to you, I need to know right away."

With that, he left me standing with Addy and Lachlan who was still bleeding, and not doing anything about it. "You need a Band-Aid," I said offhandedly. "Let me get one." I turned and moved tiredly to the door

Darkest Before Dawn

of the shelter.

He needed more than a Band-Aid, but hey, I wasn't his nanny. He punched the code in and I glared at Addy. Why would she do this? I was pissed! I pushed past him and stopped dead in my tracks as I took in the changes.

Where my father's office had been was more of Lachlan's men, pointing at pins on the white board that held a map of our town. The children's area had been changed as well, and was now a cafeteria. Food was piled on tables, as if it had an endless supply. Candles burned while the lights shined at full power.

"What the friggin' bloody monkey fucks!"

"Emma, it's okay. They brought fuel, food and other supplies with them," Addy's voice was soft behind me.

"It's not okay, Addy! There's not a friggin' store to run down to when the supplies are gone. You let them into our home— my home! This is ours! This is the friggin' sanctuary for people who need to be helped and they don't need help! You let a bunch of hot ass men inside, and we already have one baby too many! Why?" I choked on the tears. "We were doing fine with what we had! We protected each other, and we got shit done, Addy. Why would you take this away from me?"

"Emma, tis nae like that, lass," Lachlan said gently.

"Take your lass and shove it!" I yelled as an overload of emotions flooded over me. "You don't get to come in here with your dinnae fret, and dinnae lass this, and cannae be so bad! This is mine. I helped my father build it! It's all I have left of him." A traitorous tear slid down my cheek and I angrily swiped at it.

"Ye cannae get mad at the lassie fer thinking ye were dead. She asked fer help and we came tae do that. She isnae as strong as ye, Emma; she was scared," he offered reasonably.

"I'm going to bed—" I felt betrayed, and my head swam with too many emotions, too much turmoil with what had happened. Tears slid down my cheeks unchecked as I moved as swiftly as my legs would carry me through the shelter to my room. Luckily, it was still there and hadn't been given over to one of Lachlan's men or something. I fell on the bed without closing the door, and crashed hard.

Chapter FIFTEEN

Addy shaking my shoulder was my wakeup call the next morning. She had been crying for a while, judging by the puffiness of her eyes. I sat up and tried to recall where I was. Home. I lay back down on my pillows and turned to face her. She sniffled, and started apologizing profusely.

"Addy, enough crying, I get it, but I don't think you understand what you've done," I mumbled, trying to snuggle back into the bedding.

"You were dead! I was afraid to be alone. What happened to Mom and Dad was awful, and your dad was gone, I didn't know what to do. Lachlan was sweet; he and his men offered to protect us. It seemed like a good plan, Ems, we buried you," I rolled over and stared at her blankly. They'd buried me? What the hell was she talking about and how creepy was that shit?

"Emma?" Grayson peered at me from the doorway

before he ran for the small bed and jumped on me. His exuberance was contagious and for a brief moment, I forgot my resentment. "I knew you weren't dead. I told them you'd never leave me. I told them," he whispered as he sobbed in my arms.

"I know brat, but they had good reason to think I wouldn't make it," I replied with tears thick in my throat. I hadn't even thought about what Grayson would have gone through. I'd been selfish, but the idea of men such as Lachlan and his men taking over the shelter put me on edge.

"I love you, Emma, to the moon and stars," he whispered as his sobs ebbed.

"I love you beyond the moon and all its glory. I love you brighter than the stars could ever burn in the sky, brat," I answered back.

I looked over the top of Grayson's head to find Addy watching us with an uncertain look in her soft brown eyes. I nodded to her, and before I could blink, she'd wrapped herself around us and started crying again.

"I'll never leave you two, you know that. I understand why you did what you did, Addy, but I don't know them and I sure don't trust them."

"I didn't sleep with him. I slept with his brother," she blurted.

"You were sitting on his lap…?"

Darkest Before Dawn

"They share, but I wasn't into that, well, I might be. I was really tempted," she admitted as my eyes widened as I moved to plug Grayson's ears. "His men do it as well, but only Kyra took them up on it."

"Uh, okay…" I said unsure of what to say about it, and I wasn't quite sure we should be talking about this in front of my baby brother and his virgin ears. I had read enough to know a lot of the kinks of sex, and I'd enjoyed the books, but that didn't mean I'd be jumping on the ménage sandwich bandwagon anytime soon. "So basically they came in, took over, had an orgy, and decided to stay awhile?"

"It sounds really bad when you put it like that," she said and her face fell again.

"It is okay, Addy. Maybe it's time to allow others to help. We were barely pulling it together, and I'm tired of being on the losing end. I was reminded not too long ago that I expected people to be like they were before the world went to hell, but they're not. There are a lot more evil ones out there than I ever realized and the more that come here, the more I wonder what the hell we're fighting for. It will be nice having more men around to do the heavy hitting and lifting for a change."

"You're sure? 'Cause I can kick them out; now that we have you, Emma, we can make it." Addy's soulful eyes snapped eagerly with her words.

"And maybe you can finish my training?" Grayson piped up hopefully. I narrowed my eyes for a moment at him.

"Uh, let me get situated and we'll talk about that," I glanced back at Addy, resigned to what needed to be done. "As long as they keep their kinky fuckery to themselves, I'm fine with them staying. No one goes into my father's rooms. They are off limits to outsiders. Other than that, if they can help out, they can stay."

A little while later, I was standing in the shower, the water running over my naked body—it felt blissfully good. I was still standing beneath the spray of water when Lachlan stepped in, and joined me. He was naked, and his hands pulled me close against his chest.

"I've been watching ye, lass," he rumbled as I jumped from beneath the water with surprise by his silent entry. "Yer as stubborn as a newly born bairn, ye are."

"You're naked, and in my shower," I pointed out as I tried to ignore what he was pointing at me. His cock was hard, and I could smell his anticipation burning in his veins. Jaeden's had been a missile, but Lachlan certainly was a close second and I could have sworn the thing winked at me.

"Oh aye, yer in it during my scheduled time so I figured ye were making peace with me," he smiled as his eyes slid over my naked body.

Since when did we have scheduled showers? The only schedule we had was five minutes per body, and he had come in and taken over. He had some nerve!

Darkest Before Dawn

"Is that what you thought? Let me just ease your mind. I had no intention of showering with you. I figured no one would be here since water restrictions were set to keep the pumps from going out. You should learn the schedule, and show it to your men. This is my shelter, Lachlan; you and your men are guests. You will follow the rules so that it continues to run, and work smoothly. " I pulled the towel off the rack and wrapped it around my curves.

My heart was racing, and as he moved closer, I felt the tingle in the pit of my stomach which normally only responded to Jaeden's touch.

"Yer nae really expecting Jaeden tae follow through with ye, are ye, lass? He's nae that kind of man; he fucks his prey and then leaves them heartbroken. He will only break ye, and leave ye when he's had his fill."

"I'm pretty sure that's none of your damn business," I whispered.

His arms pinned me against the wall, as he lowered his mouth to mine. I could have struggled, and should've. I didn't though, because I wanted to see if I responded to him as I did with Jaeden. Lachlan's mouth was soft, as he moved over my lips seeking entrance. I opened my mouth and kissed him back. While there was a steady thrumming sensation in my core; it was nothing like I felt with Jaeden.

It wasn't until he picked me up and growled against my mouth, that I stopped him. "No, put me down, now!"

Amelia Hutchins

I panicked a little and tried to push him away.

Instead of putting me down, he rubbed his cock over my slick heat and smiled. "I could make ye mine, bonny Emma, so fucking easily. One thrust and ye would be mine," his voice came out as a rough snarl that scared me.

"I said no, Lachlan. I don't want this to be my first time," I whispered as I listened to his heart as its beat increased with my words.

"Yer a bloody maiden," he smiled as his eyes searched my face.

"I'm a virgin, yes," I replied as his mouth crushed forcefully against mine but I didn't kiss him back this time. I turned my head away from him with the stark realization that I wanted my first time to be with Jaeden. Even if he left me afterwards, I wanted him.

"Ye want the leech?"

"Why do you call him a leech?" I asked as I fixed the towel and slipped my slippers back on. He barked a short laugh.

"If ye havenae figured it oot yet, ye should ask him, but when he breaks yer heart, Emma, and he will, I'll still want ye."

I blinked. Would he break my heart? What if I just wanted meaningless sex with him? "What if I break his heart?" I asked with a devious smile on my lips.

Darkest Before Dawn

"Then I'll want ye even more, sweetheart." He grinned wickedly.

I dressed and left the shelter to visit the scene of the crime. Memories were coming back at a slow trickle. Some of it I figured was delirium, because well, it just had to be. I could think of no other reason for me to have those images in my mind, except that I knew what pain medicine could do to the human mind. It played tricks, and made you hallucinate. The only other *logical* explanation was they were both screwing with my head and that was too awful to think of.

I stood on the cliff with a new outlook. One, I was changing and I wasn't sure it was a good thing. Two, I was becoming hard and cynical and I hated that I was. Three, life wasn't a certain thing. I could die at any moment and if I did, I'd go with so many regrets. I didn't want to die before I experienced Jaeden, or found pleasure in his touch. I wanted to leave my mark in this new world, and I could sense something coming.

It was as if there was a storm brewing, and we were standing on the edge of it. I could taste the tension, thick in the air, and I could sense that a lot more people would die. Innocent people would die. I closed my eyes as the wind blew my hair, and when I turned around, I knew I'd find him standing there.

He was dressed in a white V neck shirt. His jeans were slung low over his narrow hips. He'd pulled his hair back, but loose strands had worked their way out of the thin leather band. He wore a necklace, dangling from it was small silver disc medallion with a raven carved into it.

He said nothing, just watched me as I took him in. I stepped closer to him and was about to tell him what I'd just figured out, but his eyes grew hard. "You've fucked that dog?" his words were harsh, but the anger I felt in him was harsher. "I leave you alone for one fucking night after saving your life, and you fuck him?"

"I didn't fuck anyone," I snapped irritably.

"No? Then tell me why the fuck you smell like wet dog?"

Wet dog? I rolled my eyes and laughed. One, because I hadn't been anywhere near a damn dog, and two, he was jealous. "I haven't been around any dogs for a long time; besides, I took a shower just a little while ago." I looked off in the distance, still trying to get a handle on the way my senses were over compensating. "Speaking of which, Lachlan kissed me and I kissed him back," I replied honestly.

"Why?" he demanded crisply.

"Because I wanted to see if he made me feel what I do when I kiss you," I said quietly as his eyes narrowed.

"And does he?"

"No, his kiss was nice, but it doesn't make me…" What? Wet? Swoon? Want to rip his clothes off and check out his wood? I could still see myself becoming a

Darkest Before Dawn

woodpecker and pecking Jaeden.

"Wet?" he asked as he stepped closer. "My kiss makes your sweet, succulent petals *wet*."

"Yes," I shook my head as I turned back towards the cliff. "He said you would break me, and then break my heart. Was he right?"

I didn't flinch as his arms wrapped around me from behind or when he pulled my body back and close to his. "Come with me somewhere?"

"Where?" I asked as I felt his hands as they rose to palm my breasts.

"To a little place I found," he whispered against my ear.

"I should get back to the shelter. I didn't tell anyone I was going out," I admitted.

"Good; come with me and I'll take you home when we are done," he assured me as his thumbs rubbed seductively over my nipples. "I promise to be on my best behavior," his voice was sensual and far too difficult to resist.

I turned in his arms and raised myself up on my toes to bring my lips against his. His kiss was slow, and sent goose bumps over my flesh. This felt right, but I wasn't ready to just give myself to him. Yes, I wanted him to be my first, but I wanted him to prove he wanted me for more than just a *been there, done that*.

Amelia Hutchins

I moaned against his mouth as he broke the kiss and placed a soft kiss on my forehead. He clasped his fingers through mine and held my hand as he walked me through the woods, to a small little crystal blue pond. We Towners called it Haven, because it was a little haven most didn't know about in our small town.

I gave him my back as he removed some of his clothes, or at least I hoped he still had some of them on. I heard a splash as he dove beneath the water. It wasn't that deep, so obviously he'd been here enough times to know the depth. Most people didn't try to dive here; then again, Jaeden wasn't most people.

He surfaced and shook the water from his long hair and gave me a glimpse of his impressive back. It was all muscle. Thick black tattoos that were Celtic in their design, from the look of it, covered his shoulder blades. My eyes drifted down to the gentle curve of his ass, and I bit my lip as heat burned inside my abdomen. He had quite a few scars, and I absently wondered where he'd gotten them. Had he been hurt in a war? He fought like a warrior, so maybe he'd been active in the military.

He turned, and my mouth went dry as the Sahara Desert as I watched him move toward the water's edge. His abs looked as if he worked out every freaking day! He had more of a swimmers body, but *damn!* I was pretty sure they didn't make men like him anymore, especially since there was a massive shortage of people these days. This man screamed sex from his every pore. Even as unknowledgeable as I was in that department, I wanted him to be my professor and teach me the kink. I

Darkest Before Dawn

was such a freak…

"Join me," he said and I twisted my lips up into a smile. I'd planned on swimming a little later today, so at least I'd dressed for it.

I met his eyes and caught the silent sparkle of laughter in them as I kicked out of my boots, and started working the buttons on my pants. "Turn around," I said shyly.

"Don't think so," he smirked, and continued to watch me. I rolled my eyes as I pulled off my shirt and jeans and left them folded on the shore. I gave a quick tug to fix the bottoms of the swimsuit. The suit had a pink and black skull-print halter bikini top. Little black bows joined the cups to the halter and the matching bottoms had black ruffles on the butt. "Skulls," he mused.

"I was going through a phase when the world went to hell," I explained.

He laughed as I stepped into the water. I met his gaze, and immediately wished I hadn't. The turquoise blue in his eyes reminded me of the pictures of the Caribbean oceans that I'd always wanted to visit. The depths in them were a cove of treasure I could easily get lost in. I made myself ignore him and focus on how cold the water was.

"This is freezing," I shivered a bit as I made my way in slowly. Of course I'd known it would be, since it was fed from a natural spring that ran beneath the ground. I screeched as he splashed my back with the icy water. I turned and glared at him. "Why did you bring me here?"

He smiled, but refused to answer. Instead he moved closer to me as his eyes moved over my pale flesh. "Do people always have to have a reason to bring you places?" he asked as he moved closer to where I stood.

"We're sorta stuck in limbo, and most of the world's population is dead from what I can tell, and you want to swim? Are you sure you're not from California? Maybe you'd like to find some waves after this, surf a bit?" I asked as I turned around to look at him better. This was a waste of time. And yet, here I was in the water with him. Worse part was I didn't want to leave here, or him.

My eyes skimmed his body until they focused on his thin patch of happy trail, again. I moved them lower and my mouth went dry. "Please tell me you're not naked."

"I'm not naked," he purred and lunged towards me. He grasped my arms and pulled me against him until I could feel with my thighs that he'd lied. He was seriously naked. *Very naked!* Unlike when I'd been in the shower with Lachlan, Jaeden being naked both terrified and turned me on.

"Oh my God! You're naked!" I shrieked as I tried to push him away.

"Of course I'm naked," he whispered huskily against my ear. "I'm bathing, and can't do that in clothes, now can I?"

I turned the color of freshly picked Washington Red

Darkest Before Dawn

apples as he moved closer against my body if it was even possible. My jaw trembled as I looked up at him. "I'm not going to sleep with you," I blurted. Hadn't I just decided I was? I could do it now, but I still felt uncertainty as Lachlan's words filled my mind with doubt.

"Who says I want to fuck you right now, Emma?" the gleam in his eyes told a different story.

"You're naked!"

"I'm bathing; I like being clean. You joined me for my bath, little one. That's all this is. Nothing more, your virtue is safe…for now," his tone was teasing as though this was just a misunderstanding. Not.

"I thought we were swimming—" I stopped as the bushes at the edge of the brush rustled.

"Get behind me, Emma, now," he ordered. I thought it might be good if I did as he asked, but only because I knew I couldn't make it to any of my weapons before whatever it was in the bushes greeted us.

Lachlan and his men moved from behind the bushes and walked in our direction. I noted the lessening of tension in Jaeden's back and peeked from behind him. "Lachlan," he said in a neutral tone.

"Emma," Lachlan said as his eyes grew hard at the sight of me in the pond with Jaeden. "Ye didnae tell anyone when ye were leaving."

"I don't need to check in to leave," I replied a little harsher than I had intended to.

"I see Jaeden's wasting nae time in getting ye into bed. I thought the kiss we shared would have at least made ye ponder yer options," he ground out.

"She knows her options, pup," Jaeden replied easily as he brought me around and held me in front of him like a shield against his nudity. I had to stop the cry that leapt to life in my throat as something hard and protruding pressed against my ass and my lower back.

"That better be a knife," I hissed.

"It can penetrate supple flesh, and go *very* deep…if that's what you're asking, sweet girl," he murmured in my ear.

I tried to pull my ass away, but his hands came down to settle on my hips. "I'd hold still, Emma, unless you plan on giving them a show. I'm not shy but I'd like it to be just the two of us when we fuck."

I swallowed past the dryness in my mouth. I'd put myself in this position, and it sucked. I held the other men's eyes as they watched us. Lachlan smiled, and nodded his head in my direction. Knowingly. Could he tell that Jaeden was naked, and that I'd kissed him? I could sense the tension between the men, and I was stuck in the middle of them, literally.

"Emma needs a real man, Jaeden, one who can show her what stamina is all aboot," Lachlan continued.

"My stamina is just fine, pooch," Jaeden replied genially.

"Ah, well a parasite such as yerself, does have persistence going fer it," Lachlan grinned and his men laughed behind him.

I blinked at their banter. Pooch? Parasite? What the hell was up with the names? I decided they needed to come up with better ones if they were going to insult each other.

"Why do we nae let the lass decide on whom is more adapted tae serve her needs?" he taunted.

This is where I probably should have said something, instead the hardness against my back pushed against it and the silkiness of it made the butterflies in my belly fight to get out. I absently arched my back and pushed my ass up until Jaeden's fingers pushed harder against my hips. "Do that again and you'll be losing the bottoms of this skimpy suit here and now, and I won't be sorry," he warned in a heated whisper. Jaeden's arm's wrapped around me protectively as Lachlan stepped closer. He turned me in his arms, and I swallowed as I felt his heated flesh against mine.

"I say we fuck this bitch," one of Lachlan's men who I'd met earlier today, called out. His twang sounded more Midwestern, rather than the Scottish burr like Lachlan and many of his men had. Dawson had given me the creeps then, and was doing so again. "Show her the difference between us, and I'll bet she'd take us all with that sweet body."

"He would nae touch ye, Emma lass. Nae, I'd cut off his balls if he tried it," Lachlan growled and snapped an angry order to Dawson.

I heard a scuffling noise, and then a deep growling noise from an animal. I turned to look at what was happening but Jaeden's arm tightened, pinning my body tightly against his chest. My head was held immobile with the other. It was then I realized that his member was pressing against my navel, pushing against my piercing. I tried to move, but his grip only tightened.

I glanced up to watch his face as his eyes narrowed on the men in front of us. Another moment passed, and his grip loosened enough that I could pull away from him. I turned, looking to where Dawson had stood, the only thing in that spot were scraps of cloth I hadn't noticed before. What the *hell?*

I looked at Lachlan and the other men, who had their arms crossed and were still watching us closely. I chanced a glimpse at Jaeden, and then stepped away from his naked form.

"Run along; you're interrupting us," Jaeden ordered them with a smirk framing his lips.

"I'd tread carefully with her, Jaeden; she's unlike those sluts ye normally fuck. She deserves someone who will protect her, and doesna have tae follow orders."

"Is that so? Let me guess, you're that man?" Jaeden

continued as his cock pressed against my flesh again.

"She'll know everything soon enough," Lachlan warned as he turned and walked away. His men closed ranks around him as they walked into the dense forest that surrounded the little pond.

"You guys really don't like each other, do you," I stated.

"He's a means to an end. As I told you, we were friends once, but that was in another place and time," he said with a wolfish grin on his lips. "Why didn't you kick them out of your shelter, Emma?" he continued.

"Because I'm tired of being alone and they did step up and help everyone while I was gone," I said tiredly. I started toward the edge of the water, but didn't make it there before Jaeden pulled me back to him. "You have a serious issue with personal space."

"You're not alone, you have me," he whispered with a serious look in his beautiful eyes.

"That's not what I meant. I'm tired of holding everything together. Addy likes them, and the girls don't seem to mind that men are around."

"Did anything unusual happen to you last night?"

I turned my eyes to the water's surface, and the waves that kissed his naked flesh. "I don't know, Jaeden. Should something have happened to me?" I asked, imagining my hands running over his bronzed flesh instead of the water. I licked my lips absently as he moved to stand closer, since I'd backed up yet again. The tip of his cock broke the surface of the water like a periscope, and God help me, I couldn't look away from it. I gasped as his hand cupped my chin and tipped my face up.

"Emma, if you keep staring at my dick I won't be able to control the urge I'm fighting right now. I'm trying to be a gentleman."

"What urge is that?" I asked before I could think better of it.

"This urge," he said and pulled me close to his body as his hands dropped to my thighs and pulled me up and out of the water until my legs wrapped around him. His lips found mine and kissed me intensely, as if he was starving for my kiss.

I moaned against him until his hand pulled on the bottoms of my suit. I pulled away and shook my head. "No, Jaeden." He leaned his forehead against mine. He remained silent as he dropped me slowly back into the water. "I'm sorry, I'm not like that. I'm not some bimbo who will just jump in bed with you."

"It's just fucking, Emma," he said softly. "Jeg ønsker å begrave min kuk så dypt inne i deg, søt jente." *

"What language is that? Scandinavian or something like Viking, right?" I asked with a guarded look burning in my eyes. I didn't trust him, and yet I felt pulled in his direction. As if something was pushing us together. As

Darkest Before Dawn

if forces I couldn't understand were at work here. Even after everything we'd been through, I still felt the need to guard myself against him. He gave a slight nod of his head, and a small smile stole across his lips.

"Norwegian," he acknowledged.

"Jaeden doesn't exactly sound like a name from Norway." Okay, now his friends Bjorn and Sven were starting to make sense.

"Changed it; you wouldn't be able to pronounce my birth name," he quipped.

"And it was?" I pried.

"Járngrímr, it means iron. It's a mouthful and while back home it was a fairly common name, here in the states it wasn't something I wanted to listen to people trip over saying."

I moved from the water and gave him my back as he worked his way up to where his clothes lay. He was silent as he dressed. I shoved my legs into my jeans and turned toward him as I felt his eyes on me.

My eyes feasted on the tendrils of water that dripped from his immaculate chest. I looked up to his right pectoral where a raven was perched, tattooed into his flesh. "The raven, what's it stand for?" I asked noting the outline for the map of Scandinavia on this other peck.

"In mythology it was used for a gateway between

life and death, but most who saw the raven believed that it was linked to the God Odin. They believed the raven was his eyes and ears in the realm of the living, so they would always appear in pairs before a great battle. In the Pacific Northwest, it was a talisman to the Indians."

"Is that why you have two of them?" I asked, noting the one on his arm was perched on a skull. I'd absently stepped closer to him, now within touching distance; if he noted this, he did well hiding it. I lifted my hand and ran it over raven and moved it to the script-looking words. "And this?" I asked as his flesh tensed beneath my touch.

His hand flew to mine, and gripped it hard as his eyes watched my response. "Careful, Emma, I'm trying very hard to be a gentleman and walk away from you. Don't make me do something we might both regret later."

I smiled. "You sound way older than you look," I turned and headed back for my shirt—but didn't make it there before his hand pulled me back. "Emma, how many men have you laid with?" My jaw opened in surprise at his question, seeing that he seemed to be pretty singular in what he wanted.

"Not sure why you're asking, Jaeden, didn't you say it's just fucking?" I teased, but froze when I caught a flash of anger in his eyes as the muscle in his jaw ticked wildly. His grip tightened on my arm, which caused my eyes to flare in panic. I was heading into fight or flight, and the only thing that kept me from running away was his own eyes widening as he realized his grip had tightened painfully on my arm. His features softened for a moment and then confusion registered on his face.

"Emma, you should go," he muttered distractedly as he dropped my arm and turned to bend over and grab his remaining clothes. "Du bedre kjøre hjem, før jeg glemmer hvem jeg er og ta det jeg vil ha." **

My jaw dropped at the tinge of anger in his voice and sudden shift in personality. I watched his back as I wondered what the heck had just happened. What had I done wrong to make him act like this?

~~*

*"*Jeg ønsker å begrave min kuk så dypt inne i deg, søt jente."*

"I want to bury my cock so deep inside you, sweet girl."

~~*

**"*Du bedre kjøre hjem, før jeg glemmer hvem jeg er og ta det jeg vil ha."*

"You better run home, before I forget who I am and take what I want."

Chapter Sixteen

The next week seemed to go by slowly, but it was very productive as everyone worked together to help gather supplies. Lachlan's people melded easily with our group. I hadn't seen Dawson since that uncomfortable incident at the pond and wondered where he had been sent, or if I needed to worry that he would be back.

Lachlan remained his usual likable self; often trying to charm or tease me, yet I could sense that some of it was an act. His men had also been watching me closely everywhere I went. It was as if they knew something wasn't quite right with me and they were prepared to take action if I should step one toe out of line. Secretly, I was uncomfortably afraid that they might jump the gun and do me in as I also knew in my heart that something *wasn't* right with me.

Mental snapshots of bizarre images kept flashing through my mind and I was terrified to speak to Addy or anyone else about it. No matter how hard I had been

Darkest Before Dawn

trying to adjust since the missing weeks, I still couldn't get comfortable. I felt like I'd been crawling out of my skin, as if something I couldn't put my finger on was changing along with my senses. It was growing worse with every passing day.

One afternoon, Lachlan suggested that we might want to boost everyone's spirits by having regular Friday night parties, which I'd thought was idiotic but it had a positive vibe and effect on the people that I just couldn't argue with.

Tonight I'd dressed in my old scavenging uniform of mask, black fatigues, and combat boots to patrol the area and make sure that everyone was safe. I didn't join in on the frolicking, for lack of better description, much to Lachlan's irritation. He tried to convince me that I could use a night off, but seriously, it wasn't safe here anymore and while I could agree with his reasoning for the party, I couldn't enjoy myself.

Earlier in the week, we'd found bodies savagely dismembered and left in places that suggested we were meant to find them. It was as if someone was baiting us, or trying to scare the shit out of us…and it was working. Except for this evening, when Lachlan set up a sound system and brought everyone outside to party. He'd even supplied alcohol, which I thought should be saved for medical purposes…His men had laughed as if it was one of the funniest things they'd ever heard.

I walked through the crowd of people until I reached the tree that had the best view of the land that surrounded the shelter. I climbed it with purpose and sat on one of the highest branches that would hold my weight. I looked out at the silent woods, noting each of the sentries Lachlan had posted to safeguard the group. My mind wandered as I kept watch and as usual, my thoughts came around to Jaeden.

He'd either forgotten about me, or decided I wasn't worth the chase anymore. I hadn't seen him at all this week and I actually missed him. All the way back to the shelter, he barely spoke to me and seemed to be bothered about something, and I wasn't sure if it was something I had said. I also noticed that since that afternoon, Lachlan had been trying to impress me.

It was working, and with each passing day, I did warm up a bit more to him. But, there was still this sick infatuation I had for Jaeden. I felt as though there was in invisible string that kept pulling me to him, several times I almost found myself heading in the direction of the estate he and his men had appropriated, only to catch myself and try to find something else to occupy myself with. Each of them had qualities I was drawn to, yet really had no experience with. Lachlan was self-assured, charming, smart, and protective. While Jaeden had those qualities as well, he was also crass and demanding. If I was smart, I'd go with Lachlan, who I knew would be gentle with me for my first time. But I didn't want gentle, I wanted Jaeden and his friggin' dirty mouth.

The things he'd done to me, and the way he demanded I do things was intensely hot. I'd known he was into control, and I'd give him as much as I could, which wasn't much...but I was willing to try.

A movement in my peripheral caught my attention, and the hair at the back of my neck stood up. All of my senses were screaming at me that something wasn't as it should be. Alert. Defend. Fight. I looked down to the group who was dancing and drinking. "Idiots," I growled as I started to descend from the trees. I sniffed the air and my body vibrated with a sense of dread that I couldn't interpret. Something was moving through the woods at an alarming speed. I hit the ground with a thud and kicked out as the first red eyed wolf broke from the thicket.

It was so quick that I wasn't even sure I'd killed it. As if a switch was flipped, everything began to move in slow motion for me, and I could see in the dark as well as I could in the day. One second I'd kicked out at the first wolf, and the next I'd brought two knives out of my pants, and had driven a blade into a second wolf's guts. Another one lunged, and I barely avoided being hit by its wicked claws, and the knife I'd held fell to the ground. I heard screaming, but ignored it as I brought my hands up, grabbed with sure hands, and snapped the wolf's neck.

The next one bit my arm, and I could have sworn I'd heard the bone snap, but couldn't have since my arm felt fine. I palmed the waistband of my pants, brought out the small Sig Sauer, and shot it at point blank range. Blood splattered over my face and God knew what else. A fifth one lowered its head and growled. I moved forward to strike at it, but it took off before I could.

I looked back at the group which was now gone and only Lachlan and his men remained. They stood staring at me as if I'd grown horns and a tail. I looked from them to the dead wolves and blanched. My heart stopped beating. My blood ran cold, because there were no wolves at my feet—they were humans. I choked on tears as I took in the carnage, wondering if I was losing it.

"I killed wolves, not humans. Not humans," I whispered brokenly. I was losing it. I squeezed my eyes shut and opened them as I fell to my knees. "You saw it, right?"

"Emma, ye should come away from them," Lachlan whispered, as if the dead would rise. He held his hands out to me and I stared blankly.

"I killed them, but I swear they were wolves! How is this possible?" I whispered. My voice sounded small and scared. I'd killed wolves; they'd had fur! The fur had shed on me and I still had it on my friggin' clothes!

Lachlan pulled me up but I shoved him away. I was covered in blood, and fur! Fucking fur! I turned and left them standing there. They could figure out what I'd done, but I had to get away from this. Now. I started running and didn't stop until I dropped to my knees. I looked up to find Bjorn looking down at me.

"You okay?" he asked cautiously.

Darkest Before Dawn

"I killed them," I cried.

"Who?" he asked as he dialed numbers into a phone.

"The wolves, but they weren't wolves, they changed...to humans...which is crazy, because wolves can't change into humans. Right? It's crazy! One minute they were wolves and I killed them and then they were human, which is impossible!"

"You killed wolves?" Bjorn asked.

"Emma?" Jaeden's voice reached my ears and I bolted into his arms. "Whoa, you're safe."

"I killed them," I said as my hands trembled and my body shook.

"Killed who?"

"I killed four wolves that had red eyes. I killed them, but they changed...I'm losing it, right?" I whispered against his chest. Safe; I felt safe here.

"You killed four rogues?" he asked cautiously.

"No, I killed four red eyed wolves that changed into humans!" Was he missing the whole *they turned into human* part?

"Impossible," an Irish accent said from less than a foot away from us. I could sense I had heard it before, but I couldn't place it.

I looked at the newcomer with trepidation pulsing

through me. Every fiber of my being said to run away from this man. He had inky black hair, with startling violet eyes. I got a chill just looking at him. He looked ancient and yet not a day over twenty five at the same time. My skin crawled while my insides turned hot with need, as if I'd been with him before and far more intimately. Jaeden's body seemed to stiffen up.

"She's stunning, Jaeden," he said as he stepped even closer.

I buried myself in Jaeden's arms as if he'd protect me. "She is," he confirmed. Then to my shock, he held me out as if to allow his friend a full inspection of my attributes. I struggled against Jaeden's hold, as tears tried to push through. "Let me go!" I shouted, and Jaeden did as if my skin burned him. "What the hell is wrong with you?" I shouted as I took a small step backwards.

"Why did you come here, Emma?" Jaeden asked in a terse tone.

"My bad," I said as I turned with as much dignity as I could and left him with his men.

I made it about twenty steps before Lachlan stepped from the woods and headed straight for me. I stopped and shook my head, warning away from him. The last thing I wanted was someone else who may suddenly run hot and cold on me. I had no idea of where to go, but after the dick move Jaeden just pulled, I just needed to get away from here.

"Emma, are ye okay?" he asked and when I nodded

Darkest Before Dawn

he continued on without me. I turned and looked back to find Jaeden glaring at me. I flipped him off and started towards the woods. Tears began to slide down my face at Jaeden's behavior; what I had done tried to sink in, too. I say *tried* because I was either going crazy, or men had actually looked like wolves, which again, crazy. That kind of shit only happened in the movies.

I moved quickly into the outer edges of the woods and froze, because that same tingly warning hit me. I looked around the silent trees and stepped back into the clearing. I could feel the eyes from the men on me, but worse, I could sense a cold, malevolent evil watching me. I had no warning, but somehow I managed to side step the huge wolf that burst from the thicket. I reached for the knives, only to find the straps empty.

The wolf spun around and I kicked its jaw as my entire body spun from the blow. I punched out, and the yelp of the animal was sickening. It lunged again, but this time I was ready and I used both hands to grip its neck and twist it using its own weight against it, violently. The sharp snapping of bones made my stomach momentarily lurch.

I watched emotionlessly as it transformed to a tall brown haired man, whose neck and head were at odd angles to each other. I swallowed the sob that tried to leave my throat and turned to find the small group of men watching me in shocked silence. Some friggin' help they'd been. I flipped them all off, as a sob escaped and I tried to put as much distance between myself and them as I could.

Maybe I was dreaming, or maybe I was actually dead and this was my hell.

*~*Jaeden*~*

All week, I had tried to stay away. It wasn't supposed to be like this. The words we had at the pond rang in my head; it *was* just supposed to be fucking. No attachment, nothing different than any woman before her. Except Astrid. Astrid was once an obsession, and now I find that despite my vows, the feelings I have for Emma are far stronger than anything I had ever felt for Astrid. The pond was a sharp wake-up call that I was getting in far too deep with her, and I couldn't allow myself to get in that far. I had orders, and they always came first.

She'd run to me. The knowledge was heady. The reminder came back to me that I couldn't let this get any deeper. I didn't want to feel for her. I didn't want to chance her getting too close and feeling the sting of betrayal again. My heart knows she's loyal to her core, but everything Astrid did destroyed any chance of having faith in women again. I wanted her, but I had to re-establish what our relationship would be. I wasn't going to be her love; that much I was sure of. Fucking; that's all it could be. That's all I could allow. Bond or no bond.

This want. This attachment. Desire. Fuck it, this obsession wasn't something I could deal with, or would chance happening again. If she wanted a quick, unattached fuck, I wouldn't say no, but that's all it would be. She should hate me for how I held her up for Shamus to inspect her. As if she was there for the taking. The last time he'd seen her, her body had still been behaving as if she was still in the thrall of change and had been unaware of him. It gutted me to offer her to another male, but it had to be done.

I hated that I allowed myself to want her this badly. I despised it, that she was in the shelter with Lachlan and his pack of mongrels. I hated that I wanted to keep her. The longing and anticipation, like a fucking green horn with his first voyage across the ocean. This coldness I felt, I deserved. This eternal fucking hard-on I had for her, again it was deserved for thinking I could have her.

"We got company," Shamus's voice broke into my thoughts as I watched the wolf move to Emma; concern was written all over his face. Instead of throwing herself at him as I thought she would, she warned him away with an angry hand. I narrowed my eyes at her response. She's almost cold to him, as he said something and then continued walking to us.

"She took on a fucking rogue squad an win. She disna see the change an noo she thinks she's losing it. She fucking fought like a banshee possessed." I hadn't heard him rattled like this before; to the point that his burr was so thick his words were almost unintelligible.

"That's impossible and you know it," Shamus spoke the words before I could.

"Aye, ye dinna think I ken it!" he spat.

I turned and leveled her beautiful ass with a killing glare. My senses felt the attack before the others. She moved with inhuman speed, as she dodged the giant brown wolf. Her hands moved to her knives, only to grasp air. I moved to lunge to her aid, but Shamus grabbed me and refused to allow me to pass; his sharp word was binding as my sire. I fisted my hands at my sides, helpless to do anything but watch as the wolf spun with lightning fast speed. It lunged at her, only to have her kick its jaw so hard that it stopped mid-attack. I watched her small frame shake, then the wolf's head swiveled and it stumbled momentarily with a pained yelp as she followed through with a punch to its side that seemed to carry more strength than her small body should have been able to deliver.

"Watch this," Lachlan's calm voice was laced with anticipation.

I glared at him briefly before turning my eyes back at Emma. She moved much like we do, and there was a cold, calculated precision to each move she made. The wolf lunged at her again, but this time she wrenched its neck sharply, snapping it in one deft move. As the carcass slumped lifelessly, her eyes filled with tears, and I wasn't sure if anyone else noticed. Her eyes grew wide with horror as the wolf transformed back to its human shape with his death.

She turned as a sob racked her small form, and flipped us off. That's my girl. She's fire in the midst of a storm, brave when most would cower. She's stubborn to the mother fucking core. I turned to Lachlan and leveled him with a glare that would make most men cower and that niggling jealousy roared to life, and I couldn't hold back any longer. .

"Have you fucked her?" I snapped, and watched as his eyes lit up with deviltry.

"Does it matter?" he laughed.

"Answer the fucking question," I demanded, but he just smiled.

"Boys, simmer down. That human just took down a rogue alpha, and instead of figuring out who should be fucking her, you should be figuring out if we should allow her to live. She had a full transfusion of Jaeden's blood, and yet she didn't change into one of us, and I know she smells too fucking hot to be a fucking wolf. Figure out what the hell she is, and how to bring her to our side, or kill her. That's what you should be worried about," Shamus said as the voice of reason.

"Take her, Jaeden. She'd give up anything for him, do anything, tell us anything," Sven pointed out with a wicked twinkle in his eyes.

Lachlan shook his head. "She's done nothing but distance herself from the entire shelter in the last week. She eats with us, and tries tae avoid conversation. She goes oot on runs, but she does it alone. She makes lists and stockpiles supplies. It's almost like she's on auto mode, and unable tae shut it off." He catalogued her daily movements thoughtfully and I hated that he knew every aspect of her daily routine.

"Maybe she doesn't care for your company?" I offered.

"She deals with me just fine, Jaeden, and several times a day. She's breaking away from her group, as if she's protecting them from herself. Ye changed her, even if ye didnae turn her. She's not the same as she was when I first got tae town." His eyes bored accusingly into mine.

"I'll go to her," I whispered as I moved through them and headed to where I knew she would be. The change may not have occurred, but I could feel her presence inside of me as if it had. I could feel her in me, as if I'd sired her; the bond was minimal and limited, but there. She'd gone back to the cliff, where this had all begun.

I watched her from the trees as she kicked the ground where she'd gone over, and then teetered on the edge. My heart pounded faster as she held one foot over the edge as if she was considering jumping. She moved back and swiped angrily at her tears.

I could feel her walls closing down as her mind tried to grasp what she'd done. I stepped out from behind the trees and headed to her. I could tell that she felt me as I moved closer, and I felt the bond as it reached for her, but she was stronger than most. She was resisting it. She somehow managed to hold it at bay, but barely.

"Emma, come away from the cliff," I whispered and

flinched as she leveled me with a nasty glare.

"Go to hell, and take your fucked up shit with you!"

"I deserve that," I replied.

"You're damn right you do! You held me up as if I was yours to give away! I came to you for help and you threw me to the wolves!" she blinked as if her choice of words were sour.

"What do you think is happening between us, Emma? Did I make any promises to you?" I snapped, and watched as her eyes narrowed and leveled me with a cold look. "You asked me once if Lachlan and I were friends; we aren't. He used something of mine that I cared for; he was just one of a long line of betrayals that stemmed from the same poor decision. I made a vow to never allow myself to be in the same situation for it to happen again."

"Something?" she spat out. "I'm not a fucking something! I'm a friggin' human being! How dare you treat me like that just because you have some fucked up shit going on in your head. News flash, Jaeden! I'm not yours to give away! I'm not fucking anyone! Not now, not tomorrow, and not ever! That also includes you!"

"You've not fucked anyone?" I asked carefully.

"It doesn't matter! There's so much more happening right now! You need to get your friggin' priorities straight. I killed a wolf who was a man! In what friggin' world is that right? I'm going crazy!" she swiped angrily at tears. "I'm afraid to be around my friends and my brother because I'm seeing shit! I have dreams that scare the shit out of me, as if I'm actually in them. I don't know what you did to me, but you should have let me die!"

My heart clenched at her words. I watched her face carefully and took a shot at the truth. She deserved this; the only question was how she would react to it. "Werewolves," I said simply and watched as her eyes flew to mine.

"Okay, no wonder why I liked you so much, you're crazy too!" She sniffed as she wiped at the tears again. "You're so full of shit, Jaeden. But thanks for playing along with my crazy mindfuck of a day."

I laughed, but was empty. I flashed my fangs and, startled, she stepped back towards the cliff. I reached out and pulled her to me. She fought against my hold, and it took everything I had to pin her. This small woman was now a match for me or any of my men. She went still suddenly, as something else caught her attention. She looked at me, then to where Lachlan stood in wolf form. His green eyes gave him away.

"Holy shit," she said. "I went to sleep and woke up in Twilight!" she laughed, and continued. "Oh! I get to be Bella!" she giggled more. "Oh, wait, Twilight was like, PG, can we kick it up to an adult version and so help me God, Jaeden if you sparkle, I want to see that penis pulling off a disco ball in the sunlight!"

Darkest Before Dawn

Yeah, it was very possible she'd been damaged in the fall. I shook my head at her strange hysteria, and I had absolutely no idea what she was talking about. I think she was making fun of me, which stung. I finally spelled it out for her and I'm not sure what I expected, but it certainly wasn't this.

The wolf nodded and left her to me. Everything in his bearing told me that it was only for now. Her shoulders shook, and I felt her pain. The confusion of everything I'd just thrown at her. The shock at everything she had experienced tonight. Her soul pulled at mine, shredding my resolve and my legs moved towards her against my will. I walked up and stood beside her, slipping my hand through hers, threading my long fingers through her delicate ones.

"Lachlan, and his men," she started hesitantly. "I didn't kill any of his men tonight, did I?" she asked and then her shoulders released the tension they'd held in them.

"No; his people and my people are fighting against those packs. It is a long story, but know that we will protect you and your people, Emma."

"Did you ever find the wolves that killed Bonnie and Jillian?" she asked with a guarded look in her eyes.

"We found the squad that killed them about two weeks after their deaths. I put them down, personally. They hurt you, maybe not physically, but like most things rabid, they needed to be put down."

"This can't be real, right? I'm dreaming," she whispered brokenly.

I pulled her to me, and tilted her chin. "Does this feel like a dream?" I asked, before lowering my hungry lips to hers. She was silk to my leather, innocence to my brutality. My tongue pushed past her teeth, and the noise she made started a maelstrom in my balls, and tightness coiled in my stomach. I groaned as I deepened the kiss, while her arms wrapped around my waist.

I wanted nothing more than to lay her on the ground and ravish her body. I picked her up and approved of how her legs wrapped around my waist. Her hands gripped my hair, as if she was afraid I would remove my mouth from hers. Not a fucking chance. I kissed her harder, my nostrils flaring with the scent of her sweet nectar as it dampened her pussy.

I pulled away, my eyes searched hers for the one answer I needed. She didn't give it. She unwrapped her legs and pulled away instead. "You can't be real, because that would mean you really did feed me your blood to save my life. That I wasn't hallucinating…"

"I did, and would do it again in a heartbeat, Emma," I whispered through fangs that slid further from my gums with anticipation. Her eyes focused on my mouth, and I watched as her small hand lifted to my mouth and stopped.

"Can I see them?" she questioned, and I nodded. "Do they hurt?"

Darkest Before Dawn

"Only when I deny them the sweet taste of you," I replied with a crooked smile breaking across my lips.

"Do you want to taste me?"

"Yes," I replied with my heart racing at the mere idea of tasting her sweet, intoxicating blood again.

"How does it work?" she asked with a shyness that I hadn't seen with her before.

"I'd kiss your flesh, and caress it with my tongue. My saliva would release a numbing agent, to prevent you from feeling pain from my bite. I would pierce your skin, and I'd feed from your blood."

"Does sex and feeding really go together?"

"Yes," I replied hoarsely, as I wondered where she's taking me with her questions.

"So if I allowed you to feed from me, I'd have to allow you more?"

"No, but I'd want more. I'd want you at my mercy."

"What does that even mean?" she asked innocently.

"I'd want to control you. I'd want to dominate you, to have your full submission in the bedroom, Emma. For a woman to submit to a man in the bedroom is one of the ultimate gifts she can ever give him. To give her body and mind to him, and trust him enough to satisfy her needs."

"It sounds kinky," she whispered with wide eyes. "Way more than I think I could commit to," was her sultry reply as I clasped her chin between my finger and thumb.

She gasped, and I smiled at the sweet sound of it. "You've already had a taste of what I can offer you. The spanking, when your pussy filled with the proof of what it made you feel? You were soaked for more abuse, and then when you came in my mouth…That Emma, is what I need from you. I could teach you everything, if you'd just let me."

She nodded as though she was considering it. "Maybe one day," she swallowed. My insides clenched at her soft words. I'm not a nice guy, not since the day Astrid betrayed me, and then fed me to the wolves, literally. I had made a vow to never let myself get that involved with a woman again. Not even Emma with her supple curves, and her wide eyed stares.

Even now she pulled at me, her soul knowing me as though she was fated to become mine, and it was fucking strong. I hated that I wanted her, that I was trying to tempt her, even knowing she could rip me apart. I'd been there, and hated the idea of it happening again.

Shamus wanted her. He'd said it as soon as he heard about her. She was a cock magnet, and a fucking hot one at that. Raphael hadn't even made it this far north yet, but I was sure he'd want in on her as well. He was my best friend, but also had a fondness for fiery redheads.

Darkest Before Dawn

I can't afford any distractions right now, not with the rogue wolf packs moving in to test our defenses. Testing us, as they convert her kind into theirs. She could die tomorrow, and I couldn't take the chance of her becoming a weakness. I had to get her back to her people and I needed to circle back to mine. The thought of the mutt being so close to her was like choking on my own sword, but unless she was prepared to take only what I can give, he was her best protection.

Chapter SEVENTEEN

A week had gone by since my little world was rearranged, and I'd stayed away from men in general. My head was a cluster fuck of things which I'd never imagined I needed to be worrying over. Like the fact that I was in some major lust with a vampire, who didn't seem to have a sunlight allergy, and I was currently living with a werewolf.

There were times I noticed the reality of what they were and I also noticed that I typically would have one of them tailing me. Like Landon, the youngest of the wolves and the one who always thought the floor was more interesting than whatever it was that I had to say. Oh, I probably wouldn't have noticed them before, but since my cliff-diving resurrection, I felt like I noticed everything.

So many questions I had for them... However, they were a tight lipped bunch, and Lachlan wasn't quite like Jaeden and the men who followed him, that much I could sense. However, I had clearly been changed after I had fallen. The unknown of what I had changed to was bugging the shit out of me.

We'd begun the first steps of gathering supplies that we would need to winterize the shelter and this allowed me multiple opportunities to slip away from the main group. I told Addy that I needed to go out alone today because I wanted time to think, but I'd ended up at my old house, going through my dad's office. There were pictures that had been left behind and now had a thick layer of dust on them. I ran my finger over one absently and then wiped it on my pants.

I scoured through the filing cabinets, but found nothing. I was putting things back when I heard the front door open and close. Addy was in the front room, looking up at a picture of me standing in a meadow that was hung above the mantel.

"I remember taking that; you looked so happy," she said as she wiped at tears. "You were just standing there in the meadow, and the flowers were in full bloom. The baby doll dress looked perfect on you," she continued. "Your father asked that I give him a copy. He said you looked just like your mother."

"I remember," I said as I stepped closer to her. "What's wrong?" I asked. She hardly ever cried. I could sense her sadness as surely as I could sense Jaeden's moods.

"I miss my parents," she whispered brokenly.

"I miss my dad," I admitted. "He's dead," I said and realized it was the first time I'd admitted it out loud.

"He might be okay, Emma," she lied to keep the pain at bay. It was weird; I just *knew* stuff like this now.

"You don't have to protect me. I know he's dead. He wouldn't have left us alone for this long if he was still alive," I replied. Deep down I'd known when he'd left the shelter that he wasn't coming back. I'd felt it in my soul, and as he'd left, I'd said my goodbye and made my peace with him. "What's really wrong?" I asked, knowing my best friend enough to know this wasn't just melancholy.

"Liam broke it off, said he wanted to spend time with Kyra. How am I supposed to live in the shelter knowing he's with her?"

"You want me to kick them out?" I offered, and I would. I'd kick them all out without a second thought for her. I was the person who'd help her hide the body if she needed it, because that was what best friends did for one another.

"No," she said as she wiped her tears away.

"Okay, well then suck it up buttercup," I said as I punched her arm. "I'm pretty sure those guys love trying to hump every girl they can in the shelter. Did he make any promises or lead you on? I will so neuter him if he did." She shook her head and giggled at me. "C'mon Addy, you weren't ready to get married and have puppies yet," I chided.

Darkest Before Dawn

"Puppies?" she snorted.

"Never mind," I said as I looked away and paid a little too much attention to the little mementos on the mantle.

"Did you get the rest of your stuff? Oh, and the jewelry box I think you hid when we were twelve?" she asked.

I smiled; I'd forgotten all about it. I'd hidden it under the floorboard with my other personal items to keep them away from Grayson and Dad's prying eyes. In the small wooden box was a pendant my mother had given me. She'd made me promise to never take it off. I broke that promise within a week of her death; wearing it was just too painful. I knew it was still there, without even entering my room.

I walked into my room and noticed that someone else had been in my room, judging from the streaks in the dust. I looked around and found other signs that someone had been there, such as my underwear drawer was open and empty. Someone had stolen my panties? And my perfume? They'd also taken the senior portrait that had been on my dresser.

I ignored the nagging feeling of being watched and lowered myself to the floor, then popped up the floorboard to retrieve the wooden box. Inside the box was a cut lock of my hair and my mother's, which had been braided together. A beautiful sterling silver necklace, which my mother had given me when I'd turned ten. I'd taken it off the day of her funeral and placed it in the box. I opened it and allowed my fingers to caress the silver pendant. The etched 3-D detail was the image of a spreading tree, which I'd always loved. The detail was incredible, but I couldn't really tell what type of tree it was.

There were words scribbled on the back, but they were in another language, which I couldn't read. I smiled and pulled it out of the box and placed it around my neck. The moment I did, I felt something inside of me open and a weight lift off of my chest. I gently ran my hand over the locket, and dug further in to find my diary, and photo albums.

"It's beautiful," Addy said.

"My mother gave it to me."

"I'm going over to head over to my house, so I can grab a few things. Meet you out front in an hour?" she asked.

"Sure," I said as I as I placed the few things into my bag. I rifled through my closet next, stuffing only a single dress and leather jacket inside. I made my way out of my room and went to the very back of the house to the room that had been closed since the day we'd learned of my mother's death.

It was my mother's home office and it hadn't been locked, or sealed shut…it just hurt too much for us to go in there and eventually it had just been forgotten. I knew I had to hurry; an hour wasn't very much time before

Darkest Before Dawn

Addy was going to be back.

I opened up one of the curtains and watched as dust met the light and created a cascade of motes through the air of the room. There was a fine layer of dust that covered the papers piled on the desk as well, a good sign that no one else had disturbed this place in a while.

I sat in the old leather chair and picked up one of the many pictures that had been forgotten on the dusty desk. My finger swiped across it, and a single tear slid down my cheek as I looked at the four of us. Me, Grayson, Mom and Dad before our world had been ripped apart. If they were here, they'd know what to do to keep us all safe.

I tried the desk drawer, and found it locked. Strange; what reason would they have had to lock it? I scooted the chair away from the desk and looked beneath the drawer for the key. My mad normally used magnetic locks that stuck to drawers in the other office, so there was a good chance one would be in here as well.

My eyes landed on the little key box but as I went to stand, I caught sight of the floorboard. Just like the one in my room, it looked hollowed out. I kneeled back down and knocked on it before I pulled it up and stuck my hand inside and felt carefully around.

I swallowed as my hand hit something hard. I pulled the large metal box out of the floor and eyed it warily. What could be so important that they'd hide it in the floor? It too needed a key, which when I stuck my hand back inside, I felt around the corners of the hole and found a small desk key hiding against the far recess of it. No key for the box though.

I lifted the box to the desk and looked at the tree symbol with an uneasiness that made my skin crawl; it was the same tree that was on the pendent I now wore around my neck. My finger absently trailed over the raised symbol. "Beautiful," I whispered. I set the box away from me and placed one of the many pictures over the top of it. I made quick work of the drawers, unlocking them all.

Documents had been filed alphabetically in the drawer, and as I looked through the drawer, a recorder caught my eye. I clicked it on, and sat it on the desk while I continued to look through the drawers. It wasn't until my mother's voice filled the room that I choked on tears.

Emma shows restraint, but she's still young. The Elders have asked that she be brought in to be tested. Her blood showed promise, and yet she's not like us. As if her father's DNA has tainted the strain. Dagan wishes to see if she worth saving.

I've already taken steps to prevent them from becoming infected in the event the virus reaches here. I've begun preparations to leave; Dagan has suggested that it's time. I do hate leaving them, but Emma is only a child in her mind, her father has refused to acknowledge what she is and spoils her as if she's a regular kid.

Darkest Before Dawn

Grayson shows no signs of being one of us; he's slow and even at his tender age, he should show the signs. It is my hope that Emma will become what is needed by the time I return. The virus should harden her. It should force her to adjust and defend her brother. If not, it will be a sign that I have failed us and my directive.

I stopped the recording with trembling hands. How had my mom known about the virus? She'd been buried over ten years before it had even surfaced. Or had she? My heart was about to burst from my chest as I pushed the recorder into my pocket and pulled open the second drawer and pushed the files out of the way, I found more tapes. I opened my bag and dropped several of them into it, before opening the last drawer.

Inside of it was info on the bunker and a manila envelope with my name on it in my father's sloppy handwriting. I looked from the envelope to the bag now full of tapes. I decided to read the letter or whatever was in the thing later. Right now I needed to find the damn layout and everything Dad had done to the shelter.

I had finished packing my bag when I walked out of the office and into the front room. Jaeden was sitting in a darkened corner; I felt him before I actually saw him. I stopped and looked at him silently. Had he heard the recording? Did he know?

"Emma," he whispered as he leaned his long frame into the light. His eyes took me in and narrowed. "What's wrong?"

"Nothing," I said but even I could hear how troubled I sounded.

"Want to talk about it?" he asked as he stood up and moved towards me.

"No," I replied, feeling my heart race at his nearness. I hated that he had this effect on my body. "Ever find something that makes you question everything you've ever known?" I blurted it out and felt the tears pooling in my eyes.

"No," he said smoothly. He watched me as I felt my world crumbling beneath my feet. Just the small bit I'd listened to was disturbing, and I wasn't sure how to process it. I felt as if my entire life had been turned upside down and torn apart.

What had she meant by what she'd said about me becoming what is needed? What the hell was needed? Had she known about Rh Viridae or was she referring to a different virus? Worse yet, her words hinted that there was a vaccine to the virus she was talking about. I felt sickened by her words. I wanted to stop thinking about it, but her words seemed to be playing on repeat inside of my head.

I turned to Jaeden and fought the urge to claim his lips. One kiss, one single kiss from him could end the turmoil playing in my mind. "Kiss me," I whispered and watched as he stepped closer, but didn't make a move to kiss me.

"Emma, are you trying to use me to forget about

Darkest Before Dawn

whatever happened?" he asked and for a brief moment, I thought I caught a flash of pain in his eyes. It was brief, so brief, that I had to have imagined it.

"And if I was?" I asked, feeling bolder now because the need to empty my mind was immense.

"You'd regret it, later. I want you, Emma, but not this way. Not to be used because you wish to forget something."

I glared at him, and closed the gap between us. His mouth was ready the moment mine touched it. His hands wrapped around me and lifted me up and against him. He pushed me against the wall, and I moaned against his hot, demanding mouth.

I moved my hips like a slut in a whorehouse who wanted to get paid. His hands held the back of my head as he deepened the kiss. We were so lost in the kiss that we failed to notice when Addy walked in on us, or even when she cleared her throat.

Jaeden was the first to break the kiss, which pulled a regretful moan from my lips. "Get out, Addy," I growled, fully intending to finish what I'd started.

I'd decimate this house. I'd do it in every room, except Grayson's. I wanted to stop being the responsible one, and just forget what I'd heard, and what my parents may or may not have been involved in or known about.

"Emma," she growled right back. "I get the whole *want-to-fuck-the-Adonis-looking-male*, but there's sorta a pile of dead bodies in my house!" I turned and took in her wide eyed look of shock.

I closed my eyes. "There are dead bodies everywhere," I sighed.

"These ones are moving!" she snapped. "Get the fuck out of Hussyland and get over whatever the hell is going on with you. You need to come see this shit!"

"If they're dead, they can't move." Unless they were vampires, like the man I still had my legs wrapped around, with a protruding cock pressed against my happy place.

"Yeah, I thought the same thing…right up until one asked me to end his pain," she said.

Jaeden's turbulent blue and green eyes smiled at me. As if he wasn't bothered at all by being interrupted. I could have screamed, but the knowledge of undead bodies was feeding my curiosity bug.

"Lead the way, Addy," I said as I dropped my legs from around Jaeden's waist. Once she was out of earshot, he growled and pulled me against his tall, hard frame.

"This isn't over, Emma; you've awoken a beast, and he's fucking hungry…" He slapped my ass and I barely managed to keep from yelping. "I'm going to fuck you soon, hard, and for hours. By the time you leave my bed, you'll know who you belong to. You'll never question it again." I glanced up in confusion at his curious choice of words.

"Are you back to that kinky shit again?"

"Absolutely," he smirked.

Chapter EIGHTEEN

At Addy's house there wasn't just a pile of bodies, these people seemed to be between life and death. They had pulses, but barely. Some could talk, while others only moaned and made eerie sounds that raised the hair on the back of my neck. Each body had a single bite mark, which looked infected.

"Animal bites?" I asked Addy as I examined a girl who didn't look a day over sixteen. She had dirty blonde hair, and huge brown eyes. She had tears running down her face, as she rocked in a fetal position on the floor of Addy's bedroom.

"You remember that one werewolf movie we watched? Mmm, what was it called…An America Werewolf in Paris? It almost looks like those kind of bite marks….or am I just fantasizing at like the worst possible time? Totes, right?"

"Totally, Addy…the word is totally, not totes," I

Darkest Before Dawn

mumbled distractedly.

"Emma, those straight-up look like wolf bites, right?" she continued.

"That's because that's exactly what they are," Lachlan said grimly as he strolled into the room and looked down at the girl.

"But werewolves don't exist," she argued.

I almost laughed at the irony of her telling a genuine werewolf that he didn't exist. Would she freak out? I hadn't, but it still felt more like a dream than reality to me. I could feel the heat of the vampire's eyes on me, as well as the posturing between the two. I chanced a peek at Jaeden, and then Lachlan.

Both seemed to be fully aware of my arousal, and the state of wetness in my panties. Could Lachlan smell as well Jaeden, and did he guess at what had gone down between us? Was this really my life? Discovering newly changed werewolves, and then lying by omission about it to my best friend?

"Lachlan's a werewolf, and Jaeden's a vampire," I blurted it out and smiled as she sighed dreamily. Whelp, that was off my chest.

"Oh em Gee! You're Bella!" she screamed excitedly with a disbelieving look in her eyes as she laughed. "Wait, you didn't like Twilight. Does Jaeden sparkle? Does his *dick* sparkle? Does Lachlan like doggie style more than any other style?" She laughed some more, until she realized we were all watching her waiting for it to fully sink in. "Oh my God, Emma! You bitch! Wait, you're not a bitch right? You're still you, no running around on all fours or sucking down O positive?"

I rolled my eyes. "Didn't like Twilight, they needed to buy a clue...I'm not a werewolf, and no, I don't suck down bags of blood."

"Oh fucking hell! You're all serious!? Is that how you got healed and didn't die?" She looked floored. It was sinking in, and with it, I knew the way her wheels inside her mind were turning. "You could have fucked a vampire and you didn't?"

"It's not as simple as that," I said as I leveled her with an irritated look. It was my best shut-the-hell-up look.

"Why not? I'd jump on it!" she admitted.

I rolled my eyes at her antics. "It's kind of a big decision which hasn't actually come up."

"So you want to bone her, but you didn't make her immortal?" Addy leveled Jaeden with are-you-fucking-serious look.

"Addy!" I growled.

"No, don't you Addy me, Emma. If he can bone you, he can damn well reward you for it."

Jaeden shook his head and awarded with me with

an *is-she-for-fucking-real* look. I rolled my eyes, and was almost relieved when the girl who'd gone silent on the floor started up again. Lachlan leaned over her, and spoke in some weird language, and then sat back on his haunches.

I kneeled down beside her, and placed my palms on her arm…and everything changed.

I was no longer inside the house with them. Instead, I was transported to a dark alley, filled with corpses. No, they weren't corpses. They'd all been bitten. I looked around, unable to leave the dark corner where I had hidden. I looked through the throngs of the changed and swiped angrily at the tears on my cheeks.

My family was in there, my brother, sisters, and my mother. I needed to find them, but how could I? There were so many of them, and each one moaned with pain from what the men had done to them.

"Two hundred," one of the stragglers said as he punched numbers into a hand held device. "At least ten percent should live through the change. Jeb got a decent number changed in Seattle. The rest of the west coast is ours."

"Braden will be pleased."

"And the pack in Newport? Lachlan and his men are there. Jaeden as well; does he have a plan to deal with them?" The man said to the guy still hidden in the shadows.

Amelia Hutchins

"We have a gift for them, one which should level the playing field. We've taken Seattle, and now Wenatchee. Soon we will move inland, right to their little stronghold."

I stepped back, but my foot caught on a metal pipe. My heart hammered against my ribcage as I turned to run, but before I could even take a few steps, I'm grabbed and held against a hard body. He growled in my ear, right before he shoved me to the ground.

"Well what do we have here?" he sneered as the man from the shadows stepped out, to look down at me.

"I get her first," he said as I took in his cold, empty eyes. He smiled and shoved the other man away, then pushed me down, holding me there. Fangs protruded from his gums. I screamed for help, but only grunts of pain and moans filled the stale, dirty alleyway. He watched as I struggled against him, his eyes ice blue and filled with lust as they took in my helpless state.

"No! No, stop. Please, I just want my family!" I shouted, but no one would hear me, they'd all been bitten. My skirt is hiked up, and the panties are ripped off harshly. I'll never save my family like this. Never. I had to be strong, had to get away. I had to live through this and kill them.

He pushed into me, and pain ripped through my entire body. I screamed, and screamed though there's no one left alive to help me.

"Emma!" I was back in Addy's room, on the floor

Darkest Before Dawn

and wrapped in Jaeden's arms, my eyes locked with the innocent girl who'd survived that hell.

"They are changing us into monsters," I whispered brokenly as Jaeden and Lachlan both watched me.

"What the fuck was that?" Jaeden demanded.

"I...uh...I was her. I was there. She was searching for her family," I replied. Had that just really happened? "How did you do that?" I asked her, but she had closed her eyes. "I was her! She was..." I stopped. I wouldn't tell them what had happened to her. That was her story. "Save her."

"It doesna work like that, lass," Lachlan said grimly.

"Make it!" I snapped. I wanted her to live, so she could have her revenge. I felt it to my bones, as if it had happened to me. More so, I needed to know what the hell she'd done to make me see her past.

"Emma," Jaeden whispered.

"Turn her, do something!" I demanded but neither of them moved. Addy sat huddled in the corner, sobbing as she watched me. Why was she upset? She hadn't seen what I had, hadn't had to mentally feel a rape that hadn't actually happened to her. It had felt real, the pain had been staggering, but now, back inside of myself, I felt no pain. I only felt the need to give her revenge.

"Emma, she's dead," Lachlan said as he reached up and closed her eyes. "They were all left here tae die. None of them were strong enough tae survive the change."

"Then why turn them?" I asked as a single tear slid down my cheek.

"What they are doing is a bit like trial and error. Only some humans can survive it, and live through the wolf attaching tae their soul. The rogues have been trying tae increase their numbers by biting as many people as they can. Because of what the rogues are, less survive their bites than if they had been bitten by a werewolf that was born tae it."

"They know we're in Newport," I said brokenly. "There's a vampire with the wolves, working with them. He said they have a plan for us, for you," I said as I lifted my eyes to Jaeden's.

"We know about the plan," Jaeden said. "Raphael is with them. He's been scouting the pack for months and has reported on the traitor."

"You guys could stop this, so why haven't you?" I asked.

"You explain the facts of life, Jaeden. I have more tae put down," he growled as he straightened up to leave.

I watched as Lachlan walked out, but Jaeden was staring at me as if I was an alien. He narrowed his eyes and lifted his hand to mine. Was he serious? Were *they* serious? The world was seriously nucking futs!

"Emma, I will not discuss this in front of the human."

"Anything you have to say to me, you can say in front of her."

"I want to fuck you," he said as the cocky smile slid into place.

"I need air, Emma. You have it out with Adonis while I go toss my cookies in the closest bush," Addy said as she slid up the wall on wobbly legs.

"Addy—"

"No, Emma. I can only process so much shit in one day. If I have to learn anything else today, my head is going to explode."

Jaeden waited until she was gone before he began speaking. "Lachlan knows more about this than I do, but I will tell you as much as I can. I do know that when a human is bitten, they begin to change immediately, but it takes a while for it move through their body and complete the transformation. It is extremely painful for most during the first change. Some can live through it and handle the virus that is carried in the werewolves' bites. The wolf spirit that attaches to the human DNA is a type of bacterial infection. Most of the humans who survived the flu were AB negative. We think this flu may have been introduced by a pack of rogues to get rid of those least likely to survive the change. These rogues started out by accident. We were told that it started a few centuries ago with a human who was legitimately changed by a born werewolf. A love match we understand and the pack alpha agreed to the change against his better judgment," Jaeden said carefully before he adjusted his position and leaned his back against Addy's bed, pulling me close to his chest.

"Just because some humans can be changed—doesn't mean they should, and many become unstable, as is what happened in this case. She died, and he became increasingly resentful at having to hide in the shadows. Not being born into that life, he didn't understand why they keep to the strict rules and would stay away from humans whenever possible. We understand how he feels about it, that with the werewolf's strength it should put them in positions of power—not hiding away and refusing to be involved with human concerns. He eventually rebelled and fought against the pack or the family that was responsible for changing him. He began his own agenda and set about aligning himself with humans that had money and power and manipulated them to his thinking and eventually changed them. In turn, they have been converting steadily over the years, increasing their numbers. The eyes of the rogues are red because we believe that Braden, the werewolf responsible for this mess and the first few he changed, became—more. We aren't entirely sure what they were enhanced with, but we have our suspicions, and it is transferable in their bite. Werewolves like Lachlan are born wolves that have been fighting against them and each day they become outnumbered. He and others in his group are pedigrees, for lack of a more descriptive word, while the rogues are essentially mixed breeds. Lately the rogues have been attacking the un-mastered vampires. Those are the ones who have been allowed their freedom for services and granted release from their sires. They are now seeking refuge with us as well as other large groups and bringing information with them. We're at war, Emma. The vampires are fighting for humans, while the rogues are trying to turn them. We have a few traitors here and there who think that rogues have the right idea, but for the most part, we are united."

"Why? Why change all humans?" I asked as my mind replayed what he'd said.

"If the world recovered from this, they'd have to hide or face being hunted down and killed. The humans still outnumber them and what is left of the government wouldn't rest until they found a way to govern us. The rogues won't allow that. We believe they started this, as a way to even the odds and tear the government down. It's also a way to be the one remaining race. If they change over the humans who are left, we will have a very difficult time trying to feed. Imagine what would happen if the cow didn't want to be milked and could fight back?" he raised an eyebrow and smirked at me.

"So they want it to be their world," I whispered. "They tried to eradicate an entire race just to kill you?" He hadn't said that, but yeah, my brain added it up and came out with its own equation.

"Smart girl," he said as he moved closer to where I stood. "You would think that was what they had planned, but I don't think they'd thought it out that far. They didn't seem to recognize our people as a threat until we came out of the woodworks and started protecting our food source."

"*Your* food source? Is that all that the human race is to you?" I seethed at his reference to my kind. "That's just cold."

"No. You have many other uses," he smiled.

"Can you for once get those dirty thoughts out of your head? This is serious!"

"The world is always falling apart. It always has some catastrophe which it's teetering on. The only way your kind goes on living, is when you are oblivious to it. So do you want to live, or have to worry about what might happen tomorrow?" he asked.

"Honesty is always better than sugar-coated bullshit."

"Not always. Not if you stop living because all of your time is spent worrying about everything that may or may not happen. I've lived a long time, Emma; I was human once too, and most humans, if they really thought about it, would decide that not knowing is better than knowing what's coming for them."

"And that might be true, but right now we are dealing with fucking genocide! It may not have started that way, but it's getting there pretty quick. If what you are saying is true, and sorry, I like to check my facts; we are staring extinction in the freaking face! I've been to a lot of houses around here, and no one's home. Even with those that came into the shelter in the past couple weeks, a lot of the people that we knew were hiding in town and in the cabins in the woods have vanished. And by vanished, I mean there's blood but no bodies, and those people that were dumped at Addy's house weren't those people. I've seen those red eyed bastards; I've fought them. We're out of time."

Chapter NINETEEN

I spent the next few days dealing with an emotional Addy, who was now prone to random outbursts, most of which seemed to include me and a vampire, a werewolf, and a bed. She'd been pretty singular in her focus since I'd updated her with everything I knew about Jaeden and Lachlan and everyday took a gigantic effort and exercise in patience to get her off the subject of vampires and werewolves, and back to her duties. I also had her swear not to discuss it outside of my room where others would hear her or discuss the subject with any member of our resident wolf pack. The last thing I needed was the others freaking or doing something stupid like lashing out at Lachlan or his men.

It had been a trying time for both of us and I knew Addy had been missing her parents and she was far more affected by the bodies in her home than she was letting on. Then there was the discovery I made in my dad's room that left me angry, frustrated, and confused. After finding the disturbing tapes and papers in my mother's

Darkest Before Dawn

office, I broke into my father's room this morning and found a concept map on his wall, the entire wall. He had my picture on top of his concept map, and then pictures of my mother, and some of the people she worked with. There were also pictures of my brother, my friends, and many others. All of them laced with red yarn that connected them together like a web of some sort. I'd been sitting in his room for hours just trying to make sense of it.

The question marks doodled with a sharpie above the pictures of some of the people we'd allowed inside the shelter bothered me. I'd listened to the tapes more, only to feel nauseated as they progressed. The truth was ugly, and hard to swallow. What was said in my mother's own voice rocked my little sheltered world. She'd known about Rh Viridae, and knew it was going to be put into play.

She kept saying I needed to be ready, but ready for what? She spoke of Lycans—the pure bred werewolves—as well as the rogues. She had known other creatures existed, and that Newport would be the most likely gathering point if the two came to an all-out confrontation. She'd explained how it had been chosen as a stronghold because it was a tactical place and easily held if the need arose.

She barely mentioned my brother and hardly anything about my father. She was fixated on me, and that I become what was needed. I sounded more like a science project than a child she'd loved. I hated that it played with my head, and left a bone-deep coldness inside of me that no heat could warm.

I was numb, and my brain kept telling me it wasn't true, but the tapes were real. I could hear us playing in the room next to her office, and Dad calling her name from the other room during the playback. She'd been planning this for a long time. The word Sentinel kept coming up, as if it was a badge of honor, *her* badge of honor to be exact. I couldn't tell if it was some sort of club or cult she secretly belonged to.

My entire life had been a lie. She had admitted to taking Sentinel lovers with the best genetic markings to father her children. According to what my mother said in the recordings, neither Grayson nor I had belonged to her husband. The man we called Dad. He'd been nothing more than a cover for her secondary life. She had mentioned multiple encounters with one Sentinel that she described as exceptionally strong when she became pregnant with me and she had hoped to have him be part of the potential daddy-pool for Grayson; however her group had lost contact with him and another donor had been substituted. I was experiencing an emotional information overload. I'd hidden the tapes beneath the mattress in my father's room, and left them there.

I was just heading to the media room to follow up on the supply group's reports for the day when Grayson caught my eye. He would be devastated if he ever found out about the tapes and what they said.

"Emma, you look sad," Grayson said as he approached me.

Darkest Before Dawn

"I'm not sad," I lied. I was devastated, but I was also pissed.

"Oh, I thought you were sad because Addy left us."

"What?" I asked confused. She hadn't left; last I'd seen her this morning, she'd been on a full-blown immortality kick. Which I'd told her was crap. Hadn't she watched the same movies I had? Immortality came with a heavy price. Usually ending with death in some horrifying way. Common sense said it was just a bad idea.

There it was. Addy had more than likely left the safety of the shelter to try and talk one of the vamps into giving her immortality. They'd give her something all right, probably more than she bargained for, and probably take a little sip while they were at it. Freaking great! I mentally pulled up my big girl panties and smiled even though I didn't feel like it. "Grayson, you know how Addy is. Sometimes she just needs a little space. We stopped by her house a few days ago. It probably reminded her of how she lost them."

"She has us, and I'm not stupid, Emma; she likes some stupid boy. You girls are seriously weird."

I blinked at Grayson and wondered when the hell he'd grown up. His hair needed a cut, and his eyes seemed sharper. He was no longer the child I'd been pretending he was. Somewhere between me trying to shelter him and keep him safe, he'd been growing up and I'd been missing it. I felt my heart as it clenched with the simple loss that could never be filled.

"When did you get so wise?" I asked with a sad smile.

"I told you I could help out, Emma. I'm not a child anymore."

"I'm your sister," I whispered as my mother's words played through my mind. "It's my job to protect you and keep you protected."

"Smothered isn't the same thing and you know it; that's what I loved about Dad, he didn't smother or shelter me. Besides, he's dead. It's my turn to protect you," he snapped.

"Grayson," I said as a single tear slid down my cheek. My heart shattered as my eyes filled up. He may have grown up, but he was still young and he certainly wasn't strong enough for what I was dealing with. I barely could deal with it.

"It's true, Emma. He left and he's been gone too long. He wouldn't leave us like this; he'd come back for us."

"He left you with me, and he knows I'd give my life to protect you. He left us with training and weapons. Enough to keep us protected, and enough food to feed us for a while, not that it would feed the masses we'd brought in after he left. We don't know that he's dead. There were a lot of calls for help, and you know how he is. He wouldn't leave anyone behind. Not if he could

Darkest Before Dawn

find a way to bring them."

"Stop lying to me! I'm smart enough to listen to the whispers. He's dead, Emma; dead and he's never coming back!" he yelled before he turned and stormed away from me. I swallowed a sob as I watched his retreating back.

"He could still be alive," Maggie said softly from behind me. I wasn't sure how much she'd overheard, or why she chose now to speak, but her words seemed as hollow to me as mine must have had sounded to Grayson.

"No, Grayson is right. He would have contacted us. He would have moved mountains to let us know he was alive. He's out there, dead. I just hope he was given a proper burial. He kept us alive, my father..." I paused as the voice from the recording played in my ear. He wasn't my dad. The man who'd stood beside me and raised us to survive wasn't my father. "...My father is dead."

He may not have been my blood, but he was my father. He'd taught me to know the difference between a boy and a man. A boy could make a child, but it took a man to raise them. I shared DNA with some stranger—well two, if you counted my traitorous, murderous mother. She'd been a part of the virus, not directly, but she'd kept it secret when it shouldn't have been.

I squared my shoulders and leveled Maggie with a steady gaze. "I'm going to find Addy, who seems to have run off. She had a little scare the other day, and I think it's got her upset. Grayson said she left a little while ago, but I should be able to find her. Keep a watch on my brother?"

"You know I will, Emma. You don't have to ask me," she said with a comforting smile on her face.

"Thanks," I said as I headed to my room to redress, and grab a bug-out bag. It was getting dark outside and I needed it in case I got stuck outside for the night. "Lock the shelter down by ten, if I haven't returned by then, I'll find a place to pass the night."

"Be safe," she said as she placed her hand gently on my shoulder.

"Always am," I breathed as I pulled away and closed the door.

I undressed quickly, and redressed in black. I had on loose fitting fatigues, with the Kevlar vest a hoodie tunic T-shirt that had a skull on it. My mind was on those damn tapes, and how Grayson would react to them. I slipped on the lightweight boots and stood up to do a check of my weapons.

They needed to be cleaned, but with everything going on, I'd been neglecting them. I tied my hair in a tight bun and hid it beneath the hooded shirt, and reached for the mask. I'd been leaving it off when going out lately, but my gut told me to bring it along.

I pulled on the bug-out bag and left the shelter with

Darkest Before Dawn

a heavy heart, knowing I'd have to face Jaeden, and ask him to *not* make my best friend immortal. In the movies, vampires were always reluctant to sire humans, but these vampires were nothing like the ones in books and movies, so who knew what they would do? Just being around Jaeden and some of the guys, my imagination was a pretty fertile place to imagine all sorts of wild scenarios.

I left the shelter without looking back. After the scene with the people at Addy's house, Lachlan and his men had come back to the shelter to grab equipment and then left to scout for any signs of new rogue packs in or around Newport. I wished he was here right now, because Addy seemed to have a thing for him, and might not have run to the vamps without speaking to him first. Jaeden hinted that the werewolves were immortal too, so she might have paid more attention to him than she ever would me.

The walk to the estate was tedious, and surprisingly silent. It wasn't until I reached the border of the woods and stepped into the clearing that the night came alive. I watched as men and women danced, and played around the leaping flames from the torches that surrounded the estate and tent city that had sprung up around it.

Were they serious? A friggin' party? Music pumped through several speakers while some of the people ground their bodies together, in perfect sync with the pulsating beat. I wondered how many of these people were vampires and how many were humans that they had collected and travelled with them. Jaeden mentioned a while ago that he had over three hundred and fifty men and I wasn't sure that was still the case as there seemed to be a lot more people here than that. There was a beautiful blonde that was currently in front of Jaeden, scantily dressed with her hips swaying seductively. My heart clenched as I took in the way he watched her.

The pair had history, and even from where I stood, I could feel it. His eyes were hooded as he silently watched her. It took every ounce of willpower I had to tear my eyes from them to look for Addy. I mean I get it, he was a hot-blooded male, and she was Barbie on steroids. I was just me; nothing special, nothing compared to her blonde perfection.

I stepped from the bushes and felt them before I saw them. Sven smiled with a wicked grin as I pulled off my mask.

"Emma, did you come to donate for the party?" he asked good-naturedly as he moved in even closer. His bright blonde hair was left long tonight with some of it pulled into a small herringbone braids at the sides of his head.

"Hardly," I said, "I seemed to have misplaced my best friend."

"Mmm, the sweet blonde," he said as he licked his lips suggesting that he knew her better than he should. "She's very enchanting, that one is."

"Where is she?" I demanded.

Darkest Before Dawn

"Last I saw, she had Bjorn and Aydan in one of the tents," he said, and turned to leave me standing at the edge of the woods.

I marched across the clearing, ignoring the looks I was getting for crashing the party. So help me, if she was offering sex for immortality, I was going to slap her. I made it about twenty feet before a large man stepped in front of me. He was about the same build as Jaeden, if a little taller, with shoulder length black hair and startling blue eyes. He was beautiful and yet the sharpness in his eyes told me he was so much more than just a pretty face.

"Mademoiselle," he said as he caught my hand and kissed it. "Such beauty," he said as a wicked smile spread across his face.

I turned to catch Jaeden watching us as the Barbie continued her bump and hump the pole routine. I turned back to the black haired man who I assumed was a vamp and smiled. "Thanks, but I'm only here to find my friend and leave."

"Please, stay and drink with me," he said with a sparkle in his eyes. I was sure he'd left hundreds of hearts broken in his wake. He had player written across his forehead.

"I'm flattered—"

"Raphael," Jaeden's voice said from behind me. I hadn't even seen him move, but a quick glance to where the pumped up Barbie stood glaring directly at me proved he had. She took long angry strides in my direction, which made my heart increase its rate, and once again I backed close to Jaeden for protection without knowing it until I was pressed against him.

"I have something that belongs to you," Jaeden whispered against my ear. "Come with me if you want it back," he said. I didn't wait; I turned and left Raphael and blondie watching us as we left them.

"You shouldn't have come here, Emma," Jaeden growled once we were out of earshot of the others, at least I hoped it was and wondered how far they could hear.

"Addy is here; you should have expected me."

"I wasn't aware that you knew she had slipped out, much less that you would think of looking here first."

"Addy's been on a tear about you guys for the past few days, so it was a good guess that she was probably here."

"And you came to beg me not to change her into the monster I am?" He raised a questioning eyebrow.

"Pretty much," I shrugged.

"What would you give me to keep her mortal?"

"Are you bartering with Addy's life?" I snapped angrily.

"I'm not a good person, and I want you. I'm willing

to play the bad guy as long as it ends with you at my mercy," he murmured in my ear, his nose slightly grazing my neck.

I snorted. "So you want me in your bed helplessly chained, and Addy stays human?" The mental picture made heat form in my limbs which traveled directly to my pussy. Oh yeah, I was a slut around him.

"Yes. That's exactly what I want."

"So basically you want me, in exchange for my best friend?" I asked as he held me locked against his body uncaring of who was watching us now.

"If you actually think you can barter sex for my best friend, that makes you a monster. Not the fact that you're a vampire."

Chapter Twenty

"Come in, Emma," he purred as we reached his office.

"You want me to come into your office right after you told me you wanted me chained to your bed? I'm not an idiot, Jaeden."

"Never thought you were," he smiled as he moved to close the door, leaving me no choice but to enter the office.

"You know your mood swings are seriously giving me whiplash."

"Is that so?" he asked as he closed the door and moved to his desk, leaning casually against it.

The room was huge, and opulently decked out in old Viking era pictures and designs. My heart hammered wildly from being alone with him, I shouldn't have followed him to this office. There was a chemical reaction between us, one that made me a brainless

Darkest Before Dawn

hussy. My knees were weak, and my heart hammered against my chest. I could already feel the moisture pooling between my thighs from the thought of what he'd already done and what else he could potentially do to me. It was simple seduction, which he was skilled in.

"I want to make a deal with you," he purred with a thin layer of silk in his tone.

"What kind of deal?"

"I want you," he smiled as I sucked in air.

I swallowed past the sudden dryness of my tongue. "Excuse me?"

"I want you," he stood to his full height using his tall frame for intimidation. His blue-green eyes raked over my face with interest. "We've played cat and mouse enough; I want to taste you and touch you at my leisure. I want to see what is under here again," he said as he reached out and ran his long, tapered finger over my left breast. "To put it bluntly, Emma, I want to fuck you. I think I have made that clear on multiple occasions."

I jerked back at his words, which splashed through me like ice water. His eyes sharpened as he watched my reaction while he calculated his chances. "I'm no whore, Jaeden. If you're asking me to trade myself for Addy, you won't like what my answer is."

"You've never been with a man before, have you?" he asked watching my face closely. I ignored his question and the tattle-tale blush that crept over my face. I watched his beautiful mouth as it tipped up in the gentle creases and turned into a mocking grin. "No, you've never been with anyone, have you? You're still a blushing virgin." His eyes sparkled with mirth, and the knowledge that he was right on the mark. His hand came up to remove a stray lock of hair that had fallen over my reddening cheek.

"You have no idea how rare you are. Do you? Such untouched beauty, just begging to be taken. I want to be the first one who watches those eyes as you discover pleasure, to be the first male to drive you to the brink and watch as you fall over the precarious cliffs of pleasure. To watch as those eyes grow large with wonder as your sweet body trembles from its first sexual release. Allow me to be your first and I promise to show you pleasure so hot, deep, and profound that you willingly seek out my bed again."

"Just a little self-adsorbed, Jaeden; who says I want you to be my first?"

He said nothing, but his seductive eyes missed nothing. I was unable to back away from him; my eyes had locked on those lips. Lips I'd kissed, and barely managed to remember to breathe. I'd barely survived them and with every kiss, it was getting harder to stop him. There was something magnetic about him that made me want him, badly. I felt safe with him, even though I shouldn't. He'd managed to save my life on several occasions.

But the main thing that entered my mind now, was

that I wanted him. I simply did. I wanted him like I needed air, but there was still that tingle in the back of my mind that told me to run. It screamed that he was dangerous, and more. It was common sense warning me that I wouldn't walk away from this being the same ever again. He'd change me, and I wasn't sure I was willing to allow it yet.

"I can see it in your eyes, Emma, and I didn't offer to be just your first, I'm asking to be your first and, I have decided, your last. I want to part those sweet thighs, taste the sweet petals of your flesh, and teach you what it's like to be seduced by a creature like me."

"And if I say no?" I asked as his body pressed against mine to show me that his need had made his pants become even tighter, as it pushed against my belly.

"Then someone else will most likely take it from you. You already know your answer. You just refuse to admit it." He whispered against my ear as his lips curved against my neck, where he kissed me softly. "You want me, little one. I can smell your desire already. So strong desire, sweet and inviting as it drips from your sweet pussy. Tell me, are you wet already? Are those sweet panties soaked from the need to be fucked?" His words were crude, but his hands moved down my body and sent a thrill of excitement and fear racing over my skin, tightening my nipples in anticipation as my back arched for his touch.

"I want to taste you, all of you," he growled low and throatily as his hungry fingers pressed against my moist heat. I cried out as he applied the slightest pressure, "here," he whispered huskily as his mouth covered mine. The kiss was hard; and demanding. When he pulled away, I had to hold on to him or chance falling to the ground. "I want you. I want you so fucking bad that I would kill for it," he growled as he then continued to kiss me. His mouth lifted from mine a second before a knock sounded.

I shook my head, dispelling the spell of sexual seduction he'd wrapped me in. If he'd continued, I would have given him what he wanted and the way his eyes watched me, he knew it as well. More knocking from the other side of the startled me.

"Don't move," he ordered me as he moved his well-muscled body out the door and locked me in.

The moment he left the room, I grabbed for a pen and paper on his desk and scrawled out a message before booking it through the open window. I eyed the message on the crisp white paper before I started the descending from his roof.

~Never going to happen Viking~

I mentally kicked myself as I shimmied down the gutter downspout, thinking about what I'd written. Oh yes, I wanted him, in all sorts of naughty ways; I just didn't want to be forced into anything. I could search for Addy by myself.

It also didn't help that the tingly, twitchy sensation that I had the night of the Friday wolf crashing party was back in full force. Being surrounded by vampires on their home turf might be a good reason for the creepy crawlies, but I had a feeling that it was something more than that.

I made it to the ground with a soft thud, but the moment my feet hit the grass, something hit me so hard on the side of the head that I was stunned for a moment and staggered briefly as the world spun. Before I could get my balance, rough hands pulled me up and held me firmly. When I looked up, it was to find blonde Barbie watching me coldly.

"If you'd just fucked him and allowed him to get you out of his system, this wouldn't be necessary," she growled as she forced open my mouth and pushed something inside. I gagged on the nasty bitter taste, and tried to spit it out as I fought against her and the arms holding me. She was pressing me against someone who felt like a clingy mountain behind me, sandwiching me to prevent me from stomping on his instep, elbowing, or head butting as she held my nose and mouth closed with her hands. "Swallow it whore," she snapped. She had a thicker accent than Jaeden, but it was the same lilt, as if they spoke the same dialect once.

Her nails bit into my flesh as her eyes flashed with anger. She hated me. I struggled to get away, but whoever it was that held me was stronger than I, and the more I struggled against him, the more he moaned, as if he was getting off restraining me. I choked on whatever it was she'd shoved in to my mouth, until she seemed satisfied that it must have been gone.

She forced my mouth open and peered curiously in, I assumed to see if I had swallowed or cheeked it. "Damn," she murmured to her companion. "She doesn't have any fangs. I heard them say Jaeden had given her his blood. She is strong like one of us, but no fangs." Viking Barbie looked a little confused as she looked down at me then her eyes narrowed.

"If you are still human, you had better hope that dose doesn't kill you." She nodded to the man still holding me. "Pick her up and take her to his room," the woman said coldly, a little too nonchalant about the killing part for my taste.

Panic hit me as I was roughly yanked from my feet and cradled in the arms of a giant bald man with dark skin. Whatever they'd given me was fast acting, because my head had begun to swim. Or maybe it was from the knock on the head. What the hell was with people clocking me in the head these days?

"What the hell did you give me?" I slurred. Within moments, my head wasn't feeling the slightest bit of pain anymore; as a matter of fact, it was becoming a giant balloon and the building and the trees surrounding it were spinning around me.

"Just something that will make you...more reasonable." She smiled and nodded at me knowingly as we moved around the other side of the estate and opened the door to a back entrance. She was nice enough to hold it open for the man carrying me. "I have very good hearing, and I have been listening in to everything

Darkest Before Dawn

he said to you since you arrived. He is fascinated with you; you won't give him what he wants," she laughed mirthlessly. "My warrior always did adore a challenge. So, I give him what he wants and he will forget about you, just like all the rest he's done this with, and then I'll have my husband's attention back," she pouted. My eyes flew to hers in disbelief. I knew they had history—but married? I could hear my heart pounding in my ears.

She'd drugged me to have sex with Jaeden? She was friggin' crazy! I tried to wiggle out of the big man's arms. "Please don't do this," I was begging. I wasn't losing this war this way. I couldn't! "You can have him!"

"Oh you see, we play this game a lot," she said as she smiled conspiratorially. "He pretends he doesn't want me and goes to other women to make me jealous. He has a huge appetite and plays with many women. You are different; you he watches for hours when you don't know he's there. It's like he's obsessed with you, but, like the others, you will be out of his mind as soon as he's played with you. I do hope you like it rough; my husband has a certain kink he's come to like," she smiled cheerfully.

"You're fucking crazy!"

"No, I just want my husband to get bored with you; he always does," she said simply. "I play with his friends and it makes him insane with jealousy." She grinned dreamily. "Then he plays other women to get me back. It makes for a very good game. This time I plan to beat him to it and leave you for him as a gift. That way he thanks me," she continued.

"Then take him! Don't put me in the middle of your damn games!"

"I will, right after I let him fuck you senseless." She seemed to have some sort of crazy logic about what she was doing that didn't make the slightest bit of sense to me. The whole passive-aggressive thing just wasn't working even in my foggy little world. Warmth filled my body and my arms felt loaded down with lead, and my legs seemed to be made of jelly and wouldn't cooperate with my will to run away. An alien had taken over my body, and I was floating over it, watching. I was sure of it.

Or, I'd taken a wrong left and landed my ass in Crazyville, which was only one mile away from Hussyland.

She removed my clothes with a knife as her friend held me in place. She fought with the kevlar before figuring out it wouldn't budge; she became frustrated and yanked it off without undoing the sides almost ripping my arms off with it.

"I heard Jaeden tell you that he wanted you tied up, so that is what we will do," she said with a soft giggle, like this was all some sort of big joke we were playing on Jaeden. My mind was becoming too foggy to care with what was happening to me or the planet.

I was unceremoniously tossed on the bed, *his* bed. She pulled a box out from a hidden panel in the wall as the dark skinned male, who seemed only able to moan, held me down. His eyes were as black as midnight, and he had protruding fangs that looked too big for his mouth.

She called out instructions, which the male followed, tying me to the bed posts, forcing my legs to stay spread open. I was about to scream, but she shoved a gag that had a ball in it into my mouth. I shook my head as she tried to secure it around my head. She had immense strength; her hands were rough, and unforgiving. Tears slid from my eyes as hopelessness set in.

She blindfolded me, and I felt her fangs as they punctured the flesh of my breast. How could another woman do this? To another woman! I couldn't move as her fangs bit me in several more places. When she finished, she made a hissing noise.

"She's delicious." She hummed it as if it was a lullaby. "Put the bow on her pussy, and start the music. It's time to fetch my husband."

Music started as the door closed. I choked on the gag, and waited for Jaeden to save me from this fucked up circus ride. I could feel blood dribbling from Viking Barbie's many bites. Time passed, and I felt increasing changes to my body as it grew heated and wet. Sweat covered my face, as the pulse and pain from the bites blistered my mind.

"I told you, Astrid, I don't want anything from you…" Jaeden's voice stopped at the door. His breathing hitched in his lungs, and then came the anger. "You fucking whore! What the fuck have you done?"

She started chattering at him excitedly, but it sounded like that language Jaeden spoke those few times to me, so I couldn't make out a word. Jaeden's voice was dangerously calm as he responded to her. Her voice ranged from flirty and coy to petulant to pleading. For a fleeting moment I thought they sounded like the Swedish Chef from the Muppets and I lapsed into a mixture of snorts and giggles from the gag, but I couldn't have cared less. I was on fire. Sweat beaded at my nape, and I needed something.

"Get out of here, Astrid. Now, before I take your head like I should have done instead of marrying you," Jaeden's voice hadn't changed; it was still calm and composed.

The door slammed with a shuddering blow that sounded as if it had shattered. My skin prickled with the sensation of his eyes taking in Astrid's handiwork. I gagged on the ball in my mouth again and it seemed to bring him out of whatever he was doing, because his hand touched the skin of my face and I moved my head and pressed closer to it for more.

It was magical. His hands were magic; the moment they touched my skin, the pain eased. The moment the gag was off, he removed the blindfold and looked down at me. "I'm so sorry she did this. Stupid, manipulative bitch she is; this wasn't what I wanted. Never like this." His softly spoken words held a world of anger in them.

Darkest Before Dawn

I looked up at him dizzily. "You were going to make me do this for Addy though; you said you were willing to be the bad guy if it got you what you wanted," I accused. "Now you have me."

"Is that why you left my office? I said I wasn't a good person, and I meant it, Emma. I wanted you to come to me willingly, but you just wouldn't let yourself go. I was bluffing and hoping you would push yourself that last little bit so you could finally let go. You unravel me, sweet girl. You make me need you like this, but never when it's not of your own free will." His hand moved my loose hair out of my face. "Sweet girl, I've wanted you like this since the first moment I heard your sultry voice. I wanted you to beg me for your precious release. I learned a long time ago that forcing a woman is an easy feat. Getting a real woman to come to you and beg for it? Now, that's a precious thing. That is all I wanted with you, not whatever fucked up shit Astrid has going on in her head about what she thinks I want," he said softly as his head shook grimly.

"Is crazy ass Viking Barbie your wife?" My voice was so small and sounded as if it belonged to someone else.

"She was once, a long time ago," he admitted. "I have done very stupid and rash things which I have regretted because of her. Right now she seems to exist just to make me lose my mind." He smiled weakly and I couldn't explain the sense of relief that his words created in me. My stomach turned over and the fuzzy feeling in my head threatened to take me under.

"Something is wrong with me, I feel sick," I whispered.

"You're not sick. She gave you drugs. One's that make you need…sex," he swallowed hard as he got the words out. "The only way to relieve the pressure is to give you release."

He hadn't untied my legs, and I was acutely aware of that fact. "Untie me?" I whispered through cracked lips. I was burning up, and I could feel the fever spreading to other parts of my body. "Jaeden," I whispered again as I met his eyes.

"You need to understand one thing, Emma; you can't leave. If I don't help you soon, you will be in agony for however many hours it takes for this to wear off."

"So basically you have to fuck me?" I snapped angrily as tears flooded my eyes.

"No, but I will make you come…which can give you the same relief. This doesn't have to be an all or nothing thing. I can make you come so many other ways, Emma, that you'll find release and won't have to feel the pain."

"But you won't take my virginity?"

"No, not unless you ask me to, but even then I might not. I want you, but not like this. I wanted you to ask me to take it, to take you."

"I'm on fire," I cried as fiery pain shot through my

body, making my back arch.

"Tell me when that fire touches you…" his fingers trailed over my core, "here."

Chapter
Twenty-One

*~*Jaeden*~*

She was spread out and exposed, bared exquisitely before me. Fucking Astrid took her will away, and she didn't even know what was coming. Unimaginable pain would engulf her if she didn't allow me to give her release…many releases at that.

I should have killed Astrid for this, and if she wasn't protected by Shamus, I would have. Emma didn't deserve to be involved in our war, Astrid's endless attempts to get me back. Seeing the Moor poised above Emma's sweet flesh with his fangs scraping her skin had been enough to get him killed, but Astrid knew the laws. She knew that without my claim on her, that Emma was fair game. Unprotected.

To claim her before this would have involved me

doing it without her consent, and even with as dark and uncaring as I was, I wanted her permission. No, I needed it. She wouldn't have agreed to it, and probably still wouldn't.

The sight of her strung up and her open, untouched flesh had my cock pulsing and straining to get free, to bury the need I felt in that creamy white flesh. Those rose-tipped nipples just begged to be sucked.

"Listen to me. I need you to decide something before you get too far out of it. Do you want me to find Lachlan to do this, or do you want me to do it?" She looked up at me with dizzy confusion in her beautiful blue eyes.

"You, Jaeden, I only want you. Promise me you won't allow anyone else in here," she cried, and I felt my useless heart clench. My cock jumped once to remind me he was there with us. *Down boy; she's untried and not ready for you.* I didn't smile, because she wasn't really willing. She was a victim of my murderous ex-wife, who just couldn't accept that she was a manipulative, adulterous, whore. One I could give less than a shit about.

"You're sure? I can find the wolf for you," I asked cautiously, wondering if I had just lost my mind by trying to do the right thing. It was something I found myself doing more frequently since meeting her. Had I really just offered to find Lachlan to fuck the pain away, when I wanted nothing more than to drive my rock hard cock balls-deep in her tightness?

"I said you!" she screamed, and her body pooled with intense heat. Her core flooded with moisture that my mouth watered to taste. Her unique scent alone was enough to drive me over the edge, but she was different than the others I sought out to find relief with. Emma had an innocence to her that couldn't be faked.

"I need to close the wounds, Emma," I whispered as my fangs slid into place. Fuck, she's addictive. Unlike any other female I've ever come across, and they number in the tens of thousands. I've fucked my way through countries, trying to forget what Astrid had done, what she was.

Tonight I had almost forgotten it, almost allowed her back in for a mere second. Her subtle curves and the hunger had mixed with the knowledge that Emma was in close proximity to the wolves. Jealousy; I was fucking jealous over a mere mortal, or whatever she was. I knew she wasn't one of us. It was another first for me. Most women sought me out, and I used them as they wished to be, but sweet Emma, she'd had a perfect *no* planted on her perfect lips from the get-go.

I leaned my mouth over and closed the wounds on her ample breasts. Next, I leaned over, making sure to gently stroke her pussy with my fingers to test where she was with the aphrodisiacs. Her hips rose to my caress, drawn to it from the subtle relief my touch had awarded to her. I leaned over and placed my mouth on her inner thigh, perilously close to her sweet honey.

Knuckles grazed her flesh as her mound pushed

Darkest Before Dawn

up again and the bonds strained with her movement. I watched as fire burned in her eyes. If I didn't know any better, I'd say that whatever Astrid had given her wasn't very long lasting. She was covered in sweat, but at the same time, I could smell the drugs pushing through her system and out of her pores.

"Emma," I whispered, and allowed the hoarseness in my voice to caress her skin. I leaned over and licked the bite from Astrid that's right above her sweet, drenched pussy. She bucked her hips at the connection, and I gave up trying to hide how fucking turned on I was.

Her legs were spread wide, and her ass and pussy were right there, inches from my tongue. One taste. One single fucking taste and I'd end up fucking her until she was sore from it. I pulled out a knife, and cut her legs free; her breathing hitched as each leg fell to the bed.

She'd been too much temptation with those legs up and parted, her sweet honey dripping for my greedy eyes to feed upon. I stepped back from the bed, watching as she realized I'd left her hands bound. I smiled as I crossed my arms and pulled my t-shirt up painfully slow.

I loved the sounds she made as I bared my own my flesh to her. Those sweet hisses and hitches of her breath as she watched me strip to nothing. I kicked off the boots I wore, and met her eyes. My hands smoothed down my chest, right until I hooked my thumbs through the buckle of the belt I wore. I took my time undoing it, wondering how it would feel across that sweet ass.

She bit gently into her lip and I didn't dare take my eyes from hers. Full control. I needed it. I had it. Fucking craved it from her like a junkie craves a fix. She was mine now; tonight I would have her. *I will make her mine.* She'd leave this room owned and sore from what we had done.

"Tell me, Emma. In your mind, what am I doing to you? Fucking your sweet body nice and slowly, or am I fucking you senseless? Should I make you work to come, or should I give you one for free?"

She swallowed, and the noise made me harder, if that was even possible. I loved taking my time as I revealed to her what she would be having tonight. I told her I wouldn't be rough for the first time, but I could see it in her sweet blue eyes. She wanted it. There was a hunger for me in them, and it was fucking erotic. Intense need that couldn't be faked, and the beautiful intensity I saw in hers floored me.

In all of my time as an immortal, I'd never wanted to fuck anyone as I did her. I wanted to rip her open and see what she's made of. I wanted her submission. Many times, it wasn't about what I wanted or needed. Not directly. Because I was the dominant one here, always. I was the fucking master. What I wanted from her was total obedience, and to allow me to control her pleasure in every sense of the word. I wanted her to be good, to be of use, to obey, and to *scream* for me. I wanted to please her, to make her boneless from how many times she would come for me.

Darkest Before Dawn

"Jaeden," she whispered my name as I kept her eyes locked with mine.

"After I take you the first time, Emma, we will no longer be Jaeden and Emma. You will be mine; you will please me and obey me, and for that, I will reward you with what I decide you deserve. My cock. My tongue. My fingers. I pick how you come for me, and when you can."

"That sounds...dark," she replied breathlessly.

"Everyone has a dark side, Emma. What I'm asking is if you want to come play with mine. My dark side is begging me to allow you inside of it, to make you my prey. It makes me believe things that shouldn't be possible, like this; you being tied to my bed right now. This feels like a dream. A really fucking good one that I've dreamt about since I first laid eyes on you. So, tell me, Emma. Can I have you?"

She smiled. She fucking *smiled*. Most women flinch when I tell them I want their obedience. Most have difficulty giving up control and yet this blushing little virgin was grinning with an eagerness in her eyes for me to take control. I shook the surprise off as I snapped the belt in my hands and watched as her eyes glazed over with heat. "You want that, don't you?" I asked, watching as her legs slid further apart.

Her pussy was soaked, and the smell was heady. I wanted to bury my face in it and suck that tender flesh until she begged me to come. Not yet, not until she was ready. Her pupils were no longer dilated from the drug, but from need.

"I want you, Jaeden," she replied to my earlier question.

"Do you feel the drugs?" I asked, curiosity sneaking in. She shakes her head, and I grin. "No?"

"No," she answered with the hottest voice I'd ever heard from a woman. "I don't think it's working anymore."

My heart hammered in my chest, knowing if she put a stop to this now, it would just about kill me. I stood, still clad in jeans. They fit loosely over my hips and my cock is probably the only thing holding them on. I waited for her to demand to be released, but she just watched me. As if she was deciding our fate.

"Do you want me to let you go?" I asked, even though doing so would leave me in agony.

"No," she said with a shy smile that spread across her lips.

"Jesus, woman," I groaned, and had to actually force myself to remain on my feet instead of falling to my knees with relief. "You're sure? I won't be able to stop once we've started, Emma. If you don't want this, tell me now."

"I already told you. I want you, Jaeden, only you."

Darkest Before Dawn

*~*Emma*~*

I wanted him, and he'd seen it in my eyes. The expression he'd just made had created a need so dark and tempting inside my mind that I wasn't leaving this room with my V-card intact. "Addy," I whispered through the dryness of my lips.

"I gave the order moment she got here that she wasn't to be bitten, or turned. I can't keep them from fucking her, though."

"Why didn't you just tell me that?" I asked.

"Because I wanted you, and Astrid was here, willing. She is always willing. The moment I watched you with Raphael, I knew it wasn't her I wanted. It was you. The entire time she danced, I was imagining you. Just like this," he smiled as the words came out filled with lust.

"I'm not going to untie you," he said with darkness in his eyes that both thrilled and scared me. His pants hung loosely on his hips, but the bulge was there. He wanted full submission, and I'd decided to give it to him this once.

"You don't have to, but Jaeden. I am scared," I admitted.

"I know," he said as he leaned against the bedpost and smiled heatedly, "but what better way to make you perfect for me than to teach you from your first orgasm how to fuck me right? I'm going to give you pain tonight, Emma. It will be mixed with pleasure, and when you are wet enough to take me, I'm going to fuck you until you scream my name. At that point, I'm going to keep fucking you until you beg me to stop. The only question in my mind is if you will be able to handle it?"

I swallowed, fear rising in my chest. "Um, I have no idea if I can handle it."

He smiled and approached the bed with his belt held in both hands. "I'm going to end up taking you hard. I like to fuck, a lot, and I like the person I fuck to know I've been inside of them for days afterwards. If it gets too painful, or it's too much for you to handle, tell me and I'll try to slow down." His voice was just a rough rumble.

"Try?"

"Yeah, try. Emma, I'm very old, and in my day we fucked to claim. We fucked to please our women and keep them sated for weeks after we'd gone to sea. My point is I'm going to fuck you hard and fast. I'm going to make damn sure you know it was me who fucked you. Understand?"

Chapter Twenty-Two

My heart accelerated. My pussy was soaking wet, and the moment he removed his pants, I wanted to scream, *stop!* I had to bite my tongue to keep from saying it. He placed the belt beside the bed, and pulled my ankles to him.

"I've imagined what this would be like a million times, sweet girl. The noises you'd make for me, and the sweet taste of your flesh," his mouth lowered to kiss one ankle and then the other one. "The way you'd scream as I pumped my cock into your tight sheath," his fingers slid further up until they held my thighs and pushed them apart. My hands strained to touch him, but he locked his eyes with mine and all thoughts of anything other than where his lips would go next evaporated from my mind. He kissed my inner thighs, trailing his tongue in an erotic pattern of swirls and kisses. "I'm going to fucking destroy you, Emma, until you want no other man. You'll be begging me for more, demanding I fuck your tight pussy because you want no other but me between your legs," he growled huskily.

Maybe the drugs were still going strong in my bloodstream, because sweat was pooling between my legs, as well as the back of my neck. My hips had begun to rock with need, and as his hands slid further up until he held my thighs apart, his mouth hovered over the one place I craved him most.

"You want me to kiss you here?" he rasped as his tongue slid over my wet heat. I cried out with need, and made other inhuman noises. "Fuck, you taste better than the last time I kissed you here."

I was shocked that he'd kissed me there again, for all of about two seconds before it was replaced with need. Addy once told me men didn't normally go down there with eagerness, yet he went straight for it. My hands held the rope as he controlled my legs, which tried to trap his head in place the moment that hot, seductive tongue had touched my flesh.

"Open your legs, now," his voice was stern and held an air of authority. I immediately obeyed him, but it wasn't because he had control. At least that's what I told myself. "Look at yourself," he continued. "Look at how wet that sweet pussy is from just one lick," he said, as he indicated just how wet he'd made me. "I'm going to make you come, and I want you to watch me do it," he said as he moved to place pillows behind my head.

I braced for the part which would hurt, and embraced it. Only he had no plans of penetrating me. Yet. He sat between my legs and stroked his cock slowly; the silken skin had swollen, leaving a monster of a cock in its

Darkest Before Dawn

place. I'd watched R-rated movies, and yes, even some XXX-rated ones, and I was pretty sure I could make the educated guess that they seriously didn't make men like him anymore. I'd now seen it a few times, and was pretty sure I hadn't imagined its magnitude.

"You were made for it," he said guessing where my thoughts had gone to. "You'll take it all and more if I tell you to."

"That thing isn't normal," I whispered.

"Says the twenty-one year old virgin?" he smiled.

"Are you going to do it?" I asked unsure of how he planned to make me come, and if he'd be inside of me for it. I just knew there was a serious pressure in the lower part of my body and I felt like a needy bitch. I wanted him to make it happen again, and by happen, I meant right freaking now.

"It's not going to be fast, Emma, I told you that. I'm going to need to prepare you for me, and that's going to take time...which I plan to enjoy. Have you ever sucked a cock?"

I blinked. "Virgin?"

"Fuck, this is going to be so much fun. I'm going to enjoy this far more than I thought I would. I think this may actually take days to do properly," he said with a devilish grin on his face.

I had a feeling by the time I left him tomorrow, I'd

be hardly able to walk. He reached up and pinched one nipple and then the other, his eyes never leaving mine. His other hand pushed against my pubic bone with just enough pressure that heat flared in my core.

"You know one of the good things about being a vampire, Emma?"

"What?"

He focused intently on what he was doing to me, "I can hear your heart speed up when you're afraid, or when you like something. For example, you like it. You get turned on waiting for it to turn from pain to pleasure," he whispered as he bit his lower lip seductively.

"Pain is not a good thing," I whispered.

He smiled. "No?" he asked as his hands left my body and he lifted both of my legs up. My ass was fully exposed. I felt a bead of trepidation as his hand slapped my flesh sharply.

I cried out, and yes, for all of ten seconds I wanted to slap him for doing this to me as I had the first time. Only, I felt my heart beat faster with anticipation for the pleasure it would bring. The next one burned my flesh, and yet my pussy grew wetter as it had the first time he'd done this. The next one was harder, but no longer painful. The sound of his hand as it smacked my flesh burned my ears but his hand against my flesh was pleasurable. I'd surely have a red ass in the morning, but the moment his hand massaged it, I moaned with pleasure. He pulled his hand away and slapped it harder,

Darkest Before Dawn

this time he allowed his hand to slap between my legs with the perfect weight behind it.

"Fucking hell, you're a natural at this, sweet girl," he said with a heavy accent this time. He released one leg and his fingers slid over my very wet opening. "You're already wet enough to fuck."

I pushed myself against his fingers, but he removed the hand. He leaned over me and smiled as his mouth claimed mine in a kiss of total domination. When he pulled away, he smiled, but the darkness was back.

"Who is in control?" he asked.

"You are," I replied.

"What do you want me to do to you?"

"Everything," I answered, surprising even myself.

"You don't know what you are asking for, but I damn well plan to show you."

His head lowered to my breast, where his fangs scraped across the skin painfully. I watched him as he lifted those sea green eyes to mine and bit into the soft tissue of my left breast. Pleasure erupted from deep inside of me, shaking my entire world, and spinning it from its axis. I moaned as he took the first pull, and then another. It was over as quick as it had started. He flicked one nipple, which was as hard as a pebble, and then the other.

"Good girl," he said as he moved from the bed and placed a full size standing mirror at the end of the bed so I could see myself and him when he rejoined me. His smile was devastating as he watched my reaction to my own nakedness. "That's what you look like to me, Emma, absolutely perfect. Do you see how much I want you? And why I want you?"

I looked as if I'd been replaced with some sultry pinup girl. My nipples were bright pink from where he'd flicked them. My core was exposed to his greedy eyes, and even from where I lay, I could see the slick mess he'd created. My hair was a mess, but it looked as if I'd planned it right down to the last strand. My lips were swollen, as if I'd spent the last hour doing nothing but kissing him.

I tore my eyes from myself as he rejoined me on the bed. He was hard, and ready. But he didn't use it yet. Instead, he smiled as one hand parted my core and the other inserted one finger, and then another. "So fucking slippery with need; can you see how wet you are? Can you hear it? Hear the sound it makes as I fuck it, and fill it with my fingers? You'll take more, and you'll beg for it, Emma. By tomorrow this sweet flesh is going to be swollen and sore from me fucking it. You'll remember it for days, and then right when your sweet pussy starts to recover, I'll fuck it again, only harder."

"Mmm, yes," I murmured around moans. He inserted another finger, and then his thumb slid over my clit and I twisted in his hold.

Darkest Before Dawn

"Part your legs, now," he growled and I tried my best to do as he asked. The noise of his fingers as they entered and parted my flesh eventually took over. "Fuck them," he encouraged, and then smiled. "Like this," he instructed as he pushed them inside, only to use his other hand as he slid it beneath my ass and lifted and then lowered at a steady pace. "Like that, now don't take your eyes from mine. I want to see you as this pussy clenches against my fingers, and your sweet juices building to take more. Feel the way it's sucking against them as it begs for more?" he stopped the hand which remained under my ass, as he inserted another finger until it was painfully full. "Fuck, you're so tight."

"Jaeden," I whimpered as I felt the growing tension coil in my belly.

"Let it go, and come for me, Emma, come hard."

I shattered. My body felt boneless as blackness filled my mind. Stars erupted as my body continued rocking, even though his hand had stopped moving. I tried to keep my eyes locked with his, but I couldn't see anything. I was still in that euphoric state when I felt him move between my legs.

I moaned as I felt him nudge my legs further apart. "I can't wait any longer to be inside of you," he growled before he pushed his cock inside of me.

There was pain. So much pain that I cried out as my body pushed away from his where he was tearing me apart from the inside. He groaned as I screamed, my nails cut through the soft tissue in the palm of my hand. "We don't fucking fit! Get that damn thing out of me!" I wailed.

"Emma, stop moving," he replied gutturally. "There's a lot of blood."

"Odin, Mercy, Fucking, Glory! Holy Satan's golden dick, that shit hurts!" I babbled as I tried to get away from that thing.

He laughed. He fucking *laughed!* His grip had tightened so I couldn't move away from him. I tried to stop the need I felt to get him out of me. I could smell my own blood, and when I looked up at him, it was to find his eyes glowing red and his fangs dangerously long. No wonder he'd sounded all guttural and shit. I was fucking Dracula! It put an entirely different spin on Vlad the Impaler!

He pulled out a fraction and moved it back inside. Tears trailed down my cheeks. His eyes locked with mine as he reached up and tore the ropes that held my hands in place easily. His hands captured mine, as he gathered my wrist in one of his large hands, brought them down against my stomach. His other hand lifted one leg, and then the other, until they both rested on his shoulders. He pulled out and began moving slowly.

"You fit me like a glove," he growled.

"No shit! Dude, you ripped me open, that thing is never gonna be the same again!"

Darkest Before Dawn

He gave me a wicked grin. "I believe I told you that that was my plan from the start of this, didn't I?"

After a few moments of his gyrating hips, it stopped hurting and started to feel good. No, wait, it started to feel really good. The pleasure began to spike and throb. I bucked against him for more as my eyes closed. "Oh hell," I growled, matching his own tone. "That's nice."

"Fuck, you're so sweet," he whispered as he pulled out to the tip and then drove his cock deep inside. "Too sweet, Emma, you need to come for me."

As if he needed to remind me? I was falling over that cliff like a cliff diver on steroids. It took exactly three more moments of him rocking those hips for me to find my happy place and jump. My nipples hardened and slick heat filled my center right before I detonated and screamed his name to the throaty sound of his laughter.

I felt his body tense as his cock pushed inside harder, and then my legs were pushed to my shoulders and he let loose. The sound of flesh meeting flesh was erotic and filled the room. His grunts met my moans and I exploded again. I'd heard that virgins didn't get off the first time normally, which, let's just say, helped me keep my V-card for so long. What the fricking hell was the point in doing it if only he got off? Jaeden was proving everything but the pain part wrong.

"Good girl," he whispered as he claimed my lips. His entire body went tight and new warmth filled my center. He was coming, and his eyes held mine captive as I watched his pupils dilate with pleasure. And, after a few moments, his fangs retreated back to a normal size. This sexual tension between us had been leading up to this moment, and right now, I didn't regret my choice.

When he was finished, he got up and walked his very firm, very sexy naked backside across the room and retrieved a cloth. I watched him leave the room and return with it wet. He washed the blood from between my legs and then kissed the sensitive nub which now felt severely swollen.

He crawled onto the bed and lay beside me, pulling my body close to his. "Thank you for the gift, Emma. It was worth the chase, and the blue balls to get it."

"I gave you blue balls?"

"Woodpecker."

I blushed, but barely concealed the sultry smile from him. Fricking woodpeckers. "I'm glad I saved it for you." I said as sleep overtook my eyes and mind.

"Get some rest; round two starts soon," was the whispered warning that filtered through my foggy brain.

He pulled me close and tucked me into the protection of his arms. I slept, blissfully unaware of anything else in the world except for how cherished I felt locked in his embrace.

Chapter Twenty-Three

I was sore. As in, I wasn't sure walking was an option. I'd soaked in his tub sometime before dawn, since he said it would help. Guess what. He lied. He'd taken me until I was pretty sure my bones had melted and my organs had been beaten to mush with his magic stick. I'd screamed for more *just as he said I would*; had he warned me about the day after, I probably would have run away screaming instead. Last night, he had put a new meaning of stamina in my mental dictionary. It must have been at least two hours of him rocking my body until he came completely undone, and that had been the last of six other times he'd taken me.

I had just woken up when I heard an angry hiss. I popped open one bleary eye to find Astrid's unhappy face competing with the early afternoon sunlight for first place of 'things I would rather not see today'. In the bits and pieces Jaeden had shared last night, one of which was the tidbit that he'd given her a divorce declaration in front of witnesses' centuries ago, but she refused to be sent away. He also recommended that I stay away from her, not just because he said she was unbalanced, but because she was protected by Shamus and it was something he couldn't go against. I'd been sharp enough to notice it was a sore subject and it was best to let it go—for now, at least.

"What are you still doing here?" she demanded in a shrieking tone.

"Awe, are you sad that your little Spanish fly crap didn't work the way you thought it would?" I asked as I pulled the sheets around me and glared at the bitch.

"He will want you gone by the time he returns. He never wants to see the bitches he fucks afterwards, so run on home." She shooed her hands at me as she walked over to the only dresser in the room and pulled out female clothes.

Why would Jaeden have her clothes in his room? I narrowed my eyes as she walked back over and tossed the worn jeans and tank top at me. "Obviously it won't be an exact fit since you look more like a boy." She sniffed disdainfully.

Did she really just go there? "Well yeah, but not all women come out of a plastic mold from the Mattel factory. Some of us are actually real."

"Is that a compliment?" she narrowed her cold blue eyes on me with a threat bared in them.

"Not at all," I smiled as I used my best fake-bitch

voice.

"He's mine," she sneered.

"Please, he was pretty clear that he got rid of your ass long ago. I think it was something like…he would rather fuck a flying monkey before he would touch you again." Yeah, I was being catty and poking the bitch, but there was no way I was going to let her push me around or intimidate me.

"You think you're the first woman to catch his eye? I've watched hundreds of you walk into his room and you all have had one thing in common. He never fucks you again. Period. He chased me through the fjords of Norway and married me. I was his love and he showed it by making me his wife. This is all just a game and you are only here to piss me off; remember it." She glared at me with a nasty little smirk. "What? You think he didn't help me plan this little charade to get you in to his bed? I'm always in his plans; now get the fuck out of *my* bedroom."

I swallowed down my retort as last night's events replayed in my mind. Had they set me up? No, he'd been too willing to get Lachlan if I'd wanted him and he had warned me she was cuckoo. I grabbed the clothes she'd tossed on the bed and dressed quickly before grabbing the pile of my things that were salvageable. I swallowed past the rage that was quickly taking root where the shame had been. Jaeden might have left, but he hadn't sent her in here; she was bitter and it showed in her words. She'd be too easy to kill, but the fact that

I was at an estate, surrounded by vampires soured that idea.

"Where is he?"

"Gone," she answered as her big mountain of a servant moved into the room silently and stood behind her. In the little bit that Jaeden had shared, he said that Astrid had acquired the Moor around the time Shamus was in Spain; he was originally a eunuch slave that had his tongue cut out. She found him in a slave market, purchased and turned him. He was extremely dangerous and would do anything for Astrid. As much as I resented his involvement, I couldn't help but feel sorry for him.

"Where?" Didn't they hand out brains at the Mattel factory?

"He left for Seattle this morning," she said coldly.

He'd left? Without a freaking word! Bastard. "My friend?"

"Well-serviced; she's somewhere down with the other cows I'm sure."

"Cows?" Was this bitch for real?

"Your kind," she said sickly sweet.

"My *kind* keep *your* kind alive, remember that, Barbie."

I managed to keep in the sheer rage I currently felt for Jaeden and the need to bury this bitch out back,

Darkest Before Dawn

which was looking really good in my head right now. I'd given myself to him and he'd left like thief in the night without so much as a goodbye or thank you. I mean, I realize it wasn't the best timing or planned at all, really, but was a little heads up too much to ask after I'd been pretty damn understanding about his crazy, Barbie doll looking ex-wife drugging me. So why the hell would he leave without saying anything?

I rounded the corner and left the manor in an angry huff. I found a very embarrassed Addy sitting outside one of the massive tents that surrounded the estate.

"You look pissed, Emma," she said warily.

"Are you done here? Or I don't know, do you need to fuck a few more guys before I can take you home?" I snapped. I regretted it, but I was trying not break down and become some sniveling little sissy who cried over a little spilled…blood. It was a vicious cycle, one that happened whenever I cried when I got pissed, and I hated it.

"Emma, what the hell is wrong with you?" Addy demanded as she rushed to keep up with me.

"I slept with Jaeden," I snapped as I spun to face her and then turned and started forward again, leaving her wide eyed with her mouth hanging open.

"You hussy!" She squealed happily and I swear she skipped a little. "Are you okay, Emma? It's a big step… you little slut!"

"*Me?* I heard you were being passed around! What the fuck is wrong with you! Why the hell would you leave the shelter to be changed?"

"I didn't come here to be a vampire, I came to ask them questions about them being vampires, and yeah, I'm pretty sure I was plastered and then shit happened and well, I'm pretty sure I had three and none making deposits in the same—"

"Eww, too much info!" I plugged my ears as I beat feet through the woods as if I was running a marathon. We made it to the little clearing where the jagged rocks were, when I smelled the first sign of smoke. My heart dropped to my feet as I ignored Addy's questioning look and took off in the direction of the shelter.

"No," I screamed as I ran the rest of the way with what little strength I had from not sleeping. Adrenaline kicked in as I stopped cold in front of the shelter. Bodies were charred and littered around the front of it, burned beyond recognition.

"Grayson!" I screamed as loud as my voice would go, pain lanced through me with the realization that I'd been screwing a vampire while the shelter had been under attack. "Grayson! Answer me!"

"Oh my God. Who would have done this?" Addy asked as her eyes searched the charred walls of the entry to the shelter.

"Grayson!" I shouted as I stumbled into the charred opening of the shelter, but beyond that point it wasn't

Darkest Before Dawn

burnt. It was spattered in blood, and Grayson was there, sitting beside Maggie. "Grayson, oh my God," I said as I fell to my knees beside him and pulled him into my arms.

"Where were you?" he accused, tears tracked down his cheeks. "You talk all this shit about protecting us but where the hell were you when we needed you!? Emma, where the hell were you! You left us!"

"I need to get Maggie to the medical center. Help me, Grayson," I pleaded as I swiftly turned his rage against me into help. I deserved it, I got it. I'd fucked up, big time. "Who did this?"

"I don't know, I didn't see. Maggie hid me, and locked me in your bedroom. I just heard the screams, oh, Emma, the screams were so bad. They were looking for us I think. Maybe Dad is alive? Maybe he sent them. Maybe it went bad, and he thought they were good guys."

"Grayson, dad wouldn't send anyone who would attack us to find us," I assured him. It didn't bode well for us either way. "They take anything? Food, supplies, weapons...anything like that?"

"I don't know, I just heard them."

"Okay, help me get Maggie up, Addy, check for pulses on those people outside. Try to get everyone organized—those who are wounded worst, in for treatment first. I'll do what I can."

Amelia Hutchins

I did a surface test on Maggie, which included running my hands over her looking for any blood wounds, or anything protruding. She had blood leaking from her chest, and a lot of it. Grayson brought the gurney I'd stolen from the med center, and together we hefted Maggie up and on to it.

When we got her to the sterile room, I stripped out of my clothes and into the scrubs before I washed and put on gloves and a surgical mask. It wouldn't be perfectly sterile, but I had some pretty good antibiotics I'd taken from the CDC when they'd deserted their post. I put on the surgical headset, and flipped on the light before working to intubate her after I discovered she'd stopped breathing.

I had been finishing my training to be a surgical tech so I knew I was in way over my head. However, I was Maggie's only chance right now and I was working against the clock, since I didn't have a time-line and I was pretty sure the Golden Hour was well over by now. I sealed the room with the pedal and set to work the moment I got her hooked up to the machines to read her vitals.

I removed her clothes, and then quickly rewashed and gloved my hands. I couldn't allow her to die, even if it meant fighting God for her soul. I'd asked her to protect my brother and she'd ended up hurt because I'd given in to temptation.

I was startled when Lachlan pounded on the door. His eyes were filled with worry, but I spared him only a

Darkest Before Dawn

quick glance before getting to work. The red light was on outside the door, so hopefully he could figure out that this was a sterile room.

He was male, so it was possible he wouldn't.

I cut into her side and searched for the wound, only I couldn't find anything. I was so busy in the task at hand that I didn't hear Lachlan when he entered or when he stepped on the suction tube pedal and started assisting. I looked up at him and almost moaned with relief when it became apparent that he knew what he was doing. He was scrubbed, gloved, and gowned just like I was.

"I don't really know what I'm doing," I admitted as I continued to search for a visual on the bleed.

"I do, ye will need tae assist me, Lass."

"So, you could have helped your brother with that trap on your own?" I asked sourly.

"Aye, I wanted tae see if ye would, or if ye would leave him tae die. I also wanted to ken what ye were aboot in the house," he said and cracked a little grin behind the mask which dimmed as he took in the damage of Maggie's body.

We worked for hours, neither one of talking more than was needed. He didn't ask what happened and I didn't ask where the hell he'd been. I couldn't because he'd flip it back on me and I wasn't ready to admit what I'd been doing while my people were being slaughtered.

Maggie was stable when we placed her in in the nearby recovery room and started on the next person, and then the next. It felt like days before Addy finally told us that no one else had made it long enough to need surgery. The shelter still had residents, but all had been wounded, had fled, or had been hidden on the other levels and weren't discovered by our attackers.

No supplies had been taken, nor had they come for our things. Had they come for me and my brother? I felt sick at the senseless acts, because I couldn't think of anyone who'd want us dead, but there were always people trying to take what others had by force, and the possibility of the attackers being sent by my dad were close to zero.

"Lass, what the hell happened?" Lachlan asked as Liam fell in step beside him.

"I don't know. I wasn't here," I croaked as tears choked my words.

"Where were ye?" he asked gently, but I could hear it in his voice that he already knew.

"I fucked up, okay? I'm human unlike everyone else here!" Tears slid from my eyes as I turned around only to find Jaeden standing in the doorway. "Close the doors," I snapped and took off to wash the blood from my face and body.

"Emma?" he called as he got closer.

"Go back to your wife! Leave me alone, Jaeden.

Darkest Before Dawn

Just get the hell out of here. I can't deal with you and this right now," I growled angrily as yet another body was brought inside to be prepared for burial. They'd been burned with gas, which meant we could actually bury our own for once. I couldn't handle him and do what needed to be done at the same time. I felt like two different people, or as if I had to be in order to be around him.

There was me with him, where I was careless and a little wild. Then there was me when I was here, and I had to be in full control, I had to lead. I didn't know how to be both at the same time, and even if I didn't believe his murderous, plotting whore of a wife, he'd left me without so much as a goodbye, and well, then there was the guilt I felt for being with him, instead of the people I was supposed to protect.

"What the fuck happened here?" Jaeden asked me, and then Lachlan when I refused to answer him.

"I dinnae smell any other vamps, or wolves. This was human or something *else*," Lachlan said as I left them to discuss it without me.

"No human could have done this," I heard Jaeden hiss at Lachlan as I retreated.

No, but whatever kind of monster *I* was, could have done this. Easily. From the timeline where Lachlan and his men had left, and from what Grayson and the other residents had told me, it had taken seconds to do this much damage in the attack.

We were getting caught up in an all-out war with rogue werewolves, but now I had to face the fact that I was going to have to find the person who had done this and kill them. I felt a bone deep coldness inside of me that would never go away. I'd done this. My careless, selfish actions had brought this upon us. Whoever it was had come to do harm, and had killed people who trusted me. Whatever the fuck they were, I wanted nothing from dirt bags that would harm innocent people.

Chapter Twenty-Four.

I'd slipped away to the shower room to get away from the males and the stench of the day. My mind was a mess of confusion and my heart felt as if it was bleeding. We'd been attacked, and I'd been in his arms for it. I couldn't have stopped it from happening, but I could have given them a fight. Grayson told me it happened in the early morning hours, which meant the door had to have been opened by someone inside.

They shouldn't have gotten through the doors, period. After I showered and changed into a fresh set of scrubs, I sat on one of the shower benches and pulled my legs to my chest as I mulled through the different scenarios. The thought that someone inside had allowed this to happen haunted me. Maggie was obviously off the list, and Lachlan and most of his men hadn't been present for the attack. Those wolves he had left behind to protect the shelter had been wounded in the defense of it. The number of people on the shelter's roster made it difficult to narrow down who had betrayed us.

I kept thinking over the concept map my father had in his room, and the lines which pointed to various people from around town. Others he'd suspected enough to question their motives, and their interactions with my mother. Some of those people had been in the shelter, and they'd made it through the attack without so much as even a scratch.

I didn't need to know who had attacked us; it was becoming obvious to me. Whoever had done this came looking for something specific. Could it have been Grayson and I? That created a shit storm of questions. No one would want us unless we served a purpose. My mother had chosen our fathers specifically for their DNA and what part it was supposed to play in her fucked up scheme. I had a bad feeling about her and that entire situation, but this? Attacking women and children, which the shelter was full of? That was something I could never get past. This was unimaginable.

We had several dead, and none had been the girls I'd trained, but they'd been wounded and unable to assist the others to safety. Three wolves had also been wounded, which told me it had to be someone with knowledge of the supernatural since they'd been shot with silver nitrate. Lachlan had been quick to see it and show me how to heal them in case it ever happened again when he wasn't here. He'd proven useful, and skilled in the sterile room. He obviously had medical training, and I would almost bet he'd earned his doctorate at some point in his long years.

I felt Jaeden's presence, and could sense his anger.

Darkest Before Dawn

If it was directed at me, I couldn't have cared less. I was hollow, and cold inside. My only thought was for the innocent lives that had been lost. I was blaming myself, and with good reason. I'd lost sight of what was important, and had become some brainless hussy who could think of little else, but him.

"This wasn't your fault, and you can't shoulder the blame," he said as he sat beside me. He had left a small gap between us. Probably for the best. "You left before I could return this morning."

"Your wife sent me home, right after you'd finished using me. She was even generous enough to give me something to wear before she told me to get out of her bedroom. You should really put a muzzle on that bitch." Ouch, I sounded as cold as I felt.

"Is that what you think? That I used you, Emma?" his tone may have been soft, but I could hear the anger and possibly some hurt in it.

"Just like all the others she bragged about you two doing this to," I said through clenched teeth. "Go away, Jaeden."

"Not like this. Not when you believe that load of shit, and certainly not with you here shouldering the blame for this attack. You're planning to hunt them down, but if they could do this, they had to have the numbers and cunning to do it. Let us help you."

"You've helped me enough," I said bitterly.

"So we're going to play it like that? You regret staying with me last night," he said with a cold smile.

I shoved my hair away from my face and leveled him with a look of cold disdain. "You've had your fun. Run back to Barbie, because I'm done playing around. I have one job to do and that's this shelter. I shouldn't have been with you, and I knew better. I don't belong in your world any more than you belong in mine."

"If that's what you want, Emma, fine; you can think like that tonight, but not forever." He leaned close and his husky voice in my ear sent sparks to other parts of my body, even after everything that had happened. "I'm not done with you though. I've tasted your desire and I'm not finished with you by a long shot. I understand the need to grieve, but you are too strong and stubborn; you don't need to do the tough stuff alone," he said reasonably.

"So what? You'll just take it?" I snapped as I held back the tears of hopelessness I felt. He pulled slightly away to stare at me with hurt and angry eyes.

"You think so little of me that you think I'd take you with force? If two people meet and share a connection as we do, it changes us whether we want it or not. What we did last night wasn't even the tip of the iceberg. You changed me, deeply and irrevocably. I get that right now you're blaming yourself for being with me instead of where you were needed, but what the fuck could you have done? Addy told me what your brother said, and it sounds to me like they were here for something which

Darkest Before Dawn

they didn't find. *Someone* they didn't find. You're not safe here, and I can protect you. The thing is, Emma, you must make a choice—to take a chance and trust me, or you could end up getting everyone you're trying to protect killed."

"It's not that simple!" I cried.

"It is!" he shouted, getting to his feet. "I've lived for over a thousand years, and I've watched people make stupid decisions; let me help you. Let me protect you from whatever is trying to find you because I promise you, they know what they are doing, and this wasn't just someone wanting what you have. This was personal. They have someone inside of this shelter, someone helping them to get to you. The people who were burnt? Your enemy knew that harming them would hurt you. That it would make you careless, and reckless to avenge them. Don't be stupid. Life doesn't always give you second chances, so take the first one. You were meant to die or be taken last night. Don't give them another shot at you."

"Get out," I said no longer able to hide the tears. "Get out!" I screamed through tears that choked me. I hated him in this moment. He was wrong; I could have made a difference. Not one single bullet had been fired in defense, because like him, I was the general in my army. If I'd been here, this would have ended differently.

We wouldn't have been so defenseless. I was pushing him away. I couldn't even look at him without seeing the dead I'd have to bury this evening. He turned and left me sitting on the bench, and I sobbed. I thought he'd gone, but he wrapped his arms around me and held me through the worst of it.

When I thought I could cry no more, he placed his hands on my face and I did the same to him. I felt the weird sensation of being weightless, as if my entire world had faded away, and maybe it had. Before I knew what happened, I was transported from the showers to the crusades. Or at least, I think it was the crusades, going off the armor they wore and the ancient scene around me.

I looked around, and wondered at just who I'd slipped into this time. Last time it had been the battered woman, and I'd felt her pain. I looked down at my hands and bent my fingers. Manly fingers were covered in blood. I didn't have long to wait to figure out who I was when Sven walked up and spoke in Jaeden's language and this time I could understand. It had to be part of the craziness I was experiencing.

He continued speaking as he pointed to a pile of dead, cataloguing losses and gains, while a woman was screaming at Bjorn while he took her by force from behind. I didn't feel sick as I should have; instead I felt pride consume me as I walked over to join in the debauchery.

The woman was terrified, but eventually her frightened screams turned to pleasure as Bjorn gave her what she wasn't prepared for—his fangs. He drank deeply, and my own fangs responded. This was war, and in war there were spoils. Fucking King of England, this was not a war to recover the Holy Land for Christians; it was a sacking, plain and simple and to the victors go spoils.

"My turn," I announced and watched as Bjorn shifted to his side, pulling her around without stopping what he was doing. The only indication he'd heard me was from his short respite of feeding from her.

"She'll take us both," he growled and rocked his hips as she moaned with the movement. "Won't you?" She nodded at his words and I smiled coldly. I liked my women willing, but none had been as willing when we'd come to their shores at the beck and call of the king to claim their lands and loot their riches.

"What's your name?" I asked of her as Bjorn spread her open for me to see his victory.

"Elizabeth," she barely got out as I undid the tie of my trousers and pulled out my throbbing cock.

"I'm going to join my friend, do you mind if I fill you as well?" I asked, needing her to say yes. In all my years I'd never taken a woman who had told me no. Even war couldn't change that, and when she screamed yes, I parted her legs and thrust inside of her willing pussy.

Men lay dead around us, their lifeless eyes staring into oblivion as we claimed their women. I watched as Sven undid his trousers, and pulled out his cock, and pressed it against her lips. She took it, even as he raised her hand to bite into her succulent wrist and drain her.

"Do not empty her; she deserves to live after she's taken us all. Sven, if you wish, change her and place her in the ground," I growled as Bjorn and I continued to fuck her tight holes together. This was often how we decided who our camp followers would be. Bloodlust often took hold after this much blood was spilled, and the result would leave me hard for days if not satisfied.

"Agreed, this nice of an ass is well deserving of my vote," Bjorn said as he picked up his thrusting pace and Sven moaned in pleasure.

Seriously fucked up! I shook it off, but instead of being back in the shower as myself, I was still Jaeden and the people in the memory were dressed like something from a Renaissance Fair.

I watched as Astrid stood, watching my men, as they took willing partners wherever was convenient as was their custom. She turned and looked at me as I fought against one of the many men I was training. As her eyes sought me, I swung my sword with more vigor.

I hated that the pain was still there, even after all the time that had passed. I put her aside; renounced her, yet every time I caught sight of the woman, it was like rubbing an open wound with salt. Time may have lessened the desire I had for her, but the pain of her betrayals still stung. I swung again, only to catch sight of her naked flesh as she started to remove her gown.

I turned and had to keep my emotions in check, one

Darkest Before Dawn

slip and she would think I still struggled against the desire I had once felt for her. There was no way I would touch that viper now. It was bad enough to know what she had done; now, I was witness to her whoring ways. She got more cock than any of the camp followers and made sure I knew each time she accepted a new lover betwixt her legs.

Her creamy breasts became fully exposed and I clenched my fist with the need to pinch her nipples, hurt them. I have become dark with my needs, hating to be touched, or touching others. Fucking is one thing, but I no longer accept the same whore into my bed twice. I use them, and discard them quickly. Feelings are nothing more than a weakness, as I learned with Astrid.

I wanted our child, an heir to raise and love, and she'd killed him. He had been in her way of being fucked by every cock that held any value back when we were human. I stepped closer, and then reminded myself that I made her immortal, and I made that choice. She is my reminder as to why I should never trust, why I should hold myself back and take my time assessing a situation from all angles and why I have to hold my anger in check and not do anything rash. I renounced her in a fit of rage and Shamus saved her life by claiming her; redirecting the bond I had tried to sever. After what she pulled with the wolves, I would have killed her—no—should have been allowed to kill her. Now she runs amok and I have no say. Instead of reining her in, Shamus seems to find her lunacy amusing.

I can already feel my cock growing with the need

to carnally punish her. She knows it. She can read me easily as she pushes the skirt from her hips and moves toward me. I shake my head, warning her that I want nothing to do with her. She smiled calculatingly. Her direction changed and she walked to one of her many lovers, one of Shamus's captains. Her long nails dug into his shoulders as she pushed him to his knees and then gripped his hair. She shoved his face between her legs, and he obeyed with enthusiasm as her servant watched them.

Sick fuck would do anything to fuck her, but he lacks the tools to get the job done. I turned and left the bitch with her lover, and made my way to the camp followers. It will take more than one whore to get me off tonight.

I wanted to scream at what I was being forced to watch. It was sick! It was demented and I was jealous of some camp whore who he was going to use, and I was him! I blinked and in that time, I was transported again.

I shook my head as the landscape changed and I looked around a bloodied battlefield and then down at what was impaled on my blade.

A child of no more than ten winters lay bleeding, with a gaping wound in his chest.

"Is it not enough to kill the men, but now he would have us slaughtering children?" I demanded as I turned to Shamus as he ran is sword through the boy's protector. Smoke poured out of the destroyed manor nearby. In this memory, Shamus was dressed like a

Darkest Before Dawn

knight from the Middle Ages. It came to my mind that the dead were Normans that had been systematically invading England. *I should have been standing with the king. Harald Hardrada, supporting his conquest of the north; however, our sire was Anglo-Saxon so we were here in the south, carrying out his will.*

"Dead sons never seek revenge, Jaeden."

"He was no more than a lad, one who wouldn't even remember us being here when he grew to be a man," I argue.

"It's been nigh over a hundred years since you lost your son, and yet you still blame Astrid for killing your seed. You hunted down the midwife responsible for assisting her, and removed her head. Your anger with her had nothing to do with the vow of chastity you'd taken, but everything to do with what she'd done to gain the lovers. What do you think that noble's son would do to the monsters that removed his father from his throne when he becomes a man? By killing this child, you've prevented him from hunting us. Do not blame me for this choice, for I, like you, follow orders. We were ordered to kill his bloodline, and so we have."

"You think he'd come after us? He is naught but a child!" I growled angrily.

"A child who would seek us out. Get it together and let it go! You would also be wise to release your dispute with Astrid. I have taken that traitorous bitch wife of yours to stop the issue you have had with her; she's in

my protection for now."

"I released her for a reason," I snapped.

"Oh aye, you were a hot-headed neophyte yourself who rashly released her. Not realizing she could run to our enemies. You would have regretted killing her, maybe not right away, but you are not as cold as you think. What she has done is unforgivable my friend, but if you had killed her, and you would have, you would have lost that last little shred of your humanity, and we need it."

"What she did to me, to our child, what she continues to do to torment me— deserves to be taken from her flesh every day for the rest of her miserable existence."

I blinked at Jaeden and the shower room came back into view, and then I pulled further away from him. "Get out and don't come back, Jaeden. I don't have time to deal with you and your crazy ex-wife today. I have to bury my people, which, to me, is a lot more important," I whispered through the pain. I was pushing him away and we both knew it.

"I'm sorry that she drugged and deceived you but I'm not sorry that I fucked you. She's been warned from touching you again. Shamus has taken her with him south," he ran his fingers through his tousled hair. "I'm sorry you saw that, but I didn't show you those memories, not voluntarily, I would never have wanted you to experience that. You can't be completely human if you are able to do that, so be careful of who you touch.

Darkest Before Dawn

I'm putting Cayla on watch whether you want it or not. She's a little out there, but she's good in a fight. I know you don't want me right now, and I'll give you space. But I told you, Emma, that this thing between us would be unlike anything you've ever known. I want you, and that didn't go away just because I fucked you. You'll get your time to think, but I have found that patience isn't something I have very much of with you."

I watched him as he walked out of the shower room, and his footsteps faded down the hall. I tried for hours to push him from my mind, but even as I stood in the cemetery with wolves guarding us as night descended, I thought of nothing but him. I thought of everything I'd seen in those memories, and wondered why I had been shown them. It felt as if I'd been given that vision for a reason, but it was beyond my grasp to know exactly why. They could have been moments he felt remorse over, but who was I to say to say if he had?

I had to consider the fact that he wasn't human, which was insane. He told me he wasn't like that anymore, but could I believe him? Nothing made sense, and everything was wrong. I headed to my room in a numb state, but he was there, sitting on the floor against my bed, with no shirt on.

"I'm not leaving this room until you understand a few things. One, I'm very old and I've done a lot of shit that was bad. I never said I was a good person. Not once. I do what's needed and often. Many of those memories were moments where I was caught up in bloodlust, and while I can't say it didn't happen again and often, I can tell you it hasn't happened in more than a century. I'm sorry about the people who died here. The innocent dying is something I don't relish. I get that you probably don't want me here, but I'm not leaving until I know you're all right."

I wasn't sure how much I could trust him right now. I got that he was trying to help me, but seeing him like that had been a wake-up call. He wasn't human and vampires were not romantic; they could kill you! Like freaking dead style, really dead, you get my meaning.

"I can't do this with you, not today. Not right now, after everything that's happened."

"Fine, but this thing between us isn't finished. As I said, I'm not done making you scream for me, and the thing between me and Astrid? She killed that a long time ago."

"Jaeden, right now I only need to be held, not fucked. I lost friends today, ones who depended on me to keep my head, and protect them. You're a distraction I just can't afford."

"Emma, I'll hold you. Come," he said as he moved over and held his hand out to me. I crumpled against his wide chest and let the tears loose that I'd been trying so hard to hold at bay, and even though he remained silent, his arms and hands gave comfort and his silent support.

The moment my eyes closed, I had nightmares about his past life, and in the middle of the night, I had to ask him to leave. It was too much, too soon. He wasn't free of evil doings and right now, I needed time to think of what I'd seen, and how to get past seeing it.

He had done some pretty horrible things, and yet he hadn't done anything that wasn't understandable or forgivable considering what he had seen and experienced in his life. I didn't know the context of why or how he'd been doing those things in the memories, only that he had. I needed to consider my next step, and concentrate on securing the shelter and protecting the people in it.

I wasn't me when I was around him, and right now, I needed to be the prepper girl everyone made fun of. She was tough, and never wavered from responsibility. I had to be that girl again. That meant I was going to have to let Jaeden go.

Chapter
Twenty-Five

Days turned to weeks and then an entire month had gone by in the search for who had betrayed us. Time was never ending, and every day I thought of Jaeden. It didn't help that he would show up once a day and leave a present for me, along with a card that had the exact number of hours and minutes of how long we'd been apart written on it. I missed him terribly and the ache was pulling and nagging at me to go to him, despite what my rational mind told me. I was still working through it as best as I could, and while I may have needed him, the time apart was getting me back to what was important.

I'd become accustomed to Lachlan being beside me in everything I did. It was as if he'd become my strength. Although I was itching to ask him every silly werewolf and vampire question inspired by books and movies that spun around in my fertile imagination, I held back for now and observed. I wasn't sure if it was because I was afraid of offending him, or if I was secretly afraid of the truth. Eventually I would have

Darkest Before Dawn

to ask. As it was, we had five people who I no longer trusted, but we couldn't just come right out and accuse them, since they'd just deny it. Torture wasn't an option either, since that would create panic—or worse—with the remaining occupants of the shelter.

We'd started watching them, but it hadn't gone unnoticed. Time would tell who'd betrayed us, but we were up against both it, and winter. I stopped going out for supplies, and I'd started depending on others to pull their weight, and the residents had rallied beautifully, pulling in a steady stream of food that we would need despite the temperatures dropping. I felt bad as the thought of not having to feed the few who had died, slipped to the back of my mind.

"Addy, have you seen Grayson? I can't find him and he's not in his room," I asked as I passed her in the hall. She'd been hanging out with Liam, who she seemed to have a thing for again. Or he had come sniffing back.

"He was with Cat and Sarah about an hour ago," she said before giving her full attention to Liam who was whispering in her ear.

I left them to make a list of things we'd need to add to our winter stores, when things went really bad.

I saw the door to my father's room had been opened a sliver, and light coming through it. I approached carefully and pushed it open. The moment I did, my heart dropped, and I was trembling. Pictures had been removed from the wall, and across my own picture in red marker was the word *liar* in Grayson's handwriting. "No," I whispered as I turned to the bed where the tapes were scattered on the blanket along with the recorder.

I left the room in a huff only to plow right into Lachlan who placed his hands on my shoulders to steady me. "What's wrong, Lass?"

"Grayson, help me find Grayson!" I shouted as everyone around us stopped what they'd been doing and looked at me.

"He left, Emma," Cat said quietly. "He and Jimmy left a little while ago. They wanted to see if there were any good comic books left in town."

"You just let him walk out!" I shouted with enough anger to make poor Cat cringe. "He's only a child; did you miss the memo where we were fucking attacked?"

"Emma, that isnae helping," Lachlan said as he placed a calming hand on my shoulder.

I felt sick. Jimmy had been on our top five list, and I'd been leaning towards him as the guilty party. "Lachlan, could you send your men out to track him but tell them to keep their distance? The rest of you, suit up. Lachlan?" I asked after he'd shouted out orders and his men had left to track Grayson's scent.

"Emma?" his voice was a rough growl as he sniffed Grayson's sweatshirt to get his scent.

"Have you ever heard of the Sentinels?"

Darkest Before Dawn

His eyes narrowed on me. "What kind?"

I blinked, and stammered. "Uh, I don't know. The name came up and I didn't know that there were different kinds. I sorta assumed that they were like you guys."

He shook his head thoughtfully. "Nae, should I have?"

"I guess not," I said as I pulled on my gear and slipped the knives and guns in the waiting pouches and holsters. "I'm going for Jaeden, he can cover more ground than we can."

"Ye sure he wants to see ye? Ye did ask him tae leave and ye never once responded tae him, lass."

"I know, but I at least have to try. It's Grayson. I'd do anything for him." Jaeden might be upset, but he knew why I was holding back and he *had* been here every day. I hoped that was worth something.

I rode the Ducati to the property line of the estate and covered the rest of the ground on foot. I ignored the surprised looks from the vampires as I made a beeline for Jaeden who was near the front of the manor with several other vampires including Shamus and Raphael. They were lounging on the benches near the entry and a female was submissively at Jaeden's knees. She wasn't touching him, but I could tell he was doing his best to ignore her presence. Astrid was standing a few feet away from them, watching him closely.

I was almost to him when she saw me and cut off my path. "Oh I don't think so," she sneered.

"Get out of my way," I said with urgency.

"He doesn't want you, I told you, it was a game we play and he has been very *aggressive* with me since he finished with you," she taunted suggestively.

It had been only a month since I'd been in his bed, but then again, he was a hot-blooded male and while I considered it a possibility, if he had gone back to her, then fuck him. Somehow seeing some of his memories, I seriously doubted he'd gone back to that well. I met his eyes and watched as Shamus stood up to intervene but Jaeden stopped him.

"You know what Barbie? Screw off. I don't care if you're together. I just need his help to find my brother," I growled with meaning, knowing he'd hear me.

Shamus smiled wickedly at Jaeden and took a few steps towards us. Astrid placed her hand on my shoulder and dug her perfectly manicured fingernails into my exposed flesh and I yelped, right before I whirled around and punched her, sending her flying across the wide expanse of lawn. I looked down at my hand and then back up to where she was sprawled with her ass in the air and struggled for a moment to sit up.

Jaeden got to his feet, ignoring Astrid's angry huff of breath as he did so; his eyes were hard on her as he approached us. Shamus looked surprised at the outcome of the scuffle, but Jaeden looked as if he'd known how it

Darkest Before Dawn

would end before it began. He was walking towards me when she stood up to try again.

"Enough, Astrid, go to your master. You should stop telling lies to poor Emma."

"Honestly, Jaeden, just fuck them both. They're willing to fight over your cock, why not use it in bed?" Raphael said smoothly, as if this was normal behavior.

Had no one else noticed that I'd just hurled a vampire across the lawn? No, just me? She moved with inhuman speed, but it was as if I predicted it, and it seemed as if it all happened in slow motion. I watched as she approached me, her body contorted as if she was running towards me, but again, in slow motion. The moment she reached me, I side stepped and she flew full tilt into a pile of debris that had been behind me.

The entire yard exploded back into real time as she screeched her anger and hatred at me. I blinked to where she stood back up and moved to attack again, but Shamus blocked her way. "Did you see that?" I asked, confused at how I'd managed to best her. This was like the night with the rogue wolves all over again.

"See what, Emma?" Jaeden asked, narrowing his eyes at me. "You tossing Astrid on her ass? Yes, we saw it."

"No. The whole world just slowed to a halt?" Hadn't it?

"No it didn't," he said as tried to draw me away from

Shamus and Astrid. He was looking way too sexy for his own good. He wore a leather jacket with a V-neck shirt beneath it. His pants were held up with a studded belt that matched his leather boots. He looked as if he'd been through hell since I'd last seen him. "What happened to your brother?" he asked carefully.

"I need help," I pleaded, not giving a crap who thought I was pathetic; this was my brother who I'd raised. "He's in danger."

"Why me, why don't you just ask your wolf?" he asked coldly. His eyes remained hard, but for a brief second, I caught sight of pain in their blue-green depths.

"You know what? Lachlan was right. I'll find him without your help. You can go right to hell, Jaeden," I said as I gave him my back only to come face to face with Shamus. "I'm leaving."

"Are you? I'm curious about you, and very willing to help you for a price," Shamus said with a light Irish accent. "I'd like to know more about you, sweet Emma."

"I'm not interested at this time," I said politely. This guy scared the shit out of me, and I didn't want to piss him off or offend him.

"At this time?" he asked as his eerie purple eyes watched me.

"I'm leaving," I said as I looked over my shoulder to find a very angry Jaeden glaring at me.

Darkest Before Dawn

I made it to my bike before he grabbed my arm and spun me around. "Why did you come here when you have an entire pack of wolves at your beck and call?" he growled.

I ripped my arm from his hold. "Go back to your life; I can find him alone," I snapped with enough anger to turn him to ash. I'd just wasted my time when I could have been searching for Grayson. The cool crisp air was doing little to cool my temper.

"I'm not with her, nor will I ever be again. You can't walk into my camp and demand I help you after a month of you acting like what we did didn't happen. I have been brutally honest about who and what I am. I've been to your shelter once a day since you threw me out; did the wolf tell you that?"

"I needed time, Jaeden, I told you that. I didn't come here for you. I came here for help. You told me to let you help and I'm asking you for it now. He's my brother and he's with someone who allowed people inside the shelter to kill them. You told me to trust you, so here I am, and what do you do? You let your friggin' Barbie doll attack me. That doesn't make me want to trust you. I knew you came each day, but if you can't handle me taking a little time to come to grips with all of this and get my priorities straight, then maybe it's for the best we just part ways."

"You didn't even acknowledge I was there. All I got was Lachlan telling me to get lost with your scent all over him. So tell me, Emma, just how close did you and

Lachlan become in the last month while you pretended I didn't exist, because according to him, you guys were pretty fucking close."

"I've been with one man in my entire life if that's what you're asking, Vampire. It was you, in case I was so forgettable."

"I've thought of nothing else." He surprised me by saying that with a delicious grin on his lips. "I was made to believe you'd gone to him and accepted him in my place."

"Uh, because I'm such an easy catch, right? Or because I'm just so fucking easy, Jaeden?"

He laughed but his eyes drank me in as if I was the most exquisite thing he'd ever seen before. "I should've known you wouldn't choose a dog over me. Not after the way you screamed my name."

"I don't have time for this, Jaeden. I have to find my brother," I said as I shifted the bike and kicked the stand up. "You can either help me because you want to, or don't. Personally I don't give a shit because you already know I'd give you anything for him."

"I was pissed at the idea of you and the wolf, and before you accuse me of it, I knew you'd win against Astrid. You have something inside of you that's scratching its way to the surface. You're as dark as me, and it's fucking sexy as hell, probably because you can't even see it yet."

"Jaeden, I need to find my brother and then you can be sexy and all dark and shit. First things first; focus."

"Promise?" he asked.

"One night, that's all I'm going to promise at this time and that's only if we find him, because nothing in this world is more important than finding him."

"Then let's go find your brother. Cayla has him in her sights at the clearing over at Priest River," he said as he pulled the bike out of my grasp and straddled it as if he owned it.

"Cayla?" I asked, confused as I climbed on the bike behind him and wrapped my arms around his waist.

"She's been watching the shelter all month, just like I said she would. She told me he'd left, and who he'd left with, but I thought nothing of it. She decided to follow them when she thought something was off about one of them, other than how bad he smelled."

Chapter Twenty-Six

It felt right to be with him. I felt the flicker of my heart as I snuggled against his back. We'd just hit the bridge when he pulled the bike to the side of the road and parked it. We climbed off, and I looked around and watched as Lachlan and his pack walked up shirtless, and with purpose.

"They're just beyond the bridge," Lachlan said as he met us. "There is also a vampire tracking them."

"Cayla was watching the shelter when they left. She thought it seemed off that they'd be out in only a pair, since most left in large groups, so she followed them to the clearing," Jaeden offered.

"The people there are holding him and another man, but it's unclear what they want," Lachlan continued. "We didnae dare breach the clearing and chance them panicking while they had the boy."

Darkest Before Dawn

Several different visions rapidly flashed before my eyes. It was as if my mind was showing me photographs of an event. Jimmy was there, along with quite a few men who seemed to be holding Grayson prisoner. My mother was also there and she looked very good for a dead person, but there was another face I recognized and I felt as if my heart was being crushed when I saw it.

"Me," I said woodenly as it sunk in. I was what they wanted, because if my mother hadn't been insane, I was her newest Knight. The first time I'd listened to the recording it hadn't made sense. She talked about Sentinels like they were pieces of a board game, one they'd been trying to figure out how to cheat on. "They're here for me."

"You can't know that, Emma," Jaeden said as he stepped protectively towards me.

"Is there a woman with the same color hair as mine over there?" I asked Lachlan.

"Aye, there is."

"Emma," Addy called softly as she walked up beside Liam.

"Why are you here?" I asked with a feeling in the pit of my belly that said we had too many pieces on our side. "Go back to the shelter. You're the only one I trust to keep it safe."

"I couldn't, not after I listened to one of those

tapes. I'm so sorry she did this, and the pain she put you through! I couldn't let you do this without me. You know I use humor as a barrier, but I love you. I couldn't let you do this without you knowing it. It's me and you, always me and you, bitch."

"What tapes?" Lachlan and Jaeden both asked together.

"My mother's tapes, the ones she made right before she faked her own death," I admitted. "They're the reason why Grayson left the protection of the shelter with Jimmy," I swallowed the anger. As an afterthought, I smiled at Addy. "I love you too, hooker."

"I thought your mother was dead," Jaeden said as Lachlan nodded his agreement.

"Yeah, me too," I said as I took in the looks of uncertainty and regret as they put it all together. I'd had time to cope with my mother being a murderous bitch, maybe not a long time, but enough to not want them to look at me like this. "Don't do that; I'm sure you all had a fucked up family at one time. Turns out, mine happens to be a lot more fucked up than I thought."

They smiled as if I'd hit it on the head with my mental hammer. I was about to say more when voices erupted inside my head. My hands rose to my temples as I listened to them.

"So, what's the plan?" Jaeden asked, but I ignored him.

Darkest Before Dawn

"She's coming, soon. Right now she's standing with a vamp and a few mutts."

"And the vampire watching us now, when do we kill her?"

"Soon; make no commotion that will spook Emma, we need her."

"We'll have her Trina, she belongs to us."

"Can she hear us?"

"No."

"Not yet, but she will once we've ended her mortal existence."

"What are they saying?"

"Emma just asked them if they had a plan."

"Emma?" Jaeden asked and my eyes lifted to his. "You okay?"

"Did she hear us? Why's she spooked?"

"Sorry, I'm just worried about Grayson," I said, hoping it led the strangers who obviously could hear us, astray. "What's your plan?" Because it sure in the hell wouldn't be the plan I went with now.

"Justin, come away from them. The vampire will sense you if you get too close."

"No! I want to know his plan. It will give us an advantage."

"Very well, but the moment you have it, pull away from them."

There were three other people who I could hear, but I couldn't give it away. They'd believed we were unaware that they could hear us, but I had a plan. I listened absently as Jaeden and Lachlan quickly sketched out a plan, and wasn't surprised when Jaeden's men and Shamus showed up.

"Shamus," Jaeden said carefully.

"Can it; I love a good fight, you know that," Shamus said before his eyes flickered to mine.

I wondered what had happened to make their friendship so rocky, but I had inkling she was busty, blonde, and bitchy. Shamus was her master, as Jaeden had called him, and she hadn't seemed happy at all about it. I was about to speak when I was given something I couldn't quite understand. A vision of my future, and it was pretty damn grim.

"Emma?" Lachlan said narrowing his eyes at me.

"Pull back; that's a direct order, Justin."

I could see other people's past memories could I now see the future? They called Justin, back, whoever he was. I still didn't trust that they couldn't hear us. The voices were crystal clear, and sounded close. If they

Darkest Before Dawn

could hear us, they already knew what our people had just planned. Grayson's life was at stake. I wondered if they were like me, with the voices in my head; I'd have to come up with my own plan. I reviewed each scenario I'd seen in the vision and everything I had heard and made a decision.

I walked up to Jaeden and Lachlan both and touched their cheeks with my hand. I pushed every ounce of willpower I had into them, and prayed it worked. I watched their eyes turn from surprise, to wonder as they watched what I had just seen. It was working! Shamus watched us until he stepped forward with narrowed eyes and reached out to touch my face.

His eyes narrowed and then grew wide with excitement. "Well I'll be, a fecking unicorn," he whispered as he smiled, lost in the vision I was giving them.

There were three scenarios in the vision, none of which had gone the way I wanted them to. I included the part where they'd been discussing the plan, and it being overheard, but that wasn't the disturbing part. The disturbing part was the choices I made in each scenario.

When they'd finished watching it, I held my hands out for everyone else to watch it as well. They now knew we were being watched, and they knew what I would do. Jaeden had been given the warning for Cayla, who popped out of the brush and walked towards us. She had long blonde hair with vibrant pink streaks pulled into a ponytail, and pink Converse high-tops. Not exactly

Amelia Hutchins

what I would call covert, but she had managed to be undetected by my people and the wolves for over a month. A thin waif of a teenage boy with dark shaggy hair and pale skin followed close behind her.

"Why did you call me back?" she asked and looked right at me. Her eyes smiled and she held out her hand to mine. "I'm Cayla, your stalker. Nice to finally meet you; this is Nery, my best friend and also your stalker."

"It's nice to meet you," I said as I held out my hand and grasped hers tightly. Her eyes narrowed and Nery touched my skin with ice cold-fingers that made me hesitate and the vision wavered. She'd seen enough of it to know we were being watched.

"Emma, I don't want you to do this," Jaeden warned.

"I have to," I said as I turned to find Addy who'd also watched the vision with tears in her eyes.

"You don't have to do this, Emma, please," she sniffled as Liam held her to him.

"I have to do this; I love you, Addy, and this isn't goodbye. It's only the beginning for me. When Grayson makes it this far, you take him home and protect him. Promise me," I whispered through unshed tears.

"No more," I said as the chatter started back up. I turned to Jaeden and smiled. "Rain check on that thing we discussed?"

He glared, because well let's face it, my plan sucked.

Okay, it only sucked if it didn't work. As in, if it didn't work, I wouldn't be coming back, and that sucked hard and blew at the same time. Worse—the option I had chosen was the best chance of the three scenarios and we all knew it.

I turned to move in the direction of my conniving mother, but strong arms pulled me back and then Jaeden's lips found mine. His kiss wasn't a goodbye, it was toe curling and beautiful. "This isn't goodbye, Emma," he whispered as he pulled away and leaned his forehead against mine as we both caught our breath. I smiled weakly at him and stepped away from his arms.

"I'll miss you all, take care," I said because shit was getting deep with Addy and she'd begun crying hysterically. Liam pulled her into his arms as I retrieved the crossbow from its harness on the bike. I walked across the bridge without looking back.

I was going to save Grayson.

I wasn't going to see any of them ever again if this shit didn't work.

Chapter Twenty-Seven

I walked into the clearing with as much as confidence as I could muster. There were about eight men in the clearing with my mom; they allowed me in and closed ranks around me. I knew more were hidden in the trees, but I didn't give any indication that I knew. All of them seemed to range in ages from twenty to thirty but none of them looked a day over that. My mother looked as she had the last time I'd seen her; the only person who looked aged was my dad.

He was battered and bruised as if they'd beaten him.

"Emma," she said.

"Grayson, are you okay?" I blatantly ignored her.

This had to happen exactly as I'd seen it.

"You're nothing but a liar; Mom didn't die," he sneered.

Darkest Before Dawn

"Yes, she did. For us she did, Grayson. She didn't raise you and she damn sure wasn't the one there when you were sick or when you got hurt. I was, you know that. I know you know that. Deep down, you know who was there for you; look what she's done to Dad. Mom's the liar here; she played us all." I looked at her coldly.

"You think you raised him? I've watched you this entire time, Emmalyn. I've known every step you've ever made. Imagine my surprise to find out my daughter who I bred to become a warrior is nothing more than a vampire's whore," she sneered.

"Well imagine my disappointment when I discovered my mother was nothing more than a deceitful, murderous, adulterous whore. Sorry, Mother, but after a review of your tapes, I think you have being a disappointment down to an art form."

"She's beautiful, Trina," one of the taller males said. He was the one who held my dad by the hair with a blade to his throat. I swallowed the pain of seeing him after all this time. His face was ashen but his eyes were on me with pride. Blood trickled from his nose, but other than the occasional bruises, he looked okay.

"Dagan, meet your daughter," Trina said with anger in her eyes. "I only wish she'd been more of what we had hoped for."

Dagan was shorter than my dad, with eyes close to mine in color. He was handsome, with wavy dark auburn hair, but there was a coldness to him which left me wanting more in my gene pool. His hold tightened on my dad's hair, as the blade pressed harder on the skin revealing a thin red line of blood as if he just remembered he held it in his grasp.

"Is he really my father or just part of the daddy donor pool?" I mocked. "So, why am I here?" I looked back at my mom, dismissing the male altogether. DNA did not make a father; raising kids with love and protecting them did. "You wanted to check in on us and be all motherly? Mmm, no, you wanted to check your chess pieces and see if they were good enough to play with now. We're ready to play, Mother, but the thing is, we don't give a fuck about your games. You came into my house and shook it; you had innocents killed. That's just something I don't see myself getting over anytime soon."

"Get ready, if she makes a move, take her down. Don't hurt her, not yet." I had a mental image of my mother's voice flash across my mind.

"Trina, there is something more here—she's stronger than we can see. She's playing with you." Dagan replied on the same mental path as he replied to her.

"So, we gonna stare at each other all day or what?"

"The vampires and wolves have pulled back; they've abandoned her."

"She's still planning for them to help her. It's time for her rebirth. Either she is really one of us, or she's dead. Someone shoot her."

Darkest Before Dawn

Well shit! I stood perfectly still which was hard considering I knew what was coming, and I really wasn't looking forward to it. I looked to my dad with pleading eyes.

"I love you, Dad; don't ever question it or wonder okay? No matter what, you will always be my dad."

"Love you Emma, always," he said as I watched the pride light up his eyes, and for the first time I had ever seen, this tough as nails man had tears in his eyes.

The sharp crack of a handgun being fired shattered the stillness of the clearing and pierced my arm. My dad cried out, but I didn't dare move. I didn't cringe, because this was how I had seen it. I simply looked down and back up at her.

"Nice shot, but want some pointers?" My dad was staring at me like I was crazy. "Rest your sight level with the divot on the gun and you might actually kill something with it."

Pain! Oh, the fucking pain! Fucking bitch was so dead! I remained still as I brought my gaze back to my mother, who had the audacity to smile with pride. As if she had played a part in making me some sort of badass! I chanced a look at Grayson and saw his eyes as he watched me with a silent plea in them. Yeah, he'd just been clued in that he'd been played, just like I told him.

"She came, as you predicted," Trina said to my brother.

Amelia Hutchins

He sniffled; this had to be hard on him, since he'd never met our mother, and now he had to meet this traitorous bitch instead of the mom I had told him stories of. Stories of the person I thought my mother was—all of it a lie, as it turned out. "It's going to be okay, Grayson. I love you," I said, wondering what my mother planned to gain by this.

"Isn't this sweet?" Dagan sneered.

"I'm going to kill you, very slowly," I told him as I shot him a murderous look.

"Enough; it's time for you to choose between the two, Emma. Which one shall live and who shall die?" Trina asked coldly.

"Easy answer, I would never choose between them. I love them both," I said as I tried to figure out her move. This wasn't part of what I had seen in the vision and my faith in what I was doing faltered a little.

"A Knight would choose the innocent. A pawn would choose to run. A Queen would pick that which could be of most use to her," Trina growled.

"A human would pick her loved ones," I said giving nothing away, or at least I hoped I wasn't.

"She's chosen, I've never seen a postulant choose outside of the three," Dagan said with a puzzled look.

"Kill him," Trina sneered and I watched as Dagan slit my dad's throat. I almost lost it, but I'd seen it happen.

Darkest Before Dawn

Three times to be exact. He died in every scenario I was shown. My heart shattered and there was certain calmness came over me as the Sentinels watched.

The sky thundered as lightning slashed across it, as if forces in nature or in the universe were aware of what was going to happen and approved. It had been what my mom and the Sentinels wanted, but as I'd always been told, you should be very careful for what you ask for. I knew the pain was coming before it hit, so I had time to prepare for it mentally.

Shots rang out from the tree line as I moved toward my brother, but a sickening pelting noise made me pause as sharp pain and an extreme burning sensation shot through several places around my heart. Dagan watched me, and I knew from the look in his eyes that this wasn't my death. It was a rebirth to them, their kind.

I could hear their mental chatter and they didn't seem to know that I'd already died, and been reborn. This would be my second death, the cliff being my first. My eyes shot to Jimmy who looked at me grimly. He must have thought Addy was exaggerating when she told everyone at the shelter that I was dying. He probably thought I was at the estate being a vampire's plaything. No wonder my mother said I was a vampire's whore. I could do this; I could handle it for Grayson. I could handle anything to save him.

Right? It was too much! It felt as if my entire body was being torn apart. My veins pushed poison through them, and the entire time, I somehow managed to stay upright. The bullets had been laced with something, ensuring death would be swift. I swallowed until I couldn't, and the air left my lungs in an exhale.

"She's amazing," Trina whispered with pride.

I closed my eyes and tried to think of what Dad would have said if he'd seen me like this. I discarded the thought quickly and focused on the process. I listened to their thoughts, and then to the others around me.

I could feel Jaeden as if he was with me, a part of me, but then I'd seen it in my vision. I had his blood, and it had done something to us. I felt the glyphs as they seared the skin inside my forearms, showing my rank in the army I was currently staring down. Thankfully, it was soon to end. Grayson was too young for it to happen to him, and right now he was fighting them to get to me.

I looked up and met Trina's eyes. Grayson broke free, as my vision changed so that I could now see an outline of everyone's heat signature. This was an improvement in the vision I experienced when I fought the wolves and I knew from my visions that my blue eyes now had a luminous glow to them.

"She's not a Knight, Trina, she's a fucking Guardian," someone whispered.

Wait, what? Knight was so much cooler than Guardian.

"Move!" she screamed, her eyes flashed in a blue luminous glow that matched mine, and the Sentinels

Darkest Before Dawn

scattered and melted into the woods, Dagan grabbed Grayson and strong armed him into one of the waiting cars in the distance and I was frozen, unable to make myself move through the pain.

"Now!" I breathed, barely above a whisper, but Jaeden still felt it and the woods exploded with life.

They attacked as a well-oiled unit, but the car that held Grayson in it sped off before anyone could stop it. I screamed for Jaeden to get Grayson, but the car was gone before I could get the words out.

Lachlan in wolf form broke away from the scuffle and darted to my frozen form. He whined and then howled, which brought a very blood-covered Jaeden to me.

"Emma," he whispered as he stared into my eyes.

"They took Grayson." I'd failed. I was alive, but the plan had failed. The change had taken longer than my vision showed me it would; I watched in silence as the wolves and vampire tore the only two remaining Sentinels apart. It didn't look like they were going to save anyone for interrogation, that much I could see.

"We will help you find him," Jaeden said with promise buried in his tone. "We will all help you find him." Jaeden picked me up since I was basically stuck standing in place and unable to move from lack of strength.

In my first vision, I'd seen Dagan kill my dad, and I

had been shot several times and underwent the change. I broke free of the change, then killed them all and saved my brother. The other vision had been them killing me when I'd tried to save my dad. The third option showed they'd killed my dad, and taken me and Grayson to some underground lab. I hadn't seen what did happen in any of the visions, but I'd learned from it.

One: My visions weren't perfect, they seemed to more like tactical simulations that allowed me to assess best-case scenario.

Two: I was a Sentinel Guardian, but without google or another Sentinel to explain what that meant, that knowledge was pretty much useless.

Three: I heard voices inside my head when the Sentinels were close to me, and I could use that to find my brother.

Four: My dad was really dead now.

Five: My mother was going to die by my hand, well; she was going to be buried and hidden in some shithole of a grave that had maggots and other things in it and she wouldn't enjoy it— not a freaking second of it.

Chapter Twenty-Eight

It was kind of anticlimactic. I hadn't discovered very much information of what I was, and the glyphs on my forearms itched a little as they set and healed. They looked a little like an intricate lacy infinity symbol on the inside of each forearm, but I had no idea as to what they signified other than a rank. As I sat in my dad's room before the small service that Addy was putting together, I realized I couldn't put my thoughts and emotions together, much less a service for my dad. I found a bunch of journals in the room while looking for clothes for him to be buried in. I started skimming the entries of one, and found references to him meeting Shamus.

"Is everything okay?" Lachlan popped his head in the doorway, concern in his eyes.

"Yeah, I'll be out in a few minutes."

He nodded and left. I watched as Jaeden walked by, carrying a load of supplies he'd brought. It was odd; as

Amelia Hutchins

I saw him in the shelter, interacting with my people and bringing in supplies, he looked so right doing it, like he belonged with us. I had no idea where that thought came from.

"Emma, it's time." Jaeden had come for me, pulling my mind from my distracted musings.

I stood and hid the journal back in my dad's drawer before heading with Jaeden and Lachlan to the makeshift morgue with my dad's best blue shirt and jeans. Sven was waiting to replace the blood soaked clothes he'd died in and when I handed them off to him, I spun around and leveled Shamus with a look.

"You knew my dad?"

"Yes," Shamus smiled as he said it. "He had been doing some research on the internet that was very specific," he shook his head and made a task-tsk noise of disproval, "which of course, didn't go unnoticed by the elders, so I came here and met him to see if he was a threat or not. I liked him immediately upon meeting him. I saw the fight in him, and knew he'd be perfect for building a 'safe haven' so to speak, if it came to that. You see, once your father understood why I was here and what I was, he told me of a virus that would be put into play soon; that it was going to wipe out much of what I hold near and dear, if you get my meaning. Now usually someone spouting nonsense like that, I wouldn't have paid much mind to, but a little taste and I knew everything he said was true." He flashed me a cheeky grin. "So, I gave him a wee bit of help

Darkest Before Dawn

and sent much of the funding used to build this Ark. Do not misunderstand me, Emma. It was for purely selfish reasons. He would attract humans, it was inevitable, and my kind need food. I made a choice to invest in him, and it made sense since this was a secure location that would be easy to hold. Years later when the virus did hit, we only had to had come here and work on the defense of the area. I had already secured the food." He finished smugly.

"Well then," I said, at a loss of anything better to say. Food, he'd secured food. And by food, he meant my friends. Peachy! "Wait, you were here before too?" I asked Jaeden who smiled at me.

"I had a peek at you from a distance once. I'm pretty sure it was Addy taking pictures of you in a field of flowers. You didn't turn in my direction, but from the scent I caught of you, I knew I'd want to have you. Your scent has changed now that you are grown; it is even more enticing now," he said as his eyes twinkled naughtily.

I blinked. I'd wondered that day if I'd ever do anything good with my life, or find love. And the entire time I'd been plotting my life, a vampire had been watching me. Death had been watching me from afar and I'd not even known it.

"Did I meet you?"

"No," he said with a sexy smile that made me think otherwise. "But I knew I'd have you if you hadn't been among the dead here."

"Nice, so you plotted my deflowering before you even met me?"

"I never take chances. I did way more than plan your deflowering since I hadn't expected you to have a flower," he replied with a husky timbre and heat in his eyes.

"Right," I said as I spun around to find my dad had been laid out on a makeshift slab. "He knew what I was, and what my mother was."

"He was a very smart man," Shamus said as he stood beside me. "He did this entire shelter alone, and he finished it without asking for help or more money than was needed to get this place operational. He was intelligent enough to know that you were special before anyone else did. He sent me a letter when you graduated high school, and he said you had started a job in the medical field, and that you'd be an asset to my people should anything happen to him."

"So what do you know of Sentinels?" I asked Shamus.

"Nothing, nothing except rumors and myth," he answered, and dismissed me.

"It looks like you all got pretty up close and personal with some rumors and myths today," I quipped, and Shamus rolled his eyes and a made a rude noise. "So what do we know of the rogue wolves?" I countered.

Darkest Before Dawn

"Jaeden shared with me what he told you; we don't know much beyond that. Information keeps coming in all the time, so we are always reassessing." He shrugged.

"I haven't made it through all of the tapes, the ones my mother made and hid," I whispered as the implications of what she'd been up to filtered through me. "There's a little information on one of the tapes that has some stuff about the wolves, not much though, but maybe one of the others might have more." I shook my head sadly as I looked at my dad's body. "The entire time she was with him, she was planning his death."

"You can't know that," Shamus said.

"No, I wouldn't have known that, but she was cocky. She documented everything. It is rambling and I don't understand most of it, but it may be the way we figure out where she is and what her plans are."

"Maybe," Jaeden said cautiously. "Right now, Emma, we need to bury your father."

I turned around and looked at the man who'd raised me. He'd done it right, and he'd never asked for anything. He had even figured out what I was, and kept detailed notes. I'm not sure if he ever meant to show them to me, but I was going to go through every journal to see what he had discovered about me and what he knew of my mom's plans. He'd protected so many people and our little town, and he'd only been a mere mortal. He figured out a lot of what was going to happen; he knew he couldn't stop it, but he still did what he could to save people. And they'd repaid him by calling him crazy.

I knew there was no easy way to figure it out, and I was going to have to listen to those damn tapes sooner or later. I'd spent so much time grieving for her that it seemed unreal that she was back, and a total psycho.

The funeral service that Addy planned had been beautiful, but what Jaeden and the men had done brought fresh tears to my eyes. Some of Lachlan's men played the bagpipes, while Jaeden and his men had built a Viking funeral pyre. Instead of the ship, they settled for building a scaffold over what looked like a tomb, overlooking the shelter that he'd built. Sage had been placed on the scaffolding, and he'd been placed on top of that so when the torch was set to the pyre, his ashes would drop to the tomb below.

It was a surreal thing to watch, and know that I was finally able to bury him. I'd thought him dead this entire time, but at some point he had run into her. Now she had my brother, and the knowledge that she did was sickening.

The funeral wrapped up and Jaeden made his way to me with a purpose in his stride. "Emma, come," he said as he grabbed my hand and pulled me behind him.

We'd just cleared the trees when he pulled me against him and kissed away the tears on my cheeks. "I hated watching you today. That shit can't happen again," he ordered.

"You're not my boss; not here, not now."

Darkest Before Dawn

"We will see about that," he grinned. "I'm taking you home with me, so go say your goodbyes. I want you tonight, and you gave me your word, so go be a good girl and let them know you won't be home until tomorrow night. I'm about to show you what it really means to be fucked by someone like me, little girl."

He swatted my ass as I turned to go do as he asked. Addy was giddy at the fact that I was going to be gone for a night, and Kyra had agreed to hold down the fort since Maggie was still in the common room, recovering. I gave Lachlan last-minute instructions that he would probably ignore and do what he felt was best, and with that, I left hand in hand with Jaeden.

It wasn't until we reached his room that I started doubting coming here. He walked us in and closed the door, sealing us in as he locked it.

"Last time was nice, but I'm not promising that. I'm going to fuck you until those pretty little toes curl." The carnal grin playing about his lips held a world of promise in it.

"Is that so?" I asked, sultry as friggin' hell. I blinked at my tone.

"Oh yes, Emma, because I'm pretty damn sure you're immortal, so I don't plan on being gentle in my fucking."

"You called what you did before, gentle?" I turned my back on him with a naughty grin on my lips.

Amelia Hutchins

"Yes," he growled as he pushed me away from the door with his body. "I'm going to push you until you want me to stop; no, you'll beg me to stop." His hands slipped down my sides, to my hips as he slowly pushed me with his body towards the bed. His lips and nose softly grazed my neck. "I won't, of course, because you're mine now, Emma. I made you into a woman last time and now I'm going to make you into my pretty little fuck toy," his lips fanned my ear, as he cupped and tested the weight of my breasts. "I'm going to bring you to the edge of orgasm, but I won't let you fall," his mouth drifted over and kissed the flesh at the nape of my neck. His voice was a soft growl that sent a little shock through my body. "Not for the first couple of times, and your body is going to want it, crave it even," his hand slipped around and cupped my already throbbing sex.

"You're going to try and stop it from happening, and it's going to add to your excitement, because it's going to let me know that you're ready to succumb to it, but I know when to pull away, when to wait it out," he pressed his fingers against the wetness he was creating and smiled against my neck. "You'll beg me to come, and your body will become sensitive and that sweet pussy will want to be punished more, until it's a soaking fucking mess for me to feast upon. You're going to realize how fucking helpless you are, and how much you want and need to come." His tongue swirled where his lips had just been, sending a shiver racing down my skin with anticipation. "It's going to be a slow tease, a merciless one that courses through your body. By the time I'm finished with you, you'll whimper and shiver

Darkest Before Dawn

as you are kept at the height of desire."

I swallowed a moan, but it came out anyways, as a needy gasp. He stepped closer, and his eyes turned red as his fangs slid from his gums abruptly. "No hiding what I am tonight, Emma. Tonight you get me, faults and all. I'm fucking dirty and I have a filthy mouth but I'm good with it. I'm going to give you one orgasm because I smell it on you already, building for me just from my words alone. After that, I'm going to torture you and make that pussy weep to come for me. Only then will I fuck it, and not just once, Emma, but for the next twenty four hours straight, you'll be in my bed with me, coming as I see fit."

I gulped down air, unable to get enough. He moved with inhuman speed. His hands were rough but it was okay; I wanted it rough, and I wanted everything he said he would do to me—everything and more. My clothes had been stripped from my body as well as my bra. I shook with the knowledge that he'd removed it all in a blink of an eye. He left my panties on and flipped me up onto the bed, sitting on all fours.

It wasn't until I was on the bed, and had my ass in the air, fully exposed to him that he growled his approval from deep in his chest. His hands grazed over my ass and lower, to the soaking mess his dirty mouth had created. He ripped the panties off, and placed them in his pocket as if he'd wanted them as a trophy. He parted my flesh and allowed his fingers to sink in slowly, until they were buried inside of me, and then he pulled them out...slowly. He leaned over me, and placed his one hand under my chin as he lifted my face until I was forced to look at him.

"Good girl," he whispered with a hoarse voice. "I think you like this a lot. Being at my mercy, begging me to allow you to come. I have dreamt of this sweet pussy being soaking wet and weeping with the need to be fucked since the last time I had you here. I imagined how hard I would fuck it, and how loud you'd scream for me."

Fuck! He was seriously skilled in dirty talk! He turned me over, and my hands itched to touch him. Like this, he could see everything I had, and take whatever he wanted.

I moved to touch him, but he pushed me down on the pillows that rested against the headboard and his hand wrapped around my throat possessively. "You'll lie there and take it, little one. Be my good girl—" he said before he leaned down and nipped at one nipple, then the other, drawing it in until it grew hard from his hot mouth. His fingers found my core and plunged inside, pulling a deep moan of pleasure from my throat where his other hand held me down by my throat still. "Fucking hell, good girls aren't this wet, Emma."

"Jaeden," I cried as his fingers continued to drive inside of me to a slow beat only he could hear and control. "I need to come!"

"Of course you do, Emma," he rumbled as he brought his face up until his lips fanned over mine. "You're right on the edge, because that's where I want you. You're so fucking close to coming but I changed my mind, I'm not ready for you to, not yet. You're so close though, so fucking close that it's driving you crazy. Every touch makes the hair on the back of your neck stand up; every caress sends a rush of shivers down your spine, and it feels like an electrical current is running through your soul." His voice was a seductive, taunting purr. "I love you like this, and I'll keep you right here as long as it pleases me. Teetering right on the brink of coming... Tell me, Emma, how does it feel to know I control when you come?"

"Please," I begged, because let's face it, between the dirty talk, his hand around my throat holding my ability to breathe in the balance, and his fingers? I was in trouble and he was in full control of every facet of my body. He had control, hell, he had my obedience.

"Not yet," he said before he pressed his lips against mine. "Kiss me," he ordered and I opened my mouth further, but his kiss was savage and hungry, as if he couldn't get inside my mouth far enough. His fangs scraped over my tongue and then I felt the slice of flesh, but no pain accompanied it. I moaned against his hungry mouth as the kiss of my blood lingered in taste. He'd cut my tongue, only to heal it with his own saliva without taking his mouth from mine.

His hand pulled away from my core but he continued to hold my throat and I realized he wanted me to watch him, and by doing this, he had my full attention, but it was also a show of control, his way of telling me he had all control of me, and would use it. He pulled his mouth away from mine, and he smiled before his hand loosened, and he started working my neck over with his mouth. His lips pressed against my neck, and opened. I waited for the pierce, but it didn't come. Instead, he sucked against the vein, and released it. Sucked, nipped, licked and repeated it until I felt my clitoris as it pulsed in sync with what his mouth was doing, if it was even possible. It was erotic, and the wetness which had pooled between my legs was proof of just how much control he held over my body.

I pulled back but it was only a second of hesitation. Too many emotions were warring inside of me, with how I felt, and what he was doing to me.

"What are you afraid of, Emma? I can feel you pulling back, and I don't like it," he growled as his mouth lifted from my neck.

"I'm afraid of falling," I replied honestly. I was terrified of loving him, and falling with him could hurt me and change who I was irrevocably. He could destroy me.

"I'll catch you, Emma," he whispered against my ear huskily. "Always."

A single tear fell from my eyes but he caught it with his lips and kissed my cheek tenderly. He then sat up and pulled me close. "No more fears, not in this bed. Do you trust me?" he asked.

"Yes," I answered without hesitation.

Darkest Before Dawn

"Do you really, or are you just placating me?"

"I trust you, Viking," I said with more force behind it. More conviction.

"Give me your arms then," he ordered and watched as I hesitated. "This takes trust," he added as he watched me move my arms to him. "I won't hurt you, but I do plan to use you like my own personal fuck toy, and after that, I'm going to make love to you."

He yanked my hands up and tied them together tightly at the wrist. He then secured the nylon rope to the headboard where a metal hook had been drilled into it since last time I'd been here. "Is that too tight?" he asked as he looked down at my body with a naked hunger that made me whimper. "I'm going to take that as no," he said as his lips on one side of his mouth rose into a cocky grin. "Spread your legs and show me how wet you are," he whispered and I did, as if his words could control my legs. "Fuck, you're so beautiful like this, all tied up and helpless."

"I need you to get to it," I growled with a hunger of my own. "I ache."

"Test the bonds, Emma, and don't talk unless I tell you to. I need to know if you are comfortable with being tied to my bed, because trust needs to be between us before I can start ravishing you. Without it, this is just fucking and I want more with you. If you just want to be fucked, tell me now and I'll do it. I'll ram my hard cock so far into this sweet pussy that you'll feel me when you sleep tonight. If you want more, you'll wait until your mind is ready for me, because at that time, your body will follow it into the abyss of pleasure I have planned for you."

I bit my lip because while I wanted to come, I wanted more with him too. I wanted more than just sex; I wanted mind blowing, fuck my world up, make me ache for days sex. I wanted him soul-deep, and I had a feeling that by the time he was done with me, we'd be there—together.

"Don't worry sweet girl, I plan to fuck this pussy until it comes for me, soon."

I moaned and bucked my hips invitingly as his fingers trailed over the thin patch of hair that was nestled there. He pulled my legs apart and smiled down at how wet I was from just his words alone. "You're drenched, is that for me?"

"Yes," I said while making incoherent moaning noises. His fingers entered my core, but just the tips of them. He smiled as he pulled them back out and flicked my clit with one and then entered with three fingers, but again it was only the tips poised at my opening. He was going to make me work for it.

"Go ahead, try to move, Emma. I want to watch you suffer with the need to be fucked. You should see how sexy you are like this. I can see you want to move so badly, as if it would give any relief at all, and maybe you wouldn't feel so helpless," he whispered as he

Darkest Before Dawn

pulled those deliciously naughty fingers away from my opening. I had to work to get that little bit of pressure back inside of me. "The fact is, my naughty little fuck toy, you *are* helpless. There is absolutely no escape for you right now. Go ahead, scream to come. I want to hear it, beg me to let you come."

"Jaeden, make me come, please? I need it so bad," I begged, but I knew what he wanted. He wanted me to scream his name in need. That was what he wanted from me; he wanted the primal, no holding back scream that I'd given him the first time he'd fucked me. He pulled his fingers away until the very tips touched my opening again, as if he was punishing me.

"Emma, tell me who your body belongs to. Then maybe I'll give this soaking wet pussy just what it craves, maybe. Look me in the eyes and listen to what I'm saying to you. It's going to be sore by the time I'm done with it, red and abused, and I promise you, it will still want more. You'll take everything I give you tonight, now beg for it."

The moment he placed the fingers barely inside of me, I did it. I begged until he smiled and leaned his head down to suckle one nipple. He swirled his tongue around it and played with it as I squirmed and begged. He moved to the other nipple and swirled, licked and played with it for a few delicious moments and then he bit down around my nipple with sharp fangs as his fingers pushed fully inside of me. He thumbed my clit and I detonated, screaming his name until my voice was hoarse from it. He pulled at my nipple with his mouth, feeding as I exploded again and yet my mouth kept saying his name over and over again like a benediction.

"Good girl; keep going, keep coming for me. Don't you dare stop coming; you're my little orgasm doll tonight, so I want to see this sweet pussy dripping with come before I finally fuck it. That's it, my pretty little fuck toy, fuck you're so hot. So fucking hot," he moaned. I shook my head, begging for something, even though I didn't know what, not until he said it. "I can see you, Emma, and no, I won't stop because you're not done coming for me yet. You were just begging for this orgasm and now you're begging for it to stop? I don't think so; can you feel how slick with your juices my fingers are?"

I was soaking wet, he was right. That wasn't the problem. It was the fact that it was one solid body shaking orgasm that had me sobbing actual tears from pure ecstasy, but I felt as if I was falling and he'd been right, I feared passing out because blackness had replaced my vision and the only thing I could see was an expanse of stars that seemed to be exploding. It felt as if I had left his bed, and floated in the abyss he'd spoken about; there was pain here. Pain and pleasure from coming too hard, too fast; I wanted it to stop, but at the same time I didn't.

"Do you feel how sensitive this sweet pussy is now? How wet and ready it is for my hard cock?"

"Jaeden," I moaned hoarsely as I drifted back to earth. The plea was naked in my eyes. I wanted it

Darkest Before Dawn

to stop, but couldn't form the words. I couldn't form anything; it was as if my mind had turned to mush from the sheer magnitude of that orgasm.

"Look at me when I'm talking to you...if you keep looking at me with that plea for me to stop one more time I am going to turn you over and spank your sexy little ass. Now, come again and this time, don't break eye contact with me. I want to see your eyes when they grow vacant from pleasure." His other hand held my throat again, tender but with enough pressure to assist me in doing as he'd told me to. "Now, tell me who taught you to come that hard, good girl?"

"You did," I breathed through swollen lips that wanted nothing more than to taste him.

"Part your legs, and beg me to fuck you, Emma." His dirty mouth was my undoing, and the moment he lowered his body and claimed my clit with his tongue, flicking and kissing it, I bucked my hips in response, riding his face. He slid his fingers over my opening, and I screamed for even more of him.

"You feel that, Emma?" he whispered as he continued, only breaking up his words as his tongue sucked and nipped at the soft, sensitive nub that seemed to hold his attention. "Every time my finger slips up and down and over this honey," he dipped his fingers inside so I would catch his meaning. "And I move them slower and slower, until your tortured arousal, your sweet fucking wetness lets it slip within you, like this." He plunged them deep inside of me. "Every time they get close, this sweet pussy with all its wetness trying to suck them inside, to fuck them."

"Yes!" I was mindless, and this was torture. If he hadn't tied my arms, I'd be riding him like a freaking horse at a rodeo, because I was in pain with need for him. Achy didn't even begin to describe how I felt.

"That wasn't a question, my sweet little toy. I hope you're ready." He pinned me down, holding my bound hands just above my head until he was poised between my thighs. He smiled, and then flipped my body over, until once again I would have been on all fours, but with bound hands, I was forced to lay there with my cheek to the bed and my ass exposed in the air.

His hands landed on my ass, as he rubbed the sensitive flesh he found there. "Someday soon, I'm going to fuck you here," his thumb dipped inside and I tensed as if he'd lit a fire cracker with a short fuse. "You'll like it, too." He leaned over me and I listened as the sound of his pants being unzipped sounded like music to my ears. I tensed as the tip of his cock pressed against the flesh that just had his fingers in it, but then he lowered it to the sleek wetness of my pussy.

His lips pressed against my ear as he told me to take it, and I moaned as he fed his cock to my greedy opening, inch after glorious inch. His hand held my face in my place. He didn't allow me to move as he entered my body; he watched my expressions with an eagerness I could feel. He whispered encouragements as he filled me until I could take no more of him. When I moaned

Darkest Before Dawn

and cried out, he laughed, the sound seductive and erotic as it rumbled against my ear. Then he whispered seductively, "We aren't finished, little girl. I have more for you." There was more? He plunged in deep and I screamed. It made me wetter which allowed him in even more, and I trembled around his cock, his massive cock that was buried deep inside of me.

"You're about to come for me again, are you ready?" he teased as he leaned back and slapped my ass hard while his other hand grabbed a handful of hair and pulled.

It was overwhelming, and erotic. I felt dirty and yet I wanted him to do worse. I wanted him to use me without remorse. I wanted to feel his worst, and know his best. I didn't care what he did, because my world was spinning off its axis, and he was the center of my universe in this moment.

I had a fire inside of me, and I wanted to believe in it, in this, in myself. I wanted to tether the fire I'd seen burning in his eyes when he looked at me, the way the world spun out of control and atoms collided together for a cataclysmic event when we touched. That's why I was here, that was why I was with him. That's how I felt with him. Only Jaeden. There was something so achingly beautiful inside me when I was with him that it terrified me and made my world spin off its axis. Nothing else mattered. Nothing mattered but him and the fire that was burning in his eyes.

He went stiff behind me and swore violently as his

hands tightened, as if he was surprised by his release. "Fucking hell, Emma, you make me helpless and come like a stripling every time I am with you."

"Good," I growled with pride, but I could already feeling him moving again.

"Too bad I'm not done. You're not sore enough, little Valkyrie. Not by a long shot. Now, scream for me, more. Scream until every male in this area knows who this sweet fuck toy belongs to."

Chapter Twenty-Nine

He kept his promise, and for twenty-four hours, I was everything he said I would be. I was sure as I eased into my clothes the next evening that I would feel the soreness into next week. Jaeden quietly led me through the estate, and stayed with me on the walk home. Everything seemed as if it had changed since last night. He seemed distracted, as if something was bothering him. I left him alone as he didn't seem like he was ready to share what was going on in his mind.

When we'd reached the half-way point, he stopped and looked around us and his posture grew stiff. He narrowed his eyes and tilted his head, as if he was listening to something.

It wasn't until a black SUV pulled behind us from the direction we had come, that his shoulders dropped and his head shook as he turned and looked at me. He was angry at something, and I caught a look of resignation as it crossed his face.

"Jaeden?" I asked, looking around us for any sign that something was off. I could see nothing, but he was reacting to something.

"Emma, go home. I have to leave. Now," he said abruptly as he turned to leave.

"What the hell?" I demanded as he started to walk away. "What's wrong with you?" I followed him a few steps.

"Some of the elders have arrived; word has gotten out about what happened at the bridge yesterday. This is very bad, Emma. I have a good deal of explaining to do and I don't want you anywhere close to me," he said and stopped again as he seemed to think on something more and then let out a stream of what sounded like irate curses. "Tell Lachlan the rogues we were concerned with are closer than we thought," he continued bitterly and moved towards the SUV as I stood there, stunned and frozen at the sudden change. Jaeden sniffed the air and called out.

"Take her home wolf; I can smell you in the bushes, Lachlan. Keep her safe." Jaeden opened the passenger door as Lachlan and his men came out of the woods. "She's yours to protect now." His angry eyes were the last thing I saw as he closed the door firmly.

"Emma," Lachlan said as he tried to pull me away from where I stood, too confused and hurt to move. "Lass," Lachlan said as he picked me up and began to carry me. "Emma, breathe."

Darkest Before Dawn

It didn't matter. Nothing did. He was gone. He'd left me. I'd lost my dad, and Grayson, and Jaeden had been the only person I knew who could possibly help me track down the Sentinels who had taken my brother.

~~*

Three weeks later.

"Emma, is this enough silver? Lach and Liam have pilfered every jewelry store from Seattle to Spokane it seems," Addy asked. "Pretty ballsy if you ask me, like Superman handling kryptonite." She giggled.

"Looks good, and with the bars of silver from the bank, we should have enough for a war with the rogue packs, if it actually comes to that." It was looming over us, and only a matter of time before they attacked. It was as if they could sense that the vampires had abandoned us.

Jaeden was gone, and by gone, I mean every vampire that had been camped out at the estate had vanished without a trace. We had been left to fight the rogue packs alone, as well as look for my brother. Lachlan was sweet, and was trying to fill my days with busy work, but nothing filled the void Jaeden had left inside of me. I was able to keep my mind busy during the day, but at night he would haunt me.

Only the thought of protecting the people here—and eventually finding Grayson—gave my mind ease. I wasn't willing to just fall in line and sleep with one of the guys to pass the hours as the others girls had been, but hey, not judging. After all, it seems I'd been a vampire's plaything. I had no room to judge anyone.

"They're back!" Aydan shouted, and we all grabbed guns and moved to the door. This was becoming an everyday thing, but unless they tried to breach the doors, we normally just stood at the ready. Today there seemed to be more of them, as if they'd actually expected us to come out.

"They can't get in here, so hold back. If they manage to be hiding explosives in their fur, we might have something to worry about." I watched as our wolves agreed, if not a little unwillingly. I knew they itched to fight them, but it wasn't time. They were testing us, looking for weakness.

I turned and walked back to my room in silence. My room was now my research center for finding Grayson. I had my mother's tapes in the room, and every day, I listened to them for clues I may have missed the day before. I read from the journal my dad had left for me, and wondered how he'd discovered so much in such a short amount of time.

Every night since he left, I dreamt of Jaeden and wondered if he ever thought about me. On the way back to the shelter the day Jaeden left, Lachlan explained that the elders were the lawmakers for the vampires and if they said they'd do something, they would. Anything they ordered was carried out with brutal efficiency. How Shamus convinced them that my dad was an asset and not a threat was nothing short of miraculous. My worries about the elders escalated when I found some damning information on one of my mom's tapes and I had to confide in Lachlan.

Sentinels, it turned out, were hunters of vampires or any other creature that became out of control and a threat to humans. Their powers made them judge, jury and executioner all rolled into one, which explained quite a bit of changes I had been going through. Sentinels were invisible death. No wonder Shamus said that Sentinels were just rumor and myth. If the elders knew more about Sentinels than Shamus indicated, I had very little hope that Jaeden would be back unless it was to kill me.

~~*

Winter had arrived and snow was piling up, which meant most of the animals for meat were in hibernation. I spent most of the morning hours hoping Grayson was being fed, and taken care of. Our mother was a cold calculating bitch, so it was doubtful. My only hope was that she wanted him alive, because if she did, she'd have to feed and take care of him.

Days went by, and eventually the rogue pack gave up on an all-out attack. They had not managed to get through the shelter's defenses, but they had made it impossible to go out at all. Maggie had developed an infection after she'd sustained a new injury; she'd been trying to overdo it with the need to make up for the time she was down. Her immune system was still compromised from surgery and she'd spiked a fever.

I waited as long as I could before I finally made the decision.

"I'm going for medicine," I told Addy as she walked into my room as I was dressing in white camo snow pants and a hooded jacket that had fur trim. "The antibiotics I have aren't doing the trick for Maggie."

"Emma, you know it's not safe out there. Those asshole rogues are still around."

"And they won't leave, but look; if I don't go, she's dead. I can't let them force us to hide forever. I'm going to slip out and Lachlan, Aydan, and a bunch of his guys are going to distract them. It's not like I'm just running out there and yelling here I am, *bite me*! We actually have a plan."

"Emma, you've done nothing but walk around here like a flipping zombie for the past two months! I'm not losing you; if you wanna go, you take me with you!"

"Addison Kathryn Stokes, I will duct tape you and toss your ass in the pantry. I have a couple of things working in my favor these days; you don't." I blinked. She blinked. I looked up to find Lachlan watching us as I finished slipping my pack on.

Darkest Before Dawn

"Two girls, duct tape, that sounds kinky as fuck," he said with a cocky smile on his lips.

"Men," I said as an image of Jaeden plagued me. I wasn't over him, and the fact that I'd fallen after I'd tried so hard not to was driving me insane. His face haunted my sleep, and in it, he was always making love to me. The last time we'd gone at it, his hands had been gentle. It was more than fucking; he'd kissed me everywhere, and whispered things I'd never expected to hear from a man, and it was that time that I kept replaying in my head.

"Emma, we're ready," he said ignoring my eyes that I had dramatically rolled just for him. "Keep rolling those eyes, lass, and I'll make your toes do the same."

"Excuse me?" I asked.

"Like this," he said with a cocky grin right before he pulled me to him and kissed me until my toes did just as he'd threatened to make them do. He was sweet, and for the first time since that incident in the showers months ago, I allowed his tongue to push inside, and when I did, he deepened the kiss. My body responded, and I allowed him to move his hands down my back as I placed mine on his chest.

It was an amazing kiss, but it didn't make me delirious or lose my mind like Jaeden's kiss did; not even close. Lachlan had skill, but it wasn't similar or even close to the way Jaeden's made me feel. I felt my core growing wet, and stopped him. "I'm—"

"It's okay, lass; it's a start, aye? He's gone, but you're still here," Lachlan said with a knowing smile, as if he approved of how I'd reacted to his kiss.

I on the other hand was appalled at my behavior. I knew Jaeden was gone, but he'd stolen my heart and taken it with him. His departure had been so abrupt and unexpected that it had left a hole inside of me. If I slept with Lachlan, that's all it would be, fucking. I just wasn't made like that. I had an ache between my legs that only Jaeden could fill and a hole in my heart that only made it worse.

I walked to the door where I kissed Addy on the cheek and watched as Lachlan and a few of his men started to strip down for the change. Watching an entire group of hot men strip down to nothing while we watched them? Priceless.

"Take it in," he said cockily and then shifted to wolf form right in front of us. It looked like it should've been painful, but the turn from human to wolf was effortless, as if a single thought could bring it on.

I'd never asked him about it, and figured it was none of my business. I liked that he flirted with me, but still gave me space to decide if I wanted it to go further between the two of us. There wasn't that chemical reaction of atoms and molecules exploding when we touched, and that was what kept me from moving forward.

I opened the door and watched as the wolves fanned

out in an aggressive formation and left the shelter to give me an actual shot at saving Maggie. I turned and looked at Addy with a small smile.

"I love you, bitch," I said and wiggled my eyebrows.

"Don't do that, Emma, you better come back to me. I can't do this without you."

"*I'll be back*," I said in my best Arnold Schwarzenegger impression.

Chapter
THIRTY

It was a frozen wonderland outside. Inside the shelter, it was easy to forget how winter was in the Pacific Northwest. The trees had shed their leaves and layers of snow had replaced them. The sun was bright through the many trees that stood silently in the forest. The only sounds were my boots as they crunched against the snow, and my breath as I huffed out little clouds in the freezing air with each step.

It had taken me an hour and a half just to travel through the three feet of snow that had blanketed the forest floor. I was just nearing Newport as the sun started to set. "Just wait for me," I told it. I clicked on the flashlight I'd brought and headed into the dark, frozen hospital.

It took another thirty minutes to just search through the many bottles and packets of medicine that someone had disturbed. Between the pile of bottles in the pharmacy, and the ice that had found a home with

Darkest Before Dawn

all of the broken windows, it was hell. I finally found what I had been looking for and smiled with victory. Lachlan and the others had yet to find me or radio that they'd gone back to the shelter. We learned early on that they couldn't carry walkie-talkies with them when they shifted, so we had tried to talk Maggie into making them little doggie pouches or something to carry a radio or walkie-talkie in. Lachlan and his men didn't think it was very funny.

I walked back outside and considered my options. The ice across the lake should be frozen enough to walk on by now, and without hearing from Lachlan, I didn't dare go the way I'd come. I made the decision and headed towards the lake, but when I was almost there, I caught sight of an elk, standing proudly as he nosed the snow for the grass just beneath it. If I hadn't gone through the change, I would never have seen him in the dark.

It was surreal. Sure, I'd seen many of them, but none this close. I smiled at it, and moved to step closer when the first wolf attacked it. I paused and looked around me, only to find more wolves coming out of the woods. I turned and ran with everything I had, tripping over the branches that hid beneath the snow's deceptive depths. My bag weighed more than it should have, so I dropped it knowing the pills I needed for Maggie were safely in my zippered pocket.

The wolves' intent must have originally been the elk; otherwise my early warning system would have gone off. Well that was a bit of a flaw with that kind of alarm. I looked back as they continued to give chase. I had no option but to try and outrun them. There were no trees close enough for me to climb, no place for me to hide. I heard the packed snow crunch under the heavy weight of one of the wolves, but refused to look back.

It wasn't until I slid on ice that I paused. I turned and looked at the wolves that had stopped at the edge of the lake. I could hear the ice cracking in the distance. I turned and ran for the other side of the lake, knowing there wasn't a chance in hell I'd actually make it, but knowing it wouldn't kill me. Or at least, I hoped it wouldn't. I had survived the cliff and bullets meant to kill me, so my odds were pretty good.

I made it half way when the ice gave out.

My last sight was the wolves turning tail, leaving me to my icy tomb.

I struggled against the icy depths, my heart pounding in my ears as water filled my lungs. Gravity was a bitch, I could feel hypothermia taking hold, and knew the moment I lost the fight. They say you get this replay of your life when you die, but I'd died twice now, and I didn't see anything either time. I'd be damned if the third wasn't the same.

I wondered at why I wasn't awarded the images, or why I kept being cheated of death. Too much had happened in such a short time, that it would be so easy to just let go. I considered it for a moment, but right when I had been willing to give up hope, he came to me.

Darkest Before Dawn

Blue-green eyes and his heated touch. I smiled, even though I'd become numb from the icy grasp of the lake. Blackness was fighting me for my mind, but there, in that moment. I found him. At deaths door, I found Jaeden. Only he wasn't dreamy, he looked pissed. The darkness won, and I knew no more.

~~*

Fire crackled from somewhere close. Warmth filled my mind and my body, and something was wrapped around me; hands rubbed over me. I was stark ass naked. Death…well let's just say that death had a hot sense of irony.

"Emma," Jaeden's voice called to me from somewhere far away.

"Mmm," I mumbled incoherent things, only to pass out again, and then do the same each time he called my name.

When I awoke again, it was to his lips touching mine, his cock pressed hard against my belly, and we'd moved closer to the fire. "I like dying with you," I whispered and opened my mouth for his kiss.

"Emma," he said again as his hands framed my face. "You are immortal my sweet, silly girl; it would have to be something very extreme to kill you now, but you do need sleep." His gentle voice sounded amused. Damn, I loved his accent.

"Okay." I needed sleepily.

I slept, but each time I woke, it became clearer. I'm not sure how long we did this for, or why we did this, but when I finally came to, it was to find Jaeden wrapped around me and blankets tucked in against us. His masculine scent filled my mind with a calmness that I hadn't felt in a long time.

"Am I dreaming?" I whispered.

"Do you want to dream of me, sweet girl?" he asked as he rubbed his massive erection against me.

"Yes," I replied and then gasped as he rolled over, pinning me to the floor. I loved this dream. It was different than before, and he felt real. His hands pinned mine easily in their larger hold. His mouth was hungry and intense as he kissed me.

His fingers parted my sex, and dipped inside. I bucked, and rocked them for more, needing more of him. It was too much, and not enough at the same time. I wanted more. I was already on the brink, and his husky laughter made me want it more. He refused to allow me release, and I started to think I'd fallen for him all over again.

Dreams were funny like that, never giving you what you wanted, and it made me wonder why they always said to chase your dreams. Um hello, dreams sometimes

Darkest Before Dawn

sucked! This one in particular had my body ready for penetration and yet dream-Jaeden was kissing my breasts slowly, as if he had all the time in the world. I knew it was wrong but I didn't care. I wanted him, and I wanted him now.

He drew me in like a moth to the flame. He made my heart race with each twitch of his massive cock as it touched my clitoris. That amazing scent of his made my mouth water with the need to taste his flesh. The trembling of his fingers as he rubbed them over my core with skilled pets and touches. Could dream-Jaeden hear my heart pounding with need? Could he feel the heat of my core as it grew slick with need for him?

He lowered his face until his mouth touched and kissed the crook of my neck, breathing me in as he did so. He leaned back and smiled, a heated gaze filling his turquoise depths. His hands released mine as he parted my legs even further. One hand came back to hold my face in place as his other one reached down to open the petals that had already grown wet with need.

"Such a beautiful sight," he whispered huskily. His fingers parted my folds which swelled with need and glistened for his greedy eyes; he knew it was only for him that I was this wet for. Only his touch made this storm of emotions and raw need saturate my core. He lowered his long frame down until his mouth hovered over the slick mess that was his. He leaned in closer until his long tongue dragged over the folds knowingly, so slowly, so thoroughly. I gasped and his lips curved into a smile that he pressed against my pussy. "Such a beautiful pussy," he growled as he moved his hand from my face and used two fingers to fill me.

I cried out as the friction mixed with longing, and my body responded to his touch. His eyes locked with mine, and his turned darker, glittering with desire. I licked my lips invitingly, but he ignored it. His touch was gentle as he held my thighs apart and continued to fuck me with his mouth. His fingers would come out, only for his tongue to take their place. I was coming undone, and I could see in his eyes that he sensed it.

It wasn't until he climbed up my body, framed my face between his large hands and looked me straight in the eyes, that he entered my body slowly; his eyes never left mine until he was buried deep inside of me. "Does that feel like a dream?" he asked with a hoarse tone.

"Yes," I cried as he began to move slowly. His hips rocked in a steady tempo that had me lost in desire. The steady rhythm, mixed with the juices between my thighs, had him increasing his fast pace. The concentration on his face as he looked at how his handiwork was bringing me closer to the edge sent me and my mind right over it.

He moved down my body until he held both of my feet in his large hands, his mouth fed greedily from my wetness with an overwhelming eagerness that created shock waves to follow the first release. My mind was coming back, and with it, the knowledge that I was actually fucking Jaeden. As in, he'd really saved me and was now fucking me silly.

Darkest Before Dawn

"You asshole!" I kicked him until he released my feet. "You mother fucker! You left us!"

"Emma," he said as he stood up to his full height as I came to my feet as well. He lifted his hands, which looked comical considering his cock was bouncing in the air. "I can explain everything if you just let me."

"You left me!" I swung out at him but I didn't have the best balance at the moment and ended up being caught by him. "You destroyed me!" He pulled me close and held me tightly.

"I had to break ties with you; the elders questioned everything about you, those Sentinels at the bridge, my loyalty—everything! They reassigned us. Shamus told them you were an asset and he made them see that you were on our side, but it took time. I have been trying to get back to you since we left, but we also had to consider the fact that this place was swarming with rogue wolves," he said softly as one of his big hands stroked my hair. "We aren't from here, but we have been keeping out of sight and picking off the rogues pretty steadily. I wouldn't have left you had there been another way, but the elders are law in my world, even above our sires. I knew it would only be a matter of time before they saw reason and I could come back to you."

"You could have told me that! I could have handled it if I'd known there was a reason!"

"Could you have? I couldn't chance a scene, or them figuring out how I felt about you."

"And just how do you feel?" I asked softly.

"Do you really need words to figure it out?" he asked as he pressed his erection at my junction.

"You scared me tonight," he whispered as he moved the hair from my face and looked down at me, "I saw the ice give way and had to save you. We've lost the element of surprise we had, but you were right; you're worth it."

"You left me," I said as a single tear slid down my cheek.

"To protect you, Emma, yes, I left you to buy time and get a plan together, because losing you wasn't an option. I have to leave again after we thin out some of these rabid mongrels, but for now, in this house, we belong together."

"Where are you going?" I asked as my heart lifted and seemed to get stuck in my throat.

"I'm going to Utah," he said with a sensual grin on his lips. "You're coming with me." A gleam in his eye told me he was dead serious.

"Why would I leave?" I asked turning my full attention on him and what he'd said. I wasn't leaving and I was curious to figure out why he thought I'd just pick up and go.

"Because they aren't holding Grayson close to here, but a lead I discovered in the last few weeks said

Darkest Before Dawn

he might be in Utah, around Provo. I also discovered another group of what I think might be Sentinels. I told you'd I'd help you and I will. I discovered more information about your mother and where she has been, but I'll tell you all that later."

"You were looking for Grayson?" I asked barely above a whisper.

"He's your brother, and I figured you wouldn't be able to leave the shelter long enough to find him; not without help anyways." His mouth tipped up. "Now, how do you plan to reward me?" he asked.

I didn't hesitate. I jumped into his arms and wrapped my legs around his waist as I kissed him like he was my world. My hands framed his face and the moan of pleasure that broke from his throat was smothered by my mouth.

Chapter Thirty-One

"So let me get this straight," I said as Addy, Lachlan, Liam and I sat around the common room of the shelter. The vampires, who had returned with Jaeden, had been settling into another level of the shelter. "You don't agree with what the rogues are doing, and you came here when you heard they were headed here?"

Lachlan nodded. "My Da went missing a while back, heard aboot this place and that he'd come here tae talk to a man, and then his trail went cold."

"And these wolves," I started, but he interrupted me.

"We deal with our own messes. These wolves are breaking a very serious code we live by. An occasional slip up, bite, or attack is normal. We can look past it, but this? This is something that we need tae stop."

"So how did you know to come here?"

"Shamus and the pack, we go back a long time.

Darkest Before Dawn

Looking fer information on my Da, we connected and shared information aboot what was happening with the rogue wolves and he told me aboot some of the elders that went missing, and we devised a plan tae find them together. His and Jaeden's maker is among the missing, and they'd be bound by blood tae find him."

Jaeden walked in and I turned in my seat to look at him as he smiled. "And why are you involved in this besides your sire being missing?"

"I'll answer questions!" Cayla chirped as she walked in with her long hair now a bright sea green with bright blue tips. The strange boy followed her with his eyes on me; it was unnerving. "What am I answering?" she asked as she took a seat beside me on the sofa. She'd made us all pause at her entrance.

I started to move over but her hand landed on mine and she smiled showing off the twin tips of her fangs. "Don't even think about it, Emmy; we're going to be great friends! I just know it, and even though you're squeamish around blood, I feel we can totally get past that! Nery says so as well."

"Uh, Cayla, I'm not squeamish around blood," I told her quietly and she shook it off like she hadn't heard me.

"Is Nery here, Cayla?" Shamus asked good-naturedly as he walked in and started to take a seat. I screamed a warning, but as I watched, Shamus sat right *through* Nery.

Cayla smiled at me. "Ask Emmy," she said as she patted my shoulder comfortingly.

I narrowed my eyes on Cayla and then Shamus; couldn't they see him? "You guys can't see him?" I asked when everyone settled in.

"No, he's her imaginary friend, Emma," Jaeden said in a matter-of-fact voice.

"Ghost?" I asked Cayla who narrowed her eyes on me. Nery reappeared, sitting next to Cayla on the other side.

"He's not a ghost! Don't say such a thing to us!" she cried as Nery rolled his eyes.

"Then how did Shamus sit *in* him," I asked ignoring the eyes watching me.

"He's special," she huffed defensively.

"It's very nice to meet you, Nery," I said realizing he was watching me expectantly.

"And you, Guardian," he smiled to show off perfect white teeth. "Cayla has been excited about meeting you."

I nodded and turned to find Jaeden looking at me with wide eyes. "Don't encourage her, because it will get a lot worse."

"What will?" I asked innocently.

Darkest Before Dawn

"Nery's opinion," he whispered with a small smile.

"Oh," I said and then narrowed my eyes on him. "You can't see him?"

"No," he and Shamus said together. "He's been with her since Shamus changed her over. It's the result of a head wound that happened just before he changed her."

"I'm sorry but I fail to see where having a...boy follow you around is from a head wound."

"You can see him," Shamus said with narrowed eyes that seemed to miss nothing.

"Yes," I agreed. "I can."

"Magnificent," he said as he watched me. "So he's real. But then, you also suffered a head wound."

"Why is she here?" Astrid asked with a pout on her lips as she sat down beside Shamus. "She's not a part of this, and I want her gone, baby," she batted her lashes and continued to pout as she draped herself around Shamus.

"Don't test my patience, Astrid. She's a big part of this, and with her help, we might be able to find the other elders and we may even be able to gain the upper hand here," Shamus snapped.

"Use the whore as bait," she said with a haughty look. "She's why that woman came here," Astrid whined. She continued to smile knowingly. "What? You thought he actually wanted to come to this little shithole? Or did you actually think his meeting you was by chance? I'm not sure which one makes you more pathetic." I felt as if I'd been kicked in the stomach.

"Astrid," Jaeden warned.

"It's the truth, Jaeden. You came here to gain a foothold, but you were also told to get into the Ark by any means necessary; job well done."

I felt nauseated, but I refused to show it. I folded my hands between my legs and gave Jaeden with a cold look. "So, are we going to actually plan the assault on the rogues you guys say are coming or just sit here and bullshit all day? If that's the plan, then I have other shit that actually needs to get done."

"Hurts, don't it?" she sniped.

"Astrid, go to the room and don't leave it until I summon you. Pack your shit while you are there, you're being sent to the elders," Shamus ordered, and I watched as her eyes grew sharp with hatred. "I'm sorry about that, Emma, Astrid lacks manners," Shamus sighed apologetically.

She didn't want to be with Shamus, and anyone with eyeballs could see it. She stood up abruptly and slammed her palms down on the table with a bone jarring boom. "He's mine! He's always been mine, and I'll be damned if this little whore takes my place! I won't go the elders, that's not fair. You know how horrible they are!"

Darkest Before Dawn

"I was yours, Astrid, right up to the point you killed our unborn child. I could have lived with your whoring, I would have gotten over it eventually, but not what you did so you could continue to whore around," he said quietly.

"Tell her the truth, Jaeden! Tell her how you fed off of whores while we were gone!"

I stood to leave the room abruptly but stopped and turned to Lachlan. "Let me know what the plan is. I don't do drama," I gave Jaeden and Astrid a withering look. "Not over something as stupid as that, not when so much is riding on this."

"Emma," Jaeden growled.

"I'll be ready with the silver when the time comes. Let me know what the plan is; I have to get my people ready."

Chapter Thirty-Two

Astrid's words replayed in my head as I sat in one of the rooms we had set up with small forges so we could melt silver and pour it into bullet molds. We had also become pretty adept at filing it down to a fine silver nitrate type of powder that we could use in landmines; needless to say, the wolf pack avoided this room like the plague.

It was a shock to learn the truth, but then again, I should have expected it. I wasn't sure why I had been surprised; Jaeden wasn't the type to do anything by chance. I still planned to go with him to find Grayson, and Lachlan had offered to go with us.

Maggie was getting better and luckily the antibiotics had been in a sealed container and hadn't been ruined by the icy water. She was at least on the mend and up and moving around, even though she should have been resting. She was a comforting presence for me as we took turns carefully pouring melted silver into the molds.

Darkest Before Dawn

"There's a very angry Jaeden that wants to speak to you outside, Emma," she said as she took a seat beside me. "You want me to send him away?" I shook my head at her as I stood up and dusted myself off. "I'll kick his ass for whatever he did this time, if you want me to," she sang out to my retreating back.

I reached the door and wiped the hair from my face before I stepped through the different doors that led out of the shelter, including the door meant to withstand explosives. I sealed the door and watched as Jaeden prowled closer, his eyes latched onto my now very hard nipples from going from the scorching room to the snowy night's chilled air.

I wore shorts, and a tank top, both white in color since it had been all I could find. I stunk, but I wasn't trying to impress him, not anymore. "What do you want, Viking?"

"What the hell are you wearing?" he asked, still unable to take his eyes from the rose colored tips that showed through both the shirt and the bra. "I can see your nipples, and it makes me want to suck them, slowly."

I crossed my arms over my chest and shot him an irritated look. "You don't get that anymore, Jaeden, not from me."

"You're upset; I get it, sweet girl. I'm a vampire though, Emma, I have to feed."

"I'm not upset that you fed from others, Jaeden. I'm

trying to figure out where we stand. You and I meeting wasn't an accident, and that makes me wonder about a lot of things."

"Emma, Shamus supported this shelter and your family, I had no idea that you were the daughter of the man who built this place when I first met you. Yes, I had my orders, and after I met you, things took on a life of their own," he said reasonably.

"Not good enough," I said. "Look, Jaeden, this thing between us? It's toxic to me. You're hot and cold and I can't do it. Not anymore. I'll go with you to find my brother and help find anyone my mother has taken from you, if she's involved in that, but us? We can't happen…" One minute I'd been talking and the next I was pressed up against the shelter with his hand over my mouth and his eyes hard on mine.

"Do you know what I am? I'm a proud Viking warrior who used to fuck for breakfast, lunch and dinner. I'm immortal, Emma, but I still have to feed. I'm sorry for doing it, but I didn't fuck them while I fed, and it wasn't them I wanted, it was you." I pulled his hand away from my mouth.

"I know what you are, but I'm not sure we can work out—ever," I said stubbornly. "I get it now, what Lachlan said about you having to follow orders, and right now I need to focus on what is important, and that's finding Grayson. Alive. So for now, I accept that we're stuck in this together, but for the foreseeable future we're going to be strictly platonic."

Darkest Before Dawn

"You think it's that easy to walk away from me? You think I buy that shit, Emma? You want me even now. It's in the curve of your lips when I say something you like, the way your mouth lingers on mine when I kiss those soft lips. That slow, deliberate way your lips maneuver down my neckline when I'm riding your body. You don't have to admit it, sweet girl, that mouth of yours gives it away every time.

"It doesn't matter what I want anymore. I have to save him and if this thing between us stops me, then *it* stops. I left the meeting because of you and the drama that surrounds you, and that can't happen again. I need to be focused on what is important, and what my people need."

"I should have kissed you longer," he said as he stepped back and turned, leaving me standing alone.

~~*

Two days later

The stage had been set and it included what I liked to think of, as an 'army' of wolves that had been changing humans into monsters. I'd listened to the tapes which had my mother's plans on them, and had taken them to Shamus to see if he could make sense of her crazy ranting ways. He had some good ideas, but we needed more time to figure them out. Time wasn't something we had a lot of, and with the rogues getting braver, we'd decided to do the fight on our own terms.

Five humans from my group stood in an open field within running distance to the shelter. Jaeden and Lachlan had planned it in advance, knowing the rogue wolves would show up if enough people's scent flowed through the air. Lachlan assured me that their scent was like candy to the rogues, and so far, they'd been unable to stay away from it.

We now considered the possibility that while my mother had been a part of what started this, the wolves were taking advantage of it for their own reasons. My mom working with the people who started this was really throwing me, because Sentinels were supposed to protect humans, from what I gathered in her tapes. She was completely contradictory. While we knew the wolves were close, I could also sense the presence of a Sentinel close by.

I had no idea how my powers worked, or why I had them, but I knew I was linked to other Sentinels; I just didn't really know what the link did or how it worked. I knew he was high up in a tree, to the left of the field, watching us. There was also the fact that I felt a connection, even though it was faint at best. As if we shared some kind of weird bond, which we felt.

It was as if we were at standoff, and it wasn't until Jaeden moved up to my side wearing only jeans and a grin, that I gulped down air as I did a double take. He wore a strap of leather across his chest, which held a shield in place behind his back. His biceps had intricate

Darkest Before Dawn

platinum bands around them, defining just how well-muscled he was. His hand gripped a large sword handle, and his eyes were on me as I took him in.

For a moment it was only he and I on what would soon become a battlefield. He didn't move closer, but didn't back away as I took an involuntary step in his direction. For a moment I forgot who I was, and didn't care that on the other side of the field was a mob of fucked-up looking wolves who wanted to kill us.

In my head, I tasted his flesh and he was between my legs, pushing himself against my body and I'd caused all of that sweat. He was shirtless, and yes, I was pretty sure his naked chest had just made me almost spasm with the heated look in his eyes alone. He looked like a magical berserker, taken from another era and placed in front of me. Here, he was all Viking, and Vikings were hella hot!

I was momentarily distracted as our wolves took up their positions behind the vampires. It was almost comical that they'd worn kilts since they'd shed them if they had to shift in the middle of a fight. Maybe it was easier on them to get dressed after the battle; those old-fashioned kilts they had on *were* one size fits all. Bare-chested Scots and shirtless Vikings, how the hell was I supposed to focus with all this testosterone bared?

"What the hell are those?" Lachlan asked, looking off in the distance.

"Wolves?" I mumbled. "Why aren't they attacking

Amelia Hutchins

Jaeden moved closer to me.

waiting for orders; they must have an alpha now," Bjorn answered.

"Emma," Jaeden said with a sardonic smile on his lips as he walked up and pulled me closer. "Kiss for good luck?"

I smiled, and crinkled my nose as I giggled at his ballsy question. I stood up on my tip toes far enough that I could kiss his cheek.

I mean really, I was always myself, but at the moment, I was with Vikings so why not be one? His men hooted with him as if I was the shit, but then one of the landmines I'd set went off. We scrambled to our positions with the humans in the lead.

"It's time," I said to the few humans I led. "We work together, and when I give the cue, you run to the shelter. Addy is waiting at the door to close it."

I held my hand up in the air, flat as I watched the wolves fall to the ground with the first of many explosions that would soon follow. It was amazing what you could do with immortals and a full night to prepare for the fight. This was going to be really cutting it close, to use silver against bad wolves and not hit the good guys was a really dicey proposition, so I'd helped Lachlan and his men clear the brush and some of the trees in front of the shelter so if the time came, they'd be able to run to safety.

Darkest Before Dawn

I watched in horror as one after another went off, and silver nitrate was set loose into the air around them. They couldn't breathe, and the pistons that had been inside of the landmines shredded their skin and when it had finished with them, only bloody corpses littered the ground.

My eyes lifted to the tree line and spotted the Sentinel watching me. He had cold blue eyes, longish brown hair, and olive colored skin. He also looked younger than the others who'd come with my mother had been. *Knight*. I smiled up at him not because I found him cute, which he was, but because I'd solved the puzzle of why my mother referred to Sentinels as chess pieces. It was because you could see it, but it was only a brief showing. One moment he was dressed in jeans, and a leather jacket and then he sort of shimmered for the briefest of seconds and then he was wearing the armor of a black knight. He shimmered again and was back to normal. I wasn't sure what it meant, if anything, because I didn't see any of the Sentinels at the bridge do that.

It made perfect sense as I thought about it, since the Knights were normally placed where there would be action. They were best used on the board where the opponent's pieces would be clustered together. It made even more sense now that they hadn't all shown up, since the Knight was the only piece who could be moved at the beginning of the game, without needing to move the Pawn.

The wolves moved through the field, but this time,

there were no landmines left, or if there were, they hadn't gone off. I closed my fist and lowered my body to aim the silver bullet filled automatic AR-15 at the field and opened fire along with the armed humans, vamps, and Lachlan's men. Another wave had been stopped from gaining the field.

"To the shelter," I screamed to be heard. "Now!" I watched as Lachlan, Jaeden and their men took the place of my people at the front of the line, protecting us from attack as we retreated. I watched as the humans made a line that ended with the last one closing the door. "Close it," I mouthed as Addy met me at the glass door. I placed my hand on hers, and smiled. "I love you, wench."

"Always," she replied.

As I turned around, it was to watch the vampires and Lachlan's men throw themselves into the fight. They took the field gloriously, battling together to rid the field of the rogue wolves. Jaeden, Shamus, Bjorn and Sven all worked together in a tag team system as they dropped wolves together. Lachlan and his pack fought in human form so they wouldn't be mistaken and killed in friendly fire. Raphael was quick on his feet, and spun with a pace I could barely keep up with. He'd shouldered his bow and now long and short swords were almost a blur around him as he cut through the wolves.

I pulled silver knives from their holsters and moved to the fray, watching as the Knight moved through the fight. I ignored the wolves and everything around me as I made my way in his direction. He too was coming for me, but there was a cold detachment to him that left me unsure of which side he was on. His icy blue eyes had a luminous glow to them and it was disorientating to watch as he seemed to blink in and out of existence around the battlefield as he advanced on me, almost like short spurts of teleportation.

"My brother," I growled when I was close enough for him to hear me.

"I know not of what you speak," he snapped.

"You took my brother, I want to know where you took him!" I screamed angrily before I moved to slice his arm open, but he dodged the attack effortlessly.

"I know nothing of your brother; I came here because you called to us. But I find you here with our enemies, and that screams traitor," he said before he moved with lightning fast speed. A long blade I hadn't seen him holding cut through my arm.

I cried out as the metal tore through my flesh. He seemed different than the others that had come with my mother. "I didn't call to anyone, you're one of Trina's flunkies," I accused.

"Trina and Dagan have betrayed our order, and are marked for death for what they have done. Any Sentinels with them have been marked as well," he growled. "You smell of her and your being here shows your guilt," he spat out before he did his super speed move again, but this time he captured me from behind. One hand was a manacle around my wrist, shoving my arm at a painful angle behind my back and then other held the long knife against my neck. "You're the vampires' whore?"

I didn't answer him; his blade was pressed against my throat. "I'm no one's whore," I finally said, and turned my head slightly to look up at him. "I was human, until I wasn't. I died, and this is what happened to me. I have no idea what I am, and you all seem to want me dead so I'm better off here, with them."

"No one claimed you?" he asked. His hand adjusted the angle of the blade slightly away from my throat. "Are you with the vampires and wolves, or are you Sentinel?" he continued. "We protect the humans, and we don't mix with other creatures. You seem to do it all; the order needs to know where you stand."

I was about to answer him, when a silver tipped arrow pierced his shoulder, and he disappeared. I looked to where Raphael stood, his bow now pointed at the ground.

"No!" I shouted as I looked around. "He knew what I was, and he wasn't working for my mother!"

Chapter Thirty-Three

I felt as if I'd failed Grayson by not being able to chase after him immediately after he'd been taken. I knew however, that giving chase before I was prepared would be foolish. I had to find out where they'd gone, and why. Running blindly after him would have given my mother the advantage. If I was going to find him, I had to be smart about it. With what I knew now, I knew I could take the advantage, and bring him home where he belonged.

We'd won the skirmish, but to me it felt empty. I'd discovered that there were others like me who didn't agree or follow orders from my mother. It gave me hope that eventually, I'd be able to find them and gain their help in killing my mother. Maybe they could help me understand these weird powers I had been given and how to use them properly. So far I kept finding what powers I had purely by accident and I sure couldn't control them.

Amelia Hutchins

I hadn't stopped to celebrate the small victory, not with Grayson's life on the line. The day after the skirmish we'd decided it was time to head out towards Provo. The journey there would long considering what we'd have to wade through to get there.

I'd packed my things and left the shelter, walking up to where the SUVs were waiting along the barren road out in front of the shelter. Addy stood off the side with Liam holding her hand. They had become very close, and I knew together they could run the shelter until I got back. Hopefully she wouldn't have any puppies while I was away.

I wished that we could just teleport there and be done with this, but from what I saw, Sentinels could travel short distances, based on that funky speed-hopping thing the Sentinel in the field was doing. But the Sentinels with my mom had clearly used cars, so I wasn't sure if they could teleport with another person. Dagan hadn't done so when he hauled Grayson off to the car. Even though we had a lead on their location, the world wasn't exactly an easy place to travel through. Jaeden and Lachlan had told me grim stories of things they had seen when they trekked up here. Things I wasn't sure anyone could be prepared for.

I glanced around at some of the familiar and unfamiliar faces that were packed and ready to go with us. "You sure you want to be sandwiched in a car with a vampire and a wolf?" Jaeden asked as he moved forward to take my trusty, handmade bug-out bag.

Darkest Before Dawn

"You sure you can handle being stuck in a car with Lachlan?" I countered with a smile.

"Nae, he isnae going tae like it," Lachlan said with a wicked smile on his lips.

"I made sure the CD player in the SUV works; hopefully he'll hang his head out the window for most of the trip," Jaeden growled as he tossed my bag into the back.

I was leaving the shelter, and it felt as if I was leaving a part of myself behind. I said my goodbyes quickly to prevent Addy from becoming too hysterical and jumped in the passenger seat. When Lachlan and Jaeden joined me, we took off and headed toward the highway.

We made it the Idaho-Oregon border with little effort, but just about fifteen miles before we reached Boise, we found a disturbing sign. Cars were packed together, and filled with remains of the dead. We got out of the SUVs and looked at the horrifying sight. Bones were being picked clean by the carrion eaters and ravens were everywhere. It was a wasteland of those who tried to escape the flu back when it began, and were trapped here instead.

"That's nae good," Lachlan stated the obvious.

"We may have to go on foot," Jaeden announced as the other SUVs stopped and joined us as we stood on the edge of the road. Raphael, Bjorn and a few of Jaeden's men unloaded and waited for his answer. Lachlan's men did the same. I watched as the few vampires and wolves that had come with us joined me with their own packs on their backs. I surveyed the area and spotted the river which headed south.

I rounded the car and grabbed the maps out of the center console and then grabbed my bag. I took a moment to say a prayer for the victims of the flu. It wouldn't be easy finding Grayson in this mess, but we would figure it out. I motioned to Jaeden and Lachlan who ambled over to see me spreading out one of the maps on the hood of the SUV.

"We can follow the Snake River; it will provide us a barrier and drinking water. I'm sure less of the people who died would have thought to follow it. And look," I said as I unfurled another map on top of the one for Idaho. "It branches off to the Raft River which takes us right into Utah."

"Lead the way, Emma," Jaeden said as he looked over my shoulder.

"Ye do ken that ye just asked the lass tae lead us to the unknown," Lachlan said as he peered over my other shoulder.

"It's all unknown in this world. Besides, she has maps and seems to be more resourceful than you. I say I'll keep her," Jaeden grinned.

I smiled at his reasoning, but in reality, we would be on the defensive side and stay away from people if we could help it.

Darkest Before Dawn

I had a vampire on my right and a werewolf on my left. I'd find Grayson; it would be getting to him that would be the hard part. With the creatures of the dark beside me, I was sure I could find him no matter where my mother tried to hide him.

We stood on the edge of a disaster, looking out into what was now our reality. People were no longer what they'd been. The entire world was forever changed, and those who were left struggled to survive. I often wondered if we didn't deserve this; we'd lost touch with the simple things in life which should have mattered the most—our humanity.

We'd become accustomed to technology and depended on it for way too much. We depended on it for all of the wrong reasons. Maybe this was our slap upside the head, a reminder of how fragile life was. This catastrophic event had made us go back to the basics, and for some, it made them stronger, while others gave in to their baser instincts and killed others to steal what they had.

It had taken total devastation to show us what mattered. There had been over seven billion people in the world before the flu hit. Billions had died, and millions more would die before the world righted itself. Hell, I was standing between a vampire and a werewolf, and I was stronger with them at my side. My dad had always known that the world would be hit with the Rh Viridae virus, but he'd also known that we'd survive it.

He'd prepared me for this, this single moment in

time where I stood with these men. He'd trained me to use my head before my heart in everything I did. He'd taught me to survive, and how to track, both of which I'd need to use now.

My dad had died to save many, and I wondered if he'd known his fate when he started all of this. He was the reason I still believed there was hope for the human race; people like him were worth saving, and even though my journey was taking me away from what Shamus had dubbed 'the Ark', I knew he was with me in everything I did to help others. He'd live on in every life that we helped, because he'd saved us and we'd be able to save them.

The wind ruffled my hair and I turned to look at Jaeden, and then Lachlan. I took the first step from the road in the direction which would take us to Utah, and away from everything I'd ever known.

It wasn't a happy ever after, but it would work for now. With them at my side, working together, I could do anything. I still felt numb, as we headed into the unfamiliar path to find my brother—together.

'Til Next Time...

About the Author

Amelia Hutchins lives in the beautiful Pacific Northwest with her beautiful family. She's an avid reader and writer of anything Paranormal. She started writing at the age of nine with the help of the huge imagination her Grandmother taught her to use. When not writing a new twisting plot, she can be found on her author page, or running Erotica Book Club where she helps new Indie Authors connect with a growing fan base.

Come by and say hello!

www.facebook.com/authorameliahutchins

www.facebook.com/EroticaBookClub

www.goodreads.com/author/show/7092218.Amelia_Hutchins

Printed in Great Britain
by Amazon